THE BILLIONAIRE AND BABIES COLLECTION

The men in this special 2-in-1 collection rule their worlds with authority and determination. They're comfortable commanding those around them and aren't afraid to be ruthless if necessary. Independent and self-reliant, they are content with their money and lack of commitment.

Then the babies enter their lives and, before they know it, these powerful men are wrapped around their babies' little fingers!

With the babies comes the awareness of what else might be missing. Seems the perfect time for these billionaires to find the women who will love them forever.

Join us for two passionate, provocative stories where billionaires encounter the women—and babies—who will make them complete!

If you love these two classic stories, be sure to look for more Billionaires and Babies books from Harlequin Desire.

USA TODAY Bestselling Author

Catherine Mann

and

USA TODAY Bestselling Author

Michelle Celmer

BILLIONAIRE'S JET SET BABIES

AND

THE NANNY BOMBSHELL

H HARLEQUIN® BILLIONAIRES AND BABIES

Recycling programs
for this product may
not exist in your area.

ISBN-13: 978-0-373-60982-6

Billionaire's Jet Set Babies And The Nanny Bombshell
Copyright © 2014 by Harlequin Books S.A.

The publisher acknowledges the copyright holders
of the individual works as follows:

Billionaire's Jet Set Babies
Copyright © 2011 by Catherine Mann

The Nanny Bombshell
Copyright © 2012 by Michelle Celmer

HARLEQUIN®
www.Harlequin.com

Printed in U.S.A.

CONTENTS

BILLIONAIRE'S JET SET BABIES

Catherine Mann

To Amelia Richard:
a treasured reader, reviewer and friend.
Thank you for all you've done to
help spread the word about my stories.
You're awesome!

Chapter 1

Alexa Randall had accumulated an eclectic box-ful of lost and found items since opening her own cleaning company for charter jets. There were the standard smart phones, portfolios, tablets, even a Patek Philippe watch. She'd returned each to its owner.

Then there were the stray panties and men's boxers, even the occasional sex toys from Mile High Club members. All of those items, she'd picked up with latex gloves and tossed in the trash.

But today marked a first find ever in the history of A-1 Aircraft Cleaning Services. Never before had she found a baby left on board—actually, *two* babies.

Her bucket of supplies dropped to the industrial blue carpet with a heavy thud that startled the sleeping pair. Yep, two infants, apparently twins with similar blond curly hair and cherub cheeks. About one year old, perhaps? A boy and a girl, it seemed, gauging from their pink and blue smocked outfits and gender-matched car seats.

Tasked to clean the jet alone, Alexa had no one to share her shock with. She flipped on another table lamp in the main compartment of the sleek private jet, the lighting in the hangar sketchy at best even at three in the afternoon.

Both kids were strapped into car seats resting on the leather sofa along the side of the plane, which was Seth Jansen's personal aircraft. As in *the* Seth Jansen of Jansen Jets. The self-made billionaire who'd raked in a fortune inventing some must-have security device for airports to help combat possible terrorist attacks on planes during takeoffs and landings. She admired the man's entrepreneurial spirit.

Landing his account would be her company's big break. She needed this first cleaning of his aircraft to go off without a hitch.

Tiny fists waved for a second, slowing, lowering, until both babies began to settle back to sleep. Another huffy sigh shuddered through the girl before her breaths evened out. Her little arm landed on a piece of paper safety-pinned to the girl's hem.

Narrowing her eyes, Alexa leaned forward and read:

> Seth,
> You always say you want more time with the twins, so here's your chance. Sorry for the short notice, but a friend surprised me with a two-week spa retreat. Enjoy your "daddy time" with Olivia and Owen!
> XOXO,
> Pippa

Pippa?

Alexa straightened again, horrified. Really? Really!

Pippa Jansen, as in the *ex*-Mrs. Jansen, had dumped off her infants on their father's jet. Unreal. Alexa stuffed her fists into the pockets of her navy chinos, standard uniform for A-1 cleaning staff along with a blue polo shirt bearing the company's logo.

And who signed a note to their obviously estranged baby daddy with kisses and hugs? Alexa sank down into a fat chair across from the pint-size passengers. Bigger question of the day, who left babies unattended on an airplane?

A crappy parent, that's who.

The rich and spoiled rotten, who played by their own rules, a sad reality she knew only too well from growing up in that world. People had told her how lucky she was as a kid—lucky to have a dedicated nanny that she spent more time with than she did with either of her parents.

The best thing that had ever happened to her? Her father bankrupted the family's sportswear chain— once worth billions, now worth zip. That left Alexa the recipient of a trust fund from Grandma containing a couple of thousand dollars.

She'd used the money to buy a partnership in a cleaning service about to go under because the aging owner could no longer carry the workload on her own. Bethany—her new partner—had been grateful for Alexa's energy and the second chance for A-1 Aircraft Cleaning Services to stay afloat. Using Alexa's contacts from her family's world of luxury and extravagance she had revitalized the struggling business. Alexa's ex-husband, Travis, had been appalled by her new occupation and offered to help out financially so she wouldn't have to work.

She would rather scrub toilets.

And the toilet on this particular Gulfstream III jet was very important to her. She had to land the Jansen Jet contract and hopefully this one-time stint would impress him enough to cinch the deal. Her business needed this account to survive, especially in today's tough economy. If she failed, she could lose everything and A-1 might well face Chapter 11 bankruptcy. She'd hardly believed her luck when she'd been asked by another cleaning company to subcontract out on one of the Jansen Jets—this jet.

Now that she'd found these two babies, she was screwed. She swept particles of sand from the seat into her hand, eyed the fingerprints on the windows, could almost feel the grit rising from the carpet fiber. But she couldn't just clean up, restock the Evian water and pretend these kids weren't here. She needed to contact airport security, which was going to land Jansen's ex-wife in hot water, possibly him as well. That would piss off Jansen. And the jet still wouldn't be serviced. And then he would never consider her for the contract.

Frustration and a hefty dose of anger stung stronger than a bucket full of ammonia. Scratch cleaning detail for now, scratch cinching this deal that would finally take her company out of the red. She had to locate the twins' father ASAP.

Alexa unclipped the cell phone from her waist and thumbed her directory to find the number for Jansen Jets, which she happened to have since she'd been trying to get through to the guy for a month. She'd never made it further than his secretary, who'd agreed to pass along Alexa's business prospectus.

She eyed the sleeping babies. Maybe some good could come from this mess after all.

Today, she would finally have the chance to talk to the boss, just not how she'd planned and not in a way that would put him in a receptive mood...

The phone stopped ringing as someone picked up.

"Jansen Jets, please hold." As quickly as the thick female Southern drawl answered, the line clicked and Muzak filled the air waves with soulless contemporary tunes.

A squawk from one of the car seats drew her attention. She looked up fast to see Olivia wriggling in her seat, kicking free a Winnie the Pooh blanket. The little girl spit out her Piglet pacifier and whimpered, getting louder until her brother scrunched up his face, blinking awake and none too happy. His Eeyore pacifier dangled from a clip attached to his blue sailor outfit.

Two pairs of periwinkle-blue eyes stared at her, button noses crinkled. Owen's eyes filled with tears. Olivia's bottom lip thrust outward again.

Tucking the Muzak-humming phone under her chin, Alexa hefted the iconic Burberry plaid diaper bag off the floor.

"Hey there, little ones," she said in what she hoped was a conciliatory tone. She'd spent so little time around babies she could only hope she pegged it right. "I know, I know, sweetie, I'm a stranger, but I'm all you've got right now."

And how crummy was that? She stifled another spurt of anger at the faceless Pippa who'd dropped her children off like luggage. When had the spa-hopping mama expected their father to locate them?

"I'm assuming you're Olivia." Alexa tickled the bare foot of the girl wearing a pink smocked dress.

Olivia giggled, and Alexa pulled the pink lace bootie from the baby's mouth. Olivia thrust out her bottom lip—until Alexa unhooked a teething ring from the diaper bag and passed it over to the chubby-cheeked girl.

"And you must be Owen." She tweaked his blue tennis shoe—still on his foot as opposed to his sister who was ditching her other booty across the aisle with the arm of a major league pitcher. "Any idea where your daddy is? Or how much longer he'll be?"

She'd been told by security she had about a half hour to service the inside of the jet in order to be out before Mr. Jansen arrived. As much as she would have liked to meet him, it was considered poor form for the cleaning staff to still be on hand. She'd expected her work and a business card left on the silver drink tray to speak for itself.

So much for her well laid plans.

She scooped up a baby blanket from the floor, folded it neatly and placed it on the couch. She smoothed back Owen's sweaty curls. Going quiet, he stared back at her just as the on hold Muzak cued up "Sweet Caroline"—the fourth song so far. Apparently she'd been relegated to call waiting purgatory.

How long until the kids got hungry? She peeked into the diaper bag for supplies. Maybe she would luck out and find more contact info along the way. Sippy cups of juice, powdered formula, jars of food and diapers, diapers, diapers…

The clank of feet on the stairway outside yanked her upright. She dropped the diaper bag and spun around fast, just as a man filled the open hatch. A tall and broad-shouldered man.

He stood with the sun backlighting him, casting his face in mysterious shadows.

Alexa stepped in front of the babies instinctively, protectively. "Good afternoon. What can I do for you?"

Silently he stepped deeper into the craft until overhead lights splashed over his face and she recognized him from her internet searches. Seth Jansen, founder and CEO of Jansen Jets.

Relief made her knees wobbly. She'd been saved from a tough decision by Jansen's early arrival. And, wow, did the guy ever know how to make an entrance.

From press shots she'd seen he was good-looking, with a kind of matured Abercrombie & Fitch beach hunk appeal. But no amount of Google Images could capture the impact of this tremendously attractive self-made billionaire in person.

Six foot three or four, he filled the charter jet with raw muscled *man*. He wasn't some pale pencil pusher. He was more the size of a keen-eyed lumberjack, in a suit. An expensive, tailored suit.

The previously spacious cabin now felt tight. Intimate.

His sandy-colored hair—thick without being shaggy—sported sun-kissed streaks of lighter blond, the kind that came naturally from being outside rather than sitting in a salon chair. His tan and toned body gave further testimony to that. No raccoon rings around the eyes from tanning bed glasses. The scent of crisp air clung to him, so different from the boardroom aftershaves of her father and her ex. She scrunched her nose at even the memory of cloying cologne and cigars.

Even his eyes spoke of the outdoors. They were the same vibrant green she'd once seen in the waters off the Caribbean coast of St. Maarten, the sort of sparkling green that made you want to dive right into their cool depths. She turned shivery all over just thinking about taking a swim in those pristine waters.

She seriously needed to lighten up on the cleaning supply fumes. How unprofessional to stand here and gawk like a sex-starved divorcée—which she was.

"Good afternoon, Mr. Jansen. I'm Alexa Randall with A-1 Aircraft Cleaning Services."

He shrugged out of his suit jacket, gray pin-stripe and almost certainly an Ermenegildo Zegna, a brand known for its no-nonsense look. Expensive. Not surprising.

His open shirt collar, with his burgundy tie loosened did surprise her, however. Overall, she got the impression of an Olympic swimmer confined in an Italian suit.

"Right." He checked his watch—the only non-*GQ* item on him. He wore what appeared to be a top-of-the-line diver's timepiece. "I'm early, I know, but I need to leave right away so if you could speed this up, I would appreciate it."

Jansen charged by, not even hesitating as he passed the two tykes. *His* tykes.

She cleared her throat. "You have a welcoming crew waiting for you."

"I'm sure you're mistaken." He stowed his brief-case, his words clipped. "I'm flying solo today."

She held up Pippa's letter. "It appears, Mr. Jansen, your flight plans have changed."

Seth Jansen stopped dead in his tracks. He looked back over his shoulder at Alexa Randall, the owner of a new, small company that had been trying to get his attention for at least a month. Yeah, he knew who the drop-dead gorgeous blonde was. But he didn't have time to listen to her make a pitch he already knew would be rejected.

While he appreciated persistence as a business professional himself, he did not like gimmicks. "Let's move along to the point, please."

He had less than twenty minutes to get his Gulf-stream III into the air and on its way from Charleston, South Carolina, to St. Augustine, Florida. He had a business meeting he'd been working his ass off to land for six months—dinner with the head of security for the Medinas, a deposed royal family that lived in exile in the United States.

Big-time account.

Once in a lifetime opportunity.

And the freedom to devote more of his energies to the philanthropic branch of this company. Freedom. It had a different meaning these days than when he'd flown crop dusters to make his rent back, in North Dakota.

"This—" she waved a piece of floral paper in front of him "—is the point."

As she passed over the slip of paper, she stepped aside and revealed—holy crap—his kids. He looked down at the letter fast.

Two lines into the note, his temple throbbed. What the hell was Pippa thinking, leaving the twins this way? How long had they been in here? And why had she left him a damn note, for Pete's sake?

He pulled out his cell phone to call his ex. Her voice mail picked up immediately. She was avoiding him, no doubt.

A text from Pippa popped up in his in-box. He opened the message and it simply read, Want 2 make sure you know. Twins r waiting for you at plane. Sorry 4 short notice. XOXO.

"What the h—?" He stopped himself short before he cursed in front of his toddlers who were just beginning to form words. He tucked his phone away and faced Alexa Randall. "I'm sorry my ex added babysitter duties to your job today. Of course I'll pay you extra. Did you happen to notice which way Pippa headed out?"

Because he had some choice words for her when he found her.

"Your ex-wife wasn't here when I arrived." Alexa held up her own cell phone, her thumb swiping away a print. "I tried to contact your office, but your assistant wouldn't let me get a word out before shifting me over to Muzak. It's looped twice while I waited. Much longer and I would have had to call security, which would have brought in child services—"

He held up a hand, sick to his gut already. "Thanks. I get the picture. I owe you for cleaning up after my ex-wife's recklessness as well."

His blood pressure spiked higher until he saw red. Pippa had left the children unattended in an airplane at his privately owned airport? What had his security people been thinking, letting Pippa just wander around the aircraft that way? These were supposed to be the days of increased precautions and safety measures, and yet they must have assumed because she was his ex-wife that garnered her a free pass around the facility. Not so.

Heads were going to roll hard and fast over this. No one put the safety of his children at risk.

No one.

He crumpled the note in his fist and pitched it aside. Forcing his face to smooth so he wouldn't scare the babies, he unstrapped the buckle on his daughter's car seat.

"Hey there, princess." He held Olivia up high and thought about how she'd squealed with delight over the baby swing on the sprawling oak in his backyard. "Did you have fruit for lunch?"

She grinned, and he saw a new front tooth had come in on top. She smelled like peaches and baby shampoo and there weren't enough hours in the day to take in all the changes happening too quickly.

He loved his kids more than anything, had since the second he'd seen their fists waving in an ultrasound. He'd been damn lucky Pippa let him be there when they were born, considering she'd already started divorce proceedings at that point. He hated not being with them every day, hated missing even one milestone. But the timing for this visit couldn't be worse.

Seth tucked Olivia against his chest and reached to ruffle his son's hair. "Hey, buddy. Missed you this week."

Owen stuck out his tongue and offered up his best raspberry.

The petite blonde dressed in trim, pressed chinos popped a pacifier into Owen's mouth then knelt to pick up the crumpled note and pitch it into her cleaning bucket. "I assume today isn't your scheduled visitation."

She would be right on that. Although why the disdain in her voice? Nobody—single parent or not—would appreciate having their kids dumped off in their workplace. Not to mention he was mad as hell at Pippa for just dropping them off unannounced.

What if someone else had boarded this plane?

Thank God, this woman—Alexa—had been the one to find them. He knew who she was, but Pippa hadn't known jack when she'd unloaded his children.

Of all the reckless, irresponsible…

Deep breath. He unbuckled Owen as well and scooped him up, too, with an ease he'd learned from walking the floors with them when they were infants. Just as he'd needed calm then, he forced it through his veins now.

Getting pissed off wouldn't accomplish anything. He had to figure out what to do with his children when he was scheduled to fly out for a meeting with multimillion dollar possibilities.

When he'd first moved to South Carolina, he'd been a dumb ass, led by glitz. That's how he'd ended up married to his ex. He'd grown up with more spartan, farm values that he'd somehow lost in his quest for beaches and billions.

Now, he itched inside his high-priced starched shirt and longed for the solitude of those flights. But he had long ago learned if he wanted to do business with certain people, he had to dress the part and endure the stuffy business meetings. And he very much wanted to do business with the Medina family based out of Florida. He glanced at his watch and flinched. Damn it. He needed to be in the air already, on his way to St. Augustine. At the moment, he didn't have time for a sandwich, much less to find a qualified babysitter.

He would just have to make time. "Could you hold Owen for a second while I make some calls?"

"Sure, no problem." Alexa stopped straightening his jacket on the hanger and extended her arms.

As he passed his son over, Seth's hand grazed her breast. Her very soft, tempting breast. Just that fast touch pumped pure lust through his overworked body. It was more than just "nice, a female" kind of notice. His body was going on alert, saying "I will make it my mission in life to undress you."

She gasped lightly, not in outrage but more like someone who'd been zapped with some static. For him, it was more like a jolt from a light socket.

Olivia rested her head on his shoulder with a sleepy sigh, bringing him back to reality. He was a father with responsibilities.

Still, he was a man. Why hadn't he noticed the power of the pull to this woman when he'd walked onto the plane? Had he grown so accustomed to wealth that he'd stopped noticing "the help"? That notion didn't sit well with him at all.

But it also didn't keep him from looking at Alexa more closely.

Her pale blond hair was pulled back in a simple silver clasp. Navy chino pants and a light blue shirt—the company uniform—matched her eyes. It also fit her loosely, but not so much that it hid her curves.

Before the kids, before Pippa, he would have asked Alexa for her number, made plans to take her out on a riverboat dinner cruise where he would kiss her senseless under a starry sky. But these days he didn't have time for dating. He worked and when he wasn't on the job he saw his kids.

With a stab of regret, his gaze raked back over her T-shirt with the A-1 Aircraft Cleaning logo.

He'd seen that same emblem in the cover letter she'd sent with her prospectus.

He also recalled why he hadn't gotten any further than the cover letter and the fledgling business's flyer—where he'd seen her headshot.

Following his eyes, she looked down at her shirt and met his gaze dead-on. "Yes, I have a proposal on your desk." Alexa cocked one eyebrow. "I assume that's why you were looking at my shirt?"

"Of course, why else?" he answered dryly. "You should have received an answer from my secretary."

"I did, and when you're not in a hurry—" she smoothed back her already immaculate hair "—I would appreciate the opportunity to explore your reasons for rejecting my initial bid."

"I'll save us both some time. I'm not interested in the lowest bidder or taking a risk on such a small company."

Her sky-blue eyes narrowed perceptively. "You didn't read my proposal all the way through, did you?"

"I read until my gut told me to stop." He didn't have time to waste on page after page of something he already knew wasn't going to work.

"And you're saying that your gut spoke up quickly."

"Afraid so," he said shortly, hoping to end an awkward situation with his best boardroom bite. A suspicion niggled. "Why is it you're here cleaning today instead of someone from my regular company?"

"They subcontracted A-1 when they overbooked. Obviously I wasn't going to turn down the opportunity to impress you." She stood tall and undaunted in spite of his rejection.

Spunky and hot. Dangerous combo.

He fished his phone from his suit coat again. "I really do need to start making some calls."

"Don't let me keep you." She dipped her hand into the diaper bag and pulled out two rice cakes. She passed one to Owen and the other to Olivia. All the while Owen tugged at her hair, watching the way the white-blond strands glittered in the light. "That should keep them quiet while you talk."

Interesting that Alexa never once winced, even when Owen's fingers tangled and tugged. Not that he could blame his son in the least.

Seth thumbed the numbers on his phone and started with placing a call to his ex-wife—that again went straight to voice mail. Damn it. He then moved on to dialing family members.

Five frustrating conversations later, he'd come up empty on all counts. Either his kids were hellions and no one wanted to watch them, or he was having a serious run of bad luck.

Although their excuses were rock solid. His cousin Paige was on lockdown since her two daughters had strep throat. His cousin Vic had announced his wife was in labor with child number three—which meant *her* sisters were watching her other two kids, in addition to their own. But damn it, he'd needed to take off five minutes ago.

Brooding, he watched Alexa jostle Owen on her shapely hip. She was obviously a natural with kids. She wasn't easily intimidated, important when dealing with his strong-willed offspring. She'd protected the kids when she found them alone on the plane. He'd seen proof of her determination and work ethic. An idea formed in his head, and as much as he questioned the wisdom of it, the notion still took root.

In spite of what he'd told her, he had read more of her proposal than the cover letter, enough to know something about her. He was interested in her entrepreneurial spirit—she'd done a solid job revitalizing a company that had virtually been on financial life support. Still, his gut told him he couldn't afford to take a risk on this part of his business, especially not now. Now that he was expanding, he needed to hire a larger, more established cleaning chain, even if it cost him extra.

But he needed a nanny and she'd passed the high-level background check needed to work in an airport. Her life had been investigated more thoroughly than anyone he would get from a babysitting service. Not to mention a babysitting service would send over a total stranger that his kids might hate. At least he'd met this woman, had access to her life story. Most importantly, he saw her natural rapport with the twins. He would be nearby in the hotel at all times—even during meetings—if she had questions about their routine.

She was actually a godsend.

Decision made, he forged ahead. "While I don't think your company's the right one to service Jansen Jets, *I* have a proposal for *you*."

"I'm not sure I understand?"

"You fly with me and the kids to St. Augustine, be Owen and Olivia's nanny for the next twenty-four hours and I'll let you verbally pitch your agency's proposal to me again, in detail." The more he spelled it out, the better the idea sounded. "I'll give you a few pointers about why my gut spoke up so quickly in case you want to make adjustments for future proposals to other companies. I'll even pass along your name to possible contacts, damn good contacts. And of course you'll be paid, a week's worth of wages for one day's work."

Was he taking advantage here? He didn't think so. He was offering her a business "in" she wouldn't have otherwise. If her verbal proposal held together, he would mention her business to some of his connections. And yes, give her those tips to help cinch a deal elsewhere. She would land jobs, just not his.

She eyed him suspiciously. "Twenty-four hours

of Mary Poppins duty in exchange for a critique and some new contacts?"

"That should be long enough for me to make alternative arrangements." There'd been a time when twenty-four hours with a woman would be more than enough time to seduce her as well. His eyes roved over Alexa's curves once more, regretting that he wouldn't be able to brush up on those skills during this trip.

"And you trust me, a stranger, with your children?" Disdain dripped from her voice.

"Do you think this is the right time to call me a crummy father?" Though he had to appreciate her protective instincts when it came to his children.

"You could just ring up a nanny service."

"Already thought of that. They wouldn't get here in time and my kids might not like the person they send. Olivia and Owen have taken to you." Unable to resist, he tapped the logo just above her breast. Lightly. Briefly. His finger damn near shot out a flame like a Bic lighter. "And I do know who you are. I read enough of your proposal to learn you've passed your security check for airport work."

"Well, tomorrow is usually my day off…" She dusted the logo on her shirt, as if his touch lingered. "You'll really listen to my pitch and give me tips, mention my company to others?"

"Scout's honor." He smiled for the first time all day, seeing victory in sight.

"I want you to know I'm not giving up on persuading you to sign me up for Jansen Jets as well."

"Fair enough. You're welcome to try."

She eyed both the children then looked back to him. He knew when he'd presented an irresistible proposition. Now he just needed to wait for her to see this was a win-win situation.

Although he needed for her to realize that quickly. "I have about two minutes left here," he pressed. "If your answer's no, get to it so I can make use of the rest of my time to secure alternative arrangements." Although God only knew what those might be.

"Okay." She nodded in agreement although her furrowed brow broadcast a hefty dose of reservation. "You have yourself a deal. I'll call my partner to let her know so she can cover—"

"Great," he interrupted. "But do it while you buckle up the kids and yourself. We're out of here." He settled Olivia back into her car seat with a quick kiss on her forehead.

Alexa looked up quickly from fastening Owen into his safety seat. "Where's the pilot?"

He stared into her pale blue eyes and imagined them shifting colors as he made her as hot for him as he was for her. God, it would be damn tough to have this jaw-dropping female working beside him for the next twenty-four hours. But his children were his top priority.

So he simply smiled—and, yes, took a hefty dose of pleasure in seeing her pupils widen with awareness. "The pilot? That would be me."

Chapter 2

Her stomach dropped and she prayed the Gulf-stream III wouldn't do the same in Seth Jansen's hands.

Turning off her cell after deleting four missed calls from her mother and leaving a message for her partner, Bethany, Alexa double-checked the safety belts for both children and buckled her own. Watching Seth slide into the pilot's seat, she reminded herself he owned a charter jet company so of course it made sense he could pilot a plane himself. She'd flown on private aircraft during her entire childhood, trusting plenty of aviators she'd never even met to get her safely from point A to point B. So why was she so nervous with this guy at the helm?

Because he'd thrown her off balance.

Boarding the plane earlier, she'd had such optimism, a solid approach in place and control of her world. In the span of less than ten minutes, Seth Jansen had seized control of not just the plane, but her carefully made plan.

The kind of bargain he'd proposed was so unexpected, outrageous even. But too good an opportunity to pass up. She needed to take a deep breath, relax and focus on learning everything she could about him, to give her an edge in negotiations.

Even knowing he must have his pilot's license, she wouldn't have expected someone as wealthy as him willing to fly himself. She'd thought he would have someone else "chauffeuring" while he banged back a few drinks or took a nap. Like her dad would have done during their annual family vacation, a one-week trip that was supposed to make up for all the time they never spent together during the year.

Not that she saw much of either of her parents even then. While on vacation, the nanny had taken her to amusement parks or sightseeing or to the slopes while her father attended to "emergency" business and her mother went to the spa.

Simmering over old memories, Alexa polished the metal seatbelt buckle absently with the hem of her shirt as she watched Seth Jansen complete his preflight routine.

The door to the cockpit had been left open. Seth adjusted the mic on the headset, his mouth moving, although she couldn't hear him as the engines hummed to life. Smooth as silk, the plane left the hangar, past a row of parked smaller aircraft until he taxied to the end of the runway and stopped.

Nerves pattered up from her stomach to the roots of her hair. The jet engines roared louder, louder still, and yet she could swear she heard Seth's deep voice calmly blending with the aerial symphony.

Words drifted back…

"Charleston tower… Gulfstream alpha, two, one, prepared… Roger… Ready for takeoff…"

The luxury craft eased forward again, Seth's hands steady on the yoke and power. Confidence radiated from his every move, so much so she found herself relaxing into the butter-soft leather sofa. Her hands fell to rest on the handle of each car seat, claiming her charges. Her babies, for the next twenty-four hours.

Her heart squeezed with old regrets. Her marriage to Travis had been an unquestionable failure. While part of her was relieved there hadn't been children hurt by their breakup, another part of her grieved for the babies that might have been.

The nose of the plane lifted as the aircraft swooped upward. Olivia and Owen squirmed in their seats. Alexa reached for the diaper bag, panic stirring. Did they want a bottle? A toy? And if they needed a diaper change there wasn't a thing she could do about that for a while. Just when the panic started to squeeze her chest, the noise of the engines and the pacifiers she'd used to help their ears soothed them back into their unfinished nap.

The diaper bag slid from her grip, thudding on the floor. Relaxing, she stared across the aisle out the window as they left Charleston behind. She also left behind an empty apartment and a silent phone since her married friends had dropped away after her divorce.

Church steeples and spires dotted the ocean-locked landscape. So many, the historic town had earned nicknames of the Holy City and the City by the Sea. After their financial meltdown, her parents had relocated to a condo in Boca Raton to start over—away from the gossip.

How ironic that her parents' initial reservations about Travis had been so very far off base. They'd begged him to sign a prenuptial agreement. She'd told them to take their prenup and go to hell. Travis had insisted he didn't care and signed the papers anyway. She thought she'd found her dream man, finally someone who would love her for herself.

Not that the contract had mattered in the end since her father had blown through the whole fortune anyway. By the time they'd broken up, her ex hadn't wanted anything to do with her, her messy family dysfunction, or what he called her germaphobic ways.

The way Travis had simply fallen out of love with her had kicked the hell out of her self-esteem there for a while. She couldn't even blame the breakup on another woman. No way in hell was she going to let a man have control of her heart or her life ever again.

All the more reason she had to make a go of her cleaning business and establish her independence. She had no other marketable skills, apart from a host of bills and a life to rebuild in her beloved hometown.

So here she was, on a plane bound for St. Augustine with a stranger and two heart-tuggingly adorable babies. The coastline looked miniscule now outside the window as they reached their cruising altitude.

"Hey, Alexa?"

Seth's voice pulled her attention away from the view. He stood in the archway between the cockpit and the seating area.

Her stomach jolted again. "Shouldn't you be flying the plane?"

"It's on autopilot for the moment. Since the kids are sleeping, I want you to come up front. The flight isn't long, but it will give us the chance to talk through some specifics about your time with the twins."

She saw the flinty edge of calculation in his jewel-toned eyes. He may have offered her a deal back at the airport, but now he intended to interview her further before he turned over his children to her. A flicker of admiration lit through the disdain she had felt for him earlier.

Giving each baby another quick check and finding them snoozing away, binkies half in, half out of their slack mouths, she unbuckled, reassured she could safely leave them for a few minutes. She walked the short distance to Seth and stopped in the archway, waiting for him to move back to the pilot's seat.

Still, he stood immobile and aloof, other than those glinting green eyes that swept over her face. The crisp scent of him rode the recycled air to tempt her nose, swirling deeper inside her with each breath. Her breasts tingled with awareness, her body overcome with the urge to lean into him, press the aching fullness of her chest against the hard wall of manly muscles.

She shivered. He smiled arrogantly as if completely cognizant of just how much he affected her on a physical level. Seth stepped back brusquely, returning to the pilot's spot on the left and waving her into the copilot's seat on the right.

Strapping in, she stared at the gauges around her,

the yoke moving automatically in front of her. Seth tapped buttons along the control panel and resumed flying the plane. Still, the steering in front of her mirrored his movements until she felt connected to him in some mystical manner.

She resented the way he sent her hormones into overdrive with just the sound of his husky voice or the intensity of his sharp gaze. She was here to do a job, damn it, not bring a man into her already too complicated life.

Twisting her fingers together in her lap, she forced her thoughts back to their jobs. "What's so important about this particular meeting that it can't be rescheduled?"

"I have small mouths to feed. Responsibilities." He stayed steadily busy as he talked, his eyes roving the gauges, his hands adjusting the yoke. "Surely you understand that, and if not, then I don't even need to read your proposal." He winked.

"Thank you for the Business 101 lecture, Mr. Jansen." She brushed specks of dust from a gauge. "I was really just trying to make conversation, but if you're more comfortable hanging out here alone, I'll be glad to return to the back."

"Sorry… And call me Seth," he said with what sounded like genuine contrition. "Long day. Too many surprises."

She glanced back at the sleeping babies, suddenly realizing they had miniature versions of his strong chin. "I can see that. What do you do to relax?"

"Fly."

He stared out at the expanse of blue sky and puffy clouds, and she couldn't miss the buzz radiating from him. Jansen Jets wasn't just a company to him. He'd turned his hobby, his true love, into a financial success. Not many could accomplish such a feat. Maybe she could learn something about business from him after all.

"You were looking forward to this time in the air, weren't you? What should have been your relaxing hour for the day has become a stressor."

"I've gotta ask…" He looked over at her quickly, brow furrowed. "Is the psychoanalysis included in the cleanup fee?"

She winced as his words hit a little too close to a truth of her own. Travis used to complain about that same trait. Well, she did have plenty of practice in what a shrink would say after all the time she'd spent in analysis as a teenager. The whole point had been to internalize those healthier ways of thinking. She'd needed the help, no question, but she'd also needed her parents. When they hadn't heard her, she'd started crying out for their attention in other ways, ways that had almost cost her life.

Her thoughts were definitely getting too deep and dark, and therefore too distracting. Something about this man and his children made her visit places in her mind she normally kept closed off. "Like I said, just making small talk. I thought you wanted me to come up here for conversation, to dig a little deeper into the background of your new, temporary nanny. If you don't want to chat, simply say so."

"You're right. I do. And the first thing I've learned is that you don't back down, which is a very good thing. It takes a strong person to stand up to the twins when they're in a bad mood." He shuddered melodramatically, his complaint totally undercut by the pride in his voice. Mr. Button-Up Businessman loosened up a little when he spoke of his kids. "What made you trade in your white gloves at tea for white glove cleaning?"

So he knew a little about her privileged upbringing as well. "You did more than just read my cover letter."

"I recognized your name—or rather your return to your maiden name. Your father was once a client of a competing company. Your husband chartered one of my planes."

"My ex-husband," she snapped.

He nodded, his fingers whitening as his grip tightened on the yoke. "So, back to my original question. What made you reach for the vacuum cleaner?"

"Comes with the business."

"Why choose this particular line of work?"

Because she didn't have a super cool hobby like he did? She'd suffered a rude awakening after her divorce was finalized a year ago, and she realized she had no money and no marketable skills.

Her one negligible talent? Being a neat-freak with a need to control her environment. Pair that with insights into the lifestyles of the rich and spoiled and she'd fashioned a career. But that answer sounded too half-baked and not particularly professional.

"Because I understand the needs of the customer, beyond just a clean space, I know the unique services that make the job stand out." True enough, and since he seemed to be listening, she continued, "Keeping records of allergies, favored scents, personal preferences for the drink bar can make the difference between a successful flight and a disaster. Flying in a charter jet isn't simply an air taxi service. It's a luxury experience and should be treated as such."

"You understand the world since you lived in it."

Lived. Past tense. "I want to be successful on my own merits rather than mooch off the family coffers."

Or at least she liked to think she would have felt that way if there had been any lucre left in the Randall portfolio.

"Why work in this particular realm, the aircraft world?" He gestured around the jet with a broad hand.

Her eyes snagged on the sprinkling of fair hair along his forearm. Tanned skin contrasted with the white cuffs of his rolled up sleeves and wow did her fingertips ever itch to touch him. To see if his bronzed-god flesh still carried the warmth of the sun.

It had been so long since she'd felt these urges. Her divorce had left her emotionally gutted. She'd tried dating a couple of times, but the chemistry hadn't been there. Her new business venture consumed her. Or rather, it had until right now, when it mattered most.

"I'm missing your point." No surprise since she was staring at his arm like an idiot.

"You're a…what…history major?"

"Art history, and being that close means you read my bio. You do know a lot more about me than you let on at first."

"Of course I do or I never would have asked you to watch my children. They're far more precious to me than any plane." His eyes went hard, leaving no room for doubt. Any mistakes with his son and daughter would not be tolerated. Then he looked back at the sky, mellow Seth returning. "Why not manage a gallery if you need to fill your hours?"

Because she would be lucky if working in a gallery would cover rent on an apartment or a lease on an economy car, much less food and economic stability. Because she wanted to prove she didn't need a man to be successful. And most importantly, *because* she didn't ever again want the freaked out feeling of being less than six hundred dollars away from bankruptcy.

Okay, sort of melodramatic since she'd still owned jewelry she could hock. But still scary as hell when she'd sold off her house and car only to find it barely covered the existing loans.

"I do not expect anyone to support me, and given the current economy, jobs in the arts aren't exactly filling up the want ad sections. Bethany has experience in the business, while I bring new contacts to the table. We're a good team. Besides, I really do enjoy this work, strange as that may seem. While A-1 has employees who handle cleaning most of the time, I pitch in if someone's out sick or we get the call for a special job. I enjoy the break from office work."

"Okay, I believe you. So you used to like art history, and now you enjoy feeding people's Evian habits and their need for clean armrests."

The deepening sarcasm in his voice had her spine starching with irritation. "Are you making fun of me for the hell of it or is there a purpose behind this line of questioning?"

"I always have a purpose," he said as smoothly as he flew the plane. "Will your whim of the week pass, once you realize people take these services for granted and your work is not appreciated? What happens to my aircraft then? I'll be stuck wading through that stack of proposals all over again."

He really saw her as a flighty, spoiled individual and that stung. It wasn't particularly fair, either. "Do you keep flying even when people don't appreciate a smooth or on-time flight, when they only gripe about the late or bumpy rides?"

"I'm not following your point here. I like to fly. Are you saying you like to clean?"

"I like to restore order," she answered simply, truthfully.

The shrinks she'd seen as a teen had helped her rechannel the need for perfection her mother had drilled into Alexa from birth. She'd stopped starving herself, eased off searching the art world for flawless beauty and now took comfort from order, from peace.

"Ah—" a smile spread over his face "—you like control. Now that I understand."

"Who doesn't like control?" And how many therapy sessions had she spent on *that* topic?

He looked over at her with an emerald-eyed sexy stare. The air crackled as if a lightning bolt had zipped between them. "Would you like to take over flying the plane?"

"Are you kidding?" She slid her hands under her

thighs even though she couldn't deny to herself just how tempting the offer sounded.

Who wouldn't want to take a stab at soaring through the air, just her and the wide-open blue rolling out in front of the plane? It would be like driving a car alone for the first time. Pushing an exotic Arabian racehorse to gallop. Happier memories from another lifetime called to her.

"Just take the yoke."

God, how she wanted to, but there was something in his voice that gave her pause. She couldn't quite figure out his game. She wasn't in the position to risk her livelihood or her newfound independence on some guy's whims.

"Your children are on board." She knew she sounded prim, but then hey, she was a nanny for the day.

"If it appears you're about to send us into a nosedive, I'll take over."

"Maybe another time." She leaped up from the seat, not about to get sucked into a false sense of control that wouldn't last. "I think I hear Olivia."

His low chuckle followed her all the way back to both peacefully sleeping children.

Alexa could hear his husky laugh echoing in her ears two hours later as they settled into their luxurious hotel room in St. Augustine, Florida.

She had seen the best of the best lodgings and the

Casa Monica—one of the oldest hotels in the United States—was gorgeous by any standards, designed to resemble a castle. The city of St. Augustine itself was rich with history and ornate Spanish architecture, the Casa Monica being a jewel. The hotel had been built in the 1800s, named for St. Monica, the mother of St. Augustine, the city's namesake.

And here she was with Seth and his babies. She could use a little motherly advice from a patron saint's mom right now.

She also needed to find some time to touch base with Bethany at work. Even though she was sure Bethany could manage—it had been her company at one time—she really did need to speak with her partner and give Bethany her contact information.

Seth had checked them into one of the penthouse suites, with a walk-out to a turret with views of the city. The suite had two bedrooms connected by a sitting area. The mammoth bath with a circular tub called to her muscles, which ached from working all day then lugging one of the baby carriers around. Then her thoughts went to images of sharing the tub with a man...not just any man...

She turned back to the room, decorated in blue velvet upholstery and heavy brocade curtains. Seth had claimed the spare bedroom, leaving her the larger master with two cribs inside. She trailed her fingers over the handle to Olivia's car seat on the floor beside the mission style sofa in the sitting room. Olivia's brother rested in his car seat next to hers.

"Your twins sleep well. They're making this job too easy, you know."

"Pippa doesn't believe in bedtimes. They usually nap hard their first day with me." Seth strode into the spare bedroom. "Expect mayhem soon enough when they wake up recharged. Owen's a charmer, so much so it's easy to miss the mischief he's plotting. He's always looking for the best way to stack furniture and climb his way out. You can see where he's already had stitches through his left eyebrow. As for Olivia, well, keep a close eye on her hands. She loves to collect small things to shove up her nose, in her ears, in her mouth…"

Affection swelled from each word as he detailed his children's personalities. The man definitely loosened up when around his kids or when he was talking about them. He seemed to know his offspring well. Not what she would have expected from a distant dad. Intrigued, she moved closer.

Through the open door, she could see him drape his suit coat on the foot of the bed. He loosened his tie further and unbuttoned his collar, then worked the buttons free down his shirt.

Alexa backed toward her own room. "Um, what are you doing?"

Seth slipped his still-knotted tie over his head and untucked the shirt. "Owen kicked his shoes against me when I picked him up after we landed." He pointed to smudges down the left side. "I need to change fast before my meeting."

His all-important meeting. Right. Seth had told her he was having dinner with a bigwig contact downstairs and she could order whatever she wanted from room service. He would be back in two to three hours. If she could get the kids settled in the tub, she could sit on the side and make some work calls while watching them. Check voice mail and email on her iPhone, deal with the standard million missed calls from her mom before moving on to deal with work. Her staff wasn't large, just four other employees, including Bethany. Her partner was slowing down, but could hold down the fort. In the event an emergency arose, Bethany would make sure things didn't reach a boiling point. So she was in the free and clear to spend the night here. With the kids.

And Seth.

She thumbed a smudge from the base of the brass lamp. "Can't have shoe prints all over you at the big meeting. That's for sure."

"Could you look in the hang-up bag and get me another shirt?"

"Right, okay." She spun away before he undressed further. She charged over to the black suitcase resting on top of a mahogany luggage rack.

Alexa tugged the zipper around and…oh my.

The scent of him wafted up from his clothes, which should be impossible since they were clean clothes. But no question about it, the suitcase had captured the essence of him and it was intoxicating.

Her fingers moved along the hangers until she found a plain white shirt mixed in with a surprising amount of colorful others. Mr. Buttoned-up Businessman had a wild side. An unwelcome tingle played along her skin and in her imagination. She slapped the case closed.

Shirt in hand, she turned back to Seth who was now wearing only his pants and a T-shirt. His shoulders stretched the fabric to the limit. Her fingers curled into the shirt in her hands, her fingertips registering Sea Island Cotton, high-end, breathable, known for keeping the wearer's body cool throughout the day.

Maybe she could use some Sea Island Cotton herself because she was heating up.

Alexa thrust the shirt toward him. "Will this do?"

"Great, thanks." His knuckles brushed hers as she passed over his clothes as if they were intimately sharing a space.

And more.

Awareness chased up her wrist, her arm, higher still as the intimacy of the moment engulfed her. She was in a gorgeous hotel room, with a hot man and his beautiful children, helping him get dressed.

The scene was too wonderful. Too close to what she'd once dreamed of having with her ex.

She jerked back fast. "Any last minute things to tell me about the kids when I order up supper?"

"Owen is allergic to strawberries, but Olivia loves them and if she can get her hands on them, she tries to share them with her brother. So watch that— hotels do the strawberry garnish thing on meals."

"Anything else?" She tried to pull her eyes away from the nimble glide of his fingers up the buttons on his shirt.

"If you have an emergency, you can contact me at this number." He grabbed a hotel pen and jotted a string of numbers on the back of a business card. "That's my private cell line I use only for the kids."

"Got it." She tucked it in the corner of the gold gilded mirror. She could handle a couple of babies for a few hours.

Right?

"Don't lose it. And don't let Owen find it or he will eat it." He unbuckled his belt.

Her jaw dropped.

He tucked in his shirttails—and caught her staring. Her face heating, she turned away. Again.

Looking out the window seemed like a safe idea even though she'd been to St. Augustine about a dozen times. She could see Flagler College across the way, a place she'd once considered attending. Except her parents refused to pay if she left Charleston. Students at the Flagler castlelike fortress must feel as if they were attending Hogwarts. In fact, the whole city had a removed-from-reality feel, a step out of time. Much like this entire trip.

A Cinderella carriage pulled by a horse creaked slowly by as a Mercedes convertible whipped around and past it.

As Charleston had the French Huguenot influence, buildings here sported a Spanish Renaissance flair, and if Seth didn't get dressed soon, she would run out of things to look at. He was too much of a threat to her world for her to risk a tempting peek.

Her body hummed with awareness even when she didn't see him. What a hell of a time for her hormones to stoke to life again.

"You can turn around now." Seth's voice stroked along her ragged nerves.

She chewed her lip, spinning back to face him, a man too handsome for his own good—or hers. "I've taken care of babies before."

Not often, but for friends in hopes she could prepare herself for the day it was her turn. A day that had never come around.

"Twins are different." He tugged the tie back over his head.

If he was so worried, he should cancel his meeting. She wanted to snap at him, but knew her irritability for what it was. Her perfect plan for the day had gone way off course, complicated even more by how damn attracted she was to the man she wanted to woo for a contract, not as a bed partner.

Memories of rustling sheets and sweat-slicked bodies smoked through her mind. She'd had a healthy sex life with her ex, so much so that she hadn't considered something could be wrong until everything fell apart. She definitely couldn't trust her body to judge the situation.

"Seth." She said his first name so easily she almost gasped, but forced herself to continue, "the twins and I will manage. We'll eat applesauce and fries and chicken nuggets then skyrocket your pay-per-view bill with cartoon movies until our brains are mush. I'll watch Olivia with small objects, and Owen's charm won't distract me from his climbing or strawberry snitching. They'll be fine. Go to your meeting."

He actually hesitated before grabbing his jacket from the edge of the bed. "I'll be downstairs in the bar if you need me."

Oh, her body needed him all right. Too much for her own good. She was better off using her brains.

Seth stepped from the elevator into the lobby full of arches that led to the bar and restaurant. He scanned the chairs and sofas of rich dark woods with red-striped fabrics. Looking further, he searched past the heavy beams and thick curtains pulled back at each archway.

Thank God, somehow he'd managed to make it here ahead of his dinner partner. He strode past an iron fountain with Moorish tiles toward the bar where he was supposed to meet Javier Cortez, a cousin to royalty.

Literally. Cortez was related to the Medina family, a European monarchy that had ended in a violent coup. The Medinas and relatives had relocated to the United States, living in anonymity until a media scoop exposed their royal roots last year.

Cortez had served as head of security to one of the princes prior to the newsbreak and now oversaw safety measures for the entire family. Landing the Medinas as clients would be a huge coup.

Seth hitched up onto a stool at the bar, waving to the bartender for a seltzer water. Nothing stronger tonight.

Jansen Jets was still a small company, relatively speaking, but thanks to an in, he'd landed this meeting. One of those "Human Web" six degrees of separation moments—his cousin's wife's sister married into the Landis family, and a Landis brother married the illegitimate Medina princess.

Okay, that was more like ten degrees of separation. Thankfully, enough to bring him to this meeting. From this point on he had to rest on his own merits. Much like he'd told Alexa. *Alexa*...

Damn it all, did every thought have to circle back around to her?

Sure he'd noticed her on a physical level when he'd first stepped on the plane, and he'd managed the attraction well enough until he'd caught her eyes sliding over his body as he'd undone his pants. The ensuing heat wave sure hadn't been a welcome condition right before a meeting.

But he needed her help, so he would damn well wrestle the attraction into submission. His kids were his number one priority. He'd tried calling his ex multiple times since landing in St. Augustine, but only got her voice mail. Life had been a hell of a lot less complicated when he was flying those routes solo in North Dakota.

There didn't seem to be a damn thing more he could do about his mess of a personal life. Hopefully he could at least make headway in the business world.

Starting now.

The elevator dinged, doors swished open and Javier Cortez stepped out. Predictably the bar patrons buzzed. The newness of having royalty around hadn't worn off for people. The forty-year-old royal cousin strode out confidently, his Castilian heritage fitting right into the hotel's decor.

The guy's regal lineage didn't matter to Seth. He just appreciated the guy's hard-nosed efficiency. This deal would be sewn up quickly, one way or another.

"Sorry I'm late." Cortez thrust out his hand. "Javier Cortez."

"Seth Jansen." He stood to shake Javier's hand and then resettled onto a barstool beside the other guy.

The bartender placed an amber drink in front of Javier before he even placed an order. "I appreciate your flying down to meet with me here." He rattled the ice and looked around with assessing eyes. "My wife loves this place."

"I can see why. Lots of historic appeal."

It was also a good locale to conduct business, near the Medinas' private island off the coast of Florida. Although Seth hadn't been invited into that inner sanctum yet. Security measures were tight. No one knew the exact location and few had seen the island fortress. The Medinas owned a couple of private jets, but were looking to increase their transport options to and from the island as their family expanded with marriages and new children.

Cortez tasted his drink and set it on the cocktail napkin. "Since my wife and I are still technically finishing up our honeymoon, I promised her a longer stay, the chance to shop, laze around by the pool, soak up some Florida sun before we head back to Boston."

What the hell was he supposed to say to that? "Congratulations."

"Thanks, thanks. I hear you have your kids and their sitter with you."

Of course he'd heard, even though Seth had only been in town for about an hour. The guy was a security whiz and obviously didn't walk into a meeting unprepared. "I like to work in time with them whenever I can, so I brought the kids and Mary Poppins along."

"Excellent. Then you won't mind if we postpone the rest of this discussion."

Crap. Just what he didn't need.

The stay here extended. Less taken care of tonight, more tomorrow and even the next day. "Of course."

Cortez stood, taking his drink with him as he started back toward the elevator. Seth abandoned his seltzer water.

They stepped into the elevator together, and Cortez swiped his card for the penthouse level. "My wife and I would enjoy having you and your kids meet us for breakfast in the morning, your sitter, too. Around nine? Great," he said without waiting for an answer. "See you there."

Holy hell. Breakfast in a restaurant with a one-year-old was tough enough. But with two of them?

He stepped out onto the top floor, Javier going right as he went left.

The closer he came to the suite's door, the louder the muffled sounds grew. Squealing babies. Damn.

Was one of them hurt? He double-timed toward his room, whipped the key card through just as the door opened.

Alexa carried a baby on each hip—two freshly bathed and wet naked babies. Her cheeks were flushed, her smile wide. "I just caught them. Holy cow, they've got some speed for toddlers."

He snagged a towel from the arm of the sofa and held it open. "Pass me one."

She handed Owen over and Seth saw...

Her shirt was soaking wet, clinging to every perfect curve. Who would have thought Mary Poppins could rock the hell out of a wet T-shirt contest?

Chapter 3

Alexa plucked at her wet company shirt, conscious of the way it clung to her breasts. She didn't need the heat in Seth's eyes. She didn't need the answering fire it stirred in her. They both had different goals for what remained of their twenty-four-hour deal. They were best served focusing on the children and work.

Turning away, she hitched Olivia up on her hip and snagged the other towel from where she'd dropped it on the sofa to chase the racing duo around the suite. "You're back early from your dinner meeting."

"You need some clothes." The sound of his confident footsteps sounded softly behind her on plush carpet.

"Dry ones, for sure." She glanced through to the bathroom. Towels were draped on the floor around the circular tub, soaking up all the splashes. "I let the babies use the Jacuzzi like a kiddie pool. A few plastic cups and they were happy to play. Supper should be arriving soon. I thought you were room service when I heard you at the door."

"They'll need cleaning up again after supper." He tugged out two diapers and two T-shirts from the diaper bag.

"Then I'll just order more towels." She plucked the tiny pink T-shirt from his hand and busied herself with dressing Olivia to keep from noticing how at ease he was handling his squirming son.

"Fair enough." He pressed the diaper tapes in place, his large masculine hands surprisingly nimble.

"Did your meeting go well?" She wrestled a tiny waving arm through the sleeve.

"We didn't get through more than half a drink. He had to postpone until the morning." A quick tug later, he had Owen's powder-blue shirt in place. He hoisted his son in the air and buzzed his belly before setting him on his feet. "I'll just call room service and add my order to the rest."

He wasn't going back to work? They would be spending the rest of the evening here. Together with the children, of course. And after the toddlers drifted off? He'd mentioned Pippa kept them up late. With luck the pint-size chaperones would burn the midnight oil.

"Too bad your dinner companion couldn't have told you about the delay before you left Charleston. You would have had time to make other arrangements for the children." And she would have been at home in her lonely apartment eating ice cream while thinking about encountering Seth on his plane. Because without question, he was a memorable man.

"I'm glad to have the time with them. I assume you can arrange to stay longer?"

"I'll call my partner back as soon as the kids are asleep. She and I will make it work."

"Excellent. Now we just need to arrange extra clothes and toiletries for you." He reached for the room phone as Olivia and Owen chased each other in circles around their father. "When I order my supper I'll also have the concierge pick up something for you to change int—"

"Really, no need." She held up a hand, an unsettling tingle tripping up her spine at the thought of wearing things purchased by him. "I'll wear the hotel robe tonight and we can have the hotel wash my clothes. The kids and I will kill time tomorrow browsing around downtown, shopping while you finish your meeting. You do have a double stroller, don't you?"

"Already arranged. But you are going to need a change of clothing sooner than that." The furrows in his brow warned her a second before he said, "My business prospect wants to have breakfast with the kids and there's not a chance in hell I can carry that off on my own. It's my fault you're here without a change of clothes."

A business breakfast? With two toddlers? Whose genius idea was that? But she held her silence and conceded to the need for something appropriate to wear.

She stifled a twinge of nerves at discussing her clothing size. She was past those days of stepping on the scales every morning for her mom to check— what a hell of a way to spend "mother-daughter" time. And thank God, she was past the days of starving herself into a size zero.

Size zero. There'd been an irony in that, as if she could somehow fade away…

Blinking the past back, she said, "Okay then, tell them to buy smalls or eights, and my shoes are size seven."

His green eyes glimmered wickedly. "And underwear measurements?"

She poked him in the chest with one finger. "Not on your life am I answering that one." God, his chest was solid. She stepped away. "Make sure to keep a tally of how much everything costs. I insist on reimbursing you."

"Unnecessarily prideful, but as you wish." He said it so arrogantly she wanted to thump him on the back of his head.

Not a wise business move, though, touching him again. One little tap had nearly seared her fingertip and her mind. "I pay my own way now."

"At least let me loan you a T-shirt to sleep in tonight rather than that stifling hotel robe."

His clothes against her naked flesh?

Whoa.

Shaking off the goose bumps, she followed the toddling twins into the master bedroom. The rumble of his voice followed her as Seth ordered his meal, her clothing and some other toiletries...

Olivia and Owen sprinted to check out the matching portable cribs that had been set up on the far side of the king-size bed, each neatly made. Everything had been provided to accommodate a family. A real family. Except she would crawl under her own covers all alone wearing a hot guy's T-shirt.

Alexa wrapped her arms around her stomach, reminded of the life she'd been denied with the implosion of her marriage. A life she purposefully hadn't thought about in a year since she'd craved a real family more than her next breath. Being thrust into this situation with Seth stirred longings she'd

ignored for too long. Damn it, she'd taken this gam-
ble for her company, her employees, her future.

But in doing so, she hadn't realized how deeply
playing at this family game could cut into her heart.

Playing pretend family was kicking his ass.

Seth forked up the last bite of his Chilean sea
bass while Alexa started her warm peach bread
pudding with lavender cream. They'd opted to feed
the babies first and put them to bed so the adults
could actually dine in peace out on the turret balcony. Their supper had been set up by the wrought-
iron table for two, complete with a lone rose in the
middle of the table. Historical sconces on either
side of the open doors cast a candlelit glow over
the table.

Classical music drifted softly from inside. Okay,
so it was actually something called "The Mozart
Effect—Music for Babies," and he used it to help
soothe Olivia and Owen to sleep. But it still qualified as mood-setting music for grown-ups.

And holy crap, did Alexa ever qualify as a smok-
ing hot adult.

She'd changed into one of his T-shirts with the
fluffy hotel robe over it. She looked as if she'd just
rolled out of his bed. An ocean breeze lifted her
whispery blond hair as late evening street noises
echoed softly from the street below. Tonight had

been the closest he'd come to experiencing family life with his children.

He hadn't dated much since his divorce and when he had, he'd been careful to keep that world separate from his kids. Working side by side with Alexa had more than cut the tasks in half tonight. That made him angry all over again that he'd screwed up so badly in his own marriage. He and Pippa had known it was a long shot going in, but they'd both wanted to give it a chance, for the babies. Or at least that's what he'd thought, until he'd discovered Pippa wasn't even sure if he was the biological father.

His gut twisted.

Damn it all, Olivia and Owen were *his* children. *His* name was on their birth certificate. And he refused to let anyone take them from him. Pippa vowed she wasn't going to challenge the custody agreement, but she'd lied to him before, and in such a major way, he had trouble trusting her.

He studied the woman across from him, wishing he could read her thoughts better, but she held herself in such tight control at all times. Sure, he knew he couldn't judge all females by how things had shaken down between him and Pippa. But it definitely made him wary. Fool him once, shame on her. Fool him twice. Shame on him.

Alexa Randall was here for one reason only. To use him to jump-start her business. She wasn't in St. Augustine to play house. She didn't know, much less love, his kids. She was doing a job. Everybody in this world had an agenda. As long as he kept that knowledge forefront in his mind, they would be fine.

He reached for his seltzer water. "You're good with kids."

"Thanks," she said tightly, stabbing at her pudding.

"Seriously. You'll make a good mother someday."

She shook her head and shoved away her half-eaten dessert. "I prefer to have a husband for that and my only attempt at marriage didn't end well."

The bitterness in her voice hung between them.

He tipped back his crystal glass, eyeing her over the rim. "I'm really sorry to hear that."

Sighing, she dipped her finger in the water and traced the rim of her glass until the crystal sang. "I married a guy who seemed perfect. He didn't even care about my family's money. In fact, he sided with my dad about signing a prenup to prove it." Faster and faster her finger moved, the pitch growing higher. "After always having to second-guess friendships while growing up, that felt so good—thinking he loved me for myself, unconditionally."

"That's how it's supposed to work."

"Supposed to. But then, I'm sure you understand what it's like to have to question everyone's motives."

"Not always. I grew up in a regular farming family in North Dakota. Everyone around me had working class values. I spent my spare time camping, fishing or flying."

"Most of my friends in private school wanted the perks of hanging out with me—shopping trips in New York. For my sixteenth, my mother flew me and my friends to the Bahamas." She tapped the glass once with a short fingernail. "The ones with parents who could afford the same kind of perks were every bit as spoiled as I was. No wonder I didn't have any true friends."

Having to question people's motives as an adult was tough enough. But worrying as a kid? That could mark a person long-term. He thought of his children asleep in the next room and wondered how he would keep their lives even-keeled.

"So your ex seems like a dream guy with the prenup…and…?"

"His only condition was that I not take any money from my family." Her eyes took on a faraway, jaded look that bothered him more than it should have for someone he'd just met. "My money could go into trust for our kids someday, but we would live our lives on what we made. Sounded good, honorable."

"What happened?" He lifted his glass.

"I was allergic to his sperm."

He choked on his water. "Uh, could you run that by me again?"

"You heard me. Allergic to his swimmers. We can both have kids, just not with each other." She folded her arms on the edge of the table, leaning closer. "I was sad when the doctor told me, but I figured, hey, this was our call to adopt. Apparently Travis—my ex—didn't get the same message."

"Let me get this straight." Seth placed his glass on the table carefully to keep from snapping the stemware in two with his growing anger. "Your ex-husband left you because the two of you couldn't have biological children together?"

"Bingo," she said with a tight smile that didn't come close to reaching her haunted blue eyes.

"He sounds like a shallow jerk." A jerk Seth had an urge to punch for putting such deep shadows in this woman's eyes. "I would be happy to kick his ass for you. I may be a desk jockey these days, but I've still got enough North Dakota farm boy in me to take him down."

A smile played at her lips. "No worries. I kick butts on my own these days."

"Good for you." He admired her resilience, her spunk. She'd rebuilt her life after two nearly simultaneous blows from life that would have debilitated most people.

"I try not to beat myself up about it." Sagging back in the wrought-iron patio chair, she clutched the robe closed with her fists. "I didn't have much practice in making smart choices about the people I invited into my life. So it stands to reason I would screw that one up, too."

"Well, I'm a damn good judge of character and it's obvious to me that *he* screwed up." Seth reached across the table and touched her elbow lightly where the sleeve fell back to reveal the vulnerable crook. "Not you."

Her eyes opened wider with surprise, with awareness, but she didn't pull away. "Thanks for the vote of confidence, but I know there had to be fault on both sides."

"Still, that's not always easy to see or say." His hand fell away.

"What about *your* ex?" She straightened the extra fork she hadn't needed for her dinner. In fact, she hadn't eaten much of her fire-grilled sea scallops at all and only half of her bread pudding. Maybe the cuisine here didn't suit her. "Does she make it a regular practice to run off and leave the kids?"

"Actually, no." Pippa was usually diligent when it came to their care. In fact, she usually cried buckets anytime she left them.

Alexa tapped the top of his hand with a whisper-soft touch. "Come on now. I unloaded about my sucky marriage story. What's yours?"

Normally he preferred not to talk about his failures. But the moonlight, good food—for him at least—and even better company made him want to extend the evening. If that meant spilling a few public knowledge facts about his personal life, then so be it.

"There's no great drama to share—" And yeah, he was lying, but he preferred to keep it low-key. He was used to glossing over the truth in front of his kids, who were too young to understand paternity questions. "We had a fling that resulted in a surprise pregnancy—" Pippa had just failed to mention the other fling she'd had around the same time. "So we got married for the children, gave it an honest try and figured out it wasn't going to work. We already had divorce papers in motion by the time the babies were due."

"If you don't mind my asking—" she paused until he waved her on "—why did you get married at all then?"

He'd asked himself the same question more than once, late at night when he was alone and missing the twins. "Old-fashioned, I guess. I wanted to be around my kids all the time. I wanted it to work." Wanted the babies to be his. "It just…didn't."

"You're so calm about it," she said with more of those shadows chasing around in her eyes.

Calm? He was a holy mess inside, but letting that anger, the betrayal, fly wouldn't accomplish anything. "I have the twins. Pippa and I are trying to be good parents. At least I thought we were."

Her hand covered his completely, steadily. "By all appearances you're doing a great job. They're beautiful, sweet babies."

The touch of her soft skin sent a bolt of lust straight through his veins, pumping pulsing blood south. He wrestled his thoughts back to the conversation, back to the care of his offspring. "They're hell on wheels, but I would do anything for them. Anything."

So there was no need for him to stress over the fact that Alexa turned him on so hard his teeth hurt. He'd been too long without sex, only a couple of encounters in the year since his divorce. That had to be the reason for his instantaneous, out of control reaction to this woman.

Gauging by the pure blue flame in her eyes, she was feeling it, too.

He was realizing they had a lot more than just a hefty dose of attraction in common. They were both reeling from crappy marriages and completely focused on their careers. Neither of them was looking for anything permanent that would involve more messy emotions.

So why not hook up? If he wanted to act on their attraction and she was cool with the fact that being together had no effect on his business decisions, this could be the best damn thing to happen to him in months. *She* could be the best thing to happen to him in months.

Yeah, this could work.

Simple, uncomplicated sex.

They had an empty second bedroom waiting for them. He always carried condoms these days. One surprise pregnancy was enough. They had moonlight, atmosphere. She was even already half-undressed. There was nothing stopping him from seeing if she was amenable.

Decision made, Seth pulled the rose from the vase and stroked it lightly down her nose. Her eyes blinked wide with surprise, but she didn't say a word, didn't so much as move. Hell, yeah.

Emboldened, he traced her lips with the bud before he leaned across the table and kissed her.

Chapter 4

The warm press of Seth's mouth against hers surprised Alexa into stillness—for all of three heartbeats. Then her pulse double-timed. Surprise became desire. The attraction she'd been feeling since first laying eyes on him, since he'd taken off his tie, since she'd felt the steamy glide of his gaze over her damp clothing now ramped into hyperdrive.

He stood without breaking contact, and she rose with him as they stepped around the small table into each other's arms. She gripped his shoulders, her fingers sinking into the warm cotton of the shirt she'd chosen for him earlier. Her defenses were low, without a doubt. The romantic meal, moonlit turret and alluring dinner companion had lulled her. Even the soft classical music stroked over her tensed and frazzled nerves. It had been so long since she'd relaxed, too busy charging ahead with rebuilding her life. Even opening up about her divorce had felt—if not good—at least cathartic.

It had also left her bare and defenseless.

The man might be brusque in the way he spoke sometimes, but, wow, did he ever take his time with a kiss. She slid one hand from his shoulder up to the back of his neck, her fingers toying with the coarse texture of his hair. Her body fit against his, her softness giving way to the hard planes of his chest. The sensitive pads of her fingers savored the rasp of his late day beard as she traced his strong jaw, brushed across his cheekbones and back into his thick hair.

His mouth moved over hers firmly, surely, enticing her to open for him. Her breasts pressed more firmly against him as she breathed faster and faster with arousal. The scent of aftershave mingled with the salty sea air. The taste of lime water and spices from his dinner flavored their kiss, tempting her senses all the more to throw reason away. The bold sweep of his tongue made her hunger for more of this. More of *him*.

How easy it would be to follow him into his bedroom and toss away all the stress and worries of the past years as quickly as discarded clothes. Except, too soon, morning would come and with it would come all those concerns, multiplied because of their lack of self-control.

God, this was so reckless and unwise and impulsive in a way she couldn't afford any longer. Scavenging for a shred of self-control, she pushed at his shoulders since she couldn't seem to bring herself to tear her mouth away from his.

Thank goodness he took the hint.

He pulled back, but not far, only a whisper away. Each breath she took drew in the crisp scent of him. The starlight reflected in his green eyes staring at her with a keen perception of how very much she ached to take this kiss further.

Her chest pumped for air even though she knew full well the dizziness had nothing to do with oxygen and everything to do with Seth's appeal. Slowly he guided her back to her chair—good thing since her legs were wobbly—and he returned to his as well, his eyes still holding her captive. He lifted his crystal glass, sipping the sparkling water while watching her over the rim.

She forced a laugh that came out half strangled. "That was unexpected."

"Really?" He placed his glass on the table again. The pulse visibly throbbing in his neck offered the only sign he was as shaken as she was by what they'd just shared. "I've wanted to kiss you since I first saw you on board my plane. At that moment,

I thought that attraction was mutual. Now, I *know* it is."

His cool arrogance smoked across the table.

A chilling thought iced the heat just as quickly as he'd stoked it. "Is that why you asked me to watch your children? Because you wanted a chance to hit on me?" She sat straighter in her chair and wished she wore something more businesslike than a borrowed terry-cloth robe and his shirt. "I thought we had a business arrangement. Mixing business and personal lives is never a good idea."

"Then why did you kiss me back?" He turned the glass on the tablecloth.

"Impulse."

His eyes narrowed. "So you admit you're attracted to me."

Duh. Denying the mutual draw would be pointless. "You know that I am, but it doesn't mean I've been making plans to act on the feeling. I think Brad Pitt's hot as hell, but I wouldn't jump him even if given the opportunity."

"You think I'm Brad Pitt-hot?"

Damn the return of his arrogant grin.

"I was just making a point," she snapped.

"But you think I'm hot."

"Not relevant." She flattened her hands on the table. "I'm not acting on the impulse any further tonight or ever. If that means you renege on your offer to read my proposal and refer me to others in the business, then so be it. I will not sleep my way into a deal."

She pushed to her feet.

"Whoa, hold on." Standing, he circled the table to face her, stroking her upper arm soothingly. "I didn't mean to imply anything of the sort. First, I don't believe you're the kind of person to get ahead in the world that way. And second, I have never paid for sex, and I never intend to."

She froze, his touch sending fresh skitters of awareness up her arm. The darkness and distant night sounds isolated them with too much intimacy.

Alexa eased back a step toward their suite and the soft serenade of Mozart on the breeze. "Have you looked into finding someone else to take care of your children?"

Still, he didn't move. He didn't have to. His presence called to her as he simply stood a couple of steps away, his broad shoulders backlit by the moon, starlight playing across his blond hair, giving him a Greek godlike air.

"Why would I need to do that?" he asked. "You're here for them."

"Our agreement only lasts for twenty-four hours," she reminded him, holding onto the door frame to bolster her wavering resolve.

"I thought we established the time frame had expanded because my meeting with Javier Cortez fell through tonight." He stepped closer, stopping just shy of touching her again. "You even rearranged things at your work to accommodate our business agreement."

He was right, and she'd allowed him to scramble her thoughts once more. She locked onto his last three words and pushed ahead. "Our *business* agreement."

"You're angry."

"Not…angry exactly. Just frustrated and disappointed in both of us."

His eyes flared with something indefinable. "Disappointed?"

"Oh—" she suddenly understood his expression "—not disappointed in the kiss. It was… Hell, you were here, too. There's no denying the chemistry between us."

Another arrogant grin spread across his face. "I agree one hundred percent."

"But back to the Brad Pitt principle." She stiffened her spine and her resolve. "Just because there's an attraction doesn't mean it's wise to act on it. I'm disappointed that we did something so reckless, so unprofessional. My business has to be my primary focus, just as you've said your children are your main concern."

"Having my priorities in order doesn't cancel out my attraction to you. I can separate business from pleasure." He held her with his laser hot gaze. "I'm very good at multitasking."

Anger did build inside her now alongside the frustration. "You're not hearing me! This thing between us is too much, too soon. We barely know each other and we both have high stakes riding on this trip." She jabbed him in the chest with one finger. "So, listen closely. No. More. Kissing."

She launched through the door and into the suite before he could shake her resolve again. But as she raced across the luxurious sitting area into her bedroom, his voice echoed in her ears and through her hungry senses.

"Damn shame."

She completely agreed. Sleep tonight would be difficult to come by as regrets piled on top of frustrated desire.▴▾

Staring off over the city skyline, Seth leaned back in his chair, staying on the turret balcony long after Alexa left. The heat of their kiss still sizzling through him, he finished his seltzer water, waiting for the light in her room to turn off.

He'd only met her today, and he couldn't recall wanting any woman this much. The strength of the attraction had been strong enough on its own. But now that he'd actually tasted her? He pushed the glass aside, his deeper thirst not even close to quenched.

Now he had to decide what to do about that feeling. She was right in saying that giving in to an affair wasn't wise. They both had important reasons to keep their acquaintance all business.

His life was complicated enough. He needed to keep his life stable for his kids. No parade of women through the door, confusing them.

He eyed his smartphone on the table where it had been resting since his four attempts to contact Pippa. She still wasn't returning his messages, and his temper was starting to simmer. What if there had been something wrong with one of the kids and he needed to contact her? She should at least pick up to find out why he was trying to reach her.

His phone vibrated with an incoming call. He slammed his chair back on all four legs and scooped up his cell fast. The LED screen showed a stored name…his cousin Paige back in Charleston.

Not Pippa.

Damn it.

Even his extended family kept in better contact with him than the mother of his kids. His cousins Paige and Vic had both moved from North Dakota, each starting their families in the Charleston area. With no other family left out west, Seth had followed and started his own business.

He picked up without hesitation. "Paige? Everything okay?"

"We're fine." His cousin's voice was soft as if lowered to keep from waking her children. Classical guitar music played softly in the background.

"The girls are both finally asleep. I've been worried about you all afternoon. How are you and the twins? I feel so bad that I couldn't help you out."

"No need to call and apologize. We prefer to steer clear of strep throat."

"Actually I'm calling about Vic and Claire…"

Oh. Hell. In the chaos with the twins, he'd actually forgotten that his cousin Vic's wife had gone into labor today. "How's she doing?"

"She delivered a healthy baby boy just before midnight. Nine pounds thirteen ounces, which explains the C-section. But Mom and baby are doing great. His big sister and big brother can't wait to meet him in the morning." Two boys and a girl. A family.

Seth scratched the kink in his neck. "Send my congratulations when you see them. I'll swing by for a visit when I get back·in town."

"I'll let them know." The reception crackled as it sounded like she moved her phone to the other ear. More guitar music filled the airwaves… Bach, perhaps? "Actually, I called for a different reason. Now that Claire's had the baby and Vic has picked up their kids, her sister Starr says she can watch the twins. They know her two kids. They'll have a blast. You could fly Olivia and Owen up early in the morning before your first meeting."

"That's a generous offer…"

"My girls won't be contagious in another day or

two once the antibiotics kick in, so I can relieve her then. No worries."

Her plan sounded workable. And yet, he hesitated, his gaze drawn back to the suite where Alexa slept. "You're all busy with your own families, and I have a plan in place here."

"You're family," Paige insisted sincerely. "We want to help."

"I appreciate that." Except he genuinely wanted his kids near him—and he wanted to keep Alexa near him, too.

The thought of cutting his time with Alexa short—it just wasn't happening. Crazy, really, since he could contact her later, after this deal was cinched. If she was even still speaking to him once she realized he never intended to give her the Jansen Jets contract.

No. His time to get to know Alexa was now. He needed to figure out this unrelenting draw between them and work through it. She was here, and he intended to keep it that way. "Thanks, Paige, but I meant it when I said I'm set. I have help."

"Hmm…" Her voice rose with interest. "You have a new nanny?"

His family chipped in most of the time, but he didn't want to take advantage so he hired a couple of part-time nannies on occasion, all of which Paige would already know about. "Not a nanny. More of a sitter, a, uh, friend actually."

"A female friend?" she pressed, tenacious as ever.

"She's a female, yes." *Definitely* female.

"That's it?" Paige laughed. "That's all you're going to tell me, eh?"

"There's not much to tell." Yet. His eyes drifted back to the suite as he envisioned Alexa curled up asleep, wearing his shirt.

"Ah," she said smugly, "so you're still in the early stages, but not too early, right, or she wouldn't be there with your children. Because, as best as I can remember, you haven't dated much and none of those women ever got anywhere near the twins."

His cousin was too insightful. The way she homed in on the intensity of his draw to Alexa so quickly made him uncomfortable.

He shot up from his seat. "That's enough hypothesizing about my personal life for one night. I need to go."

"I'm not giving up. I'll want details when you return," Paige insisted, getting louder and louder by the second. "And I want to meet her. I know you guard your privacy, but I'm family and I love you."

"Love you too, cuz."

"So you'll talk to me? Let me know what's going on in your world rather than hole up the way you did after Pippa—"

"I hear a kid," he cut her short. "Gotta go. Bye." He thumbed the off button and flipped the phone in his palm, over and over.

Guilt kicked around in his gut for shutting down Paige and for taking advantage of Alexa's help. He should send Alexa back to Charleston and then impose on the sister of a cousin-in-law because his ex-wife had dumped his kids off without warning...

Hell, his life was screwed up, and he needed to start taking charge. He'd meant it when he said he could separate the personal from the professional. But he also heard Alexa when she said this was moving too fast for her. She needed more time, time they wouldn't have if she went back to Charleston while he stayed here. He suspected once she went home, she would erect mile-high walls between them, especially once she learned he'd never planned to sign her cleaning company.

He needed longer with her *now*.

His mind filled with a vision of Alexa chasing his kids around, all wet from the tub. Warm memories pulled him in with a reminder of the family life he should be having right now and wasn't because of his workload. Having Alexa here felt so right.

It *was* right.

And so, he wasn't sending her back in the morning. In fact, he had to find a way to extend their window of time together. He not only needed her help with the children, but he also wanted her to stay for more *personal* reasons. The explosive chemistry they'd just discovered didn't come around often. Hell, he couldn't remember when he'd ever burned to have a particular woman this much. So much the craving filled his mind as well as his body.

The extension of their trip presented the perfect opportunity to follow that attraction to its ultimate destination.

Landing her directly into his bed.

Sunlight streamed through the window over the array of clothes laid out on the bed. So many clothes. Far more than she needed for a day or two.

Although as Alexa looked closer, she noticed the variety. It was as if whoever had shopped for her had planned for any contingency. Tan capris with a shabby chic blouse. A simple red cocktail dress. A sexy black bathing suit that looked far from nanny-like and made her wonder who'd placed the order. At least there was a crocheted cover-up. And for this morning's breakfast…

She wore a silky sundress, floral with coral-tinted tulips in a watercolor print. Strappy gold sandals wrapped up and around her ankles. She scraped her hair back with a matching scarf that trailed down her back.

There was a whole other shopping bag that a quick peek told her held more clothes, underwear, a nightgown and a fabric cosmetics bag full of toiletries. Once upon a time, she'd taken these kinds of luxuries for granted, barely noticing when they appeared in her room or at a hotel.

These days she had a firm grasp on how hard she would have to work to pay for even one of these designer items. What a difference a year could make in a person's life. Yet, here she was again, dancing on the periphery of a world that had almost swallowed her whole.

Steeling her resolve to keep her values firmly in place, she strode from the bedroom into the sitting area where Seth was strapping the twins into the new, top-of–the-line double stroller.

He looked up and smiled. The power of his vibrant green eyes and dimples reached across the room, wrapping around her, enticing her to move closer into the circle of that happiness. A dangerous move. She had to step away, for her own peace of mind. She wasn't wired to leap into intimacy with a stranger.

A stranger who became more intriguing by the second.

Surely a billionaire who knew how to work a stroller couldn't be totally disconnected from everyday reality. That insight buoyed her, and inspired her. Actively learning more about him would help her on many levels. Knowing more about him was wise for her work.

For work, damn it, not because of this insane attraction.

"Are you ready?" he asked.

"Yes, I believe I am." She could do this. She

could keep her professional face in place, while discovering if Seth Jansen harbored any more surprises in that hulking hot body of his.

"Glad the clothes fit. Although for breakfast with the twins, we might be better off draping ourselves in rain ponchos."

Before she could laugh or reply, his phone rang and he held up a hand. "Hold on, I've got to take this. Work call coming in."

He started talking into his cell and grabbed his briefcase off the sofa. Opening the door, he gestured her ahead. She wheeled the stroller forward, out into the hall and toward the elevator.

The fabric slid sensuously against her skin with each step as she pushed the stroller into the elevator while Seth spoke on his phone to his partner… Rick…briefcase in his other hand. Each glide of the silky dress against her skin reminded her how vibrantly in tune her senses were this morning, and, as much as she wanted to credit the sunshine, she knew it was last night's kiss that had awakened something inside her.

Something that made professional goals tougher to keep in focus.

Two floors down, the doors slid open to admit an older couple dressed casually in sightseeing clothes that still shouted Armani and Prada. They fit right in with the rest of the clientele here. Except the woman carried a simple canvas bag with little handprints painted on it and signed in childlike hand-writing. Stenciled along the top of the bag were the words Grandma's Angels. Alexa swallowed a lump of emotion as she counted at least eleven different scrawled signatures.

The husband leaned closer to his wife, whisper-ing, pointing and smiling nostalgically. The wife knelt to pick up a tiny tennis shoe and passed it to Alexa. "You have a beautiful family."

Before Alexa could correct her, they reached the lobby and the couple exited. She glanced sheep-ishly toward Seth and found him staring at her with assessing eyes as he tucked away his phone. Her mouth went dry. She grabbed the stroller, grateful for the support as the now increasingly predictable wobbly knees syndrome set in.

Ever aware of his gaze following her, she wheeled the twins from the elevator. She needed to get her thoughts in order ASAP. She was seconds away from meeting royalty for breakfast, pretty heady stuff even given her own upbringing. Seth was cer-tainly coming through on his promise to introduce her to prestigious connections. Knowing the Me-dina family could be a serious boon to her fledg-ling business.

Although she was confused by a person who invited twin toddlers to a business breakfast at a restaurant with silk, antiques and a ceiling hand-painted with twenty-four karat gold.

The clink of silverware echoing from the room full of patrons, she didn't have to wonder for even a second which pair of diners to approach. A dark-haired, aristocratic man stood from a table set for six, nodding in their direction. A blonde woman sat beside him, a flower tucked behind her ear.

The wheels of the stroller glided smoothly along the tile floor as they passed a waiter carrying plates of crepes on his tray. Alexa stopped by their table.

Seth shook the man's hand. "Javier, I'd like you to meet—"

The man took her hand. "Alexa Randall. A pleasure to meet you," Javier said with only a hint of an accent. He motioned to the elegant woman beside him. "This is my wife, Victoria."

"Lovely to meet you." Victoria smiled welcomingly, while tucking her fingers into the crook of her husband's arm. He covered her hand automatically with a possessive and affectionate air.

Good God, this place was chock full of couples swimming in marital bliss. First the elderly couple in the elevator. Now her dining companions for breakfast. She didn't even dare look at the couple feeding each other bits of melon at the table next to them.

The numbers of fawning couples here defied national divorce statistics. Although, now that she thought about it, she and Seth had enough break-ups to even out the scales.

Leaning into the stroller, Victoria grinned at the twins and spun a rattle attached to the tray. "Would you mind if I held one of these sweethearts?"

Seth pulled back the stroller canopy. "Sure, this is Owen—" he picked up his son "—and this is Olivia."

As Victoria reached down, the little girl stretched her arms up toward Alexa instead. Alexa's heart squeezed in response. So much so, it scared her a little. These babies were quickly working their way into her affection. Victoria eased back gracefully and left Alexa to settle the baby girl into her high chair beside her brother's. The adults took their seats and placed their orders, so far, with no mishaps.

As the waitress placed each person's dish on the table, Victoria spread her linen napkin across her lap. "I told Javier he really put you on the spot insisting you bring along babies, but the twins are total dolls." She tickled Olivia's chin. "Hopefully you'll warm up to me, sweetie, so I can entertain you while Alexa eats her breakfast, too."

"I think I can manage, but thank you." She reached past her smoked salmon bagel for her goblet of juice. How well did this woman and her husband already know Seth? What kind of information might she learn during this breakfast about Seth and his possible contacts?

While Javier detailed the must-see sights in

St. Augustine, Olivia and Owen fed themselves fruit—which scared Alexa to her last frazzled nerve as she watched to be sure strawberries stayed on Olivia's tray but not Owen's.

Seth shoveled in steak and eggs, spooning oatmeal into the twins' mouths, while holding a conversation. She was in awe.

And a little intimidated.

She'd almost flooded the floor last night during their bath. If he hadn't shown up early, she wasn't sure how she would have wrestled them both into clothes. Whenever she thought she'd moved everything dangerous out of their reach...

Oh, God...

She lunged for Olivia just as Seth smoothly pulled the salt shaker from her grasp. Her pulse rate doubled at the near miss with catastrophe. So much for using this breakfast to learn more about Seth from the Cortez couple. She would be lucky to make it through the meal with her sanity intact.

Victoria rested her knife at the top of her plate of half-eaten eggs Benedict. "I hope he's treating you to some vacation fun after all these stodgy business meetings are over."

"Pardon?" Alexa struggled to keep track of the twins and the conversation in the middle of a business meeting and a dining room full of tourists.

Glasses and silverware clinked and clattered.

Waiters angled past with loaded trays as people fueled up for the day ahead.

Victoria swiped her mouth with the linen napkin. "You deserve some pampering for watching the kids solo here at the hotel during the day."

"I'm helping out with temporary nanny detail."

Leaning closer, Victoria whispered, "It's obvious he doesn't look at you like a nanny."

She couldn't exactly deny that since she was likely searing him with her own glances, too. "Honestly we don't know each other that well."

Victoria waved away her comment, her wedding rings refracting light from the chandelier. "The length of time doesn't always matter when it comes to the heart. I knew right away Javier was the one." She smiled affectionately at her new husband, who was deep in conversation with Seth. "It took us a while to find our way to each other, but if I'd listened to my heart right off, we could have been saved so many months of grief."

"It's a business arrangement," she said simply, hoping if she repeated it enough she could maintain her objectivity. "Only business."

"Of course," Victoria conceded, but her smile didn't dim. "I'm sorry. I didn't mean to be nosy. It's just that given what I understand from Javier, Seth has been a workaholic since his divorce. He hasn't had time for relationships."

"There's nothing to apologize for." Alexa knew

full well she and Seth were sending out mixed signals. As much as she'd been determined to keep things professional with Seth the businessman, she found herself drawn to Seth the father. A man so tender with his children. At ease with a baby stroller. As adept at flying a spoonful of oatmeal into a child's mouth as he was at piloting a plane through the sky.

These surprise insights proved a potent attraction, especially after living with her own distant father and then the way her ex had checked out on her.

Victoria's voice pulled Alexa out of her musings.

"Honestly, my thoughts may be selfish. I was thinking ahead that if Javier and Seth settle on a contract, then I was hoping we would get to see more of each other. As much as I adore my husband, his world is narrow and he's suspicious of expanding the circle. I'm always grateful for some girl time."

"That would be lovely, thank you." Alexa understood perfectly about lonely inner circles, too much so. She felt a twinge of guilt over her thoughts about using the Cortezes for contacts.

All her life she'd been warned about gold diggers. She'd always known the chances of someone seeing through the money to love her for herself was slim. And still she'd made a royal mess. She didn't want to let the Cortez money and their Medina connections blind her to who they really were.

"I mean it. And regardless of how much time we spend visiting, let's enjoy the day…let's have fun."

Fun? She should be home, at work. She took a deep breath. This situation would help her at work. Or she hoped so.

She couldn't ignore the fact that her wish to stay right here was increasing by the second. "I appreciate how helpful you've been here at breakfast. The twins are my responsibility. We're going sightseeing with the stroller, maybe do a little shopping."

"Perfect," Victoria declared. "I'm at loose ends. I love a good walk and shopping. And after that, we can wear them out at the pool."

Alexa did have a swimsuit and she had absolutely no reason not to take Victoria up on her generous offer. No reason other than a deep-seated fear of allowing herself to be tempted back into a world she'd been determined to leave behind. A way of life embraced by Seth and his precious children. Her eyes were drawn back to the twins.

Just as Owen wrapped his fist around one of his sister's strawberries—a food he was allergic to.

Panic gripped Alexa as she saw the baby's lightning fast intent to gobble the forbidden fruit. "No! Owen, don't eat that."

Lurching toward him, she grabbed his chubby wrist just before his hand reached his mouth. His face scrunched into utter dejection as his tiny world crumbled over the lost treat. Alexa winced a second ahead of his piercing scream. Seth leaned in to soothe the temper tantrum. Before Alexa could even form the words of warning…

Olivia flipped the bowl of oatmeal straight into Javier Cortez's lap.

Chapter 5

The cosmos must have been holding a serious grudge against him because the sight of Alexa in a bathing suit sucker-punched him clean through.

Seth stopped short by the poolside bar outside the hotel and allowed himself a moment to soak in the sunlit view, a welcome pleasure after a tense work day that had started with his kid dumping oatmeal in a prospective customer's lap. Thank goodness Javier Cortez had insisted it didn't matter.

And Alexa had acted fast by scooping up both twins and taking them away for the day.

Now, she looked anything but maternal as she rubbed sunscreen down her arms, laughing at something Victoria said. The twins slept in a playpen under the shade of a small open cabana. Only a half dozen others had stayed this late in the day—a young couple drinking wine in the hot tub and a family playing with a beach ball in the shallow end.

His attention stayed fully focused on the goddess in black Lycra.

He should be celebrating the success of his day's meeting. Javier wanted him to tour the landing strip at the king's private island off the coast of St. Augustine. Their time here was done. The king's island even came equipped with a top-notch nanny for the twins, a nanny the king kept on staff for his grandchildren's visits.

And yet, Seth was all the more determined than ever to keep Alexa with him, to win her over, to seduce her into his bed again and again until he worked this tenacious attraction out of their systems. He hadn't yet attained that goal but was determined to keep her around until he succeeded.

The black bathing suit was more modest than the strings other women wore that barely held in the essentials. Still, there was no denying her sensuality. Halter neckline, plunging deeply until the top of her belly button ring showed.

A simple gold hoop.

His hands itched to grasp her hips and slide his fingers along the edges, slipping inside to feel the satiny slickness he knew waited right there. For him.

Splashing from the deep end snapped him back to reality. Damn, he seriously needed to rein in those kinds of thoughts out here in public. Even when they were alone. He needed to be patient. He didn't want to spook her into bailing on this time they had together.

He thought back to how fast she'd retreated after their kiss. She'd been undeniably as turned on as he was and yet, she'd avoided him that morning as they'd prepared for the day. Although he thought he sensed a bit of softening in her stance as the day wore on. At breakfast he'd thought he caught her eyes lingering on him more than once. He could see the memory of their kiss written in her eyes as she stared at him with a mixture of confusion and attraction.

Shoving away from the bar, Seth strode alongside the pool toward Alexa. "Good afternoon, ladies."

Jolted, she looked over at him. Her eyes widened and he could have sworn goose bumps of aware-ness rose along her arms. She yanked her crocheted cover-up off the glass-topped table and shrugged into it almost fast enough to hide her breasts bead-ing with arousal. His own body throbbed in re-sponse, his hands aching to cradle each creamy globe in his palms.

"Seth, I didn't expect you back this early."

Out of the corner of his eyes, he saw Victoria gather her beach bag. "Since you're done for the day, I take it my husband's free, so if you'll both excuse me…"

The woman made a smooth—and timely—exit.

Seth sank down into her vacated lounger beside Alexa as a teenager cannonballed into the deep end. "Did you and the babies have a good afternoon?"

"No problems or I would have called you. I wrote down everything the children ate and when they went to sleep. The pool time wore them out." She toyed with the tie on her cover up—right between her breasts.

He forced his gaze to stay on her face. "I want you to extend your time with us for a couple more days."

Her jaw went slack with surprise before she swallowed hard. "You want me to stay with you and the children?"

"Precisely."

"My business is a small operation—"

"What about your partner?"

"I can't dump everything on her indefinitely and still meet our obligations."

His point exactly as for why hers wasn't the company for Jansen Jets—hers wasn't large enough and didn't have adequate backup resources. He leaned forward, elbows resting on his knees. "I thought you were cleaning my plane to meet with me."

"That certainly was my intent—and to impress you with A-1's work." She hugged her legs. "But I do clean other aircraft in addition to my obligations to office work."

"That doesn't leave much time for a private life." Late day sun beating down on his head, he shrugged out of his suit jacket and draped it over the back of the lounger. He loosened his tie. God, he hated the constraining things.

"I'm investing in my future."

"I understand completely." His eyes gravitated toward his children, still sleeping peacefully in the playpen—Olivia on her tummy with her diapered butt up in the air, Owen on his back with his arms flung wide.

"You've achieved your goals. That's admirable. I'm working on my dream now." Determination coated each word as fully as the sunscreen covered her bared skin.

He *really* didn't need to be thinking about her exposed body right now.

Already, he was on the edge of a new deal with Javier Cortez to supply charter jets for the royal Medinas. That huge boon would take his company to the next level and free him up to set up an entire volunteer, nonprofit foundation devoted to search and rescue operations. His first love, what had drawn him into flying in the first place. That love of flying had helped him develop and patent the airport security device that had made him a mint. Once he took his business to the next level, funding and overstretched government budgets wouldn't be an issue...

So damn close to achieving all his business dreams.

Yet, still he was restless. "Let's forget arguing about tomorrow and business. We can hash that out later. Right now, I'm off the clock. I want to make the most of our time left in St. Augustine tonight."

"What exactly did you have in mind?" She eyed him suspiciously.

Had he imagined her softening on the all-business stance? There was only one way to find out.

Standing, he snagged his suit coat. "We're going to spend the evening out."

"With twins? Don't you think breakfast was pushing our luck?"

He grinned, scooping up his groggy daughter. "Trust me. I can handle this."

"All right, if you're sure."

"Absolutely." He palmed his daughter's back as she wriggled in his arms and tugged at his collar. "Wait until you see what I have planned. You'll want to dress comfortably, though. And we should probably pack extra clothes for the kids in case they get dirty."

Alexa pulled up alongside him, Owen in her arms. Seth reached for the door inside—

Until her gasp stopped him short.

"Did you forget something?" he asked.

When Alexa didn't answer, he glanced and found her staring back at him with horror. What the hell? Except as she raised a shaking hand to point, he realized she wasn't looking at him. Her attention was focused fully on Olivia.

More precisely, on Olivia's bulging left nostril.

Sitting on the edge of the hotel sofa in their suite, Alexa struggled to contain the squirming little girl in her lap while pushing back the welling panic. The whole ride up in the elevator had been crazy, with Seth attempting to check his daughter's nose and the child growing more agitated by the second.

How in the world had Olivia wedged something up her nostril? More importantly, *what* had she shoved into there?

Alexa winced at the baby's bulging left nostril. She hadn't taken her eyes off Olivia for a second during their time at the pool—except when Olivia had been sleeping. Had she woken up? Found something in the playpen? Perhaps something blew inside the pen with her?

Panic gripped her. What the hell had she been thinking, allowing herself to believe she could care for these two precious children? She willed herself to stop shaking and deal with the crisis at hand.

Seth knelt in front of her, trying to grasp his

daughter's head between his palms. "I can get this out if you will just hold her still long enough for me to push my thumb down the outside of her nose."

"Believe me, I'm trying my best." Alexa's heart pumped as hard and fast as Olivia's feet as the little girl screamed, kicking her father in the stomach. Her face turned red; her skin beaded with sweat from hysteria.

Sinking back on his haunches, Seth looked around their suite. "Is there any pepper left from last night's dinner?"

"Housekeeping cleared away everything. Oh, God, I am so sorry. I don't know how this happened—"

A crash echoed through the room.

Alexa looked at Seth, her panic mirrored in his eyes. "Owen!"

They both shot to their feet just as a pitiful wail drifted from behind the velvet sofa. Holding Olivia around the waist, Alexa ran fast on Seth's heels, only to slam against his back when he stopped short.

Owen sat on the floor, blessedly unharmed, just angry. His "tower"—which consisted of a chair, a pillow and the ice bucket—now lay on its side by the television. Handprints all over the flat screen testified to his attempt to turn on the TV by himself.

Seth knelt beside his son, running his hands along the toddler's arms and legs. "Are you okay, buddy? You know you're not supposed to climb like that." His thumb brushed over his son's forehead, along the eyebrow that still carried a scar from past stitches. "Be careful."

Picking up Owen, Seth held him close for a second, a sigh of relief racking through his body so visibly Alexa almost melted into the floor with sympathy. God, this big manly guy who plowed through life and through the skies alone had the most amazing way of connecting with his kids.

What would it have been like to grow up with a father like him? A dad so very present in his children's lives?

Standing, Seth said, "I'm going to have to take Olivia to the emergency room. Swap kids with me. You can stay here with Owen."

"You still trust me?"

"Of course," he responded automatically even though his mouth had gone tight. With frustration? Fear?

Or anger?

He leaned toward her. Olivia let out a high-pitched shriek and locked her arms tighter around Alexa's neck, turning her face frantically from her father.

Seth frowned. "It's okay, kiddo. It's just me."

Patting Olivia's back, Alexa swayed soothingly from side to side. "She must think you're going to pinch her nose again."

"Well, we don't have much choice here. I need

to take her in." He set down Owen and clasped his daughter.

Olivia's cries cranked up to earsplitting wails, which upset her brother who started sobbing on the floor. If Olivia kept gasping would whatever was in her nose get sucked in? And then where would it go? Into a lung? The possibilities were horrifying. This parenting thing was not for the faint of heart.

"Seth, let me hold her rather than risk her becoming even more hysterical." She cradled the little girl's head, blond curls looping around Alexa's fingers as surely as the child was sliding into Alexa's heart. "You and I can go to the emergency room and take both kids."

Plowing a hand through his hair, Seth looked around the suite again as if searching for other options. Finally he nodded and picked up his son. "That's probably for the best. We just have to get a car." He grabbed the room phone and dialed the hotel operator. "Seth Jansen here. We need transportation to the nearest E.R. waiting for us. We're headed to the elevator now."

She jammed her feet into the flip-flops she'd worn to the pool, grateful she'd at least had time to change out of her swimsuit, and followed Seth out into the hall. The elevator opened immediately— thank God—and they plunged inside the empty compartment. He jostled his restless son while she made *shhh, shhh, shhh* soothing sounds for Olivia, who was now hiccupping. But at least the little girl wasn't crying.

The floors dinged by, but not fast enough. The doors parted and the elderly couple they'd seen on their way down to breakfast stepped inside.

Dressed to the nines in jewels and evening wear, the woman wasn't carrying her canvas bag made by her grandchildren, but she still radiated a grandma air. She leaned toward Olivia and crooned, "What's the matter, sweetie? Why the tears?"

Lines of strain and worry pulled tighter at the corners of Seth's mouth. "She shoved something up her nose," he said curtly, his gaze locked in on the elevator numbers as if willing the car to move faster. "We're headed to the E.R."

As if sensing her dad's intent, Olivia pressed her face into Alexa's neck.

The grandmother looked back at her husband and winked knowingly. The older gentleman, dressed in a tuxedo, reached past Alexa so quickly she didn't have time to think.

He tugged Olivia's ear. "What's that back there behind your ear, little one?" His hand came back around with a gold cuff link in his palm. "Was that in your ear?"

Olivia peeked around to see and like lightning, the grandmother reached past and swiped her finger down Olivia's nose. A white button shot out and into the woman's hand. She held it up to Seth's shirt.

A perfect match. They hadn't even noticed he was missing one from near his neck.

Surprise stamped on his handsome face, Seth stuffed the button into his pocket. "She must have pulled it off when I picked her up by the pool."

Alexa gasped in awe at how easily the couple had handled mining the button from Olivia's nose. "How did you two manage that so smoothly?"

The grandpa straightened his tuxedo bow tie. "Lots of practice. You two will get the knack before you know it."

In a swirl of diamonds and expensive perfume, the couple swept out of the elevator, leaving Alexa and Seth inside. The doors slid closed again. She sagged back against the brass rail. Relief left her weak-kneed all the way back to the penthouse floor while Seth called downstairs on his cell to cancel their ride to the E.R.

Stopping just outside their door, he tucked his phone in his pocket and slid a hand behind her neck. "Thank you."

"For what? I feel like I've let you down." The emotions and worry after the scare with Olivia had left her spinning. She could only imagine how he must feel.

"Thank you for being here. Chasing these two is more challenging than flying a plane through a thunderstorm." He scrubbed a hand over his jaw. "My family tells me I'm not too good at asking for help. But I gotta admit having an extra set of hands and eyes around made things easier just now."

His emerald-green gaze warmed her along with his words. Given her history with men, the whole trust notion was tough for her. But right now, she so desperately wanted to believe in the sincerity she saw in his eyes. She felt appreciated. Valued as a person.

Giving that much control to another person scared her spitless. "You're welcome."

She thought for a moment he was going to kiss her again. Her lips tingled at the prospect. But then he glanced at the two children and eased back. "Let's get the diaper bag so we can move forward with our night out on the town."

Blinking fast, she stood stock-still for a second, barely registering his words. They still had a whole night ahead of them? She was wrung out, as if she'd run an emotional marathon. With her defenses in the negative numbers, an evening out with Seth and his children was too tantalizing, too tempting a prospect. Hell, the man himself was too tempting. Not that she had the choice of opting out.

She just really hoped the evening sucked.

The evening hadn't sucked.

In fact, Seth had followed through with the perfect plans so far, starting off with a gourmet picnic at a park near a seventeenth century fort by the harbor. The children had toddled around, eaten their fill and gotten dirty. So precious and perfect and far more normal than she would have expected.

Then Seth had chartered a carriage ride through the historic district at sundown. Olivia and Owen had squealed with delight over the horse. And the last part of the outing hadn't ended in a half hour as she'd expected.

Once the kids' bedtime arrived, Seth had simply paid the driver to continue down the waterside road while the children slept in their laps. The *clop, clop, clop* of the Belgian draft's hooves lulled Alexa as she cuddled the sweet weight of Owen sleeping in her arms.

The night was more than Cinderella-perfect. Cinderella only had the prospect of happily ever after. For tonight, Alexa had experienced the magic of being a part of a real family during this outing with Seth and his children.

Although Cinderella's driver likely wasn't sporting ear buds for an iPod. Alexa appreciated the privacy it offered as she didn't have to worry about him eavesdropping.

Being a part of a family taking a magical moonlit carriage ride presented a tableau she'd dreamed about. The way Olivia nestled so trustingly against her father's chest. The obvious affection between him and his children during their picnic. He'd built a relationship with them, complete with familiar games and songs and love.

But even as she joined in this family game for now, she couldn't lose sight of her real role here. Or the fact that Seth Jansen was a sharp businessman, known for his drive for perfection and no-nonsense ways.

She knew he wanted her. Could he be devious enough to use his children to keep her here? She thought of earlier, by the pool, how he'd focused all that intensity on her. His eyes had stroked over her, hot and hungry.

Exciting.

There'd been a time when she couldn't show her body in a bathing suit—for fear people would find out her secret, because of her own hang-ups. She'd worked past that. She'd come to peace with herself. But as her thoughts drifted toward the possibility of intimacy with another person, she faced the reality of sharing that secret part of herself, to explain why she had such extensive stretch marks in spite of never having had a child.

Even though she'd found resolution inside, it wasn't something she enjoyed revisiting.

She rested her chin on Owen's head, Seth sitting across from her holding Olivia. "How did your business meeting go?"

"We're moving forward, closer to a deal than

before. My gut tells me there's a real possibility I can land this one."

"If he hasn't ended the negotiations, that's got to be a positive sign." She settled into the professional discussion, thinking of how far she'd come from her teenage years of insecurity.

"That's my take." He nodded, then something shifted in his eyes. "It appeared you had fun with Victoria today."

More memories of his interest at the pool, of his kiss last night steamed through her as tangibly as the heat rising from the paved road. A cooling breeze rolled off the harbor and caressed her shoulders, lifting her hair the way his fingers had played through the strands.

Her hand lifted to swipe back a lock from her face. "I feel guilty calling this work when it really has been more of a vacation."

"You've had twins to watch over. That's hardly a holiday."

"I've had a lot of help from you and Victoria." The carriage driver tugged the reins at a stop sign, a towering adobe church on the corner. "Not that any of us could stop that oatmeal incident."

He chuckled softly. "Thank goodness Javier's more laid back than I would have given him credit for."

"It was gracious of him to acknowledge that the breakfast with toddlers was his idea." She shuffled Owen into a more comfortable position as the baby settled deeper into sleep. "What made you think of taking a carriage ride to help the twins wind down?"

"I spent so much time outdoors growing up." He patted his daughter's back softly. "I try to give that to my kids when I can."

"Well, this was a great idea…" The moonlight played across the water rippling in the harbor. "The night air, the gorgeous scenery, the water, it's been quite a break for me, too."

"I never get tired of the year-round good weather here." As he sat across from her, he propped a foot beside her on the seat.

"What about January through March?" She shivered melodramatically. "The cold wind off the water is biting."

His laugh rode the ocean breeze as he opened up more as the evening wore on. "You've obviously never visited North Dakota. My uncle would get icicles in his beard in the winter."

"No kidding?"

"No kidding." He scratched his chin as if caught in the memories. "My cousins and I still went outside, no matter how far the temperature dropped, but it's a lot easier here when it doesn't take a half hour to pull on so many layers of clothes."

"What did you like to do in North Dakota?" she

asked, hungry for deeper peeks into this intriguing man.

"Typical stuff, snowmobiling, hiking, horseback riding on the farm. Then I discovered flying…" He shrugged. "And here I am now."

Yet there was so much more to him than that, this man who'd come from a North Dakota farm and made billions off his interest in airplanes.

The carriage shocks squeaked as the large wheels rolled along a brick side-road. How was it she felt tipsy when she hadn't even had so much as a sip of alcohol?

He nudged the side of her leg with his foot. "What about you? What did you want to do when you were a kid?"

"Art history, remember?" she said evasively.

"Why art history?"

"An obsession with creating beauty, I guess."

And now they were dancing a little too close to uncomfortable territory from her past. She pointed to the old-fashioned sailboat anchored near the shore with the sounds of a party carrying across the water. "What's up with that?"

He hesitated for a moment as if he understood full well she was trying to redirect the conversation. "It's a pirate ship. The *Black Raven*. They do everything from kids' parties to the more adult sort." He gestured toward a couple in buccaneer and maid costumes strolling down the sidewalk.

"Then there are regular bar hours. People come in costume. I thought about having a party for the kids there someday—during regular hours, of course."

"I can envision you in a Jack Sparrow-style pirate shirt so you wouldn't have to tug at your tie all the time."

"You've noticed that?"

She shrugged, staying silent.

"There are lots of things I hope to teach my kids." He pointed toward the sky. "Like showing them the Big Dipper there. Or my favorite constellation, Orion's belt. See the orange-looking star along the strand? That's Betelgeuse, a red star. There's nothing like charting the sky."

"Sounds like you have a pirate's soul. If you'd been born before airplanes…"

"Star navigation can be helpful if you're lost," he pointed out. "Betelgeuse saved my ass from getting lost more than once when the navigational instruments went on the fritz during a search."

She thought back to her research on him from when she'd put together her proposal. "You started your company doing search and rescue."

"I'm still active in that arena."

"Really?" Why hadn't she seen information about that kind of work? That could have been useful in her proposal. She wanted to kick herself for falling short. "I didn't realize that."

"SAR—search and rescue—was my first love. Still is," he said with undeniable fire.

"Then why do you do the corporate charter gig?" The image of Seth Jansen was more confusing with each new revelation. She hadn't expected so many layers, so much depth.

"Search and rescue doesn't pay well. So the bigger my business..."

"The more good you can do." And just that fast the pieces came together, the billionaire, the father, the philanthropist. And on top of everything he was hot?

God, she was in serious deep water here.

His gaze slid to hers, held and heated. In a smooth move, he shifted off the seat across from her to sit beside her. The scent of his crisp aftershave teased her nose, while his hulking magnetism drew her. Before she could think, she swayed toward him.

They still held both sleeping children, so nothing could or would happen. But the connection between them was tangible. His eyes invited her to lean against him and his arm slid around her shoulders, tucking her closer as the carriage rolled on.

How far did she want to take this? She hadn't forgotten his request that she extend her stay, even if he hadn't brought it up again. Then there was the whole tangle of her wanting to work for him...

And there were these two beautiful children who

obviously came first with him, as they should. She understood how deeply a child could be affected by their growing up years. She carried the scars of her own childhood, complete with fears about opening herself to another relationship, making herself vulnerable to a man by baring her secrets as well as her body.

The carriage jerked to a halt outside their hotel, and her time to decide what to do next came to an end.

Seth set his iPod in the hotel's docking station and cued up the twins' favorite Mozart for tots music. The babies had been too groggy for baths after the carriage ride, so he and Alexa had just tucked them into their cribs, each wearing a fresh diaper and T-shirt.

Leaving him alone with Alexa—and completely awake.

Their evening together had given him an opportunity to learn more about her, the person, rather than the businesswoman. Guilt tweaked his conscience. She had a life and a company and a tender heart. She also had some misguided notion she could persuade him to sign a contract with her cleaning service. He'd told her otherwise, but he suspected she believed she could change his mind.

He needed to clear that up now, before things went further.

While he would do anything for his kids, he had other options for their care now and he couldn't deny the truth. He was keeping her here because he wanted to sleep with her, now, away from Charleston, in a way that wouldn't tangle their lives up with each other. Because, damn it all, no matter how much he wanted her in his bed, he didn't have the time or inclination to start a full out relationship. He would not, under any circumstances put his children through the upheaval of another inevitable breakup.

He plowed his fingers through his hair. He was left with no choice. He had to come clean with Alexa. He owed it to her. If for no other reason than because of the way she'd been so patient with his children, more than just watching over them, she'd played with them.

Rolled a ball.

Kissed a minor boo-boo.

Wiped away pudding smudges from their faces.

Rested her cheek on a sleeping baby's head with such genuine affection while they rode in the carriage like an honest to God family.

A dark cloud mushroomed inside him. He pivoted toward the living room—and found her waiting in the open doorway. She still wore the tan capris and flowing blouse she'd had on for their picnic, except her feet were bare.

Her toes curled into the carpet. "Earlier tonight,

you mentioned extending our stay. What was that all about?"

He should be rejoicing. He had achieved exactly what he wanted in enticing her to stay.

Yet now was his time to man-up and tell her the whole story. "There's been a change in plans. I'm not returning to Charleston in the morning."

"You're staying here?" Her forehead crinkled in confusion.

He glanced back at his kids, concerned with waking them, and guided Alexa into the living area, closing the bedroom door behind him.

"Not exactly." He steered her to the blue velvet sofa and sat beside her. "Tomorrow, Javier and I are moving negotiations to the king's island to peruse his landing strip and discuss possibilities for increasing security measures."

"That's great news for you." She smiled with genuine pleasure.

Her obvious—unselfish—happiness over his success kicked his guilt into high gear. "I need to be up-front with you."

"Okay—" her eyes went wary "—I'm listening."

"I want you to come with me to the island." He tucked a knuckle under her chin, brushed his mouth over hers. The connection deepened, crackled with need. "Not because of business or the kids. But because I want *you*. I want *this*."

He hesitated. "And before you ask, I do still

intend to introduce you to the contacts just like I promised on day one. And I will listen to your business proposal and give you advice. But that's all I can offer."

Small consolation to his burning conscience right now. He truly wished he could do more for her and for her business.

Realization dawned in her eyes, her face paling. "I'm not going to land the Jansen Jets contract, no matter what I say."

"I'm afraid not. Your company is simply not large enough. I'm sorry."

She gnawed her plump bottom lip, then braced her shoulders. "You don't have to apologize. You told me as much that first day, and I just didn't want to hear you."

"The way your service is growing shows promise, and if this had been a year from now, the answer might have been different." That made him wonder what it would have been like to meet her a year from now, when his kids were older and the sting of his divorce had lessened.

"Then I go home now."

Was that anger or regret he saw chasing across her expression? It looked enough like the latter that he wasn't going to miss the opportunity to press what little advantage he had. "Or you could go with me to the island. Just for the weekend."

Her lips pressed tightly, thinning. "You may always get weekends free, but Bethany and I trade off every other one. I've already taken two days off work in the hope of a business proposition you never intended to fulfill. I can't keep imposing on her indefinitely."

"I meant what I said. I do intend to make good on introducing you to new connections and helping you beef up your presentation. Damn it, I'm trying hard to be honest with you." He reached to loosen his tie and then realized he wasn't wearing it anymore. "I'll pay the difference you need to hire temporary help while you're away—"

Her eyes went wide with horror. "You've already paid me enough. It's not about the money."

"Take it anyway. Consider it an exchange for your help with the kids. And I do need your help."

"You want me to stay for the twins?" She crossed her arms defensively.

"It's not that simple. I can't untangle my kids from what's going on between us. So yeah, they factor into this decision." They had to factor into every decision he made. "My children like you. That counts for a lot. They've seen too much upheaval in their lives already. I try to give them as much stability as I can."

"They've only known me for a couple of days and then I'll be gone." Her fingers dug into her elbows.

She had a point there. The thought of them grow-ing too attached…

Shaking his head, he refocused. His plan for the weekend was solid. Second-guessing himself would only derail things. He loosened her grip and held her soft hands in his. "I like how happy Owen and Olivia are with you."

"I adore them, too." Obvious affection tinged her words, along with regret. "But even if I agree to this crazy proposition of yours, I'll be leaving their lives when we all go home."

"Maybe. Maybe not." Where had that come from? Only seconds ago he'd been thinking about how he needed to have an affair now because in-dulging in more once they returned home wasn't an option.

Was it?

She tugged her hands from his. "I'm not ready for any kind of relationship, and I'm still not happy about the business end of things between us."

He should be rejoicing at those words. Should be. He cradled her face in his palm. "Then consider having a fling with me."

"A fling?" She gnawed her bottom lip slowly as she repeated the word. "Fling? No attachment or expectations. Just pure indulgence in each other?"

Already her suggestive words sent a bolt of lust straight to his groin. If she could seduce him this thoroughly with just a few words, what more did she hold in store with her hands, her body?

"That's the idea," he growled softly in agreement. "We pick up where we left off last night at dinner."

So he waited for her decision, the outcome more important than it should have been for someone of such brief acquaintance. But then she smiled, not full out, just a hint of possibility.

She reached, skimming her fingers down the front of his chest lightly as if still making up her mind. The feel of her featherlight touch made his erection impossibly harder.

Her hand stopped just shy of his belt, her eyes assessing, yet still holding the briefest hint of reservation. "For how long?"

He clasped her hand and brought her wrist to his mouth. Her pulse leaped under his kiss.

"For the weekend." Or more. He wasn't sure of a hell of a lot right now. But he was certain of one thing. He wanted Alexa. "Starting now."

Chapter 6

Alexa leaned into the restrained strength of Seth's touch. He was such a giant of a man with amazing control. She'd been aching for the feel of his hands on her skin since she'd first seen him. Yes, she was angry over the doused hopes of signing a contract with his company. However, in other ways, she was relieved. The end of their business acquaintance freed her to pursue the attraction between them.

As much as she wanted to attribute the power of her desire to months of abstinence, she knew she hadn't felt anything near this compulsion for other attractive men who'd crossed her path. She wanted him, deeply, ached to have him with such a craving it was all she could do not to fling herself onto him.

Even in her spoiled princess days, she'd guarded her body closely. She'd only slept with two men before her husband and no one since. Each relationship had come after months of dating. This was so out of character for her, which emphasized the tenacious attraction all the more.

The prospect of a no-strings affair with Seth, especially now that she wasn't trying to win a contract with him, was more temptation than she could resist.

She angled her face into his hard hand, turning to press a kiss into his palm. A primitive growl of desire rumbled from him in response, stirring and stoking molten pleasure deep in her belly.

Without moving his hand from her face, he leaned to kiss her bared neck. The glide of his mouth sent delicious shivers down her spine. Her head lolled back to give him fuller access.

He swept her hair aside with a large confident hand that skimmed down to palm her waist. Nipping, kissing, his mouth traced along her throbbing pulse. His chin nudged aside one shoulder of her blouse, his late-day beard raspy and arousing against her flushed skin.

His body hummed with restraint. Straining tendons along his neck let her know just how much it cost him to go slowly. His meticulous attention to detail sent a fresh shiver of anticipation through her.

She grabbed his shirt, her fist twisting in the warm cotton as she hauled him closer, urged him on. He shot to his feet and scooped her into his arms. Her fingers linked behind his neck as she steadied herself against his chest. Part of her warned that she should stop, now; but an even more insistent part of her urged her to see this through. Then maybe she would be free of the frenetic lure of this man. She could get back to the carefully planned, safe life she'd built for herself.

Seth angled sideways through the door into the spare room. Gauzy curtains hung from rings around the wrought-iron canopy frame overhead. He lowered her gently into the poofy white spread. Stepping back, he began unbuttoning his shirt while she watched—not that he seemed the least concerned with her gaze clinging to him.

In fact, he appeared all the more aroused by her appreciation. He shrugged off the shirt and unbuckled his belt, the low lighting from the bedside lamp casting a warm glow over his bared flesh.

One long zip later… Oh, yeah, he was most definitely as turned on as she was. The rigid length of his arousal reached up his rock solid abs. Golden hair sprinkled along his defined chest. He was a sculpted god of a man, and for tonight, he was all hers...

But as she devoured him with her eyes, unease skittered up her spine at the prospect of turning the tables. While she'd conquered the eating disorder of her teenage years, her body still carried marks and signs of how close she'd come to dying.

Twisting sideways, she reached to turn off the lamp and prayed he wouldn't argue. She truly didn't want to have this discussion right now. *Click.* The room went dark then shadowy as her eyes adjusted to the moonlight streaming through the sheers on the window, the thicker brocade curtains pulled back.

She waited and thank God, Seth stayed silent. Brows pinching together, his head tilting to the side offered the only signs he'd registered her turning off the light.

Swallowing the patter of nerves, she sat up and swept her loose shirt upward and over her head. As she shook her hair free, he kicked aside his pants and leaned over her, angling her back to recline against the piled pillows. His hand fell to the top button on her capris. Up close, she could see the question in his eyes as he waited for her consent.

Arching upward, she slid her fingers into his hair and tugged his mouth toward hers. The feel of him was becoming familiar as they deepened contact, her lips parting, opening, welcoming him. Losing herself in the kiss, she barely registered his deft work pushing aside her pants and freeing the front clasp of her bra.

The cool air contrasted with the warmth of his hard muscled body. Tension built inside her, a need to take this farther, faster. She tugged at Seth's shoulders, whispering her need, her desires, but he wouldn't be rushed.

He nipped, licked, laved his way down her neck and to her breasts, drawing on her tightening nipples with the perfect mixture of tongue and tug. Her fingernails grazed down his back, tendons and muscles flexing under her stroke in response.

The glide of his hand between them sent her stomach muscles tensing. He slowed, pausing to flick her belly button ring. "This drove me insane when I saw it earlier, exposed by that sexy deep V of your bathing suit. Ever since, all I could think of was touching it. Touching you."

"Then I like the way you think," she whispered, then gasped.

His tender torment continued until her head thrashed along the deep downy pillow. She hooked her leg around his, bringing his stony thigh to rest against her aching core. Rocking against him only made her more frustrated, liquid longing pulsing through her veins and flushing her skin.

The air conditioner swirled the scents of his aftershave, her shampoo and their desire into a perfume of lust, intoxicating her with each gasping breath. He angled off her, and she moaned her frustration.

"Shh." He pressed a finger to her mouth. "Only for a second."

His hand dipped into a drawer in the bedside table. He came back with a box of condoms. Thank heaven, someone had the foresight to plan ahead. She couldn't even bring herself to condemn him for assuming this could happen…because here they were, the only place she wanted to be at the moment.

Then the thick pressure of him between her thighs scattered any other thoughts as he pushed inside her. Large and stretching and more than she'd expected. She hooked her legs around his waist, opening for him, welcoming him and the sensation of having him fully inside her.

Smoothly, he rolled to his back while their bodies stayed connected. She lay sprawled on top of him. Bowing upward, she straddled him, taking him impossibly deeper. His eyes flamed as he watched her with the same intensity she knew she'd lavished on him when he'd undressed for her. He gripped her waist, and she rolled her hips against him.

Her head flung back at the pure sensation, the perfect angle as he nudged against the circle of sensitivity hidden inside her. And again, he moved, thrusting, pumping, taking her need to a whole new level of frenzy until she raked her nails down his chest, desperate for completion. She didn't know herself, this out of control woman all but screaming for release. She'd thought she knew her body and the pleasures to be found in bed. But nothing came close to this…this fiery tingle along her every nerve.

Then they were flipping position again and he was on top of her, pumping faster, the head of his arousal tormenting that special spot inside her again and again until…

Sensation imploded, sparks of white light dotting behind her eyes. His mouth covered hers, taking her gasps and moans and, yes, even her cries of pleasure into him the way she still welcomed him into her body.

The bliss rippled through her in tingling aftershocks even as he rolled to his side, tucking her against his chest. He drew the covers over them and kissed the top of her head tenderly, stroking her back. His heart thumped hard and loud against her ear in time with her own racing pulse.

What the hell had just happened?

The best sex of her life.

And as the wash of desire cooled inside her that thought scared her more than a little. Already she wanted him again. Far too much. She needed distance to shore up her own defenses. Establishing her independence after her divorce had been damn difficult. She couldn't allow herself to turn clingy or needy again—no matter how amazing the orgasm.

Once his breathing evened out into a low snore, she eased herself from his arms, needing to think through what had just happened between them. She inched off the bed, slowly, carefully, her feet finally touching the carpet.

She tugged on her shirt and panties, the fabric gliding across her well-loved body still oversensitized from the explosiveness of her release. She pulled open the door to the sitting area with more than a little regret.

"You're leaving?" His voice rumbled softly from the bed.

She turned toward him, keeping her head high. "Just returning to my room for the night."

Gauzy white curtains and his large lounging body gave off the air of a blond sheikh…. Good Lord, her mind was taking fanciful routes and fantasies.

"Uh-uh." He shook his head, sliding his hands behind his neck, broad chest all but calling to her to curl right back up again. "You're not ready to sleep together."

"I want to." God, did she ever want to.

"Glad to hear it. Hold on to that thought for our weekend together." He swung his feet to the floor and was beside her in a heartbeat. He kissed her just once, firmly but without moving, as if simply sealing his imprint on her.

As if she didn't already carry the feel of him in her every thought right now.

He stepped back into his room. "Sleep well, Alexa. We leave early for the island. Good night."

The door closing after him, he left her standing in the middle of the sitting room ready to burst into flames all over again.

From inside the chartered jet, Alexa felt the blazing sun flame its way up the morning sky on her way to a king's getaway. The Atlantic Ocean stretched out below, a small dot of an island waiting ahead.

Their destination.

Waking up late, she and Seth had been too rushed for conversation. They'd dressed the kids and raced to the lobby just as the limousine arrived to pick them up along with Javier and his wife. The luxury ride to the small airport had given her the opportunity to double-check with Bethany and clear the schedule change. Bethany seemed so excited at the prospect of new contacts, she gave two thumbs-up. So there were no obstacles to Alexa's leaving. The ride had been so smooth and speedy she'd been whisked onto the jet before she'd even fully wiped the sleep from her eyes.

Breakfast had been waiting for them on the

flight, although she'd been told they would land within a half hour. She had monitored the babies plucking up Cheerios, while nibbling on a *churro*— a Spanish doughnut. It had all seemed so normal, as if her insides weren't still churning from what had happened between her and Seth the night before.

And wondering what would happen when they landed on the isolated island for the weekend.

Her eyes gravitated to the open door leading to the cockpit where Seth flew the jet, Javier sitting in the copilot's seat. Their night together scrolled through her mind in lush, sensual detail. He'd touched her, aroused her, fulfilled her in ways she'd never experienced before. And while she was scared as hell of where this intense connection might lead her, she couldn't bring herself to walk away. Not yet.

Victoria touched her arm lightly. "They're both loners, but I think they're going to work well together."

"I'm sure they will." Loner? She hadn't thought of Seth quite that way, more brusque and business-like. Except when he was around his kids, then he really opened up. Like he had when talking to her during their carriage ride.

And while making love, he'd held nothing back.

"Are you all right?" Victoria asked.

Alexa forced a smile. "Sorry to be so quiet." She searched for something to explain her preoccupation with a certain hot pilot only a few feet away. "It's just surreal that we would go to a king's home with babies in tow."

"Deposed king—and indulgent grandfather. If it makes you worry less, he's not in residence at the moment. He's visiting his doctors on the mainland, follow-ups on some surgery he had. We'll have the island all to ourselves, other than the staff and security, of course." She replenished the pile of Cheerios on Olivia's tray. The company that had stocked and cleaned the jet had done their job well. "The twins will find anything they need already there. He even keeps a sitter on staff."

"So none of the king's family is in residence at the moment? No other children?"

"None. The other family members have their own homes elsewhere. Since the family has reconciled, they're all visiting more often."

"More air travel." That explained why they were courting Jansen Jets.

"And more need for security with all these extra trips."

That also explained how Seth fit the bill all the better with his background in search and rescue, and security devices for airports. "How scary to have to worry so much about a regular family vacation."

Victoria huffed her blond bangs from her forehead. "The press may have eased up from the initial frenzy, but they haven't backed off altogether. Even relatives have to be on guard—and stay silent at all times."

Alexa struggled not to squirm. She was used to the background checks that accompanied working at an airport. "I hear you. No speaking to the press."

"Their cousin Alys is still persona non grata after speaking to the press. She moved back to another family compound in South America. I guess you could say she's even in exile from the exiled."

"That's so sad, but understandable." Alexa had grown up in a privileged world, but these people took privileged to a whole new level.

When the silence stretched, she followed Victoria's puzzled stare and realized…Alexa closed her fist around her napkin. She'd been scrubbing a smudge on the silver tray obsessively. Her flatware was lined up precisely and she'd even brushed some powdered sugar into a tiny pile.

Smiling sheepishly, she forced her fists to unfurl and still. "When I'm nervous, I clean."

Victoria covered Alexa's hand with her own. "There's nothing to sweat, really."

Easier said than done when she'd barely survived her home life growing up. It was one thing to stand on the periphery of that privileged world, restoring order to the messes made by others. It was another thing entirely to step into the lushness of overindulgence that had once threatened to swallow her whole. But she was committed to this weekend. Literally. There was no escape.

She stared out the window at the island nestled in miles and miles of sparkling ocean. Palm trees spiked from the lush landscape. A dozen or so small outbuildings dotted a semicircle around a larger structure.

The white mansion faced the ocean in a U shape, constructed around a large courtyard with a pool. Details were spotty but she would get an up close view soon enough. Even from a distance she couldn't miss the grand scale of the sprawling estate, the unmistakable sort that housed royalty.

The plane banked as Seth lined up the craft with a thin islet alongside the larger island. A single strip of pristine concrete marked the private runway. As they neared, a ferry boat came into focus. To ride from the airport to the main island? They truly were serious about security.

She thought she'd left behind this kind of life when she'd cut ties with her parents. She'd been happy with her peripheral role, knowing what the rich needed but free of the complications of that life for herself.

Yet here she was.

Did she really want to even dip her toe in this sort of affluent world again? What choice did she have at the moment? Her gaze slid back to Seth.

No choice really given how deeply she ached to be with him again.

Or maybe she had a choice after all: the option to take control on their next encounter rather than simply following his lead.

And she would make damn sure he was every bit as knocked off balance by the experience as she'd been.

The night unfolded for Seth, full of opportunities.

He'd concluded his deal with Javier and would spend tomorrow formulating plans for the future. He was ready to celebrate. With Alexa. Hopefully she would be in the same mindset.

He closed the door to the nursery where the twins would spend the night under the watchful eye of one of the resident nannies.

Just before their bedtime, he'd tried Pippa again, on the off chance she would pick up and could wish the kids good-night. She'd actually answered, sounding overly chipper, but cut the call short once he'd attempted to put Owen and Olivia on the line. Something about the whole conversation had been "off" but he couldn't put his finger on the exact problem.

Most likely because all he could think about right now was getting Alexa naked again.

He entered their quarters. More like a luxurious

condominium within the mansion. He and Alexa had been given separate rooms in the second floor corner suite, but he hoped he could keep her distracted through the night until she fell asleep in his arms, exhausted by good sex.

Great sex.

Searching the peach and gray room, he didn't see signs of her other than her suitcase open on her bed. His shoes padded softly against the thick Persian rug past a sitting area with an eating space stocked more fully than most kitchens.

The quiet echoed around him, leaving him hyperaware of other sounds…a ticking grandfather clock in the hall…the crashing ocean outside… Through the double doors, the balcony was as large as some yards.

And Alexa leaned on the railing.

A breeze gusted from the ocean plastering her long tiered sundress to her body, draping her curves in deep purple.

He stopped beside her. "Penny for them?"

She glanced at him sideways, the hem of her dress brushing his leg like phantom fingers. "No money for no work, remember? I've done nothing here to earn even a cent. The nanny takes over the kids, and I have to admit, she's good at charming them."

"You would rather they cried for you?"

"Of course not! I just…I like to feel useful. In control."

"Most women I know would be thrilled by an afternoon with a manicurist and masseuse."

"Don't get me wrong, I enjoy being pampered as much as anyone. In fact, I think you deserve a bit of relaxation yourself." She tapped a pager resting on the balcony wall. "The nanny can call if she needs us. What do you say we head down to the beach? I found the most wonderful cabana where we can talk."

Talk?

Not what he'd been fantasizing about for their evening together. But Alexa apparently had something on her mind, given the determined tilt of her chin. He took her hand in his. Her short nails were shiny with clear polish. The calluses on her fingers from cleaning had been softened and he felt the urge to make sure she never had to pick up a scrub brush ever again.

Keeping his hand linked with hers, he followed her down the winding cement steps toward the beach. She kicked off her sandals and waited for him to ditch his shoes and socks.

Hand in hand, they walked along the shore, feet sinking into the sand as they made their way toward a white cabana. With each step closer he could feel the tension ramping up in her body.

"I'd hoped today would offer you breaks, be a sort of vacation."

She glanced up, a smile flickering. "This is paradise. I've been in some impressive mansions over the years, but even I'm a floored by this place. No kidding royalty. Your business is going to a whole new level with this deal."

"That's the plan." So why did he still feel so…unsettled? He gestured inside the cabana where she'd ordered two low lounge chairs with a small table of refreshments between them.

Her eyes flickered wide for a second before she plunged inside, choosing a chair and eyeing the wine, cheese and grapes. She'd obviously planned this chance to…talk?

She wriggled her toes in the sand and plucked a grape. A wave curled up closer and she stretched her legs out until the water touched the tips of her feet. "This truly is paradise."

He dropped into the chair beside her. "Then why are you so tense?"

"Why do you want to know?"

"Why do you think?" He poured deep red wine into two crystal glasses and let his eyes speak as fully as his words.

She took one of the drinks by the stem and sipped. "Victoria called you a loner."

"Interesting." And he wasn't sure what that had to do with anything.

"You have so much family in Charleston, I hadn't thought of you that way." The wind rippled and flapped the three canvas walls of the cabana. "You do have family there, right? You called them when you found the babies, to ask for help."

"I have two cousins—Vic and Paige. I grew up with them in North Dakota when my parents died in a car accident." He reached for his wine. "Their SUV slid off the road in a storm when I was eleven." He downed half of the fine vintage as if it was water.

"I'm so sorry." She touched his wrist lightly as he replaced his drink.

"No need to feel sorry for me. I was lucky to have family willing to take me in." He hesitated. "My parents didn't have any assets when they died. My aunt and uncle never said anything about the extra mouth to feed, but I vowed I would pay them back."

"Look at you now. You've truly accomplished the amazing."

He stared out over the dark water and the darker night sky. "Too late to give anything to them… It took me a while to find my footing. Too long."

"Good God, Seth, you're all of what…"

"Thirty-eight."

"A self-made billionaire by thirty-eight." Her laugh stroked over his senses like the ocean breeze. "I wouldn't call that a slow start."

But he was still chasing dreams around the country. "I didn't set out on this path. I wanted to fly for the Air Force, even started ROTC at the University of Miami, but lost out on a medical snafu that isn't an issue anywhere but the Air Force. So I finished my degree and came home. Ran a flight school while flying my veterinarian cousin around to farms until the family all relocated to South Carolina."

He could feel her undivided attention on him. He wasn't sure why he was spilling all of this about himself, but somehow the words kept coming out. Strange as hell since she'd been on the mark in calling him a loner in spite of his large family.

"I wrestle with wanting to give my kids everything while worrying about teaching them working class values. I think about it a lot, how to help them have their own sense of accomplishment."

"The fact that you're even thinking about it says you're ahead of the game." She reached for his hand this time, linking her fingers and squeezing. "You do well by them."

He lifted her hand to kiss her wrist. "You grew up in a privileged world but came out with a strong work ethic. Any tips?"

She laughed bitterly. "My parents had shallow values, spending every penny they inherited to indulge themselves. My father bankrupted the family trust fund, or rather I should say they both did.

Now, I have to work in order to eat like most of the rest of the world, which isn't a tragedy or sob story. Just a reality."

He'd known about her father's crappy management of the family's finances and sportswear line. But… "What about your marriage settlement?"

"We signed a prenup. My father's lawyers were worried Travis was a fortune hunter. I told Travis I didn't care about any contracts but he insisted." She spread her arms without letting go of his hands. "No alimony for either of us."

Frustration spiked inside him. "He doesn't care that you were left penniless? The jackass."

"Stop right there." She squeezed his hand insistently. "I signed the prenup, too, and I don't want your sympathy."

"Okay, I hear you."

What was she thinking right now? He wished he was better at understanding the working of a woman's mind. He'd brought her to the island for seduction, and somehow, out here tonight, they'd ended up talking about things he didn't share with others. But Alexa had a way of kicking down barriers, and he'd had as much sharing as he could take for one night.

The rush of the ocean pulling at the sand under his feet seemed as if it tugged the rest of the world with it. He'd brought Alexa to this island for a reason: to seduce her so thoroughly he could work through this raw connection they felt.

Except, as he leaned in to kiss her, he was beginning to realize the chances of working her out of his system was going to be damn near impossible.

Her hand flattened to his chest. "Stop."

"What?" His voice came out a little strangled, but he held himself still. If a woman said no, that meant no.

"Last time we did this, you were the boss." She slid from her lounger and leaned over to straddle his hips. The warm core of her seared his legs even through her cotton dress and his slacks. "This time, Seth, I'm calling the shots."

Chapter 7

Seth's brain went numb.

Did Alexa actually intend to have sex with him outside, in a seaside cabana? If so, she wouldn't get an argument from him. He was just surprised, since she'd insisted on leaving his bed the night before. He'd assumed she was more reserved given how she'd wanted to keep the light off.

Although the way she tugged at his shirttails, he couldn't mistake her intent, or her urgency.

Moonbeams bathed her in a dim amber glow. Still straddling his hips, Alexa yanked the hem free then ripped, popping the buttons, sending them flying into the sand. Surprise snapped through him just as tangibly. Apparently he'd underestimated her adventurous spirit.

Wind rolled in from the ocean across his bare chest. His body went on alert a second before her mouth flicked, licked and nipped at his nipple the way he'd lavished attention on her the night before.

He cupped her hips, his fingers digging into the cottony softness of her bunched dress. "I like the way you think, Alexa."

"Good, but you need to listen better." She clasped his wrists and pulled them away. "This is *my* turn to be in control."

"Yes, ma'am." Grinning at her, he rested his hands on the lounger's armrests, eager to see her next move.

Wriggling closer, she sketched her mouth over his, over to his ear. "You won't be sorry."

Her hands worked his belt buckle free, her cool fingers tucking inside to trace down the length of his arousal. He throbbed in response, wanted to ditch their clothes and roll her onto the sandy ground. The more she stroked and caressed, the more he ached to do the same to her. But every time he started to move, she stopped.

Once he stilled again, she nipped his ear or his shoulder, her fingers resuming the torturously perfect glide over him. His fingers gripped the rests tighter, until the blood left his hands.

Alexa swept his pants open further, shifting. As

he started to move with her, she placed a finger over his lips. "Shh… I've got this."

Sliding from his lap, she knelt between his legs and took him in her mouth, slowly, fully. Moist, warm ecstasy clamped around him, caressed him. His head fell back against the chair, his eyes closing, shutting out all other sensation except the glide of her lips and tongue.

Her hands clamped on his thighs for balance. With his every nerve tuned into the feel of her, even her fingers digging into his muscles ramped his pulse higher. Wind lifted her hair, gliding it over his wrist. The silky torment almost sent him over the edge.

The need to finish roared inside him, too much, too close. He wasn't going there without her. Time for control games to come to an end.

He clasped her under her arms and lifted her with ease, bringing her back to his lap.

"Condom," he growled through clenched teeth. "In my wallet. Leftover from the hotel."

Laughing softly, seductively, she reached behind him and tucked her fingers into his back pocket. The stroke of her hand over his ass had him gritting his teeth with restraint. Then she pitched his wallet to the ground with a wicked glint in her eyes.

What the hell?

She leaned sideways, toward the table of wine

and cheese. Pitching aside a napkin, she uncovered a stack of condoms. "I came prepared."

His eyebrows rose at the pile of condoms, a dozen or so. "Ambitiously so."

"Is that a problem?" She studied him through her lashes.

God, he loved a challenge and this woman was turning out to be a surprise in more ways than one since she'd blasted into his life such a short time ago. "I look forward to living up to your expectations."

"Glad to hear it." She tore open one of the packets and sheathed him slowly.

Backlit by the crescent moon, she stood. She bunched the skirt of her dress and swept her panties down, kicking them aside. A low growl of approval rumbled inside him as he realized her intent. She straddled him again, inching the hem of her dress up enough so the hot heat of her settled against his hard-on.

Cradling his face in her hands, she raised up on her knees to kiss him. Her dress pooled around them, concealing her from view as she lowered herself onto the length of his erection. The moist clamp of her gripped him, drew him inside until words scattered like particles of sand along the beach.

The scent of the ocean clung to her skin. Unable to resist, he tasted her, trekking along her bared shoulder and finding the salty ocean flavor clung to her skin. He untied the halter neck of her dress, the fabric slithering down to reveal a lacy strapless bra. Her creamy breasts swelled just above the cups and with a quick flick of his fingers, he freed the front clasp.

Freed her.

Lust pumped through him along with anticipation. He filled his hands with the soft fullness, the shadowy beauty of her just barely visible in the moonlight.

His thumbs brushed the pebbly tips. "Someday we're going to make love on a beach with the sun shining down, or in a room with all the lamps on so I can see the bliss on your face."

"Someday..." she echoed softly.

Were those shadows in her eyes or just the play of clouds drifting past?

Her face lowered to his, blocking out the view and his thoughts as she sealed her mouth to his, demanding, giving and taking. With the lighting dim, his other senses heightened. The taste of her was every bit as intoxicating as the lingering hint of red wine on her tongue. Burying himself deep inside her, deeper still, he reveled in the purr of pleasure vibrating in her throat.

He stroked down her spine until his hands tucked under her bottom. Her soft curves in his palms, he angled her nearer, burning for more of her, more of them together. Her husky sighs and moans grew louder and closer together. Damn good thing since he was balancing on the edge himself, fulfillment right there for the taking.

Waves crashed in the distance, echoing the rush of his pulse pounding in his ears. Sand rode the air and clung to the perspiration dotting their skin, the gritty abrasion was arousing as she writhed against him. He tangled his hand into her satiny hair and gently tugged her head back. Exposing her breasts to his mouth, he took the tip of one tight bud and rolled it lightly between his teeth.

She sighed, her back arching hard and fast, her chanted "yes, yes, yes," circling him. Wrapping and pulsing around him like the moist spasms of her orgasm. Her cries of completion mingled with the roar of crashing waves.

Blasting through his own restraint.

Thrusting through her release, he triggered another in her just as he came. The force slammed through him, powerful and eclipsing everything else as he flew apart inside her into a pure flat spin nosedive into pleasure. His arms convulsed around her with the force of his completion.

He forced his fist open to release her hair even though she hadn't so much as whimpered in complaint. In fact, her head stayed back even as he relinquished her hair, the locks lifted and whipped by the wind into a tangled mass.

Gasping, she sagged on top of him, her bared

breasts against his heaving chest. He didn't have a clue how long it took him to steady his breathing, but Alexa still rested in his arms. He retied the top of her sundress with hands not quite as steady as he would like. She nuzzled his neck with a soft, sated sigh.

He slid from under her, smoothing her dress over her hips, covering her with more than a little regret. With luck, though, there would be more opportunities to peel every stitch of clothing from her body.

For now, though, it was time to go inside. He refastened his pants and tucked the remaining condoms in his pocket. Not much he could do about his shirt since the buttons were scattered on the beach. He snagged the nursery pager and clipped it to his waistband before turning back to Alexa.

Scooping her in his arms, he started barefoot toward the mansion. She looped her arms around his neck, her head lolling onto his shoulder. Climbing the steps to their second floor suite, he walked through the patio filled with topiaries, ferns and flowering cacti. He'd enjoyed her power play on the beach. It had certainly paid off for both of them. But that didn't mean he was passing over control completely.

Tonight, she would sleep in his bed.

Alexa stretched in the massive sleigh bed, wrapped in the delicious decadence of Egyptian cotton sheets and the scent of making love with Seth. She stared around the unfamiliar surroundings, taking in oil paintings and heavy drapery.

She dimly remembered him carrying her from the beach to his bed. For a second, she'd considered insisting he take her to her room and leave her there. But his arms felt so good around her and she'd been so deliciously sated from their time in the cabana, she'd simply cuddled against his chest and slept.

God, had she ever slept. She couldn't remember when she'd last had eight uninterrupted hours. Could be because every muscle in her body had relaxed.

Yes, she knew she hadn't turned on the glaring lights, literally and in theory, by avoiding telling him about the issues in her past. But taking control last night had given her the confidence to invite Seth the rest of the way into her life.

Through the thick wood door, she heard voices in the other room; Seth's mingled with the babble of the twins. She smiled, looking forward to the day already. Except her suitcase and other clothes were in her bedroom, and she couldn't walk out there as is with the children nearby.

Swinging her feet to the floor, she grabbed her dress off the wing chair and pulled it on hastily. The crumpled cotton shouted that she'd spent the night with a man, but at least the twins wouldn't pick up on that. She could say "good morning" to them and then zip into her room to put on something fresh before she greeted the rest of the household.

At the door, she paused by a crystal vase of lisianthus with blooms that resembled blue roses. She plucked one out, snapped the stem and tucked the blossom behind her ear. Her hands gravitated to the flowers, straightening two of the blooms again so they were level with the rest, orderly. Perfect. She pulled open the door to the living area.

Another voice mingled in the mix.

An adult female voice.

Alexa froze in the open doorway. She scoured the room. Seth sat in a chair at the small writing desk, a twin on each knee as they faced the laptop computer in the middle of a Skype conversation.

A young woman's face filled the screen, her voice swelling from the speakers. "How are my babies? I've missed you both so very, very much."

Oh, God. It couldn't be. Not right now.

If Alexa had harbored any doubts as to the woman's identity, both babies chanted, "Ma-ma, Ma-ma, Ma-ma."

"Olivia, Owen, I'm here." Her voice echoed with obvious affection.

Pippa Jansen wasn't at all what she'd expected.

For starters, the woman didn't appear airheaded; in fact she had a simple, auburn-haired glamour. She wore a short-sleeved sweater set and pearls. From the log cabinlike walls and mountainous backdrop behind Pippa, she didn't appear to be at a plush spa or cruise ship getaway as Alexa had assumed.

Pippa didn't look to be partying or carefree. She appeared...tired and sad. "Mommy's just resting up, like taking a good nap, but I'll see you soon. We'll have yogurt and play in the sandbox. Kisses and hugs." She pressed a hand to her lips then wrapped her arms around herself. "Kisses and hugs."

Olivia and Owen blew exuberant baby kisses back. Both babies were so happy, so blissfully unaware. Alexa's heart ached for both of them. Her hands twitchy, she straightened a leather-bound volume of *Don Quixote* on a nearby end table.

Tension radiated from Seth's shoulders as he held a baby on each knee. "Pippa, while I understand your need for a break, I need some kind of reassurance that you're not going to drop off the map again once we hang up. I need to be able to reach you if there's an emergency."

"I promise." Her voice wavered. "I'll check in regularly from now on. I wouldn't have left this way if I wasn't desperate. I know I should have stayed to tell you myself, but I was scared you would say no, and I really needed a break. I watched through an airport window until you got on your plane. Please don't be angry with me."

"I'm not mad," he said, not quite managing to hide the irritation in his voice. "I just want to make sure you're all right. That you never feel desperate."

"This time away is good for me, really. I'll be back to normal when I come back to Charleston."

"You know I would like to have the children more often. When you're ready to come back, we can hire more help when they're with you, but we can't have a repeat of what happened at the airport. The twins' safety has to come first."

"You're right." She fidgeted with her pearls, her nails chewed down. "But I don't think we should talk about this now, in front of the babies."

"You're right, but we do have to discuss it. Soon."

"Absolutely." She nodded, almost frantically, pulling a last smile for the babies. "Bye-bye, be good for Daddy. Mommy loves you."

Her voice faded along with her picture as the connection ended. Olivia squealed, patting the screen while Owen blew more kisses.

Alexa sagged against the door frame. She'd been prepared to hate Pippa for the way she'd been so reckless with her kids. And while she still wasn't ready to let the woman off the hook completely, she saw a mother running on fumes. Someone who was stressed and exhausted. She saw a mother who genuinely loved her children. Pippa had obviously reached her breaking point and had wisely taken them to their father before she snapped.

Of course sticking around to explain that to him would have been a far safer option. But life wasn't nearly as black and white as she'd once believed.

She'd seen Seth angry, frustrated, driven, affectionate, turned on… But right now, as Seth stared at the empty computer screen, she saw a broad-shouldered, good man who was deeply sad.

A man still holding conflicted feelings for his ex-wife.

Seth set each of his kids onto the floor and wished the weight on his shoulders was as easy to move.

Talking to Pippa had only made the situation more complicated just when he really could have used some simplicity in his personal life. He and Alexa had taken their relationship to a new level last night, both with the sex and sharing the bed. And he'd looked forward to cementing that relationship today—and tonight.

The call from Pippa had brought his life sharply back into focus. She was clearly at the end of her rope. While he wanted more time with his children, he didn't want to get it this way.

And this certainly wasn't how he'd envisioned kicking off his day with Alexa.

Glancing back over his shoulder at her in the doorway, he said, "You can come in now."

He'd sensed her there halfway through the conversation with his ex. Strange how he'd become so in tune with Alexa so quickly.

"I didn't mean to eavesdrop." She stepped deeper

into the room, a barefoot goddess in her flowing purple dress with a flower behind her tousled hair.

Gracefully she sank down to the floor in front of the babies and a pile of blocks. He took in her effortless beauty, her ease with his kids. She was his dream woman—who'd come into his life at a nightmare time.

Right now, he couldn't help but be all the more aware of her strength, the way she met challenges head-on rather than running from her troubles. She'd rebuilt her entire life from the ground up. He admired that about her. Hell, he just flat out liked her, desired her and already dreaded the notion of watching her walk away.

"The conversation wasn't private." He shoved up from the chair and sat on the camelback sofa. "Olivia and Owen were just talking with their mother. Raising a baby is tough enough. The added pressure of twins just got to her. She's wise to take a break."

She glanced up sharply. "Even though she left them unattended on the airplane?"

"I'm aware that the way she chose to take that break left more than a little to be desired in the way of good judgment." He struggled to keep his voice level for the kids. For Alexa, too. He couldn't blame her for voicing the truth. "I'll handle it."

"Of course. It's really none of my business." She gnawed her bottom lip, stacking blocks then waiting for Olivia to knock the tower over. "Why don't

I take the kids for a couple of hours? Give you some time to—"

"I've got them." He watched his son swipe his fist through the plastic blocks with a squeal of delight. "I'm sure you want a shower or a change of clothes."

In a perfect world he would have been joining her in that shower. As a matter of fact, in his screwed up, imperfect world he needed that shower with her all the more. What he would give for twenty minutes alone with her under the spray of hot water with his hands full of soap suds and naked Alexa. He swallowed hard and filed those thoughts away at the top of his "to do" list.

Although to get to everything on that list he would need more time. A lot more time.

"Really, it's no trouble." She patiently stacked the blocks again in alphabetical order while Olivia tried to wedge one, the w, in her mouth. "I'm getting good at balancing them on both hips. They can run out some energy on the beach while you finish up last minute busi—"

"I said I have them. They are my children," he snapped more curtly than he'd intended, but the discussion with Pippa had left him on edge. Wrestling for control was tough as hell with anger and frustration piling up inside him faster than those blocks made a Leaning Tower of Pisa.

Hurt slashed across her face before she schooled

her features into an expressionless mask. "I'll change then, and take care of my own packing. How much longer until we leave the island?"

"We're flying out in an hour." Not that he intended to let that stop him from pursuing her. As much as he'd hoped to win her over during their trip, he now realized that wasn't going to be enough. He needed more—more time with her, more *of* her. While his relationship with Pippa had been a disaster, he was wiser for the experience now. He could enjoy Alexa in his life without letting himself get too entangled, too close.

Staring at his babies on the floor, he listened to the echo of tread as she walked away. Thought harder on the prospect of her walking away altogether.

Away, damn it.

He was going to lose Alexa if he didn't do something. He was fast realizing that no matter what his concerns about bringing a new woman into his children's lives, he couldn't let her leave.

"Alexa?"

Her footsteps stopped, but she didn't answer.

God, for about the hundredth time he wished they'd met a year from now when this would have been so much easier. But he couldn't change it. The time was now.

He wanted Alexa in his life.

"I'm sorry for being an—" He paused short of

cursing in front of his children. "I'm sorry for being a jerk. I know you didn't sign on for this, but I hope you'll give me a chance to make it up to you."

She stayed silent so long he thought she would tell him to go to hell. He probably deserved as much for the way he was botching things with her right now. Her lengthy sigh reached him, heaping an extra dose of guilt on his shoulders.

"We'll talk later, after you have your children settled."

"Thanks, that's for the best." Problem was, with Pippa, he wasn't sure how or when things in his life would ever be *settled.* All the more reason to keep his emotions in check when dealing with either woman in his life. Starting now.

Because, their island paradise escape was over. It was time to return to the real world.

Riding on the ferry out to the king's private airstrip, Alexa gripped the railing as they neared Seth's plane on the islet runway. The twins, buckled into their safety seats, squealed in delight at the sea air in their faces as they waved goodbye to the tropical paradise.

She feared she was saying goodbye to far more than that.

Her eyes trekked to Seth, who was standing with the boat captain. Not surprising, since Seth had all but shut down emotionally around her since his conversation with his ex-wife.

Alexa twirled the stem of a sea oat in her hand, then tickled the twins' chins with it. They were cute, but it would be helpful if they spoke a few more words so they could hold up the other end of a conversation. There was no one else to talk to. Javier and his wife had opted to stay on the island for a couple of extra days. Alexa envied them. Deeply. The time here with Seth before that Skype call had been magical, and she wanted more.

As smoothly as the ferry moved along the marshy water, her mind traveled to dreams of extending her relationship with Seth. Could what they'd shared be just as powerful under the pressure of everyday life? A daunting thought to say the least, especially when he had begun pulling away after his conversation with Pippa.

Thinking of that call, Alexa reached for her own phone. She should check for messages from Bethany. She'd turned her cell off last night and let it recharge—and, yes, probably because she didn't want interruptions. The way she'd made love with Seth on the beach...the way he'd made love to her afterward...

Heat pooled inside her, flushing her skin until she could have sworn she had an all-over sunburn.

Her phone powered up and she checked... No messages from Bethany, but the expected nine missed calls from her mother. Just as she started to thumb them away, the phone rang in her hand.

Her mom.

She winced.

Was her mother's perfectly coiffed blond hair actually a satellite dish that detected when her daughter turned on her phone?

Wind tearing at her own loose hair, she considered ignoring that call altogether as she had the others. But Olivia giggled and Alexa's heart tugged. If she felt this much for these two little ones so quickly, how much more must her mother feel for her?

Guilt nudged her to answer. "Hey, Mom. What's up?"

"Where are you, Lexi? I have been calling and calling." Laughter and the clank of dishes echoed over the phone line. Her parents had taken what little cash they had left and bought into a small retirement community chock-full of activities. How they continued to pay the bills was a mystery. "Lexi? Are you listening? I took a break from my 'Mimosas and Mahjong' group just to call you."

God, why couldn't her mother call her Alexa instead of Lexi? "Working. In Florida."

Crap. Why hadn't she lied?

And was the island even part of Florida? Or was it the royal family's own privately owned little kingdom? She wasn't sure and didn't intend to

split hairs—or reveal anything more than necessary to her mother.

"Oh, are you near Boca? Clear the rest of your
day," her mother ordered. "Your dad and I will drive
over to meet you."

"I really am working. I can't just put that on
hold. And besides, I'm in Northern Florida. Very
far away." Not far enough at the moment.

"You can't be working. I hear children in the
background."

She hated outright lying. So she dodged with,
"The boss has kids."

"Single boss?"

Not wading into those waters with her mother.
"Why was it that you called?"

"Christmas!"

Huh? "The holidays are months away, Mom."

"I know, but we need to get these things pinned
down so nothing goes wrong. You know how I like
to have everything perfect for the holidays."

And that need for perfection differed from the
rest of the year how, exactly? "I'll do my best to
be there."

"I need to know, though, so we have an even
number of males and females at the table. I would
just hate to have the place setting ruined at the last
minute if you cancel."

So much for her mother's burning need to see her
only child. She just needed an extra warm body at

the table, a body with female chromosomes. "You know what, Mom, then let's just plan on me not being there."

"Now, Lexi, don't be that way. And wipe that frown off your face. You're going to get wrinkles in your forehead early, and I can't afford collagen treatments for you."

Deep breaths. She wasn't her mother. She'd refused to let her mom have power over her life.

But control seemed harder to find today than usual after she'd lowered so many barriers with Seth last night.

Her mother had her own reasons for the way she acted, most of which came from having a control freak mother of her own. Holiday photos were always color-coordinated, perfectly posed and very strained.

But understanding the reasons didn't mean accepting the hurtful behavior. Alexa had worked hard to break the cycle, to get well and make sure that if she ever had a child of her own, the next generation would know unconditional love, rather than the smothering oppression of a parent determined to create a perfectly crafted mini-me.

Her eyes slid down to Olivia who was trying her best to stuff her sock in her mouth. God, that kid was adorable.

Alexa's hand tightened around the phone, another swell of sympathy for her mom washing over her. She could do this. She could talk to her mother while still keeping boundaries in place. "Mom, I appreciate that you want to have me there for the holidays. I will get back to you at the end of the month with a definite answer one way or the other."

"That's my good girl." Her mother paused for a second, the background chatter and cheers the only indication she was still on the line. "I love you, Alexa. Thanks for picking up."

"Sure, Mom. I love you, too."

And she did. That's what made it so tough sometimes. Because while love could be beautiful, it also stole control, giving another person the power to cause hurt.

As the ferry docked at the airstrip and Alexa dropped the phone back into her bag, her eyes didn't land on the kids this time. Her gaze went straight to Seth.

Chapter 8

Her stomach knotted with each step down the stairway leading from the private jet. Back where she'd started in Charleston a few short, eventful days ago.

The flight hadn't given them any opportunity to discuss what they would do after landing. The kids had been fussy for most of the journey, not surprising given all the upheaval to their routine. Seth had been occupied with flying the plane through bumpy skies.

And all those pockets of turbulence hadn't helped the children's moods. Or hers for that matter. Her nerves were shot.

Alexa hitched Olivia on her hip more securely. The early morning sun glinted off the concrete parking area of the private airport that housed Jansen Jets. She saw Seth's world with new eyes now. Before she'd viewed him and his planes from a business perspective. She'd seen his hangars at the private airport and his jets, and thought about what a boon it would be to service his fleet. Now, she took in the variety of aircraft, in awe of how much he'd acquired in such a short time.

From her research on him she'd learned that about ten years ago he'd purchased the privately owned airport, which, at that time, sported two hangars. Now there were three times as many filled with anything from the standard luxury Learjets to Gulfstreams like the one she'd flown in today. In fact, one of those Lears taxied out toward the runway now.

As she looked back at the hangars, she also saw smaller Cessnas. Perhaps for flight training like he'd done back in North Dakota? Or was that a part of the search and rescue aspect he obviously felt so passionately about?

There was so much more to Seth than she'd originally thought.

An open hangar also gave her a peek of what appeared to be a vintage plane, maybe World War II era. Not exactly what she expected a buttoned-up businessman to own. But a bold, crop-dusting North

Dakota farm boy who'd branched out to South Carolina, who'd built a billion-dollar corporation from the ground up? That man, she could envision taking to the skies in the historic craft.

She'd wanted to get to know more about Seth, to understand him, at first to win his contract and then to protect herself from heartache. Instead she was only more confused, more vulnerable, and unable to walk away.

Her feet hit solid ground just as she heard a squeal from the direction of the airport's main building, a one-story red brick structure with picture windows. An auburn-haired woman raced past a fuel truck toward the plane, her arms wide.

Pippa Jansen.

The beauty wore the same short-sleeve sweater set she'd had on during the Skype conversation earlier. She raced toward them, a wide smile on her face.

Olivia stretched out her hands, squealing, "Mama, Ma-ma..."

Pippa gathered her daughter into her arms and spun around. "I missed you, precious girl. Did you have fun with Daddy? I have your favorite *Winnie the Pooh* video in the car."

She slowed her spin, coming face-to-face with Alexa. A flicker of curiosity chased through Pippa's hazel eyes. The Learjet engines hummed louder in the background as the plane accelerated, faster,

faster, swooping smoothly upward. Owen pointed with a grin as he clapped.

Her son's glee distracted her and she turned to kiss his forehead. "Hello, my handsome boy."

His face tight with tension, Seth passed over his son. "I thought we were going to talk later today?"

"I decided to meet you here instead. After I heard the children's voices this morning, I just couldn't stay away any longer. I missed them too much, so I flew straight home. Your secretary gave me your arrival time since it related to the children." She kissed each child on top of the head, breathing deeply before looking up again, directly at Alexa. "And who might you be?"

Seth stepped up, his face guarded. "This is my friend Alexa. She took time off work to help me with the twins since I had an out of town business meeting I couldn't cancel. Your note said you were going to be gone for two weeks."

"The weekend's rest recharged me. I'm ready to be with my children again." Her pointy chin jutted with undeniable strength. "It's my custodial time."

He sighed wearily, guiding them toward the building, away from the bustle of trucks and maintenance personnel. He stopped outside a glass door at the end of the brick building. "Pippa, I don't want a fight. I just want to be sure you won't check out on them again without notice."

"My mother's in the car. I'm staying with her for

a while." She adjusted the weight of both babies, resettling them. "Seth, I'm going to take you up on the offer to hire extra help when I'm with them, and I'd like to write up more visitation time into our agreement. They've been weaned for a couple of months, so the timing is right. Okay?"

He didn't look a hundred percent pleased with the outcome but nodded curtly. "All right, we'll meet tomorrow morning in my office at ten to set that in motion."

"Good, I'm so relieved to see them. My time away gave me a fresh perspective on how to pace myself better." She passed Olivia to Seth. "Could you help me carry them out to the car? You'll get to see my mom and reassure yourself." She glanced at Alexa. "You won't mind if I borrow him for a minute?"

"Of course not." It was clear Alexa wasn't invited on this little family walk.

Seth slid an arm around Alexa's shoulder. "This won't take long." He pulled out a set of keys and unlocked the glass door in front of him. "You can wait in my office space here where it's cooler."

An office here? Jansen Jets Corporate was located downtown. But then of course he would have an office here as well.

"I'll be waiting."

He dropped a kiss on her lips. Nothing lengthy or overtly sexual, but a clear branding of their relationship in front of his ex. Surprise tingled through her along with the now expected attraction.

Pippa looked at her with deepening curiosity. "Thank you for being there for my babies when Seth needed an extra set of hands."

Alexa didn't have a clue how to respond, so she opted for a noncommittal "Owen and Olivia are precious. I'm glad I could help."

Stepping into the back entrance to Seth's office, she crossed to a corner window and watched the couple carrying their children toward a silver Mercedes sedan parked and idling. Pippa's older "twin" sat behind the wheel. Her mother, no doubt.

A sense of déjà vu swept over Alexa at the mother-daughter twin look. It could have been her with her own mom years ago. More than the outward similarity, Alexa recognized a fragility in Pippa, something she'd once felt herself, a lack of ego. Having rich parents provided a lot of luxuries, but it could also rob a person of any sense of accomplishment. Her parents bought her everything, even bought her way out of bad grades…which had been wrong.

Just as it would be wrong to write off Pippa's reckless escape from motherhood for the weekend. Yes, she was an overwhelmed mom, but she was also a parent with resources. She could hire help. There were a hundred better options than leaving her children unattended on an aircraft. Pippa's excuse about watching through a window was bogus. How could she have helped them from so far away if something had gone wrong?

Alexa's fists dug into the windowsill, helplessness sweeping over her. There was nothing she could do. These weren't her children. This wasn't her family. She had to trust Seth to handle the situation with his ex-wife.

Spinning back to the office, she studied the space Seth had created for himself. It was a mass of contradictions, just like the man himself. High-end leather furniture filled the room, a sofa, a wing recliner and office chair, along with thick mahogany shelves and a desk.

She also saw a ratty fishing hat resting on top of a stack of books. The messy desktop was filled with folders and even a couple of honest to God plastic photo cubes—not exactly what she'd expected in a billionaire's space. It was tough for her to resist the desire to order the spill of files across the credenza.

Forcing her eyes upward, she studied the walls packed with framed charts and maps, weathered paper with routes inked on them. In the middle of the wall, he'd displayed a print of buffalo on the plains tagged Land of Tatanka.

The land looked austere and lonely to her. Like the man, a man who'd been strangely aloof all day. Her fingers traced along the bottom of the frame. Even as he embraced the skies and adventure here, there was still a part of him that remembered his stark North Dakota farm boy roots.

The opening door pulled her attention off the artwork and back to the man striding into the room. His face was hard. His arms empty and loose by his sides.

She rested her hand on his shoulder and squeezed lightly. "Are you okay?"

"I will be." He nodded curtly, stepping away.

Only a few minutes earlier he'd kissed her and now he was distant, cold. Had it been an act? She didn't think so. But if he didn't want her here, if he needed space, she could find her own way home. She started toward the door leading out of his office and into the building.

"Alexa," he called out. "Hold on. We have some unfinished business."

Business? Not what she was hoping to hear. "What would that be?"

He walked to the massive desk and pulled a file off the corner. "I made a promise when you agreed to help me. Before I spoke to Pippa this morning, I put in some calls, arranged for you and your partner to interview with four potential clients who commute into the Charleston area, both at the regional airport and here at my private airstrip." He passed her the folder. "Top of the list, Senator Matthew Landis."

She took the file from his hand, everything she

could have hoped for when she'd first stepped onto his plane, cleaning bucket in hand. And now? She couldn't shake the sense he was shuffling her off, giving her walking papers. While, yes, that's what they'd agreed upon, she couldn't help worrying that he was fulfilling the deal to the letter so they could be done, here and now.

Her grip tightened on the file until the edges bent. "Thank you, that's great. I appreciate it."

"You still have to seal the deal when you meet them, but I had my assistant compile some notes I made that I believe will help you beef up your proposal." He sat on the edge of the desk, picked up a photo cube and tossed it from hand to hand. "I also included some ways I think you may be missing out on expansion opportunities."

He hadn't left money on the dresser, by God, but somehow the transaction still felt cheap given the bigger prize they could have had together.

"I don't know how to thank you." She clasped the folder to her chest and wondered why this victory felt hollow. Just a few days ago she would have turned cartwheels over the information in that folder.

"No. Thank *you*. It was our agreement from the start, and I keep my word." *Toss, toss,* the cube sailed from hand to hand. "And while I am genuinely sorry I can't pass over my fleet to A-1, I have requested that your company be called first for any subcontracting work from this point on."

His words carried such finality she didn't know whether to be hurt or mad. "That's it then. Our business is concluded."

"That was my intention." He pitched the cube side to side, images of Owen and Olivia tumbling to rest against a paperweight.

Okay, she was mad, damn it. They'd slept together. He'd kissed her in plain view of his ex-wife. She deserved better than this.

She slapped the file down on his messy desk and yanked the cube from midair. "Is this a brush-off?"

He did a double take and took his photos back from her. "What the hell makes you think that?"

"Your ice cold shoulder all day, for starters." She crossed her arms over her chest.

"I'm clearing away business because from this point on, if we see each other, it's for personal reasons only." He clasped her shoulders, skimming his touch down until she stepped into his embrace. "No more agendas. Holding nothing back."

She looked up at him. "Then you're saying you want to spend more time together?"

"Yes, that's exactly what I'm telling you. You've cleared your calendar until tomorrow, and it's not even lunchtime yet. So let's spend the day together, no kids, no agendas, no bargains." He brushed her hair back with a bold, broad palm. "I can't claim to know where this is headed, and there are a thousand reasons why this is the wrong time. But I can't just let you walk away without trying."

Being with this guy was like riding an emotional yo-yo. One minute he was intense, then moody, then happy, then sensual. And she was totally intrigued by all of him. "Okay then. Ask me out to lunch."

A sigh of relief shuddered through him, his arms twitching tighter around her waist. "Where would you like to go? Anywhere in the country for lunch. Hell, we could even go out of the States for supper if you can lay hands on your passport."

"Let's keep it stateside this time." This time? She shivered with possibility. "As for the place? You pick. You're the one with the airplanes."

With those words, reality settled over her with anticipation and more than a little apprehension. She'd committed. This wasn't about the babies or her business any longer. This was about the two of them.

She'd explored the complex layers of this man, and now she needed to be completely open to him as well. They had one last night away from the real world to decide where to go next.

One last night for her to see how he handled knowing everything about her, even the insecure, vulnerable parts that were too much like those she'd seen in his ex-wife.

* * *

Seth parked the rental car outside the restaurant, waiting for Alexa's verdict on the place he'd chosen.

He could have taken her to Le Cirque in New York City or City Zen in D.C. He could have even gone the distance for Savoy's in Vegas. But thinking back over the things she'd shared about her past, he realized she wasn't impressed with glitz or pretension. They'd just left a king's island, for Pete's sake. Besides, she'd grown up with luxurious trappings and, if anything, seemed to disdain them now.

The North Dakota farm boy inside him applauded her.

So he'd fueled up one Cessna 185 floatplane and taken off for his favorite "hole-in-the-wall" eating establishment on the Outer Banks in North Carolina. A seaside clapboard bar, with great beer, burgers and fresh catch from the Atlantic.

A full-out smile spread across her face. "Perfect. The openness, the view… I love it."

Some of the cold weight he'd been carrying in his chest since saying goodbye to his kids eased. He sprinted around the front of the 1975 Chevy Caprice convertible—special ordered, thanks to his assistant's speedy persistence. He opened the door for Alexa. She swept out, her striped sundress swirling around her knees as she climbed the plank steps up to the patio dining area. The Seat Yourself sign hammered to a wooden column was weather-worn but legible.

He guided her to a table for two closest to the rocky shoreline as a waitress strolled over.

"Good to see you, Mr. Jansen. I'll get your Buffalo blue-water tuna bites and two house brews."

"Great, thanks, Carol Ann." Seth passed the napkin-rolled silverware across the table. Alexa fidgeted with the salt and pepper shakers until he asked, "Something wrong? Would you like to go somewhere else after all?"

She looked up quickly. "The place is great. Really. It's just… Well… I like to order my own food."

"Of course. I apologize. You're right, that was presumptuous of me." He leaned back in his chair. "Let me get Carol Ann back over and we can add whatever you would like."

"No need. Truly. It's just for future reference. And I actually do like the sound of what you chose, so it's probably silly that I said anything at all." She smiled sheepishly. "You may have noticed I have some…control issues."

"You appreciate order in your world. Plenty to admire about that." God knows, his world could stand a little more order and reason these days. The unresolved mess with Pippa still knocked around in his head. "That's a great asset in your job—"

He stopped short as the waitress brought their

plates of Buffalo tuna bites, mugs of beer and glasses of water.

Alexa tore the paper off her straw and stirred her lemon wedge in her water. "Control's my way of kicking back at my childhood."

"In what way?" He passed an appetizer plate to her.

"When I was growing up there wasn't a lot I could control without bringing down the wrath of Mom." She speared the fish onto her plate. "She may have depended on those nannies to free up her spa days and time on the slopes but her expectations were clear."

"And those were?"

"Great grades, of course, with all the right leadership positions to get into an Ivy League school. And in my 'spare time' she expected a popular, pretty daughter. Perfectly groomed, with the perfect boyfriend." She stabbed a bite and brought it to her mouth. "Standard stuff."

"Doesn't sound standard or funny to me." Out of nowhere, an image flashed through his mind of Pippa sitting in the front seat of the car with her mother, both women wearing matching sweater sets and pearls with their trim khakis.

"You're right. That kind of hypercontrol almost inevitably leads to some kind of rebellion in teens. Passive aggressive was my style in those days. The problem started off small and got worse. I controlled what I ate, when I ate, how much I ate." She chewed slowly.

A chill shot through him as he recalled her ordering the blocks for his kids. Her careful lining up of her silverware. Little things he'd written off as sweet peculiarities of a woman who liked the proverbial ducks in a row.

Now, his mind started down a dark path and he hoped to God she would take them on a detour soon. He didn't know what to say or do, so he simply covered her other hand with his and stayed quiet.

"Then I learned I could make Mom happy by joining the swim team. And what do you know? That gave me another outlet for burning calories. I felt good, a real rush of success." She tossed aside her fork. "Until one day when I peeled away my warm-up suit and I saw the looks of horror on the faces of the people around me…"

Squeezing her hand softly, he wished like hell he could have done something for her then. Wishing he could do something more now than just listen.

"I'm lucky to be alive actually. That day at swim practice, right after I saw the looks on their faces, I tried to race back to the locker room, but my body gave out… I pretty much just crumpled to the ground." She looked down at her hands fidgeting with the silverware. "My heart stopped."

He clasped her hand across the table, needing to feel the steady, strong beat of her heart throbbing in her wrist. There were no words he could offer up right now. But then he'd always been better at listening than talking anyway.

"Thank goodness the coach was good at CPR," she half joked, but her laugh quickly lost its fizz. "That's when my parents—and I—had to face up to the fact that I had a serious eating disorder."

She pulled away from him and rubbed her bare arms in spite of the noonday sun beating overhead. "I spent my senior year in a special high school—aka hospital—for recovering bulimics and anorexics." She brushed her windswept hair back with a shaky hand. "I was the latter, by the way. I weighed eighty-nine pounds when they admitted me."

This was more—worse—than he'd expected and what he'd expected had been gut-twisting enough. He thought of his own children, of Olivia, and he wanted to wrap her up in cotton while he read every parenting book out there in hopes that he could spare his kids this kind of pain. "I'm so damn sorry you had to go through that."

"Me, too. I'm healthy now, completely over it, other than some stretch marks from the seesawing weight loss and gain."

"Was that why you preferred to keep the lights off?"

"When we were making love? Yes." She nodded, rolling her eyes. "It's not so much vanity as I wasn't ready to tell you this. I fully realize those lines on my skin are a small price to pay to be alive." She reached for her beer, tasted the brew once, and again, before placing the mug on the red-checkered cloth. "My stint in the special high school cost me a real prom, sleepovers with ice cream sundaes and dates spent parking with a boyfriend. But it also screwed up Mom's Ivy League aspirations for me. So I won control of something for a while, I guess."

"What happened after you graduated?"

"Dad bought my way into a college, and I married the man of their choice." She patted her chest. "A-1 Cleaning is the first independent thing I've done on my own, for me."

Admiration for her grew, and he'd already been feeling a hefty dose where she was concerned. But she'd broken away from every support system she had in place—such as they were—to forge her own path. Turning her back on her family had to be tough, no matter how strained the relationship. He could also see she'd grown away from the world Pippa still seemed to be suffocating in.

He hadn't been expecting this kind of revelation from her today. But he knew he'd better come up with the right response, to offer the affirmation she should have gotten from those closest to her.

"What other things would you like to do? Anything... I will make it happen."

She leaned back in her chair, her eyes going whimsical. "That's a nice thought. But the things

I regret? I need to accept I can't have them and be at peace with that."

"Things such as?"

"I can't go back and change my teenage years. I need to accept that and move forward."

The sadness in her voice as she talked about her lost past sucker punched him with the need to do something for her. To give her back those parts of her life her parents had stolen by trying to live out their own dreams through their kid. He couldn't change the past.

But he could give her one of those high school experiences she'd been denied.

Chapter 9

Alexa shook her hair free as they drove along the seaside road with the convertible top down. She adored his unexpected choices, from the car to the restaurant. The red 1975 Chevy Caprice ate up the miles down the deserted shore of the Outer Banks. She'd marveled at how lucky they were to get such a classic car, but then learned Seth's assistant had taken care of the arrangements.

How easy it was to forget he was a billionaire sometimes, with all the power and perks that came with such affluence.

The afternoon sun blazed overhead, glinting on the rippling tide. Sea oats and driftwood dotted the sandy beach along with bare picket fences permanently leaning from the force of the wind. Kind of like her. Leaning and weathered by life, but not broken, still standing.

She studied the brooding man beside her. Seth drove on, quietly focused on the two-lane road winding ahead of them. What had he thought of her revelations at lunch? He'd said all the right things, but she could see his brain was churning her words around, sifting through them. She couldn't help but feel skittish over how he would treat her now. Would he back away? Or worse yet, act differently?

Tough to tell when he'd been in such an unpredictable mood since talking with Pippa. That made Alexa wonder if she should have waited to dish out her own baggage? But she couldn't escape the sense of urgency pushing her, insisting they had only a narrow slice of time. That once they returned to Charleston permanently, this opportunity to fully know him would disappear.

She hooked her elbow on the open window, her own face staring back at her in the side mirror. "Seth? Where are we going? I thought the airport was the other way."

"It is. I wanted to make the most of the day before we leave." He pointed ahead toward a red brick lighthouse in the distance. "We're headed there, on that bluff."

The ancient beacon towered in the distance. She

could envision taking the kids there for a picnic, like the one they'd shared at the fort in St. Augustine. "It's gorgeous here. I love our South Carolinian low country home, but this is special, too, different. I can't believe I've never been here before."

Her parents had always opted for more "exotic" vacations.

"I thought you would appreciate it. You seem to have an eye for the unique, an appreciation for entertainment off the beaten path."

"I'm not sure I follow what you mean."

"Like when we had the picnic at the old fort. You saw it with an artist's eye rather than looking for an up-to-date, pristine park. Must be the art history major in you. This place and this car are certainly pieces of history. Did I read you right on that?"

"You did, very much so." The fact that he knew her this well already, had put so much thought into what she thought, made her heart swell. The twisting road led higher over the town, taking them farther away and into a more isolated area.

When she looked around her, she also realized… "You brought me here to make out, didn't you?"

"Guilty as charged."

"Because of what I said at the restaurant about missing the high school experience of parking and making out with a guy."

"Guilty again. It's private, bare, stripped away nature, which in some ways reminds me of North

Dakota as a whole. There's something…freeing about leaving civilization behind." He steered the car off the paved road, onto a dirt trail leading toward the lighthouse. "It's good to leave baggage behind, and it's safe to say we both have our fair share."

Nerves took flight in her belly like the herons along the shore. "Like what I told you at lunch?"

"In part. Yes." Tires crunched along the rocky road, spitting a gritty cloud of dirt behind them. "It's clear we're both members of the Walking Wounded Divorce Club, both with hang-ups. But we have something else in common, an attraction and a mutual respect."

The way he'd analyzed them chilled her in spite of the bold shining sun overhead and the thoughtfulness of his gesture. He'd pinpointed them so well, and yet… "You make it sound so logical. So calculated. So…coldly emotionless."

Stopping the car at the base of the lighthouse, the top of the bluff, he gripped the steering wheel in white-knuckled fists. "Believe me, there's nothing cold about the way I'm feeling about you. I want you so much I'm damn near ready to explode just sitting beside you."

Breathless, she leaned against her door, the power of his voice washing over her as tangibly as the sun warming her skin.

He turned toward her, leather seat squeaking, his

green eyes flinty. "Just watching you walk across the room, I imagine resting my hands on your hips to gauge the sway." His fingers glided along her shoulder. "Or when I see the wind lift your hair, I burn to test the texture between my fingers. Everything about you mesmerizes me."

Tension crackled between them like static in her hair, in his words. "Before this past weekend, I'd been celibate for over six months. Attractive women have walked into my life and not one of them has tempted me the way you do."

There was no missing the intensity of his words—or the intent in his eyes. His fingers stroked through her hair, down to the capped sleeves of her sundress, hovering, waiting. "Did anyone ever tell you what a truly stunning woman you are, how beautiful you will still be when you're eighty-five years old? Not that it matters what the hell I, or anyone else, thinks."

While she was flattered, his words also left her blushing with self-consciousness.

She resisted the urge to fidget. "Okay, I hear you. Now could you stop? I don't need you to flatter me because of what I said earlier. I'm beyond needing affirmation of my looks."

"I'm not flattering. I'm stating facts, indisputable, beyond perceptions."

She realized now that he'd brought her out to this place for a private conversation, a better place to discuss her past than a crowded restaurant. She should have realized that earlier.

"Thank you and I hear you. Skewed perceptions played a part in what I went through." Her hands fell to his chest. "But I'm over that now. It was hard as hell, but I'm healthy and very protective of that particular fact."

"Good. I'm glad to hear it, and I don't claim to be an expert on the subject. I only know that I want to tell you how beautiful, how sexy you are to me. Yet, that seems to make you uncomfortable."

The ocean breeze lifted her hair like a lover's caress, the scent so clean and fresh that the day felt like a new beginning.

"Maybe I like to speak with actions."

"I'm all about that, too." His hands brushed down the sleeves of her dress. "When I touch you, it turns me inside out to feel the curves, the silky softness, the way you're one hundred percent a woman."

He inched the bodice down farther, baring the top of her breasts.

Realization raised goose bumps along her skin as she grasped his deeper intent for bringing her here... "Are you actually planning for us to make love, here?"

He nuzzled the crook of her neck. "Do you think you're the only one who can initiate outdoor sex?"

"That was at night."

"Hidden away where no one could see us." Where they could barely see each other.

Her thoughts cleared as if someone had turned the sun up a notch. Out here, there was no turning off the lamp or shrouding herself in darkness. Oh hell, maybe she wasn't as over the past as she'd thought. She'd controlled everything about their lovemaking before.

This place, now, out in the brightest light of all, meant giving over complete control. That sent jitters clear through her. But the thought of saying no, of turning down this chance to be with him, upset her far more.

He cupped her face in both hands. "Do you think I would ever place you at risk? I chose this place carefully because I feel certain we're completely alone."

Alone and yet so totally exposed by the unfiltered sunshine. Seth was asking for a bigger commitment from her. He was requiring her trust.

Toying with his belt, she said, "Out here, huh? In full daylight. No drawing the shades, that's for sure."

"Sunscreen?" He grinned.

She raised an eyebrow and tugged his belt open. "You expect to be naked that long? You're a big talker."

His smile faded, his touch got firmer. "So you're good with this."

"I'm good with *you*," she murmured against his lips.

"I like the sound of that." He slanted his mouth over hers.

The man knew how to kiss a woman and kiss her well. The way he devoted his all to the moment, to her, in his big bold way, made her want to take everything he offered here today. She'd shared everything about herself at lunch. Giving all here seemed the natural extension of that if she dared.

And she did.

Easing back from him, she shrugged the sleeves of her dress down, revealing herself inch by inch, much the way he'd undressed for her their first time together. In some ways, this was a first for them. A first without barriers.

Her bodice pooled around her waist. With the flick of her fingers, she opened the front clasp on her lacy bra. And waited. It was one thing to bare herself in the dark, but in the daylight, everything showed, her journey showed. Her battle with anorexia had left stretch marks. Regaining her muscle tone had taken nearly six years.

Meeting his gaze, she saw…heat…passion…and tenderness. He touched her, his large hands so deft and nimble as they played over her breasts in just the ways she enjoyed best, lingering on *her* erogenous zones, the ones he must have picked up on from their time together.

She arched into his palms, her grip clenching around his belt buckle. Her head fell to rest against the leather seat. The sun above warmed every inch of her bared flesh as fully as his caresses, his kisses.

His hands swept down to inch the hem upward until he exposed her yellow lace panties. Just above the waistband, he flicked a finger against her belly button ring.

She smiled at a memory. "That was my treat to myself the first time I wore a bikini in public."

"I'll buy you dozens, each one with a different jewel."

Laughing softly, she traced his top lip with the tip of her tongue. He growled deeply in his throat. But he only allowed her to steal control for an instant before he stroked lower, dipping a finger inside her panties, between her legs, finding her wet and ready.

Her spine went weak and he braced her with an arm around her waist, holding her. She unbuttoned his shirt, sweeping it aside and baring his brazened chest to her eyes, her touch. The rasp of his crisp blond hair tantalized her fingertips.

She inhaled the scent of leather and sea, a brand-new aphrodisiac for her. "We should move this to the backseat where we can stretch out somewhat."

"Or we can stay here and save the backseat for later."

She purred her agreement as she swung her leg

over to straddle his lap. The steering wheel at her back only served to keep her closer to him. Everything about this place was removed from the real world, and she intended to make the most of it. She opened his pants and somehow a condom appeared in his hand. She didn't care where or how. She just thanked goodness he had the foresight.

His hands palmed her waist, her arms looping around his neck. He lowered her onto him, carefully, slowly filling her. Moving within her. Or was she moving over him? Either way, the sensation rippled inside her, built to a fever pitch. Every sensation heightened: the give of the butter-soft leather under her knees, the rub of his trousers against the inside of her thighs.

The openness of the convertible and the untouched landscape called to her. The endless stretch of ocean pulled at her, like taking a skein of yarn and unraveling it infinitely. Moans swelled inside her, begging to be set free to fly into that vastness.

He thrust his hands into her hair and encouraged her in a litany detailing how damn much he wanted her, needed her, burned to make this last as long as he could because he was not finishing without her. The power of his words pulsed through her, took her pleasure higher.

Face-to-face, she realized there wasn't a battle for control. They were sharing the moment, sharing the experience. The insight exploded inside her in a shower of light and sensation as she flew apart in his arms. Her cries of completion burst from her in abandon, followed by his. Their voices twined together, echoing out over the ocean.

Panting, she sagged against his chest, perspiration bonding their bodies. Their time together here, away from the rest of the world, had been perfect. Almost too much so.

Now she had to trust in what they'd shared enough to test it out when they returned home.

Seth revved the Cessna seaplane's engines, skimming the craft along the water faster and faster until finally, smoothly...*airborne.*

A few more days on the Outer Banks would have been damn welcome to give him a chance to fortify his connection with Alexa. To experience more of the amazing sex they'd shared in the front seat of the convertible, then the backseat. Except he was out of time.

He had to meet with Pippa tomorrow and hammer out a new visitation schedule. That always proved sticky since the ugly truth lurked behind every negotiation that he might not be the twins' biological father. If Pippa ever decided to push that, things could go all to hell. He would fight for his kids, but it tore him up inside thinking of how deep it would slice if he lost. Acid burned in his gut.

If only life could be simpler. He just wanted to

enjoy his children like any parent. The way his cousin Paige enjoyed hers. The way his cousin Vic was celebrating a new baby with his wife, Claire. That reminded him of what a crappy cousin he'd been in not calling to congratulate them. Paige had texted him that Claire was staying in the hospital longer because of the C-section delivery. He needed to stop by and do the family support gig.

That also meant introducing Alexa to the rest of his family. Soon. His relatives were important to him. He wasn't sure how he was going to piece together his crazy ass life with hers, but walking away wasn't an option. He also wasn't sure how Alexa would feel about his big noisy family, especially given how strained her relationship was with her own.

If only life was as easy to level out as an airplane.

Easing back on the yoke, he scanned his airspeed, along with the rest of the control panel.

Alexa touched the window, an ocean view visible beyond. "I grew up with charter jets, but I've never flown on one of these before. And I certainly didn't have a fleet of planes at my fingertips 24/7."

"This wasn't among my more elite crafts, but, God, I love to fly her."

"I can tell by how relaxed you are here versus other times." She trapped the toy bobblehead fisherman suction-cupped to the control panel. Her finger swayed the line from the fishing pole. "I can hardly believe how much we've done since waking up. Starting in Florida, stopping in South Carolina, North Carolina by lunch. Now home again."

"I still owe you supper, although it'll be late."

"Can we eat it naked?"

"As long as I have you all to myself."

She laughed softly. "While I enjoyed our time in the convertible, I haven't turned into that much of an exhibitionist."

"Good," he growled with more possessiveness than he was used to feeling. "I don't share well."

She toyed with the sleeve of her dress, adjusting it after the haphazard way they'd thrown on their clothes as the sun started to set. "I appreciate that you didn't get weirded out by what I shared with you at the restaurant."

"I admire the way you've taken everything life threw at you and just kept right on kicking back," he answered without hesitation.

He meant every word.

"I'm determined not to let other people steal anything more from me—not my parents or my ex."

"That attitude is exactly what I'm talking about."

"I'm not so sure about the kick-ass thing." Her hand fell to her lap. "It's wacky the way a piece of cheesecake can sometimes still hold me hostage. Sounds strange, I know. I don't expect you to understand."

"Explain it to me." He needed to understand. He

couldn't tolerate saying or doing something that could hurt her.

She sagged back in her seat. "Sometimes I look at it and remember what it was like to want that cheesecake, but then I would measure out how many calories I'd eaten that day. Think how many laps I would need to swim in order to pick up that fork for one bite. Then I would imagine the disappointment on my mother's face when I stepped on the scale the next morning."

What the hell? Her mother made her weigh in every morning? No wonder Alexa had control issues.

He wrestled to keep his face impassive when he really wanted to find her parents and… He didn't know what he would do. He did know he needed to be here for Alexa now. "I wish I'd known you then."

She turned to look at him. "Me, too."

Suddenly he knew exactly where he wanted to take Alexa tonight. "Do you mind staying out late?"

"I'm all for letting this day last as long as possible."

"Good. Then I have one more stop to make on my way to take you home."

Of all the places she thought Seth might take her, Alexa wouldn't have guessed they would go to a hospital.

Once they'd landed, Seth had said he wanted to

visit his cousin's new baby. Her heart had leaped to her throat at the mention of an infant. A newborn.

Her skin felt clammy as she rubbed her arms. Was she freaked out because of the baby or because of her own hospital stay? Right now, with her emotions so close to the surface, she couldn't untangle it all.

Damn it, she was being silly. It wasn't like she would even go in to see the new mom. This visit would be over soon and she could clear the antiseptic air with deep breaths outside. Seth was walking in on his own while she hung out at the picture window looking into a nursery packed full of bassinets. Her gaze lingered on one in particular, front row, far left.

Baby Jansen.

She could barely see anything other than a white swaddling blanket and a blue-and-yellow-striped cap. But she could tell the bundle was bigger than most of the others, nearly ten pounds of baby boy, according to Seth. Alexa touched the window lightly, almost imagining she could feel the satiny softness of those chubby newborn cheeks.

A woman stepped up alongside her and Alexa inched to the side to make room.

The blonde woman—in her late thirties—wore a button that proclaimed Proud Aunt. "Beautiful little boy." She tapped the glass right around Baby

Jansen territory. "Can you believe all that blond hair? Well, under the hat there's lots of blond hair."

Alexa cocked her head to the side. "Do I know you?"

The woman grinned, and Alexa saw the family resemblance so strongly stamped on her face she might as well have pulled back her question.

"I'm Paige, Seth's cousin. While I was getting coffee, I saw you walking in with him. My brother, Vic, is this baby's daddy."

It was one thing meeting his family with Seth there to handle the introductions, to define their still new relationship. This was awkward to say the least. Why, why, why hadn't she waited in his SUV outside? "Congratulations on your new nephew."

"Thank you, we have lots to celebrate. Hope you'll join us at the next family get-together." She cut her brown eyes toward Alexa. "How did the trip with Seth and the twins go? They're sweet as can be, but a handful, for sure."

Seth had told his family about her? Curiosity drowned out the rattle of food carts, the echo of televisions, even the occasional squawk of a baby.

"Nice trip. But it's always good to be home," she answered noncommittally. "The twins are back with their mother now."

Paige nodded, tucking her hair behind her ears. "Pippa's, well…" She sighed. "She's Pippa, and she's the twins' mom. And Seth's such a good daddy. He deserves to have a good woman to love him, better than…well…you know."

Sort of. Not really. And she should really cut this short and get all of her answers from Seth. "I'm not in a position to—"

Pivoting, Paige stared her down with an unmistakably protective gleam in her golden-brown eyes. "I'm just asking you to be good to my cousin, to be fair. Pippa screwed him over, literally. There are days I would really like to give her a piece of my mind, but I hold back because I love those kids regardless of whether they're my blood or not. But I don't think I could take seeing him betrayed like that again. So please, if you're not serious, walk away now."

Whoa, whoa, whoa. Alexa struggled to keep up the barrage of information packed into that diatribe. "I don't know what to say other than your family loyalty is admirable?"

"Crap. Sorry." Paige bit her bottom lip. "I should probably hush now. I'm rambling and being rude. Hormones are getting the best of me, compounded even more by the nursery and being pregnant—a whoops, but a happy whoops. And I already get so emotional with how Pippa used Seth, the way she still uses him. I'm sure you're lovely, and I look forward to seeing you again."

Paige squeezed her arm once, before rushing away in a flurry of tissues and winces, leaving

Alexa stunned. She looked back into the nursery, then at the departing woman, going over what she'd said, something about whether or not the twins were related to her. And how Pippa had screwed Seth over. Literally.

What the hell? Had Pippa actually cheated on Seth? But he'd said they split before the twins were even born. Not that a pregnant woman couldn't have an affair, but it seemed less likely... Unless... Pippa had the affair while she and Seth were dating, and it only came out later?

An awful possibility smoked through her mind—perhaps the twins weren't his biological children?

She dismissed the thought as quickly as it came to her. He would have shared something like that with her.

Her perceptions of the man jumbled all together. At first, she'd assumed he was like her wealthy parents, too often looking for a way to dump off their kids on the nearest caregiver. Yet, she'd seen with her own eyes how much he loved them, how he spent every free waking moment with them.

If what she suspected was true, why hadn't he said something to her when they'd deepened their relationship? Sure they'd only known each other a short time, but she'd told him everything. He'd insisted on her being open, vulnerable even, when they'd made love by the lighthouse.

Had he been holding back something this important? She wanted to believe she'd misunderstood Paige. Rather than wonder, she would ask Seth once the timing was right. They would laugh together over how she'd leaped to conclusions. She wanted to trust the feelings growing between her and Seth. More than anything, she wanted this to be real.

And if she was right in her suspicions that he was holding back?

Her eyes skipped to a family at the far end of the picture window. A grandma and grandpa were standing together, shoulder to shoulder, heads tilted toward each other in conversation as they held two older grandchildren up to see their new sister. The connection, the family bond, was undeniable.

She'd seen it earlier today when Seth and Pippa discussed their children. Yes, there was strife between them, but also a certain connection, even tenderness. Disconcerting, regardless. But if they still felt that way after such a betrayal…it gave Alexa pause. It spoke of unresolved feelings between them.

Steadying herself, she pressed her hand to the window. She'd ached for a real family connection growing up, yearned to create such a bond in her marriage. She knew what it felt like to stand on the outside.

And she refused to live that way ever again.

Chapter 10

He wanted Alexa in his life, as well as in his bed.

As Seth drove Alexa home to her downtown Charleston condo after seeing his new nephew, he kept thinking about how right it felt having her sit beside him now. How right it had felt earlier taking her to the hospital with him. Having Alexa with him at such an important family moment made the evening even more special. He hoped when they got to her place, he could persuade her to just pick up some clothes and go with him to his house.

Beams of light from late night traffic streaked through the inky darkness as they crossed the Ashley River. The intimacy of just the two of them in his Infiniti SUV reminded him of making love in the classic Chevy convertible on the Outer Banks. God, was that only a few hours ago? Already, he wanted her again.

And what did she want?

He glanced out of the corner of his eye. She rested her head on the window, cool air from the vent lifting her hair. Shadows played along the dark circles under her eyes, in the furrows along her forehead. He was surprised—and concerned.

"Tell me." He skimmed a strand of hair behind her ear. "What's bothering you?"

She shook her head, keeping her face averted with only the glow of the dashboard lights to help him gauge her mood. She hugged her purse to her chest until the folder inside crackled.

"Whatever it is," he said, "I want to hear it, and don't bother saying it's nothing."

"We're both exhausted." She looked down at her hands, at least not staring out the window but still not turning to him. "It's been an emotional ride since we met, a lot crammed into a short time. I need some space to think."

Crap. She'd asked him earlier if he was giving her the brush-off and now he wondered the same thing. "You're backtracking."

"Maybe."

"Why?" he demanded, considering pulling off

the six-lane highway so he could focus his full attention on her.

"Seth, I've worked hard to put my life back together again, twice. As a teenager. And again after my divorce. I'm stronger now because of both of those times. But I still intend to be very careful not to put myself in a dangerous position again."

What the hell? This wasn't the kind of conversation they should have with him driving. He needed his focus planted firmly on her.

He eyed the fast food restaurant ahead and cut over two lanes of traffic, ignoring the honking horns. He pulled off the interstate and parked under the golden arches.

Hooking his arm on the steering wheel, he pinned her with his gaze. "Let me get this straight. You consider me *dangerous*? What have I done to make you feel threatened?"

"A relationship with you, I mean—" the trenches in her forehead dug deeper "—could be...maybe the better word is chancy." Headlights flashed past, illuminating her face with bright lights in quick, strobelike succession.

Some of the tension melted from his shoulders. His arm slid from the wheel and he took her hand in his. "Any relationship is risky. But I believe we've started something good here."

"I thought so, too, especially this afternoon. I opened up to you in ways I haven't to anyone in as long as I can remember." Her hand was cold in his. "But a relationship has to be a two-way street. Can you deny you're holding back?"

Holding back? Hell, he was giving her more than he'd imagined shelling out after the crap year he'd been through. What more did she want from him? A pint of blood? A pound of flesh?

But snapping those questions at her didn't seem wise. "I'm not sure what you mean."

"You have reservations about us as a couple." She didn't ask. She simply said it.

He couldn't deny she was right on the money.

Now he had to figure out how to work around that in a way that would still involve her packing a sleepover bag to go to his place. "Would it have been better for us to meet a year from now? Absolutely."

"Because?" she pressed.

Damn, he was tired and just wanted to take Alexa to his bed. This wasn't a conversation he wanted to have right now. He didn't much want to have it ever. "A year from now, my divorce wouldn't be as fresh—neither would yours. My kids would be older. Your business would have deeper roots. Can you deny the timing would be better for both of us?"

She shook her head slowly, the air conditioner vent catching the scent of her shampoo. "You know all the reasons why I have issues. I've been completely open with you, and I thought you'd been the same with me."

A buzz started in his brain. She couldn't be hinting at what he thought…

"Your cousin told me about Pippa, how she cheated on you. I can understand why that would make you relationship wary and it would have been helpful to know that."

The buzz in his head increased until he felt like he was being stung by hundreds of bees. Angry bees. Except the rage was his. "Paige had no business telling you that."

"Don't blame her. She thought I already kn—"

"How exactly was I supposed to work that into conversation? Hey, my ex-wife doesn't know for sure if my children are actually mine." His hands fisted. "In fact, she lied to me about that all the way to the altar. Now where would you like to go for dinner?"

Her face paled, her eyes so sympathetic her reaction slashed through all the raw places inside him.

"Seth, I am so sorry."

"I am their father in every way that matters." He slammed his fist into the dash. "I love my kids." His voice cracked.

"I realize that," she said softly, hugging her purse to her stomach.

"It doesn't matter to me whose blood or biology flows through their veins." He thumped his chest right over his heart that he'd placed in two pairs of tiny hands nearly a year ago. "They're *mine*."

"I'm sure they would agree." She paused then continued warily, "Have you taken a paternity test? They certainly look like you."

He didn't need any test to validate his love for those kids. "Back off. This isn't your business."

Her blue eyes filled with tears. "That's my whole point. We may have baggage, but I'm ready to be open about mine. You're not."

"Good God, Alexa, we've barely known each other for a week and you expect me to tell you something that could cripple my kids if they ever found out?"

"You think I would go around telling people? If so, you really don't know me at all." She held up her hands. "You know what? You're one hundred percent correct. This is a mistake. *We* are a mistake. The timing is wrong for us to have a relationship."

The thought of her backing out blindsided him. "Well, there's nothing I can do about the timing."

"My point exactly. Seth, I want to go home now, and I don't want you to follow me inside, and I don't want you to call me."

That was it? Even after their encounter on the Outer Banks, the way they'd come together so magnificently, she was slamming the door in his face? "Damn it, Alexa. Life isn't perfect. I'm not perfect, and I don't expect you to be, either. It's not about all or nothing here."

She chewed her bottom lip and he thought he might be making headway until she looked out the window again without answering.

"What do you want from me, Alexa?"

She turned slowly to him, blue eyes clouded with pain and tears. "Just what I said. I need you to respect my need for space."

Her mouth pursed shut, and she turned her head back toward the window. He waited while four cars cleared the fast food drive-through window and still she wouldn't look at him. He knew an ice-out when he saw one.

Stunned numb, he drove the rest of the way to her condo, a corner unit in a string of red brick buildings made to fit in with the rest of the historic homes. Her place. Where she belonged and he wasn't welcome.

How the hell had it gone so wrong so quickly? So he hadn't told her about Pippa cheating. He would have gotten around to it soon enough.

"Goodbye, Seth." She tore open the door and ran up the walkway into her apartment before he could make it farther than the front of the car.

Frustration chewed his gut as he settled behind the wheel again. He was doing his best here and she was cutting him off at the knees. The way she'd clutched her purse to her chest, she looked like she couldn't get out of the car fast enough. She had probably mangled the folder he'd given her.

An ugly, dark thought snaked through him. That she'd wanted her new contacts and now that she had them, she was looking for a way out. She'd used him. Just as Pippa had used him.

And just that quickly the thought dissipated. He knew Alexa was nothing like Pippa. Sure, they'd come from similar backgrounds, but Alexa had broken free of the dependent lifestyle. She was making her own way in the world. Honestly. With hard work. And she'd been up-front with him from the very start.

If anything, he was the one who'd held back.

Damn it.

She was right.

His head *thunked* against the seat. He'd been carrying so much baggage because of Pippa that he might as well have been driving one of those luggage trucks at the airport. He'd screwed up in that relationship in so many ways and felt the failure all the more acutely in the face of his cousins' marital bliss. To the point that he'd even held back from fully participating in their lives. Sure he'd moved here to be with them, but how close had he let anyone get? How many walls had he built?

None of which was fair to his cousins. And it most definitely wasn't fair to Alexa.

So where did he go from here? Talking to her

now would likely only stoke her anger, or worse, stir her tears. Once she had a chance to cool down, he needed to approach her with something more than words. He needed strong actions to show Alexa how special, how irreplaceably important she was to him.

How very much he loved her.

Love.

The word filled his head and settled in with a flawless landing. Damn straight he loved her, and she deserved to know that.

And if she still said no? Then he would work harder. He believed in what they'd shared these past days, in what they'd started to build together.

He hadn't given up in his professional life. Against the odds, regardless of what people told him about waiting until he was older, more established, he'd accomplished what he set out to do.

Now it was time to set his sights on winning over Alexa.

Alexa Randall had accumulated an eclectic box full of lost and found items since opening her own cleaning company for charter jets. There were the standard smart phones, portfolios, tablets, even a Patek Philippe watch. She'd returned each to its owner.

Then there were the stray panties and men's boxers, even the occasional sex toys from Mile High

Club members. All of those items, she'd picked up with latex gloves and tossed in the trash.

But the pacifier lying beside a seat reminded her too painfully of the precious twins she'd discovered nearly two weeks ago. Memories of their father pierced her heart all the more.

Her bucket of supplies dropped to the industrial blue carpet with a heavy thud. Ammonia fumes from the rag in her fist stung her eyes. Or maybe it was the tears. Heaven knew, she'd cried more than her fair share since leaving Seth's car after their awful argument a week ago. God, this hurt more than when she'd divorced. The end of her marriage had been a relief. Losing Seth, however, cut her to the core. So much so, she couldn't escape the fact that she loved him. Truly, deeply loved him.

And he'd let her go.

She'd half expected him to follow her or do something cliché like send bunches of flowers with stock apologies. But he'd done none of that. He'd stayed quiet. Giving her the space she'd demanded? Or walking away altogether?

Her husband and parents would have shouted her down, even going so far as to bully her until she caved.

That made her question how she'd reacted that night to his news about the children. She may have grown in how she stood up for herself since the days when she'd tried to control stress through her eating habits. While she was happy for that new-found strength, perhaps she needed to grow even more to be able to return to a problem and fix it. Real strength wasn't about arguing and stomping away. It was going back to a sticky situation and battling—compromising—for a fair resolution.

And she had no one to blame but herself for condemning him because he hadn't told her all his secrets right away. How fair had that been?

Yes, he'd held back. Yet to the best of his ability, he'd lived up to everything he'd promised, everything he was able to give right now. Why was she realizing this now rather than days ago when she could have saved herself so much pain?

Most likely because she'd hidden her head in the sand the past few days, crying her eyes out and burying herself in paperwork at the office. Today was her first day actually picking up a bucket—and what a day it was with so many reminders of Seth and his kids.

She looked around the private luxury jet owned by Senator Landis, parked at the Charleston airport—not Seth's private field. But still, with that pacifier in hand from one of the Landis babies, she couldn't help but think of Owen and Olivia, and wonder how they were doing. She'd missed their sweet faces this week as well, and she liked to think they'd felt a connection to her, too, even during their short time together.

Her ultimatum had hurt more than just her. She stared into the bucket, more of those tears springing to her eyes. Blaming them on ammonia wouldn't work indefinitely.

She sank down onto the leather sofa, her mind replaying for the millionth time the harsh words they'd shared. She looked around the pristinely clean aircraft and wished her life was as easy to perfect.

Perfect?

Her mind snagged on the word, shuffling back to something Seth had said about it not being the perfect time, but life wasn't perfect. He didn't expect her to be perfect... And... What? She reached for the thought like an elusive pristine cloud until—

An increasing ruckus outside broke her train of thought. The sound of trucks and people talking in a rising excited cacophony of voices. She stood and walked toward the hatch. Bits of conversation drifted toward her.

"What's that up—?"

"—airplane?"

"P-47 Thunderbolt, I th—"

"Can you read what—?"

"—wonder who is Alexa?"

Alexa? Airplane?

A hope too scary to acknowledge prickled along her skin. She stepped into the open hatch, stopping at the top of the metal stairs. Shading her eyes, she scanned the crowd of maintenance workers and aircraft service personnel. She followed the path of their fingers pointing upward.

A World War II-era plane buzzed low over their section of the airfield, a craft that looked remarkably like the one she'd seen in Seth's hangar. Trailing behind, a banner flapped against the bright blue sky. In block red letters, it spelled out:

I Love You, Alexa Randall!

Her breath hitched in her throat as she descended the steps one at a time, rereading the message. By the time her feet hit concrete, it had fully sunk in. Seth was making a grand gesture to win her back. Her. Alexa Randall. At an imperfect time. In spite of her frustrated fears that were far from rational.

She'd thought she'd left her growing up years behind her, but she'd been hanging on to more than a need to make the world around her perfectly in order. She'd still subconsciously held onto the old, misguided mantra that *she* had to be perfect as well.

Seth had told her that didn't matter to him.

Maybe she needed to remember Seth didn't need to be perfect, either.

And she couldn't wait for him to land so she could tell him face-to-face.

The plane circled once more, message rippling for the entire airport to see. Then the craft descended, drifting downward into a smooth landing only twenty feet away from her.

The engine shut off with a rattle. The whirring rotor on the nose slowed and finally *click, click, clicked* to a stop. And there he was. *Seth*. Big, blond, bold and all *hers*.

He jumped out of the old craft, wearing khakis, hiking boots and a loose white shirt. His broad shoulders blocked out the sun and the crowd. Or maybe that was just because when he walked into her world, everything else went fuzzy around the edges.

She threw away the rag in her hand and raced toward him. A smile stretched across his face, his arms opening just as wide. She flew into his embrace, soaking up the crisp, clean scent of him.

She kissed him. Right there in front of the cheering crowd of airport personnel as he spun her around. The other voices and applause growing dimmer in her ears, she lost herself in the moment and just held tight to Seth. Even after her feet touched ground again, her head still twirled.

Moisture burned behind her eyelids, the happy kind of tears. How amazing to find her perfect love in accepting their imperfections.

He whispered in her ear. "Now maybe we can take this conversation somewhere a bit more private."

"I happen to be cleaning that plane right behind you and no one's due to show up for at least a half hour."

He scooped her into his arms—which launched another round of applause from the crowd—and he jogged up the steps, turning sideways to duck into the plane. He set her on her feet and right back into his arms.

Holding him closer, she laughed into his neck, his shirt warm against her cheek. "How did you know I was here?"

"I had an inside track on your work schedules. Senator Landis is a cousin of mine, sort of, with his wife being the foster sister of my cousin's wife… My family. There are a lot of us." He guided her to the leather sofa. "Before we talk about anything else, I need to tell you a few things."

Good or bad? She couldn't tell from the serious set of his face. "Okay, I'm listening."

"I've spent the past week working out some new custody arrangements with Pippa. The twins will be spending more time with me, and we've hired a new nanny for when they're with her." He looked down at their joined hands, his fingers twitching. "I'm not ready to run that paternity test. I don't know if I ever will be. The other guy who could be their biological father doesn't want anything to do with them. So, I want to leave things as they are for now. I just want to enjoy watching my kids grow up."

"I can understand that." She wanted that same joy in her life. The way he loved the twins made total sense to her. She'd been completely certain she would love an adopted child during her first marriage. "I'm sorry for pushing you away."

His knuckle glided gently along her cheekbone. "And I'm sorry for not being more open with you."

She cradled his face in her hands. "I can't believe the way you flew out there. You're crazy, did you know that?"

"When it comes to you, yes I am." He pressed a lingering kiss into her palm, before pointing a thumb toward his airplane outside. "Did you get my message?"

"There wasn't any missing it." She tipped her face to his.

"I meant it, every word." His emerald eyes glinting with a gemstone radiance and strength. "I should have said them to you that night. Even before that. I was so zeroed in on my need to keep my kids' lives stable I focused on the idea of making sure they didn't have a parade of women through their lives. I almost missed the bigger message knocking around in my brain."

Her arms around his neck, she toyed with his sun-kissed hair. "And that message would be?"

"Marry me, Alexa." He pressed a hand to her lips, his fingertips callused. "I realize this is moving too fast in some ways and in other ways I haven't moved quickly enough. But if you need to wait awhile, I can be patient. You're worth it."

"I know," she said confidently, realizing for

maybe the first time she did deserve this man and his love. They both deserved to be happy together. "And I love you, too. The bold way that you touch me and challenge me. How tenderly you care for your children. You are everything I could want, everything I never even knew I could have."

"I love you, Alexa." He stroked her hair back from her face. "You. The beautiful way you are with my kids. The way you try to take care of everyone around you. But I also want to be here to take care of you when you demand too much of yourself. I love the perfect parts of us being together—and even the parts of us that aren't perfect but somehow fit together. Bottom line, you have to trust me when I say I love you and I want to be with you for the rest of my life."

"Starting now," she agreed.

"Starting right this second, if you're done here."

She scooped up her bucket. "As a matter of fact, I am. What did you have in mind?

"A date, an honest to God, going out to dinner together date—" he punctuated each plan with a kiss "—followed by more dates and making out and sex—lots of sex—followed by more romancing your socks off."

She sighed against his mouth, swaying closer to him. "And we get married."

"Yes, ma'am," he promised, "and then the real romancing begins."

Epilogue

A year later

She couldn't have asked for a more romantic wedding.

And it had nothing to do with pomp and circumstance. In fact she and Seth had bypassed all of that and planned a beach wedding in Charleston that focused on family. A very *large* family, all in attendance.

Her bouquet in one hand, Alexa looped her other arm around her husband's neck and lost herself in the toe-tingling beauty of their first kiss as man and wife. Her skin warmed from the late day sun and the promise of their honeymoon in the outer banks—of Greece.

The kiss still shimmering to the roots of her upswept hair, Alexa eased back down to her toes. Applause and cheers echoed with the rustle of sea oats. She scooped up Olivia and Seth hefted up Owen. Arm in arm with her husband, she turned to face the hundred guests. Waves rolled and crashed in time with the steel drums playing as they walked back down the aisle lined with lilies and palm fronds. The sun's rays glittered off the sand and water like billions of diamonds had been ordered special for the day.

The twins, now nearly two and nonstop chatter bugs, clapped along with the guests. Shortly before the wedding, Seth had quietly seen the doctor about running a paternity test. As Alexa had suspected all along, the babies were Seth's biological children. His relief had been enormous. He'd credited her love with giving him the strength to take that step.

A love they were celebrating today.

Sand swirled around her ankles, the perfume of her bouquet swelling upward—a mix of calla lilies, orchids and roses, with trailing stephanotis. The attire had been kept casual, with pink flowing sundresses for both bridesmaids. For the men, khakis with white shirts—and rose boutonnieres that had arrived in the *wrong* color. But she knew it was a sign that they were ideal for her wedding because

the deep crimson rose was a lovely wink and nod
to the beauty of the imperfect.

And her dress… White organza flowed straight
down from the fitted bodice with diamond spaghetti
straps. No heels to get caught in the sand, just bare
feet, miles of pristine beach and crystal blue waters. A very familiar and dear World War II vintage aircraft flew overhead carrying a banner for
the entire wedding party to see.

Congratulations, Mr. and Mrs. Seth Jansen.

Cabanas with dining tables filled the beach,
complete with a large tent and jazz band for dancing later. She'd let her new caterer-cousin choose
the menu and design a detailed sandcastle wedding
cake fit for a princess. And ironically enough, she
had an entire Medina royal family in attendance
as well as the Landises, considered by some to be
American political royalty.

A play area with babysitters on hand had been
roped off for children with their own special menu
and cupcakes with crystallized sugar seashells on
top. Although already kids were playing outside the
designated area carefully arranged for them. They
were happily building a sandcastle town with new
moms Paige and Claire overseeing them. Just the
way it should be—with everyone enjoying the day.

She and Seth had wanted their wedding to celebrate family, and they'd succeeded. Even her family
was in attendance. While their relationship would

likely never be close, enjoying a peaceful visit with them went a long way in soothing old hurts.

She and Seth had spent the past year building their relationship, strengthening the connection they'd felt so tangibly from the start. She'd also spent the past twelve months building her business and confidence. Her favorite work? Servicing the search and rescue planes on the philanthropic side of Jansen Jets. It was not the whole company, but certainly the part most near and dear to Seth's heart.

They were both living out their dreams.

She looked from their applauding relatives to her new husband. And what do you know?

He was already staring right back at her, his eyes full of love. "Is everything turning out the way you wanted today?"

She toyed with his off-color rose boutonniere. "The day couldn't be any more perfect."

And the best part of that? She knew each of their tomorrows promised to be even better.

* * * * *

MICHELLE CELMER

USA TODAY bestselling author Michelle Celmer has written more than twenty-five books for Harlequin and Silhouette. You can usually find her in her office with her laptop, loving the fact that she gets to work in her pajamas. Write her at P.O. BOX 300, Clawson, MI 48017, visit her website at www.michellecelmer.com or find her on Facebook at Michelle Celmer Author.

Look for more books from Michelle Celmer in Harlequin Desire—the ultimate destination for powerful, passionate romance! There are six new Harlequin Desire titles available every month. Check one out today!

THE NANNY BOMBSHELL
Michelle Celmer

To my granddaughter, Aubrey Helen Ann

Chapter 1

This was not good.

As a former defensive center, MVP and team captain for the New York Scorpions, Cooper Landon was one of the city's most beloved sports heroes. His hockey career had never been anything but an asset.

Until today.

He looked out the conference room window in the Manhattan office of his attorney, where he had been parked for the past ninety minutes, hands wedged in the pockets of his jeans, watching the late afternoon traffic crawl along Park Avenue. The early June sun reflected with a blinding intensity off the windows of the building across the street and the sidewalks were clogged with people going about their daily routine. Businessmen catching cabs, mothers pushing strollers. Three weeks ago he'd been one of them, walking through life oblivious to how quickly his world could be turned completely upside down.

One senseless accident had robbed him of the only family he had. Now his brother, Ash, and sister-in-law, Susan, were dead, and his twin infant nieces were orphans.

He clenched his fists, fighting back the anger and injustice of it, when what he wanted to do was slam them through the tinted glass.

He still had his nieces, he reminded himself. Though they had been adopted, Ash and Susan couldn't have loved them more if they were their own flesh and blood. Now they were Coop's responsibility, and he was determined to do right by them, give them the sort of life his brother wanted them to have. He owed Ash.

"So, what did you think of that last one?" Ben Hearst, his attorney, asked him. He sat at the conference table sorting through the applications and taking notes on the nanny candidates they had seen that afternoon.

Coop turned to him, unable to mask his frustration. "I wouldn't trust her to watch a hamster."

Like the three other women they had interviewed

that day, the latest applicant had been more interested in his hockey career than talking about the
twins. He'd met her type a million times before. In
her short skirt and low-cut blouse, she was looking to land herself a famous husband. Though in
the past he would have enjoyed the attention and,
yeah, he probably would have taken advantage of
it, now he found it annoying. He wasn't seen as the
guardian of two precious girls who lost their parents, but as a piece of meat. He'd lost his brother
two weeks ago and not a single nanny candidate
had thought to offer their condolences.

After two days and a dozen equally unproduc-
tive interviews, he was beginning to think he would
never find the right nanny.

His housekeeper, who had been grudgingly helping him with the twins and was about twenty years
past her child-rearing prime, had threatened to quit
if he didn't find someone else to care for them.

"I'm really sorry," Ben said. "I guess we should
have anticipated this happening."

Maybe Coop should have taken Ben's advice and
used a service. He just didn't feel that a bunch of
strangers would be qualified to choose the person
who would be best to care for the twins.

"I think you're going to like this next one," Ben
told him.

"Is she qualified?"

"Overqualified, actually." He handed Coop the

file. "You could say that I was saving the best for last."

Sierra Evans, twenty-six. She had graduated from college with a degree in nursing, and it listed her current occupation as a pediatric nurse. Coop blinked, then looked at Ben. "Is this right?"

He smiled and nodded. "I was surprised, too."

She was single and childless with a clean record. She didn't have so much as a parking ticket. On paper she looked perfect. Although in his experience, if something seemed too good to be true, it usually was. "What's the catch?"

Ben shrugged. "Maybe there isn't one. She's waiting in the lobby. You ready to meet her?"

"Let's do it," he said, feeling hopeful for the first time since this whole mess started. Maybe this one would be as good as she sounded.

Using the intercom, Ben asked the receptionist, "Would you send Miss Evans in please?"

A minute later the door opened and a woman walked in. Immediately Coop could see that she was different from the others. She was dressed in scrubs—dark-blue pants and a white top with Sesame Street characters all over it—and comfortable-looking shoes. Not typical attire for a job interview but a decided improvement over the clingy, revealing choices of her predecessors. She was average height, average build…very unremarkable. But her face, that was anything but average.

Her eyes were so dark brown they looked black and a slight tilt in the corners gave her an Asian appearance. Her mouth was wide, lips full and sensual, and though she didn't wear a stitch of makeup, she didn't need any. Her black hair was long and glossy and pulled back in a slightly lopsided ponytail.

One thing was clear. This woman was no groupie.

"Miss Evans," Ben said, rising to shake her hand. "I'm Ben Hearst, and this is Cooper Landon."

Coop gave her a nod but stayed put in his place by the window.

"I apologize for the scrubs," she said in a voice that was on the husky side. "I came straight from work."

"It's not a problem," Ben assured her, gesturing to a chair. "Please, have a seat."

She sat, placing her purse—a nondesigner bag that had seen better days—on the table beside her and folded her hands in her lap. Coop stood silently observing as Ben launched into the litany of questions he'd asked every candidate. She dutifully answered every one of them, darting glances Coop's way every so often but keeping her attention on Ben. The others had asked Coop questions, tried to engage him in conversation. But from Miss Evans there was no starry-eyed gazing, no flirting or innuendo. No smoldering smiles and suggestions that she would do *anything* for the job. In fact, she avoided his gaze, as if his presence made her nervous.

"You understand that this is a live-in position. You will be responsible for the twins 24/7. 11:00 a.m. to 4:00 p.m. on Sundays, and every fourth weekend from Saturday at 8:00 a.m. to Sunday at 8:00 p.m., is yours to spend as you wish," Ben said.

She nodded. "I understand."

Ben turned to Coop. "Do you have anything to add?"

"Yeah, I do." He addressed Miss Evans directly. "Why would you give up a job as a pediatric nurse to be a nanny?"

"I love working with kids...obviously," she said with a shy smile—a pretty smile. "But working in the neonatal intensive care unit is a very high-stress job. It's emotionally draining. I need a change of pace. And I can't deny that the live-in situation is alluring."

A red flag began to wave furiously. "Why is that?"

"My dad is ill and unable to care for himself. The salary you're offering, along with not having to pay rent, would make it possible for me to put him in a top-notch facility. In fact, there's a place in Jersey that has a spot opening up this week, so the timing would be perfect."

That was the last thing he had expected her to

say, and for a second he was speechless. He didn't know of many people, especially someone in her tax bracket, who would sacrifice such a large chunk of their salary for the care of a parent. Even Ben looked a little surprised.

He shot Coop a look that asked, *What do you think?* As things stood, Coop couldn't come up with a single reason not to hire her on the spot, but he didn't want to act rashly. This was about the girls, not his personal convenience.

"I'd like you to come by and meet my nieces tomorrow," he told her.

She regarded him hopefully. "Does that mean I have the job?"

"I'd like to see you interact with them before I make the final decision, but I'll be honest, you're by far the most qualified candidate we've seen so far."

"Tomorrow is my day off so I can come anytime."

"Why don't we say 1:00 p.m., after the girls' lunch. I'm a novice at this parenting thing, so it usually takes me until then to get them bathed, dressed and fed."

She smiled. "One is fine."

"I'm on the Upper East Side. Ben will give you the address."

Ben jotted down Coop's address and handed it to her. She took the slip of paper and tucked it into her purse.

Ben stood, and Miss Evans rose to her feet. She grabbed her purse and slung it over her shoulder.

"One more thing, Miss Evans," Coop said. "Are you a hockey fan?"

She hesitated. "Um…is it a prerequisite for the job?"

He felt a smile tugging at the corner of his mouth. "Of course not."

"Then, no, not really. I've never much been into sports. Although I was in a bowling league in college. Until recently my dad was a pretty big hockey fan, though."

"So you know who I am?"

"Is there anyone in New York who doesn't?"

Probably not, and only recently had that fact become a liability. "That isn't going to be an issue?"

She cocked her head slightly. "I'm not sure what you mean."

Her confusion made him feel like an idiot for even asking. Was he so used to women fawning over him that he'd come to expect it? Maybe he wasn't her type, or maybe she had a boyfriend. "Never mind."

She turned to leave, then paused and turned back to him.

"I wanted to say, I was so sorry to hear about your brother and his wife. I know how hard it is to lose someone you love."

The sympathy in her dark eyes made him want

to squirm, and that familiar knot lodged somewhere in the vicinity of his Adam's apple. It annoyed him when the others hadn't mentioned it, but when she did, it made him uncomfortable. Maybe because she seemed as though she really meant it.

"Thank you," he said. He'd certainly had his share of loss. First his parents when he was twelve, and now Ash and Susan. Maybe that was the price he had to pay for fame and success.

He would give it all up, sell his soul if that was what it took to get his brother back.

After she left Ben asked him, "So, you really think she's the one?"

"She's definitely qualified, and it sounds as though she needs the job. As long as the girls like her, I'll offer her the position."

"Easy on the eyes, too."

He shot Ben a look. "If I manage to find a nanny worth hiring, do you honestly think I would risk screwing it up by getting physically involved?"

Ben smirked. "Honestly?"

Okay, a month ago…maybe. But everything had changed since then.

"I prefer blondes," he told Ben. "The kind with no expectations and questionable morals."

Besides, taking care of the girls, seeing that they were raised in the manner Ash and Susan would want, was his top priority. Coop owed his brother that much. When their parents died, Ash had only been eighteen, but he'd put his own life on hold to raise Coop. And Coop hadn't made it easy at first. He'd been hurt and confused and had lashed out. He was out of control and fast on his way to becoming a full-fledged juvenile delinquent when the school psychologist told Ash that Coop needed a constructive outlet for his anger. She suggested a physical sport, so Ash had signed him up for hockey.

Coop had never been very athletic or interested in sports, but he took to the game instantly, and though he was on a team with kids who had been playing since they were old enough to balance on skates, he rapidly surpassed their skills. Within two years he was playing in a travel league and became the star player. At nineteen he was picked up by the New York Scorpions.

A knee injury two years ago had cut his career short, but smart investments—again thanks to the urging of his brother—had left him wealthy beyond his wildest dreams. Without Ash, and the sacrifices he made, it never would have been possible. Now Coop had the chance to repay him. But he couldn't do it alone. He was ill-equipped. He knew nothing about caring for an infant, much less two at once. Hell, until two weeks ago he'd never so much as changed a diaper. Without his housekeeper to help, he would be lost.

If Miss Evans turned out to be the right person for the job—and he had the feeling she was—

he would never risk screwing it up by sleeping with her.

She was off-limits.

Sierra Evans rode the elevator down to the lobby of the attorney's office building, sagging with relief against the paneled wall. That had gone much better than she could have hoped and she was almost positive that the job was as good as hers. It was a good thing, too, because the situation was far worse than she could have imagined.

Clearly Cooper Landon had better things to do than care for his twin nieces. He was probably too busy traipsing around like the playboy of the Western world. She wasn't one to listen to gossip, but in his case, his actions and reputation as a womanizing partier painted a disturbing picture. That was not the kind of atmosphere in which she wanted her daughters raised.

Her daughters. Only recently had she begun thinking of them as hers again.

With Ash and Susan gone, it seemed wrong that the twins would be so carelessly pawned off on someone like Cooper. But she would save them. She would take care of them and love them. It was all that mattered now.

The doors slid open and she stepped out. She crossed the swanky lobby and pushed out the door into the sunshine, heading down Park Avenue in the direction of the subway, feeling hopeful for the first time in two weeks.

Giving the twins up had been the hardest thing she'd ever done in her life, but she knew it was for the best. Between her student loans and exorbitant rent, not to mention her dad's failing health and mounting medical bills, she was in no position financially or emotionally to care for infant twins. She knew that Ash and Susan, the girls' adoptive parents, would give her babies everything that she couldn't.

But in the blink of an eye they were gone. She had been standing in front of the television, flipping through the channels when she paused on the news report about the plane crash. When she realized it was Ash and Susan they were talking about, her knees had buckled and she'd dropped to the nubby, threadbare shag carpet. In a panic she had flipped through the channels, desperate for more details, terrified to the depths of her soul that the girls had been on the flight with them. She'd sat up all night, alternating between the television and her laptop, gripped by a fear and a soul-wrenching grief that had been all-consuming.

At 7:00 a.m. the following morning the early news confirmed that the girls had in fact been left with Susan's family and were not in the crash. Sierra had been so relieved she wept. But then the reality of the situation hit hard. Who would take the girls? Would they go to Susan's family permanently or, God forbid, be dropped into the foster-care system?

She had contacted her lawyer immediately, and after a few calls he had learned what to her was unthinkable. Cooper would be their guardian. What the hell had Ash been thinking, choosing him? What possible interest could a womanizing, life of the party, ex-hockey player have in two infant babies?

She'd asked her lawyer to contact him on her behalf using no names, assuming that he would be more than happy to give the girls back to their natural mother. She would find a way to make it work. But Cooper had refused to give them up.

Her lawyer said she could try to fight him for custody, but the odds weren't in her favor. She had severed her parental rights, and getting them back would take a lengthy and expensive legal battle. But knowing Cooper would undoubtedly need help, and would probably be thrilled with someone of her qualifications, she'd managed to get herself an interview for the nanny position.

Sierra boarded the subway at Lexington and took the F Train to Queens. Normally she visited her dad on Wednesdays, but she had the appointment at Cooper's apartment tomorrow so she had to rearrange her schedule. With any luck he would offer her the job on the spot, and she could go home and start packing immediately.

She took a cab from the station to the dumpy, third-rate nursing home where her dad had spent the past fourteen months. As she passed the nursing station she said hi to the nurse seated there and received a grunt of annoyance in return. She would think that being in the same profession there would be some semblance of professional courtesy, but the opposite was true. The nurses seemed to resent her presence.

She hated that her dad had to stay in this horrible place where the employees were apathetic and the care was borderline criminal, but this was all that Medicare would cover and home care at this late stage of the disease was just too expensive. His body had lost the ability to perform anything but the most basic functions. He couldn't speak, barely reacted to stimuli and had to be fed through a tube. His heart was still beating, his lungs still pulling in air, but eventually his body would forget how to do that, too. It could be weeks, or months. He might even linger on for a year or more. There was just no way to know. If she could get him into the place in Jersey it would be harder to visit, but at least he would be well cared for.

"Hi, Lenny." She greeted her dad's roommate, a ninety-one-year-old war vet who had lost his right foot and his left arm in the battle at Normandy.

"Hey there, Sierra," he said cheerfully from his wheelchair. He was dressed in dark brown pants and a Kelly-green cardigan sweater that were as old and tattered as their wearer.

"How is Dad today?" she asked, dropping her purse in the chair and walking to his bedside. It broke her heart to see him so shriveled and lifeless. Nothing more than a shell of the man he used to be—the loving dad who single-handedly raised Sierra and her little sister, Joy. Now he was wasting away.

"It's been a good day," Lenny said.

"Hi, Daddy," she said, pressing a kiss to his papery cheek. He was awake, but he didn't acknowledge her. On a good day he lay quietly, either sleeping or staring at the dappled sunshine through the dusty vertical blinds. On a bad day, he moaned. A low, tortured, unearthly sound. They didn't know if he was in pain, or if it was just some random involuntary function. But on those days he was sedated.

"How is that little boy of yours?" Lenny asked. "Must be reaching about school age by now."

She sighed softly to herself. Lenny's memory wasn't the best. He somehow managed to remember that she'd been pregnant, but he forgot the dozen or so times when she had explained that she'd given the girls up for adoption. And clearly he was confusing her with other people in his life because sometimes he thought she had an older boy and other times it was a baby girl. And rather than explain yet again, she just went with it.

"Growing like a weed," she told him, and before he could ask more questions they announced over the intercom that it was time for bingo in the community room.

"Gotta go!" Lenny said, wheeling himself toward the door. "Can I bring you back a cookie?"

"No thanks, Lenny."

When he was gone she sat on the edge of her dad's bed and took his hand. It was cold and contracted into a stiff fist. "I had my job interview today," she told him, even though she doubted his brain could process the sounds he was hearing as anything but gibberish. "It went really well, and I get to see the girls tomorrow. If the other applicants looked anything like the bimbo who interviewed right before me, I'm a shoo-in."

She brushed a few silvery strands of hair back from his forehead. "I know you're probably thinking that I should stay out of this and trust Ash and Susan's judgment, but I just can't. The man is a train wreck just waiting to happen. I have to make sure the girls are okay. If I can't do that as their mother, I can at least do it as their nanny."

And if that meant sacrificing her freedom and working for Cooper Landon until the girls no longer needed her, that was what she was prepared to do.

Chapter 2

The next afternoon at six minutes after one, Sierra knocked on the door of Cooper's penthouse apartment, brimming with nervous excitement, her heart in her throat. She had barely slept last night in anticipation of this very moment. Though she had known that when she signed away her parental rights she might never see the girls again, she had still hoped. She just hadn't expected it to happen until they were teenagers and old enough to make the decision to meet their birth mother. But here she was, barely five months later, just seconds away from the big moment.

The door was opened by a woman. Sierra assumed it was the housekeeper, judging by the maid's uniform. She was tall and lanky with a pinched face and steel-gray hair that was pulled back severely and twisted into a bun. Sierra placed her in her mid to late sixties.

"Can I *help* you?" the woman asked in a gravely clipped tone.

"I have an appointment with Mr. Landon."

"Are you Miss Evans?"

"Yes, I am." Which she must have already known, considering the doorman had called up to announce her about a minute ago.

She looked Sierra up and down with scrutiny, pursed her lips and said, "I'm Ms. Densmore, Mr. Landon's housekeeper. You're late."

"Sorry. I had trouble getting a cab."

"I should warn you that if you do get the job, tardiness will not be tolerated."

Sierra failed to see how she could be tardy for a job she was at 24/7, but she didn't push the issue. "It won't happen again."

Ms. Densmore gave a resentful sniff and said, "Follow me."

Even the housekeeper's chilly greeting wasn't enough to smother Sierra's excitement. Her hands trembled as she followed her through the foyer into an ultra-modern, open-concept living space. Near a row of ceiling-high windows that boasted a panoramic view of Central Park, with the afternoon sunshine washing over them like gold dust, were the twins. They sat side by side in identical Exer-Saucers, babbling and swatting at the colorful toys.

They were so big! And they had changed more than she could have imagined possible. If she had seen them on the street, she probably wouldn't have recognized them. She was hit by a sense of longing so keen she had to bite down on her lip to keep from bursting into tears. She forced her feet to remain rooted to the deeply polished mahogany floor while she was announced, when what she wanted to do was fling herself into the room, drop down to her knees and gather her children in her arms.

"The one on the left is Fern," Ms. Densmore said, with not a hint of affection in her tone. "She's the loud, demanding one. The other is Ivy. She's the quiet, sneaky one."

Sneaky? At five months old? It sounded as if Ms. Densmore just didn't like children. She was probably a spinster. She sure looked like one.

Not only would Sierra have to deal with a partying, egomaniac athlete, but also an overbearing and critical housekeeper. How fun. And it frosted her that Cooper let this pinched, frigid, nasty old bat who clearly didn't like children anywhere near the girls.

"I'll go get Mr. Landon," she said, striding down a hall that Sierra assumed led to the bedrooms.

Alone with her girls for the first time since their

birth, she crossed the room and knelt down in front of them. "Look how big you are, and how beautiful," she whispered.

They gazed back at her with wide, inquisitive blue eyes. Though they weren't identical, they looked very much alike. They both had her thick, pin-straight black hair and high cheekbones, but any other traces of the Chinese traits that had come from her great-grandmother on her mother's side had skipped them. They had eyes just like their father and his long, slender fingers.

Fern let out a squeal and reached for her. Sierra wanted so badly to hold her, but she wasn't sure if she should wait for Cooper. Tears stinging her eyes, she took one of Fern's chubby little hands in hers and held it. She had missed them so much, and the guilt she felt for leaving them, for putting them in this situation, sat like a stone in her belly. But she was here now, and she would never leave them again. She would see that they were raised properly.

"She wants you to pick her up."

Sierra turned to see Cooper standing several feet behind her, big and burly, in bare feet with his slightly wrinkled shirt untucked and his hands wedged in the pockets of a pair of threadbare jeans. His dirty-blond hair was damp and a little messy, as if he'd towel-dried it and hadn't bothered with a brush. No one could deny that he was attractive with his pale blue eyes and dimpled smile. The slightly crooked nose was even a little charming. Maybe it was his total lack of self-consciousness that was so appealing right now, but athletes had never been her thing. She preferred studious men. Professional types. The kind who didn't make a living swinging a big stick and beating the crap out of other people.

"Do you mind?" she asked.

"Of course not. That's what this interview is about."

Sierra lifted Fern out of the seat and set the infant in her lap. She smelled like baby shampoo and powder. Fern fixated on the gold chain hanging down the front of her blouse and grabbed for it, so Sierra tucked it under her collar. "She's so big."

"Around fifteen pounds I think. I remember my sister-in-law saying that they were average size for their age. I'm not sure what they weighed when they were born. I think there's a baby book still packed away somewhere with all that information in it."

They had been just over six pounds each, but she couldn't tell him that or that the baby book he referred to had been started by her and given to Ash and Susan as a gift when they took the girls home. She had documented her entire pregnancy—when she felt the first kick, when she had her sonogram—so the adoptive parents would feel more involved and they could show the girls when they got older. And although she had included photos of her belly in various stages of development, there were no shots of her face. There was nothing anywhere that identified her as being the birth mother.

Ivy began to fuss—probably jealous that her sister was getting all the attention. Sierra was debating the logistics of how to extract her from the seat while still holding Fern when, without prompting, Cooper reached for Ivy and plucked her out. He lifted her high over his head, making her gasp and giggle, and plunked her down in his arms.

Sierra must have looked concerned because he laughed and said, "Don't let her mild manner fool you. She's a mini daredevil."

As he sat on the floor across from her and set Ivy in his lap, Sierra caught the scent of some sort of masculine soap. Fern reached for him and tried to wiggle her way out of Sierra's arms. She hadn't expected the girls to be so at ease with him, so attached. Not this quickly. And she expected him to be much more inept and disinterested.

"You work with younger babies?" Cooper asked.

"Newborns usually. But before the NICU I worked in the pediatric ward."

"I'm going to the market," Ms. Densmore announced from the kitchen. Sierra had been so focused on the girls she hadn't noticed that it was big and open with natural wood and frosted glass cupboard doors and yards of glossy granite countertops. Modern, yet functional—not that she ever spent much time in one. Cooking—or at least, cooking *well*—had never been one of her great accomplishments.

Ms. Densmore wore a light spring jacket, which was totally unnecessary considering it was at least seventy-five degrees outside, and clutched an old-lady-style black handbag. "Do you need anything?" she asked Cooper.

"Diapers and formula," he told her. "And those little jars of fruit the girls like." He paused, then added, "And the dried cereal, too. The flaky kind in the blue box. I think we're running low."

Looking annoyed, Ms. Densmore left out of what must have been the service entrance behind the kitchen. Sierra couldn't help but wonder how Coop would know the cereal was low and why he would even bother to look.

"The girls are eating solid foods?" she asked him.

"Cereal and fruit. And of course formula. It's astounding how much they can put away. I feel as if I'm constantly making bottles."

He made the bottles? She had a hard time picturing that. Surely Ms. Cranky-Pants must have been doing most of the work.

"Are they sleeping through the night?" she asked him.

"Not yet. It's getting better, though. At first, they woke up constantly." He smiled down at Ivy affectionately, and a little sadly, brushing a wisp of hair off her forehead. "I think they just really missed their parents. But last night they only woke up twice, and they both went back to their cribs. Half the time they end up in my bed with me. I'll admit that I'm looking forward to a good night's sleep. Alone."

"*You* get up with them?" she asked, not meaning to sound quite so incredulous.

Rather than look offended, he smiled. "Yeah, and I'll warn you right now that they're both bed hogs. I have no idea how a person so small could take up so much room.", . ,

The idea of him, such a big, burly, rough-around-the-edges guy, snuggled up in bed with two infants, was too adorable for words.

"Out of curiosity, who did you think would get up with them?" he asked.

"I just assumed… I mean, doesn't Ms. Densmore take care of them?"

"She occasionally watches them while I work, but only because I'm desperate. After raising six kids of her own and two of her grandchildren, she says she's finished taking care of babies."

So much for Sierra's spinster theory.

"Is she always so…" She struggled for a kind way to say *nasty,* but Cooper seemed to read her mind.

"Cranky? Incorrigible?" he suggested, with a

slightly crooked smile that she hated to admit made her heart beat the tiniest bit faster.

She couldn't help smiling back.

"She won't be winning any congeniality awards, I know, but she's a good housekeeper, and one hel…" he grinned and shook his head. "I mean *heck* of a fantastic cook. Sorry, I'm not used to having to censor my language."

At least he was making an effort. He would be thankful for that in a year or so when the twins started repeating everything he said verbatim.

"Ms. Densmore isn't crazy about the bad language, either," he said. "Of course, sometimes I do it just to annoy her."

"I don't think she likes me much," Sierra said.

"It really doesn't matter what she thinks. She's not hiring you. I am. And I happen to think you're perfect for the job." He paused then added, "I'm assuming, since you're here now, that you're still interested."

Her heart skipped a beat. "Absolutely. Does that mean you're officially offering it to me?"

"Under one condition—I need your word that you'll stick around. That you're invested in the position. I can't tell you how tough that first week was, right after…" He closed his eyes, took a deep breath and blew it out. "Things have just begun to settle down, and I've got the girls in something that resembles a routine. They need consistency—or at least that's what the social worker told me. The worst thing for them would be a string of nannies bouncing in and out of their lives."

He would never have to worry about that with her. "I won't let them down."

"You're *sure?* Because these two are a handful. It's a lot of work. More than I ever imagined possible. Professional hockey was a cakewalk compared to this. I need to be sure that you're committed."

"I'm giving up my apartment and putting my dad in a home that I can't begin to afford without this salary. I'm definitely committed."

He looked relieved. "In that case, the job is yours. And the sooner you can start, the better."

Her own relief was so keen she could have sobbed. She hugged Fern closer. Her little girls would be okay. She would be there to take care of them, to nurture them. And maybe someday, when they were old enough to understand, she would be able to tell them who she really was and explain why she had let them go. Maybe she could be a real mother to them.

"Miss Evans?" Coop was watching her expectantly, waiting for a reply.

"It's Sierra," she told him. "And I can start right away if that works for you. I just need a day to pack and move my things in."

He looked surprised. "What about your apartment? Your furniture? Don't you need time to—"

"I'll sublet. A friend from work is interested in taking my place and she'll be using all my furniture." Her dad's furniture, actually. By the time Sierra started making enough money to afford her own place, he was too sick to live alone, so she had stayed with him instead, on the pull-out couch of the dinky one-bedroom apartment he'd had to take when he went on disability. She had never really had a place of her own. And from the looks of it, she wouldn't for a very long time. But if that meant the girls would be happy and well taken care of, it was a sacrifice she was happy to make.

"I just need to pack my clothes and a few personal items," she told him. "I can do that today and move everything over tomorrow."

"And work? You don't need to give them notice?"

She shook her head. She was taking a chance burning that bridge, but being with the girls as soon as possible took precedence. As long as they needed her, she wouldn't be going back to nursing anyway.

"I'll have Ben, my lawyer, draw up the contract this afternoon," he said. "Considering my former profession there are privacy issues."

"I understand."

"And of course you're welcome to have your own lawyer look at it before you sign."

"I'll call him today."

"Great. Why don't I show you the girls' room, and where you'll be staying?"

"Okay."

They got up from the floor and he led her down the hall, Ivy in his arms and Sierra holding Fern, who seemed perfectly content despite Sierra being a relative stranger. Was it possible that she sensed the mother-daughter connection? Or was she just a friendly, outgoing baby?

"This is the nursery," he said, indicating a door on the left and gesturing her inside. It was by far the largest and prettiest little girls' room she had ever laid eyes on. The color scheme was pale pink and pastel green. The walls, bedding, curtains and even the carpet looked fluffy and soft, like cotton candy. Matching white cribs perched side by side, and a white rocking chair sat in the corner next to the window. She could just imagine herself holding the girls close, singing them a lullaby and rocking them to sleep.

This room was exactly what she would have wanted for them but never could have afforded. With her they wouldn't have had more than a tiny corner of her bedroom.

"It's beautiful, Cooper."

"It's Coop," he said and flashed that easy grin. "No one but my mom called me Cooper, and that was usually when she was angry about something. And as for the room, I can't take credit. It's an exact reproduction of their room at Ash and Susan's. I thought it might make the transition easier for them."

Once again he had surprised her. Maybe he wasn't quite as self-centered as she first imagined. Or maybe he was only playing the role of responsible uncle out of necessity. Maybe once he had her there to take care of the girls for him, he would live up to his party reputation, including the supposedly revolving bedroom door.

Time would tell.

"They have their own bathroom and a walk-in closet over there," he said, gesturing to a closed door across the room.

She walked over and opened it. The closet was huge! Toys lined either side of the floor—things they had used and some still in the original boxes. Seeing them, Fern shifted restlessly in Sierra's arms, clearly wanting to get down and play.

From the bars hung a wardrobe big enough for a dozen infants. Dresses and jumpers and tiny pairs of jeans and shirts—all designer labels and many with the tags still attached, and all in duplicate. In her wildest dreams Sierra never could have afforded even close to this many clothes, and certainly not this quality. They were neatly organized by style, color and size—all spelled out on sticky notes on the shelf above the bar.

Sierra had never seen anything like it. "Wow. Did you do this?"

"God, no," Coop said. "This is Ms. Densmore's thing. She's a little fanatical about organization."

"Just a little." She would have a coronary if she looked in Sierra's closet. Besides being just a fraction the size, it was so piled with junk she could barely close the door. Neatness had never been one of her strong suits. That had been okay living with her dad, who was never tidy himself, but here she would have to make an effort to be more organized.

"The bathroom is through there," Coop said, walking past her to open the door, filling the air with the delicious scent of soap and man. The guy really did smell great, and though it was silly, he looked even more attractive holding the baby, which made no sense at all. Or maybe it was just that she'd always been a sucker for a man who was good with kids—because in her profession she had seen too many who weren't. Deadbeat dads who couldn't even be bothered to visit their sick child in the hospital. And of course there were the abusive dads who put their kids in the hospital. Those were the really heartbreaking cases and one of the reasons she had transferred from pediatrics to the NICU.

But having an easy way with an infant didn't make a man a good father, she reminded herself. Neither did giving them a big beautiful bedroom or an enormous closet filled with toys and designer clothes. The twins needed nurturing, they needed to know that even though their parents were gone, someone still loved them and cared about them.

She held Fern closer and rubbed her back, and the infant laid her head on Sierra's shoulder, her thumb tucked in her mouth.

"I'll show you your room," Coop said, and she followed him to the bedroom across the hall. It was even larger than the girls' room, with the added bonus of a cozy sitting area by the window. With the bedroom, walk-in closet and private bath, it was larger than her entire apartment. All that was missing was the tiny, galley-style kitchen, but she had a gourmet kitchen just a few rooms away at her disposal.

The furnishings and decor weren't exactly her style. The black, white and gray color scheme was too modern and cold and the steel and glass furnishings were a bit masculine, but bringing some of her own things in would liven it up a little. She could learn to live with it.

"That bad, huh?"

Startled by the comment, Sierra looked over at Coop. He was frowning. "I didn't say that."

"You didn't have to. It's written all over your face. You hate it."

"I don't *hate* it."

One brow tipped up. "Now you're lying."

"It's not what I would have chosen, but it's very… stylish."

He laughed. "You are *so* lying. You think it's terrible."

She bit her lip to keep from smiling, but the corners of her mouth tipped up regardless. "I'll get used to it."

"I'll call my decorator. You can fix it however you like. Paint, furniture, the works."

She opened her mouth to tell him that wouldn't be necessary, and he held up one ridiculously large palm to shush her. "Do you really think I'm going to let you stay in a room you despise? This is going to be your home. I want you to be comfortable here."

She wondered if he was always this nice, or if he was just so desperate for a reliable nanny he would do anything to convince her to take the job. If that was the case, she could probably negotiate a higher salary, but it wasn't about the money. She just wanted to be with her girls.

"If you're sure it's not a problem, I wouldn't mind adding a few feminine touches," she told him.

"You can sleep in the nursery until it's finished, or if you'd prefer more privacy, there's a fold-out love seat in my office."

"The nursery is fine." She didn't care about privacy, and she liked the idea of sleeping near her girls.

He nodded to Fern and said, "I think we should lay them down. It's afternoon nap time."

Sierra looked down at Fern and realized that she

had fallen asleep, her thumb still wedged in her mouth, and Ivy, who had laid her head on Coop's enormously wide shoulder, was looking drowsy, too.

They carried the girls back to the nursery and laid them in their beds—Fern on the right side and Ivy on the left—then they stepped quietly out and Coop shut the door behind them.

"How long will they sleep?" Sierra asked.

"On a good day, two hours. But they slept in until eight this morning, so maybe less." He paused in the hall and asked, "Before we call my attorney, would you like something to drink? We have juice and soda…baby formula."

She smiled. "I'm good, thanks."

"Okay, if you're having any second thoughts, this is your last chance to change your mind."

That would never happen. He was stuck with her. "No second thoughts."

"Great, let's go to my office and call Ben," Coop said with a grin. "Let's get this show on the road."

Chapter 3

Coop stood outside Sierra's bedroom door, hoping she hadn't already gone to sleep for the night. It
was barely nine-thirty, but today had been her first
official day watching the girls, so he was guessing
that she was probably pretty exhausted. God knows
they wore him out.

She had signed the contract the afternoon of her
second interview, then spent most of the next day
moving her things and unpacking. He had offered
to pay a service to do the moving for her, but she
had insisted she had it covered, showing up in the
early afternoon with a slew of boxes and two young-
ish male friends—orderlies from the hospital, she'd

told him—who had been openly thrilled to meet the great Coop Landon.

Though Coop had tried to pay them for the help, they refused to take any cash. Instead he offered them each a beer, and while Sierra unpacked and the twins napped, he and the guys sat out on the rooftop patio. They asked him about his career and the upcoming season draft picks, leaving a couple of hours later with autographed pucks.

Coop had hoped to be around today to help Sierra and the twins make the transition, but he'd been trapped in meetings with the marketing team for his new sports equipment line all morning, and in the afternoon he'd met with the owner of his former team. If things went as planned, Coop would own the team before the start of the next season in October. Owning the New York Scorpions had been his dream since he started playing for the team. For twenty-two years, until his bad knee took him off the ice, he lived and breathed hockey. He loved everything about the game. Buying a team was the natural next step, and he had the players' blessing.

After the meetings Coop had enjoyed his first dinner out with friends in weeks. Well, he hadn't actually *enjoyed* it. Though he had been counting the days until he was free again, throughout the entire meal his mind kept wandering back to Fern and Ivy and how they were doing with Sierra. Should he have canceled his meetings and spent that first day with them? Was it irresponsible of him to have left them with a stranger? Not that he didn't trust Sierra—he just wanted to be sure that he was doing the right thing. They had already lost their parents—he didn't want them to think that he was abandoning them, too.

When the rest of the party had moved on to a local bar for after-dinner drinks, dancing and skirt chasing, to the surprise of his friends, Coop had called it a night. On a typical evening he closed out the bar, moved on to a party and usually didn't go home alone. But the ribbing he endured from his buddies was mild. Hell, it had been less than a month since he lost his brother. It was going to take him a little time to get back into his normal routine. And right now the twins needed him. He would try to work from home the rest of the week, so he could spend more time with them. After more than two weeks of being together almost constantly, he had gotten used to having them around.

He rapped lightly on Sierra's bedroom door, and after several seconds it opened a crack and she peeked out. He could see that she had already changed into her pajamas—a short, pink, babydoll-style nightgown. His eyes automatically drifted lower, to her bare legs. They weren't particularly long, or slender, so the impulse to touch her, to slide his palm up the inside of one creamy thigh and under the hem of her gown—and the resulting pull of lust it created—caught him completely off guard. He had to make an effort to keep his gaze above her neck and on her eyes, which were dark and inquisitive, with that exotic tilt. Her hair, which he'd only ever seen up in a ponytail, hung in a long, silky black sheet over her shoulders, and he itched to run his fingers through it. Instead he shoved his hands in the pockets of his slacks.

You can look, but you can't touch, he reminded himself, and not for the first time since she'd come by to meet the girls. She was absolutely nothing like the sort of woman he would typically be attracted to. Maybe that alone was what he found so appealing. She was different. A novelty. But her position as the twins' nanny was just too crucial to put in jeopardy.

Maybe hiring such an attractive woman had been a bad idea, even if she was the most qualified. Maybe he should have held out and interviewed a few more people, made an effort to find someone older or, better yet, a guy.

"Did you want something?" she asked, and he realized that he was just standing there staring at her.

Way to make yourself look like an idiot, Coop. He was usually pretty smooth when it came to women. He had no idea why he was acting like such a dope.

"I hope I didn't wake you," he said.

"No, I was still up."

"I just wanted to check in, see how it went today."

"It went really well. It'll take some time to get into a routine, but I'm following their lead."

"I'm sorry I wasn't here to help out."

She looked confused. "I didn't expect you to help."

He felt his eyes drifting lower, to the cleavage at the neckline of her gown. She wasn't large-busted, but she wasn't what he would consider small, either. She was...average. So why couldn't he seem to look away?

She noticed him noticing but made no move to cover herself. And why should she? It was her room. He was the intruder.

And he was making a complete ass of himself.

"Was there anything else?" she asked.

He forced his gaze back to her face. "I thought we could just talk for a while. We haven't had a chance to go over the girls' schedules. I thought you might have questions."

She looked hesitant, and he thought her answer was going to be no. And could he blame her? He was behaving like a first-rate pervert. But after several seconds, she said, "Okay, I'll be out in just a minute."

She snapped the door closed and he walked to the kitchen, mentally knocking himself in the head. What the hell was wrong with him? He was acting as if he'd never seen an attractive woman before. One of his dining companions that evening had worn a form-fitting dress that was shorter and lower cut than Sierra's nightgown and he hadn't felt even a twinge of interest. He needed to quit eyeballing her, or she was going to think he was some sort of deviant. The last thing he wanted was for her to be uncomfortable in his home.

Coop opened the wine refrigerator and fished out an open bottle of pinot grigio. Unlike his teammates, he preferred a quality wine to beer or liquor. He'd never been one to enjoy getting drunk. Not since his wild days anyway, when he'd taken pretty much anything that gave him a buzz because at the time it meant taking his pain away.

He took two glasses from the cupboard and set them on the island countertop. Sierra walked in as he was pouring. She had changed into a pair of black leggings and an oversize, faded yellow T-shirt. He found his gaze drawn to her legs again. He typically dated women who were supermodel skinny—and a few of those women had actually been supermodels—but not necessarily because that was what he preferred. That just seemed to be the type of woman who gravitated toward him. He liked that Sierra had some meat on her bones. She was not heavy by any stretch of the imagination. She just looked…healthy. Although he was sure that most women would take that as an insult.

He quickly reminded himself that it didn't matter what she looked like because she was off-limits.

"Have a seat," he said, and she slid onto one of the bar stools across the island from him. He corked the wine and slid one of the glasses toward her. "I hope you like white."

"Oh…um…" She hesitated, a frown causing an adorable little wrinkle between her brows. "Maybe I shouldn't."

He put the bottle back in the fridge. Maybe she thought he was trying to get her drunk so he could take advantage of her. "One glass," he said. "Unless you don't drink."

"No, I do. I'm just not sure if it's a good idea."

"Are you underage?"

She flashed him a cute smile. "You know I'm not. I'm just worried that one of the girls might wake up. In fact, I'd say it's a strong possibility, so I need to stay sharp."

"You think one little glass of wine will impair you?" He folded his arms. "You must be quite the lightweight."

Her chin lifted a notch. "I can hold my own. I just don't want to make a bad impression."

"If you drank an entire bottle, that might worry me, but one glass? Do you think I would offer if I thought it was a bad idea?"

"I guess not."

"Let's put it this way: If the twins were your daughters, and you wanted to wind down after a busy day, would you feel comfortable allowing yourself a glass of wine?"

"Yes."

He slid the wine closer. "So, stop worrying about what I think, and enjoy."

She took it.

"A toast, to your first day," he said, clinking his glass against hers.

She sipped, nodded and said, "Nice. I wouldn't have imagined you as the wine-drinking type."

"I'm sure there are a lot of things about me that would surprise you." He rested his hip against the edge of the countertop. "But tell me about you."

"I thought we were going to talk about the girls."

"We will, but I'd like to know a little bit about you first."

She sipped again, then set her glass down. "You read my file."

"Yeah, but that was just the basics. I'd like to know more about you as a person. Like, what made you get into nursing?"

"My mom, actually."

"She was a nurse?

"No, she was a homemaker. She got breast cancer when I was a kid. The nurses were so wonderful to her and to me and my dad and sister. Especially when she was in hospice. I decided then, that's what I wanted to do."

"She passed away?"

Sierra nodded. "When I was fourteen."

"That's a tough age for a girl to lose her mother."

"It was harder for my sister, I think. She was only ten."

He circled the counter and sat on the stool beside hers. "Is there a good age to lose a parent? I was twelve when my mom and dad died. It was really rough."

"My sister used to be this sweet, happy-go-lucky kid, but after she got really moody and brooding."

"I was angry," he said. "I went from being a pretty decent kid to the class bully."

"It's not uncommon, in that situation, for a boy to pick on someone smaller and weaker. It probably gave you a feeling of power in an otherwise powerless situation."

"Except I went after kids who were bigger than me. Because I was so big for my age, that usually meant I was fighting boys who were older than me. And I got the snot kicked out of me a couple of times, but usually I won. And you're right, it did make me feel powerful. I felt like it was the only thing I had any control over."

"My sister never picked on anyone, but she was into drugs for a while. Thankfully she cleaned herself up, but when my dad got sick she just couldn't handle it. When she turned eighteen she took off for L.A. She's an actress, or trying to be. She's done a couple of commercials and a few walk-on parts. Mostly she's a waitress."

"What is it that your dad has?" he asked, hoping he wasn't being too nosy.

"He's in the final stages of Alzheimer's."

"How old is he?"

"Fifty."

Damn. "That's really young for Alzheimer's, isn't it?"

She nodded. "It's rare, but it happens. He started getting symptoms when he was forty-six, and the disease progressed much faster than it would in someone older. They tried every drug out there to slow the progression, but nothing seemed to work. It's not likely he'll live out the year."

"I'm so sorry."

She shrugged, eyes lowered, running her thumb around the rim of her glass. "The truth is, he died months ago, at least in all the ways that matter. He's just a shell. A functioning body. I know he hates living this way."

She looked so sad. He wanted to hug her, or rub her shoulder, or do something to comfort her, but it didn't seem appropriate to be touching her. So his only choice was to comfort her with words and shared experiences. Because when it came to losing a parent, he knew just how deeply painful and traumatic it could be.

"When my parents got in the car accident, my

dad died instantly. My mom survived the crash, but she was in a coma and brain-dead. My brother, Ash, was eighteen, and he had to make the decision to take her off life support."

"What a horrible thing for him to have to go through. No one should have to make that decision. Not at any age."

"I was too young to really grasp what was happening. I thought he did it because he was mad at her or didn't love her. Only when I got older did I understand that there was no hope."

"I signed a Do Not Resuscitate order for my dad. It was so hard, but I know it's what he wants. Working in the NICU, I've seen parents have to make impossible choices. It was heartbreaking. You have to hold it together at work, be strong for the parents, but I can't tell you how many times I went home and cried my eyes out. Parents of healthy kids just don't realize how lucky they are."

"I can understand how you would burn out in a job like that."

"Don't get me wrong, I really love nursing. I liked that I was helping people. But it can be emotionally draining."

"Do you think you'll miss it?"

She smiled. "With the twins to take care of, I doubt I'll have time."

He hoped she wouldn't eventually burn out, the way she had with nursing. Maybe giving her so little time off had been a bad idea. He knew first-hand how tough it was caring for the twins nonstop. A few hours off on a Sunday and one weekend a month weren't much time. Maybe he should have considered hiring two nannies, one for during the week, and one for the weekends. "You're sure it's not going to be too much?"

"Watching the twins?"

"By taking this job, you're pretty much giving up your social life."

"I gave that up when my dad got too sick to care for himself. He couldn't be alone, so we had a caregiver while I worked, then I took over when I got home."

"Every day? That sounds expensive."

She nodded. "It was. We blew through his savings in just a few months. But I didn't want him to have to go in a nursing home. I kept him with me as long as I could. But eventually it got to the point where I just couldn't provide the best care for him."

"When did you go out? Have fun?"

"I've always been more of a homebody."

"What about dating?"

The sudden tuck between her brows said her love life was a touchy subject. And really it was none of his business. Or maybe she thought it was some sort of cheesy pickup line.

"You can tell me to mind my own business," he said.

"It's okay. Things are just a little complicated right now. I'm not in a good place emotionally to be getting into a relationship." She glanced over at him. "That's probably tough for someone like you to understand."

"Someone so morally vacant?"

Her eyes widened. "No, I didn't mean—"

"It's okay," he said with a laugh. "A few weeks ago, I probably wouldn't have understood."

Dating and being out with other people had been such an intrinsic part of who he was, he probably wouldn't have been able to grasp the concept of leading a quiet, domesticated life. Since the crash that had taken his brother, his attitude and his perception about what was really important had been altered. Like tonight for instance. Why go out bar-hopping to meet a woman for what would ultimately be a meaningless and quite frankly unsatisfying encounter when the twins needed him at home?

"Priorities change," he said.

She nodded. "Yes they do. You see things a certain way, then suddenly it's not about what you want anymore."

He wondered if she was talking about her dad. "I know exactly what you mean."

"You really love them," she said.

"The twins?" he found himself grinning. "Yeah, I do. What's not to love? This was obviously not a part of my plans, but I want to do right by them. I owe Ash that much. He sacrificed a lot to raise me. He worked two jobs and put college off for years to be there for me, and believe me, I was a handful. Some people thought that because the twins aren't Ash's biological kids it somehow absolved me of all responsibility. Even their birth mother seemed to think so."

"What do you mean?"

"Her lawyer contacted my lawyer. Apparently she saw on the news that Ash and Susan had died and she wanted the girls back. I can only assume that she thought I would be a failure as a dad."

"And you didn't consider it?"

"Not for a second. And even if I didn't think I could handle taking care of the girls myself, why would I give them to someone who didn't want them to begin with?"

That tuck was back between her brows. "Maybe she wanted them but just couldn't keep them. Maybe she thought giving them up was the best thing for the twins."

"And that changed in five months? She thinks she can give the girls more than I can? With me they'll never want for a thing. They'll have the best of everything. Clothes, education, you name it. Could she do that?"

"So you assume that because she isn't rich she wouldn't be a good parent?" she asked in a sharp tone.

For someone who didn't even know the birth mother she was acting awfully defensive. "The truth is, I don't know why she gave them up, but it doesn't matter. My brother adopted the twins and loved them like his own flesh and blood. He wanted the girls raised by me, and I'm honoring his wishes."

Her expression softened. "I'm sorry, I didn't mean to snap. In my line of work, I've seen young mothers harshly misjudged. It's a natural instinct to defend them."

"Not to mention that you've no doubt heard about my reputation and question my ability to properly raise the girls."

She shook her head. "I didn't say—"

"You didn't have to." It was amazing the people who had strong opinions about his ability to be a good father. Some of his closest friends—the single ones—thought he was crazy for taking on the responsibility. And the friends with families—not that he had many of those—openly doubted his capabilities as a parent.

He intended to prove them all wrong.

"Like I said before," he told Sierra firmly, meaning every word, "priorities change. For me, the girls come first, and they always will."

Chapter 4

Sierra could hardly believe how snippy she had gotten with Coop last night.

She replayed the conversation in her head as she got the girls ready for their afternoon nap, cringing inwardly as she placed Ivy on her belly on the carpet with a toy while she wrestled a wiggling Fern out of her jumper and into a fresh diaper.

Antagonize your boss. Way to go, Sierra. Was she *trying* to get fired? Or even worse, give him any reason to doubt that she was just the twin's nanny? But all that garbage about him changing his priorities had really ruffled her feathers, and she didn't believe it for a minute, not after the way he was ogling her when she opened the bedroom door in her nightgown. And if he thought she would be interested in a man like him, he was dreaming.

Although she couldn't deny that in a very small and completely depraved way it had been just the tiniest bit exciting. And to his credit Coop had looked conflicted, like he knew it was wrong, but he just couldn't help himself. Which she was sure summed him up in a nutshell. He would try to change, try to be a good father to the twins, but in the end he would fail because that was just the sort of man he was.

But it had been an awfully long time since someone had looked at her in a sexual way, and what woman wouldn't feel at least the tiniest bit special to be noticed by a rich, gorgeous guy who was known for dating actresses and supermodels? She also didn't let herself forget that he was a womanizer, and she was one of hundreds of women he had looked at in that very same way.

She laid Fern in her crib and turned to pick up Ivy, but she had rolled all the way across the room and wound up by the closet door.

"Come back here, you little sneak," she said, scooping her up and nibbling the ticklish spot on her neck. Ivy giggled and squirmed, but when Sierra laid her on the changing table she didn't put up a fuss. She was definitely the milder mannered of the two, but she had a curious nature. Sierra was sure that left to her own devices, Ivy could get herself into trouble. There was no doubt that Ivy was more like her, and Fern seemed to take after their birth father's side of the family. Sierra was having such a blast getting to know them, learning all their little personality quirks. She realized how fortunate she was to have this opportunity and she wouldn't take it for granted. And if being with her daughters meant putting up with an occasional inappropriate glance, it was worth it.

Speaking of Mr. Inappropriate, Sierra heard the deep timbre of Coop's voice from his office down the hall. He was on the phone again. He was working from home today, or so he said. Exactly what he was doing in there, or what that so-called "work" entailed, she wasn't sure. Polishing his various trophies? Giving interviews?

Other than basking in the glow of his former fame, she wasn't sure what he did with his time.

She laid Ivy in her crib and blew each of the girls a kiss good-night, then she closed the curtain to smother the light and stepped out of the room… colliding with Coop, who was on his way in. He said, "Whoa!" looking just as surprised to see her as she was to see him. She instinctively held her hands up to soften the inevitable collision and wound up with her palms pressed against the hard wall of his chest, breathing in the warm and clean aroma of his skin. He wore the scent of soap and shampoo the way other men wore three-hundred dollar cologne. And though it was completely irrational, the urge to slide her hands up around his neck, to plaster herself against him, hit her swift and hard.

Touching Coop was clearly a bad idea.

She pulled away so fast her upper back and head hit the door frame with a thud.

Coop winced. "You okay?"

She grimaced and rubbed her head. "Fine."

"You sure? You hit that pretty hard." He reached behind her and cupped the back of her head in one enormous palm, but his touch was gentle as he probed for an injury, his fingers slipping through her hair beneath the root of her ponytail, spreading warmth against her scalp. "I don't feel a bump."

But, oh man, did it feel nice.

Nice? Ugh! This was insane. Knowing the sort of man he was, his touch should have repulsed her.

She ducked away from his hand. "I'm fine, really. You just startled me."

He frowned, tucking his hands in the pockets of his jeans, as if maybe he realized that touching her wasn't appropriate. Or maybe he liked it as much as she did. "Sorry. Where are the girls?"

"I just put them down for their nap."

"Why didn't you tell me? I'd like to say goodnight."

Honestly, she hadn't thought it would matter to

him. "I thought I heard you on the phone and I didn't want to disturb you."

"Well, next time let me know," he said, sounding irritated. "If I'm here, the girls come first."

"Okay. I'm sorry. They're still awake if you want to see them."

His expression softened. "Just for a second."

He disappeared into their room and Sierra walked to the kitchen to clean up the girls' lunch dishes. Coop really was taking this "being there for the girls" business pretty seriously. But how long would that last? It was probably a novelty, being the caring uncle. She was sure it wouldn't be long before he slipped back into his old ways and wouldn't have the time or the inclination to say good-night to the twins.

"What is this?" Ms. Densmore snipped, holding up the empty bottles from the girls' lunch as Sierra walked into the kitchen.

Was this some sort of trick question? "Um… bottles?"

She flung daggers with her eyes. "And why were they on the kitchen counter and not in the dishwasher?"

"Because I didn't put them there yet."

"Anything you use in the kitchen must be put in the dishwasher or washed by *you*. And any messes you and the children make are yours to clean."

"I'm aware of that," Sierra said, and only because

Ms. Densmore had given her this identical lecture *three* times now. "I planned to clean up after I put the twins down for their nap. Their *care* is my priority."

"I also noticed a basket of your clothes in the laundry room. I'd like to remind you that you are responsible for your own laundry. That includes clothing, towels and bedding. I work for Mr. Landon. Not you or anyone else. Is that clear?"

Sienna gritted her teeth. She was sure it bugged the hell out of the housekeeper that she was forced to feed Sierra, although Coop was right about her being an excellent cook. "The washer was already running so I set them there temporarily."

Sierra had done absolutely nothing to offend her, so she had no clue why Ms. Densmore was so cranky, so inclined to dislike her.

"As I have said to Mr. Landon on numerous occasions, I took this job because there were no children. I am not a nanny or a babysitter. Do not ask me to hold, change, feed or play with the twins. They are *your* responsibility, and yours alone."

As if she'd want her girls anywhere near this nasty old bitch. "I'm pretty clear on that, thanks."

Ms. Densmore shoved the bottles at her and Sierra took them. Then, her pointy, beak nose in the air, Ms. Densmore stalked away to the laundry room behind the kitchen. And though it was petty and immature, Sierra gestured rudely to her retreating back.

"That wasn't very ladylike."

She spun around to find Coop watching her, a wry grin on his face.

He folded his arms across his ridiculously wide chest and said, "I'm glad the girls weren't here to see that."

She bit her lip and hooked her hands behind her back. "Um…sorry?"

Coop laughed. "I'm kidding. I would have done exactly the same thing. And you're right, the girls are your first priority. The dishwasher can wait."

"I have no idea why she dislikes me so much."

"Don't take it personally. She doesn't like me, either, but she's one hell of an awesome housekeeper."

"You would think she would be happy to have me here. Now she doesn't have to deal with the twins."

"I'll have a talk with her."

That could be a really bad idea. "Maybe you shouldn't. I don't want her to think I tattled on her. It will just make things worse."

"Don't worry, I'll take care of it."

Coop walked to the laundry room and over the sound of the washer and dryer she heard the door snap closed behind him. Tempted as she was to sneak back there and press her ear to the door to listen, she put the lunch dishes in the dishwasher instead. Coop was back a couple of minutes later, a satisfied smile on his face.

"She won't hassle you anymore," he said. "If you need me, I'll be in my office."

Whatever he'd said to Ms. Densmore, it had worked. She came out of the laundry room several minutes later, red faced with either embarrassment or anger, and didn't say a word or even look at Sierra. She maintained her tight-lipped silence until dinnertime when she served a Mexican dish that was so delicious Sierra had two helpings.

Sierra was surprised when Coop invited her to eat in the dining room with him. She had just assumed that she would be treated like any other hired help and eat in the kitchen with the girls. Because surely he wouldn't want two infants around making a fuss and disrupting his meal. But he actually insisted on it. While Sierra sat at one end of the table, Ivy in her high chair next to her, he sat with Fern, alternately feeding her then himself. When Fern started to fuss and Sierra offered to take over, he refused. He wiped applesauce from her face and hands with a washcloth, plucked her from her high chair and sat her in his lap while he finished his meal, dodging her grasping hands as she tried to intercept his fork. After their talk last night, maybe he felt he had to prove some sort of point.

When they were done with dinner he switched on the enormous flat-screen television in the living room and tuned it to ESPN. Then he stretched out on the floor and played with the girls while she sat on the couch feeling a little like an outsider.

The girls obviously adored him and it scared the hell out of her. Not because she thought they would love her more. She'd reconciled her position in the girls' lives. She just hated to see the girls become attached to him, only to have him grow bored with parenting. They were a novelty, but his fascination with them would fade. He was still reeling from his brother's death, but that would only last so long. Eventually he would go back to his womanizing, partying ways. And when he did, *she* would be there to offer the stability they needed. She was the person the twins would learn to depend on.

The worst part was that he had flat-out admitted he thought that he could buy their affection by giving them "the best money could buy," but what they really needed, his love and emotional support, he wasn't capable of giving. Not for any extended length of time.

When it was time for the twins to go to bed Coop helped her wrestle them into their pajamas. He gave them each a kiss good-night, then he and Sierra laid them in their cribs.

On their way out of the room Sierra grabbed their soiled clothes from the day and switched off the light. "I'm going to go throw these in the wash."

"You don't have to do the girls' laundry," Coop

said, following her down the hall. "Leave it for Ms. Densmore."

"It's okay. I wanted to do a few of my own things, too. Unless you'd prefer I wash the twins' clothes separately."

He looked confused. "Why would I care about that?"

Sierra shrugged. "Some people are picky about the way their kids' clothes are washed."

"Well, not me."

Somehow she didn't imagine he would be. And he probably wouldn't care that she had every intention of washing their "hand wash only" dresses on Delicate in the machine.

Sierra dumped the clothes in the washing machine, noting that the room was tidy to point of fanaticism. There wasn't so much as a speck of dust on the floor or a stitch of clothing anywhere. Ms. Densmore must have been as anal about keeping the laundry done as she was with keeping the house clean.

Sierra opened the cabinet to find the detergents, stain removers and fabric softeners organized neatly by function and perfectly aligned so the labels were facing out. She grabbed the liquid detergent, measured out a cupful and poured it into the machine. She put the cap back on, ignoring the small bit that sloshed over the side of the bottle, then, smiling serenely, stuck it back on the shelf crooked. She did the same with the fabric softener, then gave the stain removers a quick jostle just for fun before she started the machine.

She walked back out into the kitchen and found Coop sitting at the island on a barstool, two glasses of red wine on the counter.

"Take a load off," he said, nudging the other stool with his foot. "I was in the mood for red tonight. It's a Malbec. I hope that's okay."

She wasn't picky. However, she had just assumed that last night's shared wine had been a one-time thing. "You don't have to serve me wine every night."

"I know I don't."

Did he plan to make a habit of this because she wasn't sure if she was comfortable with that. Not that she minded relaxing with a glass of wine at the end of the day. It was the company that made her a little nervous. Especially when he sat so darned close to her. Last night she'd sat beside him feeling edgy, as if she were waiting for him to pounce. Which he didn't, of course. He had been a perfect gentleman. Yet he still made her nervous.

"Maybe we could sit in the living room," she suggested. Far, far away from each other.

Coop shrugged. "Sure."

What she would rather do is take the glass to her room and curl up in bed with the mystery novel she'd been reading, but she didn't want to be rude.

He sprawled in the chair by the window, his long, muscular legs stretched out in front of him, and Sierra sat with her legs tucked underneath her on the corner of the couch. He was yards away from her, so why the tension lingering in the air? And why could she not stop looking at him? Yes, he was easy on the eyes, but she didn't even like him.

Coop sipped his wine, then rested the glass on his stomach—which was no doubt totally ripped and as perfect as the rest of him—his fingers laced together and cupping the bowl. "What do you think of the wine?"

She took a sip, letting it roll around her tongue. She didn't know much about wines, but it tasted pretty good to her. Very bold and fruity. A huge step up from the cheap brands she could afford. "I like it. It tastes expensive."

"It is. But what's the point of having all this money if I can't enjoy the finer things? Which reminds me, I talked to my decorator today. He's tied up with another project and won't be available to meet with you for at least three weeks. If that's not soon enough for you, we can find someone who's available now."

"Three weeks is fine. There's no rush."

"You're sure?"

"Positive. I really appreciate that you want me to be comfortable, though." The truth was, she hadn't been spending much time in there anyway.

The twins kept her busy all day, and when she was in her room, she was usually asleep.

"I meant to ask you yesterday—what's going on with your dad? You mentioned moving him to a different place."

"They're taking him by ambulance to the new nursing home Saturday morning."

"Do you need to be there?"

Even if she did, she had a responsibility to the girls. "He's in good hands. I'll be visiting him Sunday during my time off. I can get him settled in then."

"You know, you don't have to wait until Sundays to see him. You can go anytime you'd like. I don't mind if you take the girls with you."

"He's going to be all the way out in Jersey. I don't own a car and taking the twins on the train or the bus would be a logistical nightmare."

He shrugged. "So take my car."

"I can't."

"It's okay, really."

"No, I mean I *really* can't. I don't know how."

His brows rose. "You never learned to drive?"

"I've always lived in the city. I never needed to. And gas prices being what they are, public transportation just makes more sense."

"Well then, why don't I take you? We could go Saturday when he's transferred."

Huh? Why would he want to take time out of his

day to haul her to Jersey? Surely he had something better to do. "You really don't have to do that."

"I want to."

She didn't know what to say. Why was he being so nice to her? Why did he even care if she saw her dad? He was her employer, not her pal.

"You're looking at me really weirdly right now," Coop said. "Either you're not used to people doing nice things for you, or you're seriously questioning my motives."

A little bit of both actually, and it was creepy how he seemed to always know what she was thinking. "I'm sure you have other things—"

"No, I don't. My schedule is totally free this weekend." He paused, then added, "And for the record, I have no ulterior motives."

She had a hard time buying that. "You're sure it's no trouble?"

"None at all. And I'll bet the girls would like to get out of the house."

Sierra was going to remind him that she'd taken them for a long walk in the park that morning, but it seemed like a moot point. He obviously wasn't going to take no for an answer, and she really would like to be there when they moved her dad, not only to make certain he was handled respectfully, but also to see that none of his very few possessions were left behind. The pictures and keepsakes. Not that he would know either way. Maybe, she thought sadly, it would be best if she just held on to them now.

"I'll call the nursing home tomorrow and find out when the ambulance will be there. Maybe we could be there a half an hour or so beforehand, then follow them over to the new facility."

"Just let me know when and I'll be ready."

"Thanks."

He narrowed his eyes slightly. "But…you're still wondering why I'm doing this for you. You apparently have this preconceived notion about the kind of person that I am."

She couldn't deny it. He would be surprised by how much she actually did know about him. The real stuff, not the rumors and conjecture. But she couldn't tell him that.

"Believe it or not, I'm a pretty decent guy." He paused then added, "And an above-average dancer."

She would have to take his word on that. "I clearly have trust issues," she said. Fool me once, shame on you, and all of that. Maybe he didn't have ulterior motives, but that was not usually the case. And under normal circumstances she would have told him no on principle alone, but just this one time she would make an exception.

"I guess it will just take time for you to believe that I'm not a bad guy," he said.

Honestly, she didn't understand why he cared what she thought of him. Was he this personable with all of his employees? Granted she had only worked for him a couple of days, but she had never seen him offer Ms. Densmore a glass of wine or heard him offer to drive her anywhere. She was sure it had a lot to do with Sierra being young and, yes, she was what most men considered attractive. Not a raving beauty but not too shabby, either. Then again, she was nowhere near as glamorous as the women she had seen him linked to in the past. But Coop hadn't been born wealthy. Who was to say he didn't enjoy slumming it occasionally?

Well, if he thought doing nice things for her was a direct route into her pants, that just because he was rich and famous and above average in the looks department she would go all gooey, he was in for a rude awakening.

Chapter 5

Sierra stood in her dad's new room, resisting the natural instinct to step in and help as the ambulance attendants worked with the nursing home staff to get her dad moved from the gurney to his bed, where he would most likely spend the rest of his life. At least in this new facility the staff was friendly and helpful and she could rest easy knowing that her dad would be well cared for. Unfortunately the ambulance had been an hour late to pick him up and the paperwork had taken an eternity.

Coop had been incredibly patient, taking over with the twins, but that patience had to be wearing thin by now. He was sitting in the rec room with

them, and though she had fed them their lunch in
the car on the way over, they were about an hour and
a half past their nap time and last time she checked
were getting fussy. She was thankful to have been
around for the transfer, but she felt the crushing
weight of guilt for making Coop—her employer—
wait around for her.

She would have to make this visit a short one.

Once they got him situated in bed, everyone
cleared out of the room. The nurse must have mistaken her guilt for conflicted feelings about her dad
because she rubbed Sierra's arm, smiled warmly
and said, "Don't worry, honey, we'll take good care
of him."

When she was gone Sierra walked over to the
bed. The curtain between him and his roommate
was drawn, but according to the nurse, the man in
the next bed was also comatose. "I can't stay, Dad,
but I'll come back tomorrow, I promise."

She kissed his cheek, feeling guilty for cutting her
visit so short, and headed to the rec room where Coop
and the girls were waiting for her. To look at him,
no one would guess that he was a multi-millionaire
celebrity. In jeans, a T-shirt and worn tennis shoes,
pacing the floor, looking completely at ease with one
restless twin in each arm, he looked like just a regular guy. Albeit most "regular" guys weren't six-three
with the physique of an Adonis.

She would be lying if she denied it was an adorable sight, the way he bounced the girls patiently. For someone who hadn't anticipated being a dad, and had the duty thrust on him unexpectedly, he had done amazingly well. She couldn't help but wonder if she had been unfairly harsh on him. In the five days she'd worked for him she had seen no hint of the womanizing party animal. So why couldn't she shake the feeling that he was destined to let the girls down?

It was all very confusing.

"I'm so sorry it's taken this long," she told him, plucking a wiggling Ivy from him.

"It's okay," Coop said, looking as though he genuinely meant it. "Is he all settled in?"

"Finally." Ivy squirmed in her arms, so Sierra transferred her to the opposite hip. "Let's get out of here. These two are way past their nap time."

"You don't want to stay and visit a little longer?"

She figured by now he would have been exasperated with the girls' fussing and would be gunning to get back on the road for home. To his credit, though, he hadn't once complained. Not while they sat at the other nursing home waiting for the transport, or when they sat stuck in weekend traffic. But as much as she would love to stay for just a little while longer, to make sure the trip had no adverse effects on her dad physically, she had already taken up way too much of Coop's personal time.

"I'll come by tomorrow on my time off," she told

Coop, grabbing the packed-to-the-gills designer label diaper bag and slinging it over her shoulder. Coop commandeered the double umbrella stroller—top-of-the-line, of course, because when it came to the twins Ash and Susan had spared no expense—and they walked out of the building and through the parking lot to his vehicle. Earlier that morning, as she waited on the sidewalk outside his building for him to bring the car around, she'd expected either some flashy little sports car—which logistically she knew wouldn't work with two infants—or at the opposite end of the excess spectrum, a Hummer. Instead he had pulled up in a low-key silver SUV, proving once again that the man she thought she had pegged and the real Cooper were two very different people. ••••

She and Coop each buckled a twin into her car seat, and within five minutes of exiting the lot, both girls were out cold.

"So, where to now?" Coop asked.

Sierra just assumed they would head back into the city. "Home, I guess."

"But it's a gorgeous summer afternoon. We should do something. I don't know about you, but I'm starving. Why don't we grab a bite to eat?"

"The girls just fell asleep. If we wake them up now and drag them into a restaurant, I don't anticipate it being a pleasant experience."

"Good point."

"Besides, don't you need to get home? It's Saturday. You must have plans for later."

"Nope, no plans tonight," Coop said.

He hadn't gone out the night before, either. The four of them had eaten dinner together, then Coop wrestled and played with the twins until their bedtime. After they were tucked into bed, Sierra thought for sure that he would go out, but when she emerged from the laundry room after putting in her daily load of soiled clothes, Coop had been sitting in the living room with two glasses of wine. And though she had planned on reading for a while then going to sleep early, it seemed rude to turn him down after he had gone through the trouble of actually pouring the wine.

One quick glass, she had promised herself, and she would be in bed before nine-thirty. But one glass turned into two, and she and Coop got to talking about his hockey playing days—a subject that even she had to admit was pretty interesting—and before she knew it, it was nearly midnight. Though he did still make her a little nervous and the idea of a friendship with him made her slightly uncomfortable, he was so easygoing and charming she couldn't help but like him.

"On our way in we passed a deli and a small park," he said. "We could pick up sandwiches, eat in the car, then go for a drive while the twins sleep."

That actually wasn't a bad idea. If they took the

twins home now, the minute they took them out of their car seats they would probably wake up, cutting their nap short by at least an hour, which would probably make them crabby for the rest of the day. But the idea of spending so much time in such close quarters with Coop made her nervous. Not that she was worried he would act inappropriately. If he had wanted to try something, he would have done it by now, and aside from ogling her in her nightie the other evening—which admittedly was her own fault for not putting on a robe—he'd been a perfect gentleman. These feelings of unease were her own doing.

Illogical and inappropriate as it was, she was attracted to Coop, and clearly the feeling was mutual. The air felt electrically charged whenever he was near, and then there was that unwelcome little zap of energy that passed between them whenever they touched, even if it was something as innocent as their fingers brushing when he handed her a jar of baby food. And even though she had no intention whatsoever of expanding the dynamics of their relationship to include intimacy, she couldn't shake the feeling that they were crossing some line of morality.

But what the heck, it was just a sandwich. And it really was the best thing for the girls, and that was what mattered, right?

"I could eat," she said.

"Great." He flashed her one of those adorable grins. The dimpled kind that made her heart go all wonky.

God, she was pathetic.

Though she offered to go inside the deli and order the food while he waited with the girls, he insisted on going himself and refused the money she tried to give him to cover the expense of her food.

"You shouldn't have to pay for my lunch," she told him.

"If we were at home you would be eating food that I paid for, so what's the difference?"

It was tough to argue with logic like that. Besides, he was out of the car before she could utter another word.

He was in and back out of the deli in five minutes with his grilled Reuben and her turkey on whole grain. He also got coleslaw, a bag of potato chips, bottled water and sodas. They found the park a few blocks away and parked in a spot facing the playground under the shade of a tree. Sierra worried the girls might wake up when he shut the engine off, but they were both out cold.

They spread their lunch out on the console and started eating.

"Can I ask you a question?" she said.

"Sure."

"Besides being a celebrity, what do you do now? For a living, I mean. Do you work?"

Her question seemed to amuse him. "I work really hard actually. I have my own line of hockey equipment coming out, and I started a chain of sports centers a few years ago and they've taken off. We're opening six more by next January."

"What kind of sports centers?"

"Ice rinks and indoor playing fields. Kids sports are big business these days. On top of that I own a couple dozen vacation properties around the world that I rent out. Also very lucrative."

Wow, so much for her theory that he sat around basking in his former fame. It sounded as if he kept himself really busy.

"Where are the vacation homes?" she asked him.

He named off the different cities, and then described the sorts of properties he owned. The list was an impressive one. Clearly he was a very sharp businessman.

"I never realized there was such a market for rental vacation homes."

"Most people aren't in a financial position to drop the money on a home they may only use a couple of times a year, so they rent. Not only is it a lot cheaper, but also you're not locked into one city or country."

She reached into the bag of chips for her third handful.

"I guess you were hungry," Coop teased.

She shot him a look. "Be careful, or you'll give me a complex."

"Are you kidding? I think it's great that you eat like a normal human being. I've taken women to some of the finest restaurants in the city and they order a side salad and seltzer water, or, even worse, they order a huge expensive meal and eat three bites."

"Maybe this is a dumb question, but if it bothers you so much, why do you always date super-skinny women? I mean, doesn't that sort of come with the territory?"

"Convenience, I guess."

Her brows rose. *"Convenience?"*

"They just happen to be the kind of women who hang around the people I hang around with."

"You mean, the kind who throw themselves at you."

He shrugged. "More or less."

"Have you ever had to actually pursue a woman you wanted to date?"

He thought about that for a second, then shook his head and said, "No, not really. In fact, never."

"Seriously? Not once? Not even in high school?"

"Since I was old enough to take an interest in girls I was the team star. Girls flocked to me."

She shook her head in disbelief. "Wow. That's just...*wow.*"

"Can you blame them? I mean, look at me. I'm

rich, good-looking, a famous athlete. Who wouldn't want me? I'm completely irresistible."

She couldn't tell if he was serious or just teasing her. Could he honestly be *that* arrogant? "I wouldn't."

That seemed to amuse him. "You already do. You try to pretend you don't, but I can sense it."

"I think you've been hit in the head with a hockey stick a few too many times because I do *not* want you. You aren't even my type."

"But that's what makes it so exciting. You know you shouldn't like me, you know it's wrong because you work for me, but you just can't stop thinking about me."

How did he do that? How did he always seem to know what was going on inside her head? It was probably the third or fourth time he'd done this to her. It couldn't just be a lucky guess.

It was disturbing and…fascinating. And no way in *hell* could she ever let him know just how right he was. "So what you're saying is, all that stuff about you being a nice guy was bull. Everything nice that you've done is because you've been trying to get into my pants?"

"No, I am a nice guy. And for the record, if all I wanted was to get into your pants, I'd have been there by now."

Her eyes went wide. "Oh, really?"

"You're not nearly as tough as you think you

are. If I tried to kiss you right now, you wouldn't stop me."

The thought of him leaning over the console and pressing his lips to hers made her heart flutter and her stomach bottom out. But she squared her shoulders and said, "If you tried to kiss me, you would be wearing the family jewels for earrings."

He threw his head back and laughed.

"You don't think I would do it?"

"No, you probably would, just to prove how tough you are. Then you would give in and let me kiss you anyway."

"The depth of your arrogance is truly remarkable."

"It's one of my most charming qualities," he said, but his grin said that he was definitely teasing her this time.

Maybe the confidence was a smoke screen, or this was his way of testing the waters or teasing her. Maybe he really liked her, but being so used to women throwing themselves at him, the possibility of being rejected scared him.

Weirdly enough, the idea that under the tough-guy exterior there could be a vulnerable man made him that much more appealing.

Ugh. What was *wrong* with her?

"Even if I did want you," she said, "which, despite what you believe, I really don't, I would never risk it. I can't even imagine putting my father back in that hellhole we just got him out of. And without this job I can't even come close to affording the new place. So I have every reason *not* to want you."

Before Coop had time to process that, Ivy began to stir in the backseat.

"Uh-oh," he said, glancing back at her. "We better get moving before she wakes up."

He balled up the paper wrapper from his sandwich and shoved it back in the bag, then started the engine. She thought once they got moving, he might segue back into the conversation, but he turned the radio on instead, and she breathed a silent sigh of relief. She hoped she had made her point, he would drop the subject forever and the sexual tension that had been a constant companion in their relationship would magically disappear. Then they could have a normal employee/employer relationship. Because she feared Coop was right. If he kissed her, she wasn't sure she would be able to tell him no.

And she had the sinking feeling that this conversation, inappropriate as it was, was nowhere close to over.

Chapter 6

Sierra didn't hear from her sister very often. She would go months at a time without a single word. Sierra would call and leave messages that Joy wouldn't return, send cards that would come back as undeliverable. Then out of the blue Joy would call and always with the same feeble excuses. She was crazy-busy, or had moved, or her phone had been disconnected because she couldn't pay the bill. But the reality was that Joy was fragile. Watching their mother slowly waste away had damaged her. She simply didn't have the emotional capacity to handle the hopelessness of their dad's illness and dealt with it by moving a couple thousand miles away and cutting off all contact.

Sierra hadn't even been able to reach her when she learned about Ash and Susan's death, and frankly she could have used a bit of emotional support. Which was why Sierra was surprised to see her name on her caller ID that night after she and Coop put the twins to bed. She had just stepped out of the room and was closing the door when her phone started to ring.

She considered not answering, giving Joy a taste of her own medicine for a change. Sometimes she got tired of being the responsible sister. But after two rings guilt got the best of her. Suppose it was something important? And what if Joy didn't call again for months? Besides their dad and the twins, Sierra had no one else. Not to mention that it was an awesome excuse to skip the post-bedtime glass of wine with Coop. And after what had happened this afternoon, the less time she spent with him the better.

"It's my sister. I have to take this," she said, slipping into her bedroom and shutting the door, pretending she didn't see the brief flash of disappointment that passed across his face.

"Guess who!" Joy chirped when Sierra answered.

"Hey, sis." She sat on the edge of her bed. "What's it been, three months?"

That earned a long-suffering sigh from her sister.

"I know, I know, I should call more often. But what I've got to say now will make up for it."

"Oh, yeah?" Somehow she doubted that.

"I'm coming home!"

"You're moving back to New York?"

Sierra's heart lifted, then swiftly plunged when her sister laughed and said, "God, no! Are you kidding? Los Angeles is too fabulous to leave. I'm staying at a friend's Malibu beachfront home and it's totally amazing. In fact, I'm sitting in the sand, watching the tide move in as we speak."

She could just picture Joy in one of her flowing peasant skirts and gauzy blouses, her long, tanned legs folded beneath her, her waist-length, wavy black hair blowing in the salty breeze. She would be holding a designer beer in her hand with one of those skinny cigarettes she liked to smoke dangling between two fingers. She had always been so much cooler than Sierra, so much more self-confident. Yet so tortured. And she was sure that the friend Joy was staying with was a man and that she was also sharing his bedroom.

"Then why did you say you're coming home?" Sierra asked.

"Because I'm flying in for a visit."

"When?"

"A week from this coming Wednesday. They're holding auditions for an independent film that's supposed to start filming this August and my agent thinks I'm a shoo-in for the lead roll. I'll be in town a week just in case I get a callback."

"That sounds promising." Although according to Joy, her agent thought she was a shoo-in for every role he set her up for, or so it seemed.

"I know what you're thinking," Joy said.

"I didn't say a word."

"You didn't have to. I can feel your skepticism over the phone line. But this is different. My new agent has some really awesome connections."

"New agent? What happened to the old one?"

"I didn't tell you about that? We parted ways about two months ago."

And Sierra hadn't talked to her in three months. "Why? I thought he was some sort of super-agent."

"His wife sort of caught us going at it in his office."

"You *slept* with your *married* agent?" Why did that not surprise her?

"A girl does what she can to get ahead, and it was no hardship, believe me. Besides, you're not exactly in a position to pass judgment."

Technically the twins' father was a married man, but it was a totally different situation. "He and his wife were separated, and it was only that one night."

By the time she realized she was pregnant, he and his wife had reconciled. Not that she would have wanted to marry him. He was a nice guy, but they both knew right after it happened that it had been a mistake.

"So, you said you're coming to visit?" Sierra said, changing the subject.

"For a week. And needless to say, I'll be staying with my favorite sister."

"Oh." That was going to be a problem.

"What do you mean, 'oh'? I thought you would be happy to see me."

"I am. It's just that staying with me is going to be a problem."

"Why? Don't tell me you're living with someone. And even if you are, he damned well better let your baby sister stay for a couple of nights."

"I actually am living with someone, but not in the way that you think. I mean, we're not a couple. I work for him."

"As a nurse?"

"As a nanny."

"A *nanny?* You gave the girls up, what, six months ago? Isn't that, like, a painful reminder?"

"Joy, hold on a minute, I have to check something." She walked to her door and opened it a crack. If she was going to tell Joy what was going on, she didn't want to risk Coop overhearing. From the living room she could hear the television and knew he was probably in his favorite chair, engrossed in whatever sporting event he was watching. She closed her door and walked back to the bed.

"Did you get any of my messages about the twins' adoptive parents?"

"I did, yeah. I wanted to call, but…you know…"

She was sorry, but she couldn't deal with it. Same old story. "Well, the girls went to their uncle, Ash's brother."

"Isn't he like some famous athlete or something?"

"A former hockey player. A womanizing party animal. Not exactly the sort of person I wanted raising my girls."

"Oh, Si, I'm so sorry. Have you talked to your lawyer? Is there anything he can do? Can you claim he's unfit and get the girls back?"

She fidgeted with the edge of the pillowcase, knowing this next part was not going to go over well. "My lawyer talked to his lawyer, but he refused to give them up. There's nothing I can do. So I took matters into my own hands."

Joy gasped. "You *kidnapped* them?"

Sierra laughed. "Of course not! I would never do something like that. But I needed to be there for them, to know that they were okay, so when I heard that he was looking for a nanny…"

Another gasp. "Are you saying that *you're* the twins' nanny?"

"You should see them, Joy. They're so beautiful and so sweet. And I get to be with them 24/7."

"And this guy, their uncle, he knows you're their mother?"

"God, no! And he can never know."

"Sierra, that's *crazy*. What are you going to do, just take care of the girls for the rest of your life, with them never knowing that you're their birth mother?"

"I'll stay with them as long as they need me. And maybe some day I can tell them the truth."

"What about your life? What about men and marriage and having more kids? You're just going to give that all up."

"Not forever. I figure once they're in school full-time they won't need me nearly as much. As long as I'm here in the mornings and when they get home after school, they won't really need me to spend the night."

"It sounds as if you have it all figured out."

"I do."

"And this uncle…"

"Coop. Coop Landon."

"Is he really awful?"

In a way she wished he was. It would make this a lot less confusing. "Actually, he seems like a good guy. So far. Not at all what I expected." Almost too good, *too* nice. "He's really committed to taking care of the twins. For now anyway. That doesn't mean he won't eventually revert back to his old

ways. That's why it's so important that I'm here
for the girls. To see that they're raised properly."

"Suppose he finds out who you are? What then?"

"He won't. The original birth certificate is
sealed, and obviously Ash and Susan never told
him. There's no possible way that he could find
out."

"Famous last words."

She brushed off her sister's concerns. "Just be
happy for me, okay? This is what I want."

"Oh, honey, I am happy for you. I just don't want
to see you hurt."

"I won't be. It's foolproof." As long as she didn't
do something stupid, like fall for Coop. "So anyway, that's why you can't stay with me. I'm living
in his Upper East Side penthouse apartment."

"Sounds…roomy."

Not that roomy. "Joy, you can't stay here."

"Why not? You said this Coop is a good guy. I'm
sure he wouldn't mind."

"Joy—"

"You could at least ask. Because frankly I have
nowhere else to go. My credit cards are maxed out
and I have three dollars in my checking account.
My agent had to lend me the money for the ticket,
which of course is nonrefundable. If I can't stay
with you, I'm crashing on a park bench."

She would pay for a hotel for her sister if she
could, but there wasn't a decent place within thirty

blocks that was less that one-fifty a night. The expense of moving their dad had taken up all of Sierra's cash, and like Joy, her credit cards were maxed out. It was going to take her months to catch up. And though she hated the idea of taking advantage of Coop's hospitality, this could be the perfect opportunity for a dose of emotional blackmail. "I'll ask him on one condition."

"Anything."

"You have to swear that when you're here you'll come with me to see Dad."

She sighed heavily. "Si, you know how I feel about those places. They creep me out."

"Just recently I was able to move him into a really nice place in Jersey. It's not creepy at all."

"It's just the idea of all those old, sick people... ugh."

She fought the urge to tell her sister to grow up. "This is Dad we're talking about. The man who raised you, remember?"

"According to what you told me the last time we talked, he's not even going to know I'm there. So what's the point?"

"We don't know that for sure. And he probably doesn't have much time left. This could be the last time you see him alive."

"Do you really think that's how I want to remember him?"

And did she think Sierra enjoyed bearing the

brunt of his illness alone? Both emotionally and financially. "I'm sorry, but this is nonnegotiable. Either you promise, or it's the park bench for you."

Joy was quiet for several seconds, then she sighed again and said, "Fine, I'll go see him."

"And I'll ask Coop if you can stay." He had already done so much for her, had been so accommodating, she didn't want him to think that she was taking advantage of his hospitality. Yet she had little doubt that he would say yes. He seemed to like to keep up the "good guy" persona. On the bright side, Joy wouldn't be coming in for another week and a half, so Sierra could wait at least another week to ask him. Surely by then she would have worked off the last favor. She couldn't think of anything worse than being indebted to a man like Coop. There might just come a day when he called in the debt and demanded payment.

She would do this one thing for her sister's sake, but after that she would never ask Coop for a favor again.

"Dude, they're Russian models," Vlad said, but with his thick accent, *dude* came out sounding more like *dute*. "These babes are *super hot*. You can't say no."

As Coop had explained to his other former teammate, Niko, who had called him last night, he had turned over a new leaf. His days of staying out all night partying and bringing home women—even if they were *super hot*—were over. Vlad's call suggested that either he hadn't talked to Niko or he didn't think Coop had been serious.

"Sorry dude, you're going to have to count me out. Like I told Niko, I'm a family man now."

"But you find nanny, yes?"

"Yes, but I'm still responsible for the twins. They need me around."

Vlad grumbled a bit and gave him a serious ribbing for "losing his touch," but it didn't bother Coop. He said goodbye and reached down to pick up the toy Ivy had flung onto the sidewalk from the stroller and gave it back to her. The warm morning breeze rustled the newspapers on the table beside them on the café patio, and as he caught a glimpse of Sierra through the front window, standing in line, waiting to order them a cappuccino, Coop felt utterly content.

Besides, if the deal went through and he bought the team, the entire dynamic of his relationship with his former teammates would change. He would go from being their teammate and partner in crime to their boss. But he was ready to make that change.

He stuck his phone back in his shorts pocket and adjusted the stroller so that the twins were shaded from the morning sun. It would be another scorching day as July quickly approached, but at nine-thirty the temperature was an ideal seventy-five degrees. Most days, before the twins, he wouldn't have even been out of bed yet. In his twenties he could have easily spent the entire night out, slept a few hours, then arrived to practice on time and given a stellar performance. Recently though, the late nights out had been taking their toll. Parties and barhopping until 5:00 a.m. usually meant sleeping half the day away.

These days he was in bed before midnight— sometimes even earlier—and up with the sun. He had always been more of a night owl and had figured that the radical change to his schedule would be jarring, but he found that he actually liked getting up early. This morning he had woken before dawn, made coffee and sat on the rooftop terrace to watch the sun rise. He came back down with his empty cup a while later to find Sierra, still in her nightgown, fixing the twins their morning bottles.

She had jumped out of her skin when he said good morning, clearly surprised to find that he was already up. And though he'd tried to be a gentleman and not ogle her, he found himself staring at her cleavage again. And her legs. A woman as attractive as Sierra couldn't walk around half-naked with a man in the house and expect him to look the other way. And the fact that she hadn't tried to cover herself, nor did she set any speed records mixing the formula and filling the bottle, told him that maybe she liked him looking.

He glanced through the front window of the café and saw that she had inched ahead several feet in line and was only a few customers away from the counter. It had been his idea to stop for coffee and also his idea to come with her and the girls for their morning walk. He had just gotten back from jogging in the park as she was walking out the door. And it was an intrusion on her routine that had Sierra's panties in a serious twist. No big surprise considering the way she had been avoiding him the past week. He was sure it had everything to do with their conversation the day they moved her dad into the new nursing home. She could pretend all she liked, but she wasn't fooling him. She wanted him just as much as he wanted her.

A shadow passed over him and he looked up expecting Sierra, surprised to find an unfamiliar young woman in athletic attire standing by the table clutching a bottled water.

"Mr. Landon," she gushed, sounding a little out of breath. "Hi. I just wanted to say, I'm a *huge* fan."

Her long blond hair was pulled back in a ponytail and a sheen of sweat glazed her forehead. She must have been jogging past and noticed him sitting there. He wasn't really in the mood to deal with a fan, but he turned on the charm and said, "Thank you, Miss…"

"It's Amber. Amber Radcliff."

"It's nice to meet you, Amber."

Short and petite, she could have easily passed for seventeen, but he had the feeling she was closer to twenty-five. Just the right age. She was also very attractive, not to mention slender and toned. In fact, she was exactly the sort of woman he would normally be attracted to, yet when she smiled down at him, he didn't feel so much as a twinge of interest. She didn't even seem to notice that there was a stroller beside him with two infants inside.

"I've been a hockey fan, like, my *whole* life," she said, slipping uninvited into the empty seat across from him. "My dad has season tickets and we never missed a home game. I know you probably hear this all the time, but I am truly your number-one fan."

Her and a couple hundred thousand other fans. "Well, then I'm glad you stopped to say hi."

"The team just hasn't been the same since you retired. Last season was such a disappointment. I mean, they didn't even make the championships."

"I'm sure things will turn around next season." Because he would be in charge. Negotiations were currently at a standstill, but he was confident the current owner would come around and accept Coop's very reasonable offer.

Sierra appeared at the table, holding two cappuccinos and looking annoyed, not that he blamed her with some strange woman sitting in her chair. "Excuse me."

Amber looked up, gave Sierra a quick once-over, flashed her an oh-no-you-didn't look and said, "Excuse *me,* but I saw him first."

Chapter 7

Sierra's brows rose, and Coop stifled a laugh. It was like that sometimes with fans. They figured just because they'd shelled out the cash to watch him bang a puck around the ice, they had some sort of claim on his personal time.

"Sierra," he said, "this is Amber. She's my biggest fan."

Sierra set the drinks down on the table with a clunk. "Charmed to meet you, Amber, but you're in my seat."

"Oh…sorry." Amber flushed a vivid shade of pink and awkwardly stood. "I didn't realize…"

"It's all good," Coop said, smiling up at her.

"Give my best to your dad, and tell him I said thanks for being such a loyal fan. And don't give up on the team. They'll come back strong next season, I guarantee it."

She mumbled a goodbye, tripping on the wheel of the stroller in her haste to get away.

"Well, that was interesting," Sierra said, sliding into her seat.

"It's the price you pay as a celebrity, I guess."

"Are all your fans that rude?"

"Some are a bit more aggressive than others, but no harm done. Besides, without the fans, I wouldn't have had a job. There wouldn't be a league, and I would have no team to buy." He took a sip of his cappuccino. "Delicious. Thanks."

"Were the twins okay?"

"Fine. Although Ivy keeps tossing her toy on the ground."

"Because she knows you'll pick it back up again."

"They do have me wrapped," he admitted, smiling down at them. And he would no doubt continue to spoil them until they were all grown up.

Sierra was quiet for a minute, a furrow in her brow as she gazed absently at her cup, running her thumb around the edge. She had seemed distracted all morning, as if there was something on her mind. Something bothering her. He would like to know if it was something he had done.

"Penny for your thoughts," he said.

She looked up. "You don't want to know."

Whatever it was, it looked as if it wasn't pleasant. If she was about to tell him she was quitting, after so adamantly vowing her dedication to the girls, he was going to be seriously pissed off. "Is there a problem?"

"Not exactly, no."

"Then what is it exactly?"

"I need a favor. A really big one. And I want you to know that you are under absolutely no obligation to say yes. But I promised I would at least ask."

"So ask me."

Ivy started to fuss, so Sierra reached into the diaper bag for a bottle of juice and handed it to her, and when Fern saw it and began to fuss, she gave her one, too. "The thing is, my sister has an audition in New York so she's coming to visit."

"Do you need time off?"

She shook her head. "No. Anything we do together we can take the girls with us. The thing is, she would normally crash at my place. Unfortunately, I hadn't actually gotten around to telling her about my new job, so she just assumed she could stay with me. I guess she had to borrow money from her agent for the plane ticket, which is nonrefundable of course, and she doesn't have money for a hotel."

"So you want to know if she can stay with us."

"I wouldn't even ask, but Joy is a master at making me feel guilty. She threatened to sleep on a park bench."

"When? And how long?"

"She's flying in around noon tomorrow and staying a week. Which I know is a really long time."

He shrugged and said, "That's fine."

"You're sure you don't mind? Because you shouldn't be expected to invite complete strangers into your home."

"But she's not a stranger. She's your sister. And for the record, it's not a very big favor. If you asked me for a kidney, or a lung, that would be a big deal."

"But she's a stranger to you, and I feel like a dork for putting you on the spot."

He drew in a breath and sighed. Would she ever learn that he wasn't the ogre she seemed to have pegged him for? "Because we both know that deep down I'm a big fat jerk who would never do something nice for someone if not forced."

She shot him a look. "You know that isn't what I mean."

Sometimes she made him feel that way, as if she always expected the worst from him, despite the fact that in the two weeks he had known her, he had been nothing but courteous and accommodating and he hadn't once complained about anything. Someone must have done a serious number on her to make her so wary of trusting him. And trusting her own instincts.

"She's welcome to stay. And I'm not saying that because I feel obligated or because I'm trying to get into your pants."

Sierra bit her lip and lowered her eyes. "I didn't think that."

Not that he didn't want to. Get into her pants, that is. But not at the expense of losing her as the twins' nanny, and certainly not if she felt she owed him out of some sense of duty or repayment.

Ivy tossed her bottle this time, so far that it hit the chair leg of the elderly woman sitting at the next table. She leaned down to pick it up, carefully wiped it off with her napkin, then gave it back to Ivy, who squealed happily.

"What beautiful little girls," the woman said with a smile. "They look just like their mommy, but they have their daddy's eyes."

There didn't seem any point in trying to explain the situation, so Coop just smiled and thanked the woman. When he turned back to Sierra, she looked troubled. Did the idea that someone might mistake the twins for their children disturb her so much? There were an awful lot of women out there who would be happy to earn that distinction. Clearly she was not one of them.

She leaned in and whispered, "You don't think they look like me, do you?"

"I can see why someone might think you're their mother."

"What do you mean?"

"You have similar skin tone and dark hair. But do you actually look alike?" He shrugged. "I don't really see it. And other than the fact that they have two eyes, the similarities between them and me pretty much stop there." He paused then said, "However, to see you with the twins, one would naturally assume they are yours."

She cocked her head slightly. "Why is that?"

"Because you treat them like a mother would treat her own children."

"I'm not sure what you mean. How else am I supposed to treat them?"

"Susan once told me that before she and Ash adopted the girls, she would sit at the park on her lunch break and watch the kids on the playground, hoping that some day she could watch her own kids playing there. She said she could always tell which of the adults were parents and which were nannies or au pairs. The parents interacted with their kids. She said you could just tell that they wanted to be there, that they cared. The caregivers, however, stood around in packs basically ignoring the kids and talking amongst themselves, occasionally shouting out a reprimand. She said that she made her mind up then that if she ever was blessed with a baby, she would quit working and stay home. And she did."

"It sounds like she was a really good mom," Sierra said softly.

"She was. So I'm sure you can imagine how I must have felt, knowing I had to hire a nanny, when Susan was so against the idea. Knowing that there was no way I could manage it alone, be both a mom and a dad to them. Feeling as if I was letting them down, as if I had failed them somehow. But then you came along, and in two weeks time you have surpassed my expectations by leaps and bounds. I can rest easy knowing that even when I can't be around, the twins are loved and well cared for. And even though they don't have a mom, they have someone who gives them all the love and affection a real mom would."

Sierra bit her lip, and her eyes welled up. He hadn't meant to make her cry. He just wanted her to know what an important part of their lives she had become and how much he appreciated it. And that it had nothing to do with wanting to get into her pants.

He reached across the table and wrapped his hand around hers, half expecting her to pull away. "So when I do something nice for you, it's because I want you to know how much we appreciate having you around. And I want you to be as happy with us as we are with you. I want you to feel like you're a part of our family. Unconventional as it is."

She swiped at her eyes with her free hand. "Thank you."

Ivy shrieked and threw her bottle again, and this time Fern followed suit. Coop let go of Sierra's hand to pick them up. "I think the natives are getting restless."

She sniffled and swiped at her eyes again. "Yeah, we should probably get moving."

Leaving their barely touched cappuccinos behind, they gathered their things and left the café. Coop had the overwhelming desire to link his fingers through hers, but with both her hands clutching the stroller handle he couldn't have anyway.

It defied logic, this irrational need to be close to her. To do things like skip meetings and ignore his friends just to spend time with her and the twins. He could have practically any other woman that he wanted. Women who showered him with flattery and clawed over each other for his attention. Women willing to be whatever and whoever he wanted just to make him happy.

Didn't it just figure that he had to fall for the one woman who didn't want him?

While the girls napped Sierra did laundry, wishing that this morning at the coffee shop had never happened.

Did Coop have to be so darned nice all the time? That stuff about her taking care of the girls was hands down the sweetest and kindest thing anyone had ever said to her. He was making it really hard for her to not like him. In fact, when he'd taken her hand in his…oh, my God. His hand was big and strong and had a roughness that should have been unpleasant, yet all she could think about was him rubbing it all over her. If they hadn't been in a public place, she might have done something completely insane like fling the table aside, plant herself in his lap and kiss him senseless. And then she would have divested him of the tank top and running shorts and put *her* hands all over *him*. The fact that he was still sweaty, unshaven and disheveled from his run should have been a turnoff, yet when she imagined touching his slick skin, feeling the rasp of his beard against her cheek, tasting the salty tang of his lips, she'd gone into hormone overload. She didn't even like sweaty, disheveled, unshaven men.

Why was she even thinking about this?

As good as it would be—and she *knew* it would be good—it would be a mistake. She still wasn't sure why he was attracted to her in the first place. Was it convenience—because he said himself that was how he normally chose his women? And what could be more convenient than a woman living right under his roof? Or was it the thrill of the chase fueling his interest? And if she let him catch her, just how long would it take before he got bored?

Probably not very long. And after he dumped her, she would find herself heartbroken, out of a job, homeless, and, worst of all, ripped away from her children. She simply had too much to lose. She had to do what was best for them.

The spin cycle ended and she tossed the damp linens into the dryer along with a dryer sheet and set it on High, then she dumped hers and the girls' dirty clothes in the washing machine.

She poured a scoop of detergent over the clothes, then realized she was still wearing the shirt that Fern had flung a glob of pureed carrots all over at lunch. Ms. Densmore was at the market and Coop had left an hour ago for a meeting that he said would drag on until at least dinnertime, so figuring she could make it from the laundry room to her bedroom undetected in her bra, she pulled the shirt over her head, spritzed the spot with stain remover and tossed it in, too.

She shut the lid, started the machine and headed out of the laundry room…stopping dead in her tracks when she realized that Coop was in the kitchen.

For a second she thought that her mind must be playing tricks on her. No one's luck could be *that* bad.

She blinked. Then she blinked again.

Nope, that was definitely Coop, his hip wedged against the island countertop, his eyes lowered as he sorted through the mail he must have picked up on his way in. And any second now he was going to look up and see her standing there in her bra.

She could make a run for her bedroom, but she couldn't imagine doing anything so undignified, nor would she run back to the laundry room. Besides, Coop must have sensed her there because he looked up. And *he* blinked. Then he blinked again. Then his eyes settled on her breasts and he said, "You're not wearing a shirt."

She could have at least covered herself with her hands or grabbed the dish towel hanging on the oven door, but for some weird reason she just stood there, as if, deep down she *wanted* him to see her half-naked. Which she was pretty sure she didn't.

"Ms. Densmore is at the market, and I didn't think you would be home so soon," she said.

"My lawyer had to cut the meeting short," he explained, his gaze still fixed below her neck. "For which I plan to thank him *profusely* the next time I see him."

The heat in his eyes was so intense she actually thought her bra might ignite. "That explains it then."

"Out of curiosity, do you always walk around in your bra when no one is home?"

"My shirt had carrots on it from the girls' lunch. I threw it in the washing machine." When he didn't respond she said, "You could be a gentleman and look the other way."

He tossed the mail on the counter, but it hit the edge, slid off and landed on the floor instead. "I could. And I would if I thought for a second that you didn't like me looking at you."

There he went, reading her mind again. She really wished he would stop doing that. "Who says I like it?"

"If you didn't you would have made some attempt to cover yourself or leave the room. And your heart wouldn't be racing."

Right again.

"Not to mention you're giving off enough pheromones right now to take down an entire professional hockey team. And you know what that means."

She didn't have a clue, but the idea of what it might be made her knees weak. "What does it mean?"

"It means that I *have* to kiss you."

Chapter 8

"Coop, that would be a really bad idea," Sierra said, but her voice was trembling.

Maybe it was, but right now, Coop didn't care. He crossed the room toward her and she held her breath. "All you have to do is tell me no."

"I just did."

He stopped a few inches from her and he could actually feel the heat radiating from her bare skin. "You said it would be a bad idea, but you didn't actually say don't do it."

"But that was what I meant."

"So say it."

She opened her mouth and closed it again.

Oh, yeah, she wanted him. He reached up and ran the pad of his thumb up her arm, from elbow to shoulder, then back down again. Sierra shivered.

"Tell me to stop," he said, and when she didn't say a word, when she just gazed up at him with lust-filled eyes, her cheeks flush with excitement, he knew she was as good as his.

He cupped her cheek in his palm, stroked with his thumb, and he could feel her melting, giving in. "Last chance," he said.

She blew out an exasperated breath. "Oh, for heaven's sake just shut up and *kiss* me already!"

He was smiling as he lowered his head, slanting his mouth over hers. When their lips touched, and her tongue slid against his, desire slammed him from every direction at once.

Holy hell.

Never in his life had he felt such an intense connection to a woman just from kissing her. Of course, he'd never met a woman quite like her. And he knew without a doubt that a kiss was never going to be enough. He wanted more…*needed* it in a way he had never needed anything before.

She slid her arms around his neck, trying to get closer, but his arm was in the way. She broke the kiss and looked down at his crotch, which he was cupping in his free hand, then she looked up at him questioningly.

"Just in case I was wrong and you followed through on your threat."

"Threat?"

"You said that if I tried to kiss you I would be wearing the family jewels for earrings."

She laughed and shook her head. "You do realize, the fact that you thought I might actually do it makes you about a million times more appealing."

He grinned. "I told you, I'm irresistible."

"Coop, this is so wrong," she said.

He slid his hands across her bare back. Sierra sighed and her eyes drifted closed. "Nothing that feels this good could be wrong."

She must have agreed because she wrapped her arms around his neck, pulled his head down and kissed him. He might have taken her right there in the kitchen—he sure wanted to—but Sierra deserved better than sex on the counter or up against the refrigerator. She wasn't some woman he'd picked up in a bar or at a party. She was special. She wasn't in it for the cheap thrill of being with a celebrity. This would mean something to her, something profound. She deserved tenderness and romance, and when he did make love to her—which he would do, there was no longer any doubt about that—he wanted to take his time. He didn't want to have to worry about things like the twins waking up from their nap, which they were likely to do pretty soon. And though he could be content to stand there kissing and touching her until they did, Ms. Densmore could walk in at any moment. Not that he gave a crap what *she* thought, but he didn't want Sierra to feel embarrassed or uncomfortable. He really *cared* about her, which was just too damned weird.

Could he possibly be falling in love with her?

He didn't *do* love. Hell, he usually didn't do next week. To him women were nothing more than a way to pass the time. And not because of some psychological wound or fear of commitment. He hadn't been profoundly wounded by his parents' death or dumped by his one true love. He hadn't been double-crossed or cheated on. He had just been too focused on his career to make the time for a long-term relationship. He also hadn't met anyone he'd cared so deeply for that he couldn't live without them. But it was bound to happen eventually, wasn't it? What was the saying? There was someone for everyone? Maybe Sierra was his someone.

It took every bit of restraint he possessed to break the kiss, when there was really no guarantee she would ever let him kiss her again. He was giving her time to rethink this, to change her mind. But that was just a chance he had to take.

He took her hands, pulled them from around his neck and cradled them against his chest. "We should stop before we get too carried away."

She looked surprised and disappointed and

maybe a little relieved, too. "The girls will be up soon."

"Exactly. And unless you want Ms. Densmore to see you half-naked, you might want to put a shirt on."

She looked down, as though she had completely forgotten she wasn't wearing one. "It might almost be worth it to see the look on her face."

From behind the kitchen they heard the service-entrance door open. If she wanted to see the look on Ms. Densmore's face, this was her chance. Instead she turned tail and darted from the room, ponytail swishing.

He chuckled at her retreating back. Not so tough, was she?

Ms. Densmore appeared with two canvas shopping bags full of groceries. He'd told her a million times that she could just order the groceries and have them delivered, but she insisted on walking to the market and carrying the bags back herself nearly every day.

When she saw him standing there she said, "I didn't expect you home so soon."

She looked tired, so he took the bags from her and set them up on the countertop. "Meeting ended early."

While she put her purse away he poked through the bags, finding a variety of fresh vegetables, several jars of baby food and a package of boneless, skinless chicken breasts. "Chicken for dinner to-night?"

"Chicken parmesan," she said, looking curiously at the mail on the floor and stooping to pick it up. "We need to talk."

He could see by her expression, which was more troubled than sour, that there was a problem. "What's up?"

She put the chicken in the fridge, closed the door and turned to him. "I'm afraid I can't work for you any longer."

He knew she wasn't thrilled with having the twins around, but he didn't think she was miserable enough to quit. She may not have been a very nice person, but she was a good housekeeper and he hated to lose her. "Is there a specific problem? And if so, is there anything I can do to fix it?"

"I took this job because it fit certain criteria. First, there were no children and not likely to ever be any, and second, you were rarely here. I like to be alone and left to my own devices. Since you brought the twins here everything has changed. I have to cook all the time and I hate cooking." She paused and said bitterly, "Not to mention that your nanny has been *tormenting* me."

He couldn't help laughing, which only made her glare at him. "I'm sorry, but *Sierra?* She's not exactly the tormenting type."

"She plays tricks on me."

"What kind of tricks?"

"She moves things around just to irritate me. She takes the milk off the door and puts it on the shelf and she rearranges things in the laundry room. She's petty and childish."

"I'll have a talk with her."

"It's too late for that. Besides, as long as the twins are around I won't ever be happy working here again."

He was sorry she felt that way, but neither did he want an unhappy employee. Or one who couldn't appreciate two sweet and beautiful infants. "So is this your two-week notice?"

"I got a new job and they need me to start immediately, so today is my last day."

"Today?" He couldn't believe she would leave him in a lurch that way.

"Let's not pretend that you wouldn't have eventually fired me. *She* would have insisted."

"Sierra? That's not her call."

"When she becomes the lady of the house it will be, and you know that will be the eventual outcome."

Coop had no idea that his feelings for Sierra were so obvious. And she was right. If he and Sierra did ever get married, she would insist that he get rid of Ms. Densmore, and of course he would because he would do practically anything she asked to make her happy.

"Don't worry," Ms. Densmore said. "You'll call a service and have a replacement before the week is out."

She was right. He just hated the idea of training someone new. "Do you mind my asking who you're going to be working for?"

"A diplomat and his wife. Their children are grown and they spend three weeks out of every month traveling. I'll pretty much be left alone to do my job."

"That sounds perfect for you."

"With the exception of the past month, it really has been a pleasure working for you, Mr. Landon. I just can't be happy here any longer. I'm too old and set in my ways to change."

"I understand."

"I'm sure Sierra can handle things until you find someone new."

He'd seen Sierra's bedroom. Housekeeping was a concept that seemed to escape her completely. Besides, with two infants to care for, she wouldn't have time to cook and clean, too. He needed someone within the next few days at the latest.

"Dinner will be ready at six-thirty," she said. "And I'm making a double recipe so there will be some left over. You can warm it for dinner later this week."

"Thanks."

She turned and busied herself starting dinner

as Coop went to look for Sierra, to tell her what he was sure she would consider very good news. The nursery door was closed, meaning the girls were still asleep, so he knocked on Sierra's bedroom door instead. She opened it after a few seconds, and he was sorry to see that she had changed into a clean shirt.

"Have you got a minute?" he asked.

"Of course." She stepped aside and let him in. The bed was unmade, there was a bath towel draped over the chair, the desk was piled with papers and junk, and there was a pile of books and magazines on the floor next to the bed.

"Excuse the mess," she said. "I just can't ever seem to find the time to straighten up. After being with the girls all day I'm usually too exhausted to do much of anything."

Which meant doubling as housekeeper would be out of the question. "It's your room. If you want to keep it messy, that's your choice."

"I know it drives Ms. Densmore crazy, but she won't set foot in my room."

"Funny you should mention her. She's the reason I came to talk to you."

A worry line bisected Sierra's brow. "She didn't see me without my shirt on, did she?"

"Nope. But the way I hear it, you've been tormenting my housekeeper."

* * *

Uh-oh. Someone had tattled on her.

Sierra put on her best innocent look and asked, "What do you mean?"

Coop folded his arms, and though he was trying to look tough, there was humor in his eyes. "Don't even try to pretend that you don't know what I'm talking about. You know I can always tell when you're lying."

It was that mind-reading thing that he did. *So* annoying. "To call it 'torment' is an exaggeration. They were just…*pranks.* And you can't tell me that she didn't deserve it. She's so *mean.*"

"She just quit."

She gasped and slapped a hand over her heart. "She didn't!"

"She did, just now in the kitchen. This is her last day."

"Oh my gosh, Coop. I'm so sorry. I wanted to annoy her, not make her leave. This is all my fault. Do you want me to talk to her? Promise to behave from now on?"

He grinned and shook his head. "You may have accelerated the process, but she would have left eventually anyway. She said she's been unhappy since the girls moved in. It wasn't what she signed on for. I hired her five years ago, when I was still playing hockey and barely ever here. She liked it that way."

"I still feel bad."

"Don't," he said, and gestured to a framed photo on the dresser. "Is that your mom?"

She smiled and nodded. It was Sierra's favorite shot of her. It was taken in the park, on a sunny spring afternoon. Her mom was sitting cross-legged in the grass on the old patchwork quilt they always used for picnics or at the beach, and she was looking up at the camera, smiling. "Wasn't she beautiful?"

He walked over and picked it up. "Very beautiful."

"She was always smiling, always happy. And it was infectious. You could not be in the same room and not feel like smiling. And she loved hugs, loved to snuggle. She and I would curl up on the love seat together every Sunday and read books or do crossword puzzles all day long. She was so much fun, always thinking up new adventures, trying new things. And my dad loved her so much. He never remarried. He didn't even date very often. I don't think he ever got over losing her. They never fought, never bickered. They had the perfect marriage."

"She was Asian?" Coop asked.

She nodded. "Her grandmother was Chinese. I used to wish that I looked more like her."

"You do look like her."

"I actually favor my dad more. Joy looks more like she did."

"You really miss her."

She nodded. "Every day."

He walked over to where she stood, took her hand and tugged her to him. She didn't put up a fight when he pulled her close and looped his arms around her, and it felt so *good* to lay her head on his chest, to listen to the beat of his heart. He was so big and strong and he smelled so yummy. And kissing him…oh, my. It was a little slice of heaven. And now it was just going to be the two of them, alone in the house—with the girls, too, of course. The idea made her both excited and nervous. She knew that kissing Coop had been a bad idea and that letting it go any further would be a mistake of epic proportions. But couldn't she pretend, just for a little while, that they actually had a chance? That an affair with Coop wouldn't ruin everything?

No, because for whatever reason, and though it defied logic, he seemed to genuinely like her. If all he cared about was getting her between the sheets, that's where they would be right now. And if she believed for a second that his feelings for her were anything but a passing phase, she wouldn't hesitate to drag him there herself. Unfortunately, she and Coop were just too different. It would never work.

She untangled herself from his arms and backed away. "We need to talk."

"Why do I get the feeling that I'm not going to like this?"

"What happened earlier, it was really, *really* nice."

"But…?"

"You and I both know that it's not going to work."

"We don't know that."

"I don't want to have an affair."

"I don't, either. I know this will be hard for you to believe, but I want more this time. I'm ready."

If only that were true. "How can you know that? You've known me what? Two weeks?"

"I can't explain it. All I know is that I've never wanted anyone the way I want you. It just…feels right."

His expression was so earnest, she didn't doubt he believed every word he said, and oh how she wished she could throw caution to the wind and believe him, too. But there was too much at stake. "I want you, too, Coop. And I don't doubt that it will be really, really good for a while, but eventually something will go wrong. You'll be unhappy, and I'll be unhappy, then things will get awkward, and though you'll hate to have to do it, you'll fire me because it will be what's for the best."

"I wouldn't do that."

"Yes, you would. You wouldn't have any other choice. Because think about it—what are you going to do? Dump me, then bring other women home right in front of me?"

"You're assuming it won't work. But what if it does? We could be really good together."

"That isn't a chance I'm willing to take." And there was no way to make him understand why without telling him the truth. And if she was looking for a way to get fired, that was it.

"So, the job is more important than your feelings for me?" he asked.

"The girls need me more than you do. And, if I lose this job, my father goes back into that hellhole he was in. I won't do that to him."

She could tell by his frown that he knew she was right, he just didn't want to accept it.

"I could fire you now," he said. "Then you would be free to date me."

She raised her brows at him. "So what you're saying is, if I don't sleep with you, you'll fire me?"

His frown deepened, and he rubbed a hand across his jaw. "When you say it like that it sounds really sleazy."

"That's because it *is* sleazy. It's also sexual harassment." Not that she believed his threat was anything but an empty one. He just wasn't used to not getting his way, but he would have to *get* used to it.

In her jeans pocket, the cell phone started to ring and she pulled it out to check the display. When she saw the number of the nursing home her heart skipped like a stone on a very deep, cold lake. That always happened when someone called about her dad because her first thought was inevitably that he had passed away. But they had lots of other reasons for calling her. So why, this time, did she have an especially bad feeling?

"I have to take this," she told Coop. "It's the nursing home."

She answered the phone, pulse pounding, her heart in her throat.

"Miss Evans, this is Meg Douglas, administrator of Heartland Nursing Center."

"Hi, Meg, what can I do for you?" she asked, hoping she said something simple, like there was a form that needed to be signed or a treatment they needed authorization for.

"I'm so sorry to have to inform you that your father passed away."

Chapter 9

Coop changed the twins' diapers, wrestled them into their pajamas, then sat in the rocking chair with them, one on each arm, but neither made it even halfway through their bottle before they were sound asleep. It had been a busy afternoon of going first to the nursing home so Sierra could see her dad one last time, then to the funeral home to make the final arrangements. By the time they finally got home it was well past the twins' bedtime.

Ms. Densmore had left dinner warming in the oven and, in a show of kindness that surprised both him and Sierra, a note on the refrigerator expressing her sympathy for Sierra's loss. She wasn't so sorry that she offered to stay on a few days longer, though. Not that he expected her to.

He got up and carried the twins' limp little bodies to their cribs, kissed them and tucked them in. For a minute he stood there, watching them sleep, feeling so…peaceful. At first he'd believed that once he hired someone to care for the twins, life would go back to the way it had been before he got the girls. Two months ago, if someone had told him he would enjoy being a parent and be content as a family man, he would have laughed in their face. He figured he would be happy playing the role of the fun and cool uncle, showering them with gifts and seeing that they were financially set while someone else dealt with the day-to-day issues. The feedings and the diapers and all the messy emotional stuff that would later come with hormonal teenaged girls. He realized now that they deserved better than that. They deserved a real, conventional family.

Shutting the nursery door softly behind him, he took the half-finished bottles to the kitchen and stuck them in the fridge, just in case one or both of the girls woke up hungry in the middle of the night. His and Sierra's dinner dishes were still in the sink, so he rinsed them, stuck them in the dishwasher and set it to run, recalling the days when he and his brother hadn't even been able to afford a dishwasher, and doing them by hand had been Coop's responsibility. He'd had to do his own laundry and cook three days a week, too. Maybe he was spoiled now, but he had no desire to return to those days, even temporarily. And with caring for the twins, her sister's visit and planning her dad's memorial service, Sierra definitely wouldn't have time to clean and cook. He didn't even know if she *could* cook.

He made a mental note to call a service first thing tomorrow and set up interviews for a new housekeeper as soon as humanly possible.

Though he normally drank wine in the evenings, a cold beer had a nice ring to it tonight, so he grabbed two from the fridge. He switched out the kitchen light, hooked the baby monitor to his belt and walked to the rooftop terrace where he'd sent Sierra while he got the twins settled for bed. She'd balked, of course, and gave him the usual line about how he had done enough already and she needed to do her job, but with a little persuasion she'd caved. It was strange, but lately he'd begun thinking of her as not so much a nanny, but the two of them as partners in raising the girls. And he liked it that way.

The sun had nearly set, so he hit the switch and turned on the party lights that hung around the perimeter of the terrace.

Sierra looked up from the lounge chair where she sat, her knees tucked up under her chin. When they got home she had changed into shorts and a tank top, and her feet were bare. He half expected her to be crying, but her eyes were dry. The only time she had cried today was when she'd gone into her dad's room.

"Are the twins in bed?" she asked.

"Out cold before their heads hit the mattress," he said, holding up one of the two beers. "Can I interest you in a cold one?"

"That actually sounds really good, thanks."

He twisted the tops off and handed her one of the bottles, then stretched out in the chair beside hers.

She took a long, deep pull on her drink, sighed contentedly and said, "That hits the spot. Thank you for helping me with the twins today and for driving me all over the place. I'm not sure how I would have managed without you."

"It was my pleasure," he told her, as he had the dozen other times she had thanked him during the day. He took a drink of his beer and cradled the bottle in his lap between his thighs. "How are you doing?"

"You know, I'm okay. I'm not nearly as upset as I thought I would be. I mean, I'm sad and I'm going to miss him, but the man who was my dad has been gone for a while now. No one should have to live that way. For his sake I'm relieved that it's over, that he's at peace." She looked over at Coop. "Does that make me a terrible person?"

"Not at all."

"I'm worried about Joy, though."

"She didn't take the news well?"

"No, she took it a little too well. She hasn't actually seen our father in almost four years. That's why I thought it was so important she see him when she was here. Now she'll never get the chance. I'm worried that she's going to regret it for the rest of her life. I asked if she wanted them to hold off on cremating him, so she could at least see him, but she said no. She doesn't want to remember him like that."

"It's her decision."

"I know." She took another swallow of beer and set the bottle on the ground beside her.

"Is there anything I can do? Do you need anything for the memorial? I know money is tight for you and your sister."

"I'm not letting you pay for my dad's memorial, so don't even suggest it."

"So what will you do?"

She shrugged. "I haven't quite figured that out yet."

"Is there insurance? If you don't mind my asking."

"There's a small policy. But after the medical bills and the funeral costs, there won't be much left. It's going to be at least a couple of weeks before I get a check."

"How about I give you an advance on next week's salary? Or more if you need it."

She hesitated, chewing her lip.

"I don't mind," he said. "And I'm pretty sure I can trust you to stick around."

She hesitated, picking at the label on her beer bottle. He didn't get why she was so wary of accepting his help. Isn't that what friendship was about? And he definitely considered her a friend. He would like to consider her much more than that if she would let him.

"You're sure it's not an imposition?" she asked.

"If it was, I wouldn't have offered."

"In that case, I would really appreciate it."

"I'll have the money wired into your account first thing in the morning."

"Thank you."

She was quiet for several minutes, so he said, "Penny for your thoughts."

"I was just thinking about the twins and how sad it is that they won't remember their parents. At least I got fourteen years with my mom. I have enough wonderful memories to keep her alive in my mind forever. Or maybe, if the girls had to lose their mother and father, it was better now than, say, five or ten years from now. That way they don't know what they've missed. There was no emotional connection. Or maybe I'm totally wrong." She shrugged. "Who knows really."

"Losing Ash and Susan doesn't mean they won't have two loving parents."

She looked confused. "What do you mean?"

"The twins shouldn't be raised by an uncle. It's not good enough for them, either. They deserve a real family."

Her face paled. "Are you saying you plan to give them up?"

"No, of course not. I love them. I'm ready to settle down and be a family man. So I've decided to adopt them."

Sierra bit down hard on her lip, blinking back the tears that were welling in her eyes. She had wanted to believe that Coop had changed, that he would be a good father, but until just now she hadn't been sure. It felt as if an enormous weight had been lifted off her shoulders, as if she could breathe for the first time since she heard the horrible news of the crash. She was confident that no matter what happened between her and Coop, the twins would be okay. He loved them and wanted to be their father.

She looked over at Coop and realized he was watching her, worry creasing his brow. "I hope those are happy tears you're fighting," he said. "That you aren't thinking what a terrible parent I'll be and how sorry you feel for the girls."

More like tears of relief. "Actually, I was thinking how lucky they are to have someone like you." She reached for his hand and he folded it around hers. "And how proud Ash and Susan would be and how grateful."

"Come here," he said, tugging on her arm, pulling her out of her chair and into his lap. She curled up against his chest and he wrapped his arms around her, holding her so tight it was a little hard to breathe. And though she couldn't see his face, when he spoke he sounded a little choked up. "Thank you, Sierra. You have no idea how much that means coming from you."

She tucked her face in the crook of his neck, breathed in the scent of his skin. Why did he have to be so wonderful?

"You know the girls are going to need a mother," he said, stroking her hair. "Someone who loves them as much as I do. We could be a family."

"You hardly know me."

"I know how happy I've been since you came into our lives. And how much the twins love you." His hand slipped down to caress her cheek. "I know how crazy you make me and how much I want you."

Did he really want her, or was it that she was convenient? She fit into his new "family plan." And did it really matter? They could be a family. That was what the girls needed, and isn't that was this was about? "And if it doesn't work?"

He tipped her chin up so he could see her face. "Isn't it worth it to at least try?"

Yes, she realized, it was. They were doing it for the girls.

She turned in Coop's lap so she was straddling

his thighs, then she cupped his face in her palms and kissed him. And he was right about one thing. Anything that felt this good couldn't be wrong.

She circled her arms around his neck, sliding her fingers through the softness of his hair, and as she did she could feel the stress leaching from her bones, the empty place in her heart being filled again. After what had been a long, stressful and pretty lousy day, he'd made her feel happy. In fact, she couldn't recall a time in her life when she had been as happy and content as she was with Coop and the twins. That had to mean something, didn't it? She had been trying so hard not to fall for him, maybe it was time to relax and let it happen, let nature take its course. Besides, how could she say no to a man who kissed the way he did? In no time his soft lips, the warm slide of his tongue, had her feeling all restless and achy.

Although she couldn't help noticing that kissing was *all* they were doing. She was practically crawling out of her skin for more, and he seemed perfectly content to run his fingers through her hair and caress her cheeks, but not much else. And when she tried to move things forward, tried to touch him, he took her hands and curled them against his chest.

Now that he had her where he wanted her, had he suddenly developed cold feet? Had he decided that he didn't want her after all? He was aroused, that much was obvious, so why wasn't he moving things forward?

She stopped kissing him. "Okay, what's the deal?"

He looked confused. "Deal?"

"You do know how to do this, right? I mean, it's not your first time or anything?"

One brow arched. "Is that a rhetorical question?"

"You're not doing anything," she said.

"Sure I am. I'm kissing you." He grinned that slightly crooked smile. "And for the record I'm thoroughly enjoying it. Is there something wrong with taking things slow? I want you to be sure about this."

Could she really blame him for being cautious? She was sending some pretty major mixed signals. Coop, though, had been pretty clear about what he wanted from the get-go.

"I want this, Coop," she told him. "I'm ready."

"Ready for what, that's the question," he said. "Am I going to get to second base? Third base? Am I going to knock it out of the park?"

She couldn't resist smiling. Were they really using sports euphemisms? "You can't hit a home run if you don't step up to the plate."

He grinned. "In that case, maybe we should move this party to my bedroom."

Chapter 10

Watching Coop undress—and taking off her own clothes in front of him—was one of the most erotic and terrifying experiences of Sierra's entire life. He had insisted on keeping the bedside lamp on, and she couldn't help but worry that he wouldn't like what he saw. But if he noticed the faint stretch marks on her hips and the side of her belly, or that her tummy wasn't quite as firm as it had been before the twins, he didn't let it show. She was sure that he'd been with women who were thinner and larger busted and all around prettier than she was, yet he looked at her as though she was the most beautiful woman in the world.

Coop seemed completely comfortable in his nudity. And why wouldn't he? He was simply *perfect.* From his rumpled hair to his long, slender feet, and every inch in between. She'd never been crazy about hairy men, so the sprinkling of dark-blond hair across his pecks and the thin trail bisecting his abs was ideal. And all those muscles…wow.

"I've never been with anyone so big," she said.

One brow arched up as he glanced down at his crotch. "I always thought I was sort of average."

She laughed. "I meant muscular."

He grinned. "Oh, *that.*"

But he wasn't *average* anywhere. "I just want to touch you all over."

"I think we can arrange that." He pulled back the blankets, climbed into bed and laid down, then patted the mattress beside him. "Hop in."

Feeling nervous and excited all at once, she slid in beside him. And though she wanted this more than he would ever know, as he pulled her close and started kissing her, she found she couldn't relax. Not that it didn't feel good. But he'd been with a lot of women, and she was willing to bet that compared to most of them she was, at best, a novice. Her experiences with her high school boyfriend had been more awkward than satisfying, and the handful of encounters she'd had while she was in nursing school hadn't exactly been earth-shattering. Her last sexual experience sixteen months ago with the twins' father had at most been a drunken *wham, bam, thank you ma'am* that they both regretted the minute it was over.

She wanted sex to be fun and satisfying. She wanted to feel that spark, that...*connection*. The sensation of being intrinsically linked—if such a thing really existed. Yet every new experience left her feeling disappointed and empty, faking her orgasms just to be polite, wondering if it was something she was doing wrong. What if the same thing happened with Coop? What if she couldn't satisfy him, either? What if she didn't live up to his expectations?

She had herself in such a state that when he cupped a hand over her breast, instead of letting herself enjoy it, she tensed up. He stopped kissing her, pushed himself up on one elbow and gazed down at her. "Now who's just lying there?"

Her cheeks flushed with embarrassment. She was naked, in bed with a gorgeous, sexy man and she was completely blowing it. "I'm sorry."

"Maybe we should stop."

She shook her head. "No. I don't want to stop."

"You have done this before, right?" he teased. "I mean, it's not your first time or anything."

If he wasn't so adorable, she might have slugged him. Instead she found herself smiling. "Yes, I've done this before. But probably not even close to as many times as you have."

He stroked her cheek, a frown settling into the crease between his brows. "And that bothers you?"

"No, of course not. I'm just worried that I won't measure up. That I'm going to disappoint you."

"Sierra, you won't. Trust me."

"But I *could.*"

"Or I could disappoint you. Have you considered that? Maybe I've been with so many women because I'm such a lousy lay no one would sleep with me twice."

She couldn't help it, she laughed. "That is the dumbest thing I've ever heard."

"And for the record, I haven't slept with *that* many women. And not because I haven't had the opportunity. I'm just very selective about who I hop into bed with."

His idea of *not that many* could be three hundred for all she knew. And maybe that should have bothered her, but it didn't. Because she knew it was different this time. He was different. This actually meant something to him.

"What can I do to make you more comfortable?" he asked. "To assure you that your disappointing me isn't even a remote possibility."

"Maybe you could give me some pointers, you know, tell me what you like."

"You could kiss me. I like that. And you mentioned something about touching me all over. That sounds pretty good, too." He took her hand and cradled it against his chest, brushed his lips against hers so sweetly. "We'll take it slow, okay?"

She nodded, feeling more relaxed already. He had a way of putting her at ease. And good to his word he was diligent about telling her exactly what he wanted and where he liked to be touched—which was pretty much everywhere and involved using her hands and her mouth. And after a while of his patient tutoring, she gained the confidence to experiment all on her own, which he seemed to like even more. And Coop was anything but a disappointment. The man knew his way around a woman's body. He made her feel sexy and beautiful.

By the time he reached into the night table drawer for a condom, she was so ready to take that next step, she could barely wait for him to cover himself. He pressed her thighs apart, and she held her breath, but then he just looked at her.

"You're so beautiful," he said.

"Coop, please," she pleaded.

"What, Sierra? What do you want?"

Him. She just wanted him.

But he already knew because he lowered himself over her, and the look of pure ecstasy as he eased himself inside of her almost did her in. He groaned and ran his fingers though her hair, his eyes rolling closed, and she finally felt it, that connection. And it was even more intense, more extraordinary than she ever imagined. This was it. This was what making love was supposed to feel like. And whatever happened between them, as long as she lived, she would never forget this moment.

Everything after that was a blur of skin against skin, mingling breath and soft moans and intense pleasure that kept building and building. She wasn't sure who came first, who set whom off, but it was the closest thing to heaven on earth that she had even known. Afterward they lay wrapped in each other's arms, legs intertwined, breathing hard. And all she wanted was to be closer. They could melt together, become one person, and she didn't think that would be close enough.

In that instant the reality of the situation hit her like a punch to the belly. She hadn't planned it, hadn't expected it, not in a million years, but now there was no denying it. She was in love with Coop.

Coop was a disgrace to the male gender.

In his entire life he had never come first. Not once. He prided himself on being completely in control at all times. Until last night.

Watching Sierra writhe beneath him, hearing her moans and whimpers, had pushed him so far past the point of no return, a nuclear explosion wouldn't have been able to stop him. She made him feel things he hadn't realized he was even capable of feeling. For the first time in his life, sex actually meant something. He had reached a level of intimacy that until last night he hadn't even known existed. It should have scared the hell out of him, but he had never felt more content in his entire life.

"She's grabbing her suitcase right now," Sierra said from the passenger's seat, dropping her phone back in her purse. "She said to meet her outside of Terminal C."

Joy's flight had been a few minutes late, so they had been driving around in circles while Joy deplaned and collected her luggage.

"I'm glad I fed the twins their lunch early today," Sierra said, looking back at them, sitting contentedly in their car seats. "And thank you again for picking Joy up. She could have taken the bus."

"It's no problem." He reached over and took her hand, twining his fingers through hers. "Besides, I owe you for last night."

She blew out an exasperated breath and rolled her eyes. "I don't know why you're making such a big deal out of this. It couldn't have been more than a few seconds before me."

That was a few seconds too long as far as he was concerned. "I don't lose control like that."

"I didn't even *notice*. I wouldn't have even known if you hadn't said something."

"Well, it's not going to happen again." And it hadn't. Not the second or third time last night, or this morning in bed, or in the shower. Not that there hadn't been a couple of close calls.

She shook her head, as if he were hopeless. "Men and their egos. Besides, I sort of like knowing that I make you lose control."

"That reminds me, we need to stop at the pharmacy on the way home. We blew through my entire supply of condoms."

"We don't have to use them if you don't want to."

He glanced over at her. "You take birth control pills?"

"IUD."

Sex without a condom...interesting idea.

From the time he reached puberty Ash had drilled into Coop the importance of always using protection. Years before Coop became sexually active, Ash had bought him a box of condoms and ordered him to keep one in his wallet at all times, just in case. A thing for which Coop was eternally grateful, ever since one fateful night his junior year of high school when Missy Noble's parents were out for the evening and she jumped him on the den couch right in the middle of some chick movie whose title escaped him now.

Being the stickler for safety that Coop was, not to mention the very real likelihood of being trapped into a relationship with an *accidental* pregnancy, he'd actually never had sex without one. But the idea was an intriguing one.

"I've been told that it feels better for the man that way," she said.

"Who told you that?"

"The men who tried to get me to do it without one, so I'm not sure if it's actually true or not. But logistically you would think so."

He looked over at her and grinned. "I guess we'll have to put that theory to the test, won't we? Just so you know, I get tested regularly."

"As a nurse I have to," she said.

"How's tonight looking for you?" he asked.

"With my sister here?"

"What we do in the privacy of our bedroom is our business."

"*Our* bedroom?"

"She's going to be sleeping in your room, so it just makes sense that you sleep in mine. And continue to sleep there when she's gone."

"You don't think we should take things a little bit slower?"

"You didn't seem to want to go slow last night."

"Having sex and me moving into your bedroom are two very different things."

"We're living together, Sierra. Where you sleep at this point is just logistics." He gave her hand a squeeze. "We're together. I want you to sleep with me."

She hesitated for a second, then nodded and said, "Okay."

Coop steered the SUV up to the C terminal and spotted Joy immediately. She was a taller, slimmer version of her big sister, with the same dark hair, though Joy's was wavier and hung clear down to her waist. Gauging by her long gauzy skirt, tie-dye tank, leather sandals and beaded necklaces, she was the free-spirit type. A total contrast to Sierra, who couldn't be more practical and conservative.

"There she is!" Sierra said excitedly.

Coop pulled up beside her and before he could even come to a complete stop Sierra was out the door.

He turned to the twins and said, "I'll be right back, you two," then hopped out to grab Joy's bag. By the time he made it around the vehicle the sisters were locked in a firm embrace, and when they finally parted they were both misty-eyed.

Sierra turned to him. "Coop, this is my sister, Joy. Joy, this is Coop, my...boss."

Joy offered him a finely boned hand to shake, but her grip was firm. "I can't thank you enough for giving me a place to stay while I'm here. And for picking me up."

"I hope you don't mind squeezing in between the girls," he said.

"It beats takin' the bus."

He opened the door for Joy, and when both women were inside he grabbed the suitcase, heaved it into the back, then got back in the driver's side. Sierra was introducing her sister to the twins.

"That's Fern on the right and Ivy on the left," she said.

Joy shook each one of their tiny hands, which the twins seemed to love. "Nice to meet you, girls. And it's a pleasure to meet the man who my sister can't seem to stop talking about. Are you two a couple yet or what?"

"Joy!" Sierra said, reaching back to whack her sister in the leg. Then she told Coop, "You'll have to excuse my sister. She has no filter."

Joy just laughed and said, "Love you, sis."

Coop had known Joy all of about two minutes, but he had the distinct feeling that he was going to like Sierra's sister, and he didn't doubt that her visit would be an interesting one.

"You're sleeping with him," Joy said when the twins were down for a nap and they were finally alone in Sierra's bedroom…or Joy's bedroom as the case happened to be now.

"Yeah," she admitted. "As of last night."

"I kinda figured. There was a vibe." Joy heaved her suitcase onto the bed and unzipped it. "I knew he had to be hot for you to let your sister crash here."

"You don't pack light," Sierra said as she emptied the contents of her case onto the duvet.

"The guy I've been staying with is getting his place fumigated while I'm gone, so it just made sense to bring it all. Have you got a few extra hangers?"

Sierra pointed to the closet door. "In there."

Joy crossed the room and pulled the door open. "Holy mother of God, this closet is *huge*."

"I know. It's twenty times the size of the dinky closet in my apartment."

"I didn't realize that hockey players made so much money," she called from inside the closet, emerging with a dozen or so hangers.

"He's also a successful businessman. And he does tons of charity work. He sponsors teams in low-income areas and donates his time to hold workshops for young players. For someone who had no interest in having kids of his own, he sure does a lot for them." She took note of the hippie-style clothing in a host of bright colors piled on the bed and asked Joy, "Did you bring something to wear to the memorial?"

Joy made a face. "I don't do black."

Sierra sighed, watching her hang her clothes and lay them neatly on the bed to be put in the closet. "It doesn't have to be black. Just not so…bright. If I don't have anything that fits you, we can go shopping tomorrow after your audition."

"You know I don't have any money."

"But I do. Coop advanced me a month's pay so I could pay for the memorial service."

"That was nice of him." She paused then said

with a grin, "I suppose it had nothing to do with the fact that you put out."

She glared at her sister. "Not that it's any of your business, but he offered it *before* I slept with him. And only because I refused to let him pay for the memorial himself. He's always trying to do things like that for me."

"Wow, that must be rough. I know I would hate having a rich, sexy man try to take care of me. How can you stand it?"

Sierra leaned close to give her sister a playful swat on the behind. "I almost forgot what a smart ass you are."

Joy smiled. "I've been told it's one of my most charming qualities."

It could be. But then there were the times when it was just plain annoying.

"You know I like to take care of myself," Sierra said, and now that she no longer had to pay for their father's care, she could build herself a nice nest egg.

But how would that work exactly? Now that she and Coop were a couple, would he keep paying her, or would he expect her to care for the girls for free?

It was just one of many things that they would have to discuss. Like how far he wanted to take this relationship. Would she be his perpetual live-in girlfriend, or was he open to the idea of marriage some day? Would he want more kids, or were the twins going to be it for him? And if being with the twins meant sacrificing a little, wasn't it worth it?

She still wasn't one-hundred percent sure that moving into his bedroom at this early stage in their relationship was a good idea. Yes, technically they were living together, but sleeping in the same room after being lovers for less than twenty-four hours seemed to be pushing the boundaries of respectability.

"You know you're going to have to tell him the truth," Joy said.

And there lay her other problem—telling Coop she was the twins' birth mother. But what would be even more difficult would be telling him about the birth father. "I'll tell him when the time is right."

"Honestly, I'm surprised he hasn't figured it out on his own. They look just like you."

"We were at a café yesterday morning and the woman at the next table assumed we were the twins' parents. She said they looked just like me, but have their daddy's eyes."

"What did Coop say?"

"He doesn't see it, I guess."

"If you want this thing with Coop to go anywhere, you have to be honest with him."

"I'm in love with him."

Joy looped an arm around her shoulder. "Si, you can't start a relationship based on lies. Trust me. I know this from personal experience."

She laid her head on her sister's shoulder. "How did I get myself into this mess?"

"He'll understand."

"Will he?"

"If he loves you he will."

The trouble was, she didn't know if he loved her or not. He hadn't said he did, but of course, neither had she. It was one thing to feel it, but to actually put it out there, to leave herself so vulnerable…it scared her half to death. Especially when she was pretty sure that for him, his affection for her was in part motivated by his desire to do right by the twins. Was it her that he cared about, or was it the idea of what their relationship symbolized? His mental image of the perfect family.

If she did tell him the truth—*when* she told him—would his feelings for her be strong enough to take such a direct blow? And what if she didn't tell him? Would it really be so bad? What if knowing the truth changed his perception of his relationship to the girls? What if it did more damage than good? There was no way that he could ever find out on his own.

Joy took her hand and grasped it firmly, and as if she were reading Sierra's mind said, "Si, you have to tell him."

"I will." Probably. Maybe.

"When?"

"When the time is right." If it ever was.

Chapter 11

Sierra and Coop had just gotten the girls settled for the night and into bed, and he had slipped into his office to answer the phone, when Joy exploded through the front door of the apartment in a whirl of color and exuberance and announced at the top of her lungs, "I got it!"

She'd had her audition that morning and had been waiting all day for a callback, pacing the apartment like a restless panther, whining all through dinner that if she hadn't heard something by now, she wasn't going to and that her career as an actress was over. When Sierra couldn't take it a minute longer, she'd given her money and sent her out to find a dress for the memorial. Apparently she'd found one.

"That was fast," she said, setting the girls' empty bottles in the kitchen sink. "Let's see it."

"See it?" Joy said, looking confused.

"The dress." She turned to her sister, realizing that Joy wasn't holding a bag.

"I didn't get a dress. I got the *role*."

Confused, she said, "I thought if they were interested, they would have you in for a second audition."

"Normally they would, but they were so impressed with my performance and thought I was so perfect for the role, they offered me the part!"

"Oh my gosh!" Her baby sister was going to play the leading role in a movie! "Joy, that is so awesome!"

She threw her arms around her sister and hugged her, and that's how Coop found them a second later when he came out of his office.

"I heard shouting," he said.

"Joy got the part," Sierra said.

"Hey, that's great!" Coop said, looking genuinely happy for her. "I hope you'll remember us little guys when you're a big Hollywood star."

Joy laughed. "Let's not get ahead of ourselves. Although this could open some major doors for me. And honestly, I'm just thrilled to have a job. I had to give up my waitressing job to come here. If it wasn't for my friend Jerry letting me stay at his place, I would be out on the streets until filming starts."

"When is that?" Sierra asked.

"Early August in Vancouver, and we wrap in September."

"I've played in Vancouver," Coop said. "You'll love it there."

"Oh, my God!" Joy said, practically vibrating with excitement. "I can't believe I actually got it!"

Joy was usually so negative and brooding, it was nice to see her happy for a change. Sierra was about to suggest they celebrate when the doorbell rang.

"That's Vlad and Niko," Coop said, heading for the door. "Former teammates. They called to say they were stopping by."

He pulled the door open and on the other side stood two very large, sharply dressed Russian men. One looked to be around Coop's age and the other was younger. Early twenties maybe. Both men smelled as if they had bathed in cologne.

Sierra heard Joy suck in a quiet breath and say, "Yum."

"Ladies, this is Vlad," Coop said, gesturing to the older man, "And this is Niko. Guys, this is my girlfriend, Sierra, and her sister, Joy."

Neither man could mask his surprise. Sierra was assuming that men like Coop didn't usually have "girlfriends."

"Is good to meet you," Vlad said with a thick accent, addressing Sierra, but Niko's eyes were pinned on Joy, and she was looking back at him as if he were a juicy steak she would like to sink her teeth into. If she weren't a vegetarian, that is.

"You come out with us," Vlad told Coop. "Big party at the Web's place. You bring girlfriend. And sister, too."

"The Web?" Sierra asked.

"Jimmy Webster," Coop told her. "The Scorpions goalie. He's known for his wild parties. And thanks for the invitation, guys, but I'm going to have to pass."

"You must come," Vlad said. "I don't take no for answer."

Coop shrugged. "I have to be here for the twins."

"But you have nanny for twins," Vlad said.

"Actually, I'm the nanny," Sierra said, which got her a curious look from both men. She could just imagine what they were thinking. How cliché it must have appeared. The starry-eyed nanny falls for the famous athlete.

Sierra turned to Coop. "You go. I'll stay here and watch the girls."

"See," Vlad said. "Is okay. You come with us."

Instead of darting off to change, Coop looped an arm around her shoulder and said, "No can do. Sorry."

Sierra wasn't exactly crazy about the idea of him going to a party where there would be women more beautiful and desirable than her lobbying to be his next conquest, but it was something she would just have to get used to. She couldn't expect him to give up his friends and his social life just because she lacked the party mentality. "It's really okay. Go be with your friends."

"Web's parties are really only good for two things—getting wasted and picking up women. I'm well past my partying days, and the only woman I want is standing next to me."

If he was just saying that to keep from hurting her feelings, she couldn't tell. He looked as though he meant it, and it made her feel all warm and fuzzy inside.

"How about you?" Niko said, his gaze still pinned on Joy. "You come to party."

It was more of a demand than a question, which would have annoyed Sierra, but Joy smiled a catlike grin and said, "I'll go grab my purse."

"Do you think she'll be okay?" Sierra asked after they left, Joy draped on the younger player's arm. Not that she didn't think Joy could hold her own, but she didn't know the Russian guys, and she was still Sierra's baby sister. She would always feel responsible for her.

"Those guys are harmless," Coop assured her. "It looks as though she already has Niko wrapped around her finger."

"Men have always been helpless to resist her

beauty." And usually got way more than they bargained for. Joy was beautiful and sexy, but she was also moody and temperamental. It would take a special kind of man to put up with her antics. In the long term, that is.

"Why don't you come sit down?" Coop said, nudging her toward the couch.

"Let me finish up in the kitchen real quick." She had been doing her best to keep things tidy until Coop found a new housekeeper, but she'd been tied up a good part of the day finalizing the details for the memorial, and already clutter was beginning to form on every flat surface and the furniture had developed a very fine layer of dust.

"Leave it for tomorrow," he said, trying to steer her toward the couch, but she ducked under his arm. She already had a full day tomorrow.

"Five minutes," she said, heading into the kitchen.

Coop stretched out in his chair and turned on ESPN as she finished loading the dishwasher and wiped down the countertops. Ms. Densmore had kept them polished to a gleaming shine, but under Sierra's care they were looking dull and hazy. She poked through the cleaning closet for something to polish them, but after reading the label decided it was too much work to start tonight. She fished out one of those disposable duster thingies instead, but as she started to dust the living room furniture Coop looked up from the sports show he was watching and said, "What are you doing? Come sit down and relax."

"The apartment is filthy," she said.

"And we'll have a new housekeeper in a few days." He reached over and linked his hand around her wrist, pulling her down into his lap. He took the duster and flung it behind him onto the floor, creating an even bigger mess of the room. Then he pressed a soft kiss to her lips. "This should be our alone time."

And she still felt guilty for making him stay home or making him feel as though he had to. "Are you sure you're not upset about missing the party? Because you can still go."

"I didn't want to go. If it had been one of the married guys having a party, then sure, but only if we got a sitter and you came with me."

"I'm really not the party type."

"You wouldn't like a party where the couples are all married and instead of getting hammered and hooking up, they talk about preschools and which diapers are the most absorbent?"

"They do not."

"They do, seriously. I used to think they were totally insane. What could be more boring? Now I totally get it."

"I guess I wouldn't mind a party like that," she said.

"The married guys on the team are very family oriented, and I think you would like the wives. They're very down-to-earth and friendly. Everyone gets together for barbecues during the summer. We should go sometime."

That actually sounded like fun. There was only one problem. "You said it's the players and their wives, but I'm not your wife."

"Not yet. But there are girlfriends, too. The point is, it's not a meat market."

Sierra's breath backed up in her chest. Did he really just say "not yet," as in, someday she would be? Was he actually suggesting that he intended to make her an honest woman?

"We don't have to go," Coop said.

"No, I'd like to."

"Are you sure? Because you just had a really funny look on your face."

"It wasn't that. I just didn't know... I didn't realize how you felt about that. About us."

His brow wrinkled. "I'm not sure what you mean."

"I said 'I'm not your wife,' and you said 'not yet.'"

His frown deepened. "Are you saying that you wouldn't want to be my wife?"

"No! Of course not. I just didn't know that you would *want* me to be. That you ever wanted to get married. You strike me as the perpetual bachelor type."

"It's not as if at some point I decided that I would never get married. To be honest, I was jealous as hell of Ash. He found the perfect partner for himself, and they were so happy. I just haven't had any luck finding the right one for me. I may not be ready for a trip down the aisle right now, but eventually, sure. Isn't that what everyone wants?"

The question was: Did he want to take that trip with her? That was definitely what he was implying, right? And how long was eventually? Months? A year? Ten years? She'd never been in a relationship serious enough to even consider marriage, so how long did it take to get to the wedding? Or the proposal? After he got down on one knee, how long before they said *I do?*

"You know," he said, nuzzling her cheek, nibbling her ear, sending a delicious little shiver of pleasure up her spine. "You came to bed so late last night we never got to test out that condom theory."

She and Joy had sat up until almost three last night talking, and Coop had been sound asleep by the time she slipped into bed beside him. "But we have the place all to ourselves now," she said, turning in his lap so she was straddling him. She reached down and tugged at the hem of his T-shirt, pulling it up over his head. He was so beautiful, it was still a little hard to believe that a man like him would want someone like her. But she could feel by the hard ridge between her thighs that he did.

She pulled her shirt up over her head and tossed it on the floor with his. He made a rumbly sound in his throat and wrapped his big, warm hands over her hips.

"You are the sexiest woman on the planet," he said, sliding his hands upward, skimming her bra cups with his thumbs. He sure made her feel as if she were. So why did she have the nagging feeling that it wasn't destined to last, that she was a novelty, and at some point the shine would wear thin? That he was going to miss the parties and the running around.

Either way, it was too late now. She was hooked. She loved him, and maybe someday he would learn to love her, too. They could make this work. She would be such a good wife, and keep him so happy, he wouldn't ever want to let her go.

For the twins' sake she had to at least try.

Holy freaking hell.

Coop lay spread-eagled on his back in bed, the covers tangled around his ankles, sweat beading his brow, still quaking with aftershocks from what was hands down the most intense orgasm he'd ever had. Making love to Sierra without the barrier of latex, to really feel her for the first time, was the hottest, most erotic experience of his life.

"So is it true?" Sierra asked, grinning down at him, still straddling his lap, her skin rosy with the afterglow of her own pleasure. Looking smug as hell. "Is it better without a condom?"

He tried to scowl at her, but he felt so good, so relaxed, he couldn't muster the energy. "You're evil," he said instead, and her smile widened. He should have known, when she insisted on being on top, that she was up to something. That she intended to humiliate him again. But even he couldn't deny it was the most pleasurable humiliation he'd ever had to endure.

"You beat me by what, five seconds?" she said.

No thanks to her. He had obviously been having trouble holding it together, but instead of giving him a few seconds to get a grip, she had to go and do that thing with his nipples, which of course had instantly set him off.

For someone who claimed not to have much experience with men, she sure knew which buttons to push.

"It's the principle of the thing," he told her. "The man should never come first."

"That's just dumb."

"Yeah, well, as soon as I can breathe again, you're in trouble." He wrapped his arms around her and pulled her down against his chest, kissing the smirk off her face. Sierra slid down beside him, curling up against his side. It felt as if that was exactly where she belonged. Beside him. It was astounding to him what adding an emotional connection could do to crank up the level of intimacy. He had never felt as close to anyone, as connected to another person. He had no doubt that she would be the perfect wife. A good mother, a good friend and an exceptional lover. And he knew that once she met his friends, and trusted them enough to drop her guard a little, she would fit right in.

Yeah, she wasn't much of a housekeeper, and her expertise in the kitchen was pretty much limited to things she could heat in the microwave, but he could hire people to do that. In all the ways that counted, she was exactly the sort of woman he would want as a companion. She was predictable and uncomplicated…what you see is what you get. And she was as devoted to the twins, to taking care of them, as he was. Never had he imagined finding someone so completely perfect. He'd never been one to believe in cosmic forces, but he was honestly beginning to think that fate had brought them together. She had been thrust into some pretty rotten circumstances, and like him she had come out swinging. In fact, in a lot of ways they were very much alike.

So why couldn't he shake the feeling that she was holding something back? That she didn't completely trust him. He was sure it had more to do with her own insecurities than anything he had done. She just needed time. Time to trust him and believe him when he said that he wanted to make this work. That he wanted them to be a family.

But as her hand slid south down his stomach, he decided that he had plenty of time to worry about that later.

Chapter 12

When Sierra got back from her morning walk with the twins the next day, Joy was awake—a surprise considering she didn't wander in until after 4:00 a.m.—and she was dusting the living room dressed in yoga pants and a sport bra. And she somehow made it look glamorous.

"You don't have to do that," Sierra told her, taking the twins from the stroller and sitting them in their ExerSaucers.

"Someone has to do it."

"I'll get around to it."

Joy shot her a look. "No you won't. You hate cleaning."

She couldn't deny it. People would naturally think that Joy, being such a free spirit, would be the one with the aversion to cleaning, and Sierra, the responsible one, would be neat as a pin, but the opposite was true.

"If you decide to have anyone come back here after the memorial tomorrow, it should at least be tidy," Joy said.

"Well, thank you. I'm sure Coop will appreciate it."

"Consider it payment for letting me stay here. And introducing me to Niko. He's too adorable for words."

"How was the party?"

"Wild. Those hockey dudes really know how to have a good time."

Sierra walked into the kitchen to fix the twins' bottles and nearly gasped when she realized that it was spotless and the granite had been polished to a gleaming shine. "Oh my gosh! It looks amazing in here!"

Joy shrugged, like it was no big deal. "I like cleaning. It relieves stress."

She took after their dad in that respect. And Sierra was like their mom, who was more interested in curling up with a book or taking a long, leisurely walk in the park or working in the local community garden. Their home had been messy but happy. Even when they found the cancer, it hadn't knocked her spirits down, or if it had, she never let it show. Not even when she had been too sick from the chemo to eat or when the pain must have been excruciating. She had taken it in stride up until the very end.

It would be twelve years in September, and though the pain of losing her had dulled, Sierra still missed her as keenly as she had that first year. She missed her warm hugs, and her gentle voice. Her playful nature. Why sit inside cleaning bedrooms and doing homework when there was a world full of adventures to explore? Sierra only hoped that she would be as good a mother, as good a wife as her mom had been.

She poured juice into bottles and carried them to the living room for the twins. "Do you still miss her?" she asked Joy.

"Miss who?" she asked, though Sierra had the feeling she knew exactly who she meant.

"Mom. It'll be twelve years this fall."

Joy shrugged. "I guess."

"You *guess?*" How could she *not* miss her?

"You were always closer with her than I was."

"What are you talking about? Of course I wasn't."

Joy stopped dusting and turned to her. "Si, come on. Half the time she didn't even know we were there, and the other half she spent doting on you. You two were just alike, she used to say."

"Yes, she and I were more alike, but she didn't love you any less."

"Didn't it ever bother you that the entire world seemed to revolve around her? Dad ran himself ragged working two jobs, and half the time she wouldn't even have dinner fixed when he got home. We would end up eating sandwiches or fast food."

"Not everyone is a good cook," Sierra said.

"But she didn't even try. And the apartment was always a mess. It was as if she was allergic to cleaning or something. Dad got one day a week off, and he would have to spend it vacuuming and picking up all the junk she and you left all over."

Sierra couldn't believe she would talk about their mom like that, that she even felt that way. "She was a good wife and mother. Dad adored her."

"She was a flake, and dad was miserable. My bed was right next to the wall and I could hear them fighting when they thought we were asleep."

"All couples fight sometimes."

"Sure, but with them it was a nightly thing."

Sierra shook her head. "No, they were happy."

"Look, believe me or don't believe me, I really don't care. I know what I heard. I don't doubt that Dad loved her, but he *wasn't* happy."

Maybe their mom could be a little self-centered at times, but she loved her family, all of them equally, despite what Joy believed. She did her best.

If that wasn't good enough for Joy, that was *her* problem.

Joy's cell phone, which was sitting on the coffee table, started to ring and she dashed over to grab it. "It's Jerry!" she said excitedly, who Sierra remembered was the "friend" she had been staying with. "Did you get my message? I got the part!" She flopped down on the couch and propped her feet on the coffee table. "I know! Isn't it awesome... No, not until August. Maybe you can come visit me there."

There was a pause, and Joy's smile began to disintegrate. "No, I don't have anyone else I can stay with until then. Why?" Joy sat up as outrage crept over her features. "What do you mean she's moving back in? You told me that you're getting divorced!"

Another married boyfriend? What was Joy's fixation with unavailable men? Why couldn't she find a nice, single guy? One who wouldn't screw her over and break her heart.

Joy jerked to her feet, shouting into the phone, "You sleazy-ass son of a bitch. You've been planning this since before I left, haven't you? You were never going to fumigate. You just wanted my stuff out so you could move her back in. I could have had a totally hot Russian guy last night, but I was being faithful to you, you big jerk! He was young and hot and I'll bet he doesn't have any of your *performance* problems."

Whoa. Maybe this was a conversation best kept

private. Not that she thought Joy gave a damn if Sierra heard. She liked that element of drama. *Clearly.*

Joy listened, looking angrier by the second, then growled, "Take your apologies and shove them, you heartless bastard." She disconnected the call, blew out a frustrated breath and said, "Well, *crap.*"

"You okay?" Sierra asked.

Joy collapsed back onto the couch. "It's official, I'm homeless."

"I meant about Jerry. You were dating him?"

She shrugged. "I don't know if you would actually call it dating. He gave me a place to stay and I kept him company."

Sierra could just imagine what that entailed.

"I mean, I liked him, but it's not as if we had some sort of future. He's kind of old to be thinking long term."

"How old?"

"Fifty-two."

Sierra's jaw dropped. "He's *thirty* years older than you?"

"Like I said, I didn't want to marry the guy. It was just…convenient."

Sierra raised a brow.

"For *both* of us. He liked having a much younger companion to flaunt, and I liked having a roof over my head."

"You liked him enough to be faithful to him," Sierra said.

Joy shrugged. "He was a nice guy. Or so I thought."

Sierra had the feeling Joy cared about him more than she wanted to admit. "So, what are you going to do?"

"I have no idea. I gave up my waitressing job for this trip and the film doesn't start shooting until the end of August. Even if I could find another job it would be a month before I could afford first and last months' rent."

"Can't you get some sort of signing bonus?"

She shook her head. "It's very low budget. My salary will barely cover living expenses."

"So what are you going to do? Stay with another friend?"

"When you mooch off everyone you know, eventually you run out of people to mooch off. But don't worry," she said, pushing herself back up off the couch and grabbing the duster. "I'll figure something out. I always do."

Sierra was a little surprised that Joy hadn't asked if she could stay with her and Coop. Maybe she knew Sierra would say no. It was one thing to have her stay for a short visit, but for more than a month? If she had her own place, no problem, but she would never ask Coop for that kind of favor.

Joy was a big girl. She was going to have to figure this one out on her own.

Coop sat at the conference table in his lawyer's office, fisting his hands in his lap, struggling to keep his cool, to keep his expression passive.

"We agreed on a price," he told his former boss, Mike Norris, the current owner of the New York Scorpions. A price that had been a couple million less than what he wanted today.

The arrogant bastard sat back in his chair, an unlit cigar clamped between his teeth, wearing a smug smile. Flanking him were his business manager and his lawyer, both of whom were as overweight, out of shape and devoid of human decency as Mike.

"My team, my terms," Mike said. "Take it or leave it."

He knew how badly Coop wanted it, and he was trying to use it to his advantage. The paperwork had been drawn up and Coop came here thinking that they would be signing to lock in the terms. But Mike had gotten greedy. Coop should have seen this coming, he should have known the son of a bitch would pull something at the last minute.

At the price they had agreed on last week, buying the team would have had its risks, but it was still what he considered a sound investment. At the price Mike was demanding now, Coop would be putting too much on the line. His conservative nature with money was responsible for his healthy portfolio. If it were just his financial future hanging in the balance, he might say what the hell and go for it, but he had the twins to consider now. Sierra, too, although he doubted his money was a motivating factor in her feelings toward him. In fact, he was pretty sure she was intimidated by it. It was one of her most appealing qualities.

"Why the hesitation, Landon?" Mike said. "You know you want it, and we all know you can afford it. If you're hesitating because you think I'm going to back down, it ain't gonna happen." He leaned in toward the table, his belly flab preventing him from getting very close. "Just say yes and we've got a deal."

Even if he had planned to say yes, to give Mike what he wanted, that would have killed the deal.

He wanted that team, wanted it more than anything in his life, and giving it up would be one of the hardest things he would ever have to do, but it would be for the best. He glanced over at Ben, whose expression seemed to say that he knew what was coming, then Coop pushed back from the table and stood. "Sorry, gentleman, but I'm going to have to pass."

He started for the door and Mike called after him, sounding a little less smug now. "This deal is only good this afternoon. After today the price goes up again."

Mike thought Coop was bluffing. He wasn't. And though Coop wanted to tell him to shove his threat where the sun don't shine, he restrained himself. He was dying to see Mike's expression as he left, but he resisted the urge to turn and look as he walked out the conference room door and down the hall to Ben's office.

He sat down, taking long, deep breaths, fisting his hands in his lap when what he wanted to do was wrap them around that smug bastard's throat.

Ben walked in the office several minutes later, presumably after seeing the other men out.

"Coop, I'm sorry. I had no idea they were going to pull that."

Coop shrugged. "It's not your fault."

"You have every right to be furious. I know how much you wanted this."

It wasn't just about owning the team and the money that it would bring in. He cared about those guys. Mike was an old-school businessman who, until he bought the team five years ago, had never even been to a hockey game. For him it was nothing more than an investment. He knew nothing about the game and had been running the team into the ground since he took over. He didn't care about the players—his only goal was to pad his pockets. And the players knew it. They also knew that when

Coop was at the helm, things would change. They would be back on top.

He felt as if he was letting them down.

"I don't know what I'm going to tell the guys."

"You're going to tell them exactly what happened. Norris screwed you. But don't consider this over. Not yet. You should have seen Norris's face when you walked out. He really thought he had you. I wouldn't be too surprised if we get a call from him in a day or two backing down on his price."

"If he does, make it clear that I'm not paying him a penny over what we originally agreed on."

"There's something else we need to talk about," Ben said, and the furrow in his brow made Coop think that whatever it was, it wasn't good. "I didn't want to say anything before we signed the deal, and now probably isn't the best time after what happened in there…"

Whatever it was, it couldn't be much worse than what he'd just gone through. "Just tell me."

"A source at the National Transportation Safety Board has informed me that the official report on the plane crash is going to be released Monday."

Coop's heart clenched in his chest, then climbed up into his throat. "Did this source tell you what's in the report."

"They're calling it pilot error."

"No way!" Coop shot up from his seat. "No way it was pilot error. Your source must have it wrong."

"According to the report there were narcotics recovered from the scene."

"Which wouldn't surprise me in the least. Susan hurt her back a week before the trip. She ruptured a disc. It was so painful she couldn't even pick the twins up. I'm sure her doctor can confirm that. And she wasn't flying the plane."

"He said they found narcotics and marijuana in both Susan and Ash's systems."

No way. He knew that Ash and Susan smoked occasionally, but Ash would *never* take anything and then operate a plane. "I don't believe it. I know my brother, Ben. Ash would never take drugs and fly."

"We'll know more when we get a copy of the report, but if it's true, all hell is going to break loose and the vultures are going to descend. You might even want to get out of town for a few days, or even a week or two. Until things die down."

With the deal falling through he had nothing pressing to keep him in town, and frankly, he could use a vacation. "We have the memorial for Sierra's dad tomorrow, but after that there's nothing keeping me in the city. I think a trip to my place in Cabo might be in order."

"How is it working out with Sierra?"

Coop scrubbed a hand across his jaw. "Um… well, better than I anticipated, actually."

Ben narrowed his eyes. "Oh, yeah, how much better?"

A smile tugged at the corners of his mouth. "She moved into my bedroom two nights ago."

"I distinctly recall you telling me that you weren't going to sleep with her."

"It wasn't something I planned. But she's just so…extraordinary."

"So it's serious?"

"Yeah, I think so. She's everything I didn't realize that I wanted in a woman."

Ben grinned and shook his head. "I had no idea you were such a romantic, Coop. You should needlepoint that on a pillow."

"Who'd have thought, right? But she's smart and funny and beautiful, and the twins love her. And she doesn't seem to give a damn about my money."

"Should I start drafting the prenup?"

"Let's not get ahead of ourselves." Besides, he couldn't imagine making Sierra sign one of those. It would be the same as saying that he didn't trust her. He was a pretty good judge of character and as far as he could tell, she didn't have a deceitful bone in her body.

Ben eyed him warily. "You do plan to have a prenup, right? Assuming that you're going to marry her eventually."

"I'm definitely going to marry her. Eventually.

But as far as a prenup…I don't think that's going to be necessary. She's not after my money."

"Not now, maybe…"

"I trust her, Ben."

"It's not about trust. It's about protecting you both in the case of a divorce."

"That would never happen. She's it for me. I know she is."

"One of my partners specializes in divorce, and the horror stories he could tell you—"

"That wouldn't happen to me and Sierra. We both come from very stable, loving homes. We aren't products of divorce. Her parents were happily married and so were mine. Whatever problems we might have, we would work them out."

"You're rationalizing."

"I'm being realistic."

"So am I."

"To even ask would feel like a betrayal. It would be like saying that I don't trust her."

"If the two of you have such a great relationship, I would think she would understand. The least you could do is ask. If she balks, I might reconsider my position on the matter."

"She won't."

"Promise me that you'll at least consider it."

"I will. And like I said, we have no immediate plans to get hitched. I haven't even proposed yet."

"Just keep it in mind when you do."

In a way Coop wished he hadn't said anything to Ben about marrying her. What with the sour deal, the accident report and Ben's prenup lecture, Coop left his office feeling downright depressed.

But on the bright side, things couldn't get much worse.

Chapter 13

Coop caught a cab back home, getting out a block early so he could pick up a bouquet of flowers for Sierra from a street vendor. Remembering that they had never really had a chance to celebrate Joy's new job, he got her one, too. He walked the rest of the way home, the sun's heat beating down on his shoulders and back, melting the tension that had settled into his bones. Which made a week or two in a sunny locale sound even more appealing. If they left Sunday, they would be long gone before the backlash from the NTSB report hit the media.

The doorman greeted Coop as he headed inside and he had the elevator all to himself on the ride up. He opened the apartment door and the scent of something delicious tantalized his senses. Something that smelled too good to have come from a microwave. He dropped his keys on the entryway table and walked into the living room, realizing that not only was someone cooking, but also someone had cleaned. The apartment was spotless.

Sierra appeared from the hallway, jerking with surprise when she saw him standing there. "Hey! Hi, I didn't hear you come in."

At the sight of her, his heart instantly lifted, a smile tugged at his lips and all the crap that happened today, all the rotten news, didn't seem so terrible any longer. "I just got here."

"I just put the girls down for a nap." Her eyes settled on the bouquets he was carrying. "Nice flowers."

"One for you," he said, handing her the larger of the two.

"Thank you!" She pushed up on her toes and kissed him. "I can't even remember the last time someone gave me flowers."

"This one is for Joy," he said of the second bouquet. "To say congratulations. Is she here?"

"She ran down to the market. She should be back soon. In the meantime why don't I put them in water? They look like they're starting to wilt."

"It's hot as blazes out."

"I know. It was pretty warm and sticky when we took our walk this morning. Do you have a vase?"

He shrugged. "I recall Ms. Densmore setting out fresh flowers, but if there is a vase I have no idea where it would be."

He followed her to the kitchen, where she began to search for something to put the flowers in.

"Whatever you're making, it smells delicious."

"It's some sort of Mexican casserole, but I can't take credit. Joy said she was tired of carryout. But I'll warn you that it's vegetarian."

He didn't care, as long as it tasted good. Because frankly, he was tired of carryout, too. He'd been spoiled by Ms. Densmore's home-cooked meals and the five-star dining that he'd grown used to.

He opened the fridge and grabbed a beer, noticing that someone had even cleaned out the food that had begun to spoil. "The apartment looks great, by the way."

"Also thanks to Joy," she said, rising up on her toes to peer in the cabinet above the refrigerator. "She went through here like a maniac this morning."

He twisted the cap off his beer and took a long pull. "She doesn't strike me as the type who would like to clean."

"You wouldn't think it to look at her, but Joy is far more domestically gifted than I am," she said, going through another cupboard with no luck. "She says it relieves stress. And she was pretty stressed out today."

"Is she nervous about the film role?"

"No, apparently the much older guy that she was living with decided to move his wife back in, so she's got nowhere to live and no job when she goes back to L.A."

"What is she going to do?"

Sierra shrugged. "Joy is twenty-two. It's time she started taking responsibility for herself. She can't be the reckless kid any longer."

Joy may have been a bit irresponsible, but she was still family. He knew from personal experience that pursuing dreams took sacrifice, and it sounded as if this film role was the break she had been working toward. He knew Sierra wasn't in a position to help her out, and though he knew she would never ask him to help Joy, he could. In fact, he had a pretty good idea how he could do it, without actually appearing to do it.

Sierra finally found the vases in the very back of one of the lower cabinets and pulled out two. "These should work."

She set them on the countertop, then turned to him. "I almost forgot, how did your meeting go?"

"The deal fell through."

"What! What happened?"

He told her how Norris had raised his price and that he had turned him down. "Ben seems to think that he'll come around, but I'm not holding my breath."

"I'm so sorry, Coop. I know how much you wanted this."

"I'm more concerned about the guys on the team. Since Norris took over he's been running the team into the ground. They were counting on me to turn things around."

"They're your friends. They respect you. I'm sure they'll understand."

"I hope so."

As she was filling the vases with water the front door opened and Joy stepped inside, weighed down with more plastic grocery bags than one person should carry. Coop set his beer down and rushed over to help her. "I hope Sierra gave you money out of the house account for all this," he said, carrying several bags to the kitchen.

"Since I'm broke and my shoplifting days are over—" she set her bags down on the granite with a thunk "—she had no choice."

"Look what Coop got you," Sierra said, dropping Joy's bouquet into a vase.

"Well, damn, wasn't that sweet of you." Joy leaned close and inhaled the scent of the blooms. "They're lovely. Thanks."

"Originally I bought them to say congratulations, but I think they work better as a thank-you for cleaning the apartment and cooking dinner."

"It's the least I can do. Besides," she added, shooting Sierra a wry smile, "you've probably noticed my sister isn't much of a housekeeper. Or a cook."

Sierra gave her a playful jab in the arm. "And let's see you balance a checkbook or pay your rent on time."

"Gotta find a place to live before I can pay rent, don't I?"

She had just given him the perfect segue. "Sierra mentioned that your living arrangements have changed, and I wondered if that meant you might not be going back to L.A."

She collapsed on one of the stools, looking thoroughly frustrated. "Honestly, I'm not sure what I'm going to do. I want to go back to L.A., but I might have a better chance finding a job here."

"Can I offer a third option?"

She shrugged. "I'm open to pretty much anything at this point."

"Then how do you feel about Mexico?"

"You think you're pretty sneaky, don't you?" Sierra called to Coop from bed later that night when they were in their room with the door closed. It was still a little strange to think of it as *their* room, but she was feeling more comfortable there. It was decorated in warmer colors than the spare room, with traditionally styled cherrywood furniture, includ-

ing a king-size bed so huge she could get lost in it.
Though there wasn't much chance of that happening, considering that Coop was a cuddler. She was
used to sleeping alone, so sharing a bed would take
a bit of getting used to, but she couldn't deny the
pleasures of waking spooned with a warm, naked
and aroused man.

Coop stuck his head out of the bathroom, a tooth-
brush wedged in his mouth. "If brushing one's teeth
can be considered sneaky," he said around a mouth-
ful of toothpaste.

She shot him a look. "Two weeks in Mexico?"

He grinned. "Oh, *that.*"

He was gone again, and she heard the water running, then he walked out of the bathroom.

"You knew Joy didn't have anywhere to go," she
said. "And rather than making her figure this out
on her own—"

"In my defense, I had already planned to take the
trip, and I would have invited her to come with us
even if she did have a place in L.A. to go back to."
He sat on the edge of the mattress to untie his shoes.
"But yes, I'm trying to help her. Is there something
wrong with that?"

"I just worry that she's never going to learn to
be responsible, to take care of herself."

"She seems to have done okay until now. And
following your dream takes sacrifice. That I know
from personal experience."

Maybe he had a point. Besides, this way she would get to spend a little more time with Joy because who knew when she would talk to her again?

He kicked his shoes off, peeled off his socks, then stood and pulled his shirt over his head. His jeans went next, then his boxers.

Nice.

He looked so good naked, it was a shame he couldn't walk around like that all the time.

He gathered his clothes and dropped them in the hamper, then he pulled the covers back and slipped into bed beside her. But instead of pulling her into his arms and kissing her, like he normally would, he rolled onto his side facing her, wearing a troubled expression. He'd been unusually quiet all night, and she had a pretty good idea what was on his mind. He'd mentioned the accident report being released and what his lawyer's source had said it contained. And though he had clearly been disturbed, he'd seemed hesitant to discuss it. Maybe because Joy had been there, or maybe he just hadn't been ready to deal with it. But maybe now he was.

She rolled onto her side facing him and asked, "Are you thinking about Ash and Susan?"

He drew in a deep breath and blew it out. "I just keep thinking, there has to be some sort of mistake."

She hated to believe that the people she had entrusted her children to could be so irresponsible, but facts were facts. If the report said there were drugs in their systems, then there probably were.

"I *know* Ash," Coop said. "He just wouldn't do something like that."

And she knew for a fact that he didn't know everything about Ash. Everyone had secrets and did things that they weren't proud of. Everyone made mistakes.

"If it had been faulty equipment or turbulent weather…" He shook his head. "But pilot error? It just seems so senseless. How could he do that to Susan and the girls?"

"And you?"

"*Yes,* and me. After all we went through losing our parents, why would he put me through that again? I'm just so damned…*angry*."

"I felt the same way about my mom."

"But she got sick. She couldn't help that."

"Actually, she could have. Joy doesn't know this, and I don't ever want her to know, but I overheard my dad talking to his sister a few months after the funeral. My mom had a cyst in her breast a couple of years earlier but it turned out to be benign. So when she found another lump, she assumed it was a cyst again."

"But it wasn't."

She shook her head. "By the time she went to the doctor, it had already metastasized. It was in her lungs and her bones. There really wasn't much they could do."

"And if she had gone in as soon as she found the lump?"

"Statistically, there's a seventy-three-percent chance she would be alive today. I was *so* angry at her, but being mad wouldn't bring her back. It just made me really miserable." She reached over and touched Coop's arm. "I'm sure your brother didn't get into that plane thinking that something like this would happen. People make mistakes."

"Come here," he said. She scooted closer and he wrapped his arms around her, pulling her against him chest to chest, bare skin against bare skin. Nice.

She closed her eyes and laid her head in the crook of his neck.

"I just want this to be over, so I can get on with my life," he said.

"It doesn't always work that way."

"I miss him."

"I know."

He buried his face against her hair, holding on so tight it was hard to breathe. "He was all I had left."

"You have the twins. They need you."

"And I need them. I never realized how much having a child could change a man. I'm a better person because of them."

She pulled back so she could see his face. "You said before that you were worried you would let

Susan and Ash down, but you've done such an awesome job with the twins. They would be so proud
of you." She couldn't imagine being separated from
the girls, but if that ever happened, she felt confident that they would be well taken care of. Coop
would be a good dad. All the more reason for him
not to know the truth. She didn't want to risk changing the way he felt about the girls. And yes, her, too.

"This is probably a really weird time to ask this,"
he said. "But what are your feelings on prenuptial
agreements?"

The timing was a little weird. And it was the
second time that week that he'd brought up the subject of marriage. "I haven't really given it much
thought," she said. "I've never come close to getting married, and even if I had, the men I date aren't
exactly rolling in money."

"But if someone asked you to sign one?"

He looked conflicted, as if he didn't really want
to be talking about this. He had seen his attorney
that morning, so she could only assume the subject
had come up. Which meant he was discussing marrying her with other people now. That had to be a
good sign, right?

She hadn't wanted to let herself believe it could
really happen. She didn't want to get her hopes
up only to have them crushed. But it was looking as though he was seriously planning to marry

her. Why discuss a prenup with his attorney if he wasn't?

"I guess it would depend on who was asking," she said.

"What if *I* was asking?"

She shrugged. "I would say sure."

"You wouldn't be upset or hurt?"

"Considering what you're worth, I would think you were a moron if you didn't ask for one. I know you would be fair. And maybe you haven't noticed, but I'm not interested in your money."

A slow smile crept across his face. "Have I ever mentioned what an amazing woman you are?"

If he knew the truth, he may not think she was all that amazing. Learning that his brother may have been under the influence of drugs while flying would be nothing compared to the bombshell she could drop on him. And in this case, what he didn't know really couldn't hurt him. So what was the harm in keeping a secret that he had no chance in ever learning? Why, when things were so good, would she risk rocking the boat?

And if she was so sure it was okay, why did she feel so guilty? Would she ever be able to completely relax with Coop, or would she always feel the nagging feeling of something unsettled between them?

But then Coop pulled her closer, trailed kisses from her lips to her throat and down to her breasts, awakening a passion that she'd felt with no one before him. Like he said before, nothing that felt this good could be wrong. And some things were better left unsaid.

The last month had been the most blissful, most relaxing of Sierra's life. Coop's beachfront condo in Cabo San Lucas was like an oasis. And being out of the States and away from the media seemed to soften the blow of the NTSB report, which was just as bad as Ben's source had predicted.

She and Coop spent their days walking along the beach or lounging by the pool, and the twins were like little mermaids in their matching swimsuits and floating rings. They *loved* the water, howling pitifully whenever she and Coop took them out. But with all the sun and activity, they were so exhausted by evening, they began to sleep peacefully through the night, leaving the adults plenty of alone time.

They spent their evenings out on the patio sipping wine and snacking on the local fare, and after dark they built bonfires. A few days after they arrived they met a young couple from Amsterdam, Joe and Trina, who were renting a neighboring condo and had a son close to the twins' age. For the next week both the kids and the parents became inseparable. Coop and Joe went golfing together while Sierra and Trina played with the kids by the pool or took them into the village to shop.

The week flew by, and everyone was disappointed when Joe and Trina had to leave.

Sierra had hoped that the trip would mean spending some quality time with her sister, but Joy being Joy, she met a man and spent a considerable part of her time with him at his condo about a quarter of a mile down the shore.

When their two weeks were drawing to an end, no one felt ready to leave, and because Coop had no pressing business back in New York, he suggested they stay a third week. Then three weeks became four, and by the time they flew home—with Joy remaining in Mexico until she had to leave for Vancouver—July was practically over.

Everyone missed the sun and the beach and especially the pool. The twins were so despondent at first that Coop suggested they consider looking for a home upstate. Maybe something on a lake with a huge yard for the girls to play in and of course a pool. Sierra hadn't been sure if he was completely serious, but then he disappeared into his office and came out an hour later with a stack of real estate listings that he had printed out.

Life with Coop was more perfect than she could have imagined, and she was happier and more content than she'd ever been. But as close as she and Coop had become, she knew that deep inside she was holding something back. She loved Coop, but she still hadn't said the words. Of course, he hadn't said them, either, or brought up the subject of marriage again, but he'd shown his affection for her in a million other ways. She couldn't expect a man like Coop, who had never even had a steady relationship, to go all gooey and lovesick in his first few months out of the gate. These things took time. Maybe she was holding back because she didn't want to rush him, didn't want to make him feel as though he had to commit to feelings he wasn't quite ready to express. Or maybe she was holding back because of the secrets she couldn't bring herself to tell him.

"What do you think of this one?" Coop asked the week after they returned from their trip. The twins were down for their nap and Coop had called her into his office. He pulled her down into his lap so she could see the listing on his ginormous computer monitor.

"It just went on the market yesterday, and the Realtor thinks it's a great price for the area and probably won't be available for long."

The house itself was gorgeous. Big and beautiful and modern, with all the amenities they were looking for, and when she saw the listing price she practically swallowed her own tongue. "It's so expensive."

He shrugged. "It's half of what this place cost me. And after we settle into the house I'll put this place on the market. So technically I'll actually make money. The Realtor can take us through this afternoon. Maybe Lita can watch the kids for a couple of hours and we can go just the two of us."

Lita was the housekeeper Coop had hired right before they left for Cabo. She had taken care of the apartment while they were gone, and since they returned the twins had taken an immediate shine to her. Even better, she absolutely adored them. Her English wasn't the best, but she kept the apartment spotless, she was a decent cook, and most important, she had a very pleasant disposition. And having raised six kids of her own, she was also an experienced babysitter.

"Unless you don't like the house," Coop said, "In which case we'll keep looking."

"It looks really nice, but what I think doesn't really matter. You're buying it, not me."

"No, *we're* buying it. It's going to be your house as much as mine."

She wished that were true, but until they were married, it was his dime. No community property, no alimony if it didn't work out.

Coop shook his head and rubbed a hand across his jaw. "You don't believe me."

"It has nothing to do with me believing you."

"Then you don't trust me."

"It's not about that, either. We're living together, but technically we're still just dating. If you buy a house, it's going to be *your* house."

"Because we're not married."

She nodded.

"Well, maybe we should get married."

It took a second to process the meaning of his words. Had he really just asked her to marry him? She opened her mouth to reply, but no sound came out. She didn't know what to say. Was he seriously asking, or just throwing out suggestions?

"Is that a no?"

Oh, my God, he was asking, and he expected an answer. "Of course it isn't, I just—"

"Look," he said, turning her in his lap so he could look into her eyes, taking her hands in his and holding them gently. "I know this is hard for you. I know you have trust issues, and I've been trying really hard to give you space, to not overwhelm you, but I'm getting tired of holding back. I love you, Sierra. I know it's only been two months, but it's been the happiest two months of my life. I want to marry you and spend the rest of my life with you. I want us to adopt the girls together and be a real family. If it happens next week, or next year, I don't care. I just need to know that we're on the same page, that you want that, too."

More than he could imagine. "I do want that, and I had no idea you felt that way. I fell in love with you the first time you kissed me. I just didn't say anything because I didn't want to overwhelm *you*. I might have trust issues but not with you."

He grinned, sliding his arms around her. "Sounds like we had a slight breakdown of communication."

She looped her arms around his neck. "I guess we did."

"Let's promise that from now on, we tell each other exactly what we're feeling, that we don't hold anything back."

"I think that's a good idea."

He gave her a soft, sweet kiss. "So, if your answer isn't no…"

"Yes, I'll marry you."

He pulled her close and held her tight.

She loved Coop, and she wanted this, more than anything in her life. She thought about what Joy said, that they couldn't base this relationship on lies. But the truth could tear them apart forever.

Chapter 14

Things were moving fast, but Coop liked it that way.

He rolled over in bed and reached for Sierra, but her side of the bed was cold. He squinted at the clock and was surprised to see that it was almost nine, which meant Sierra and the twins were probably taking their morning walk. And he needed to get his butt out of bed. They had a long, busy day ahead of them. After a week of negotiating, they would find out this morning if the sellers of the house they wanted had come back with a reasonable offer. After lunch they had a meeting planned with a wedding coordinator—one who came highly recommended from several of the players' wives—and after that Coop and Sierra were going ring shopping. They had been scouring the Internet for a week, trying to find the perfect one with no luck. She decided that if she was actually seeing them in person, putting them on her finger, something might click. They had a list of a dozen or so places in the city to look, including Cartier, Verdura and of course Tiffany's.

Coop pushed himself out of bed, showered and dressed, then wandered out to the kitchen, surprised to find Lita sitting on the living room floor playing with the twins.

"Good morning, Lita. Where is Miss Evans?"

"Morning, Mr. Landon. She have appointment. She say she leave note for you, on your desk."

"Thanks."

He gave the twins each a kiss on the tops of their heads, then poured himself a cup of coffee and carried it to his office.

He found Sierra's note on his desk by the phone. It said that Ben had called and needed him to call back ASAP. He had been drafting a prenup, even though Coop was still opposed to the idea, but Sierra had insisted.

He sat at his desk and dialed Ben's number.

"Are you sitting down?" Ben asked.

"Actually, yeah, why?"

"I got a call from Mike Norris's lawyer this morning. He wants to talk deal."

Coop's heart stalled in his chest. "You told him I won't budge on price?"

"He knows. Apparently Mike just wants to sell. It would seem that the players have been giving him a bit of a hard time lately."

Coop smiled. He had been worried that they would be angry, but instead they had rallied around him. They knew exactly what Norris was doing and they were pissed.

"When do they want to meet?" Coop asked.

"Tomorrow at three."

"Make it eleven—that way, when the deal is locked in, you and I can go out for lunch to celebrate."

"I'll let him know. Maybe you can come a little early and look over the final draft of the prenup. We made all the changes you asked for, although I still think you're being a little too generous."

"I know what I'm doing."

"I hope so."

He hung up wearing a grin. He had a hunch that Norris would come around, but until just now he hadn't let himself get his hopes up. He still didn't want to count his chickens, but it did sound as if Norris was ready to accept his offer. Everything was falling into place. Personally and professionally. It was almost too good to be true.

He glanced over at the boxes lining one wall of his office. Susan's mother had sent them over after she packed up Ash and Susan's belongings. Things she thought Coop would want. He hadn't been ready to deal with what he would find inside them, especially after reading the NTSB report. But Sierra had been right—being angry at Ash was irrational and counterproductive.

He walked over, grabbed one of the boxes and carried it to his desk. He took a slow, deep breath, telling himself it's like a Band-Aid. You just have to rip it off.

He grabbed the edge of the packing tape and ripped. He opened the flaps, and inside he found a stack of wrapped photo frames. One by one he pulled them from the box and extracted them from the packing. He found photos of Ash and Susan and the girls together. Photos of Ash and Coop with their parents from holidays and vacations, and a 5x7 of Ash and Coop at Coop's high school graduation—Coop in his cap and gown and Ash standing beside him, beaming like a proud parent.

Swallowing back an acute sting of sorrow, he set the photo aside to hang on his office wall.

At the very bottom of the box he found the twins' baby book. Smiling, he lifted it out and flipped through the pages. At the front there were pages and pages of prebirth information, filled in, he was assuming, by the birth mother. Then there was a section recording the events of the girls' first few months, and that was in Susan's handwriting. It contained their growth charts, their sleep and eating schedules, the date of their first smile and the first time eating cereal. A couple of months ago he would have seen keeping such details as a silly waste of time, but now he found himself engrossed.

He sat at his desk sipping his coffee and reading the pages Susan had filled in, which ended abruptly after the girls turned five months. He was assaulted by guilt for not continuing on the tradition, realizing that some day the twins would probably want to look back at it, maybe even show it to their children.

He vowed that, starting today, he would go back and fill in as much information as possible from those missed months, then keep the book up to date from now on. He was sure Sierra would help him. She would remember the finer details he'd forgotten or overlooked.

Curious about the woman who gave birth to the girls, he flipped back to the beginning. He couldn't find her name, which was no surprise, and though there were a few photos of her pregnant belly, they were all from the chest down. Yet as he thumbed through the pages, reading the pregnancy milestones, he was overwhelmed with an eerie sense of déjà vu. He was sure he'd read this before. It just looked so…familiar. He racked his memory, wondering if maybe he'd seen the baby book at

Ash and Susan's place. But he was sure he hadn't. Even if it had been sitting right in front of him he wouldn't have thought to pick it up. So why did it look so familiar?

Realization hit him like a stick check to the gut, knocking the air from his lungs. No way. It wasn't possible.

He snatched the note Sierra had left him from the trash beside his desk and compared it to the writing in the baby book, and the coffee he'd just swallowed threatened to rise back up his throat. It was identical. Completely and totally identical.

Sierra, the woman he loved and planned to marry, was the girls' birth mother.

Sierra opened the apartment door, her hair clinging to her damp forehead. It was a hot, sticky morning headed toward a blistering hot afternoon. She went right to the kitchen, poured herself a glass of cold water from the fridge and guzzled it down. Then she went down the hall in search of Lita and the girls. She found them in the nursery in the middle of a diaper change.

"I'm back, Lita. Is Mr. Landon still here?"

"He in his office," she said, concern furrowing her brow. "I go to talk to him, but he look angry."

Which probably meant that their offer on the house had been turned down. Well, shoot. They had seen a dozen different places in the past week, but that was by far their favorite. Coop was going to be so disappointed.

The past week, since she said she would marry him, had been a bit of a whirlwind. He seemed determined to get them married and settled into a house as fast as humanly possible. As if he were trying to make it official before she had a chance to get away. He had even mentioned that if they were going to have more children, he wanted to do it soon, so they would be close in age. She already had her hands pretty full with the twins, but he seemed to want it so badly she didn't have the heart to say she wanted to wait a while.

She felt a little like she was on a speeding train, and even if she wanted off, it was moving too fast to jump.

Sierra walked to Coop's office. The door was closed so she rapped lightly.

"Come in."

She opened the door and stepped inside. Coop was standing by the window, looking out, hands wedged in the pockets of his jeans.

"Hey, is everything okay? Lita said you looked angry."

"Close the door," he said, not looking at her.

Something definitely was wrong. She snapped the door shut and asked, "Coop, what's the matter? Did the Realtor call? Did they turn down our offer?"

"They didn't call yet. I finally started going through one of the boxes of Ash's things."

No wonder he was upset. "Oh, Coop. That must have been really hard."

"I found a whole bunch of photos, and the twins' baby book. It's on my desk."

She walked over to his desk. A stack of framed photographs sat on one corner, and next to it, the baby book she hadn't seen in almost seven months.

"I bookmarked my favorite page. Have a look."

She picked it up and thumbed through it until she found the page, marked with the note she'd written him this morning. She saw the writing on the note and the writing on the page, and her stomach bottomed out. Side by side they were clearly identical. Her knees went so limp she had to sink down into the chair.

She looked up to see that Coop had turned and was glaring down at her, his eyes so cold she nearly shivered.

"That's your handwriting. You're the twins' birth mother."

She closed her eyes and drew in a shaky breath. Joy was right. She should have told him.

"Nothing to say?" he asked, and the anger simmering just below the surface made her heart skip.

"I can explain."

"Don't bother. Here's what I think happened. You wanted them back, but I refused to give them up and you knew you didn't have a shot in hell in court. So instead you decided to infiltrate my home, to prove me unfit."

"No, Coop—"

"But then you looked around and realized what a sweet life you could have as my wife, so you seduced me instead."

"It wasn't like that at all. I just needed to know that they were okay. Your reputation... I didn't know what kind of parent you would be. I was scared. I thought they needed me. I swear, I never intended to act as anything but their nanny. And I never wanted anything from you. You know that."

"Did you ever plan to tell me the truth?"

She could tell him she did, that she was waiting for the right time, but that would be a lie. "I was afraid to."

"Because you thought I would be angry? And feel betrayed? Well, you were right."

"It wasn't that. At least, not entirely. I was afraid it would change the way you felt about the twins. You're so good with them, and you love them so much. I thought it might change your feelings toward them. And yes, toward me."

"So you just planned to lie to me, what, for the rest of our lives?"

"You'll never know how hard it's been keeping the truth from you. And if I thought for a second that you would understand, I would have told you that very first day. But look at it from my point of view. I didn't know you. All I knew is what I read in the papers and heard on the news. I didn't even know that you had any interest in taking care of twins who you believed you weren't technically re-lated to."

His eyes narrowed. "What do you mean, who I *believed* I wasn't related to?"

Damn it. Had she really just said that?

"Sierra?"

Damn, damn, *damn.*

It was one thing not to tell him and another to lie about it. Besides, he was bound to ask about the birth father some day, and not telling him would be another lie. "Coop, you're the girls' uncle."

"I know that."

"No, I mean that you are the girls' *biological* uncle. Ash wasn't just Fern and Ivy's adoptive dad. He was their birth dad."

The room seemed to tilt on its axis and Coop clutched the edge of the desk for support. "You *slept* with my brother."

"Yes, but it's not what you're thinking."

"You have *no idea* what I'm thinking."

"Please," she said, looking desperate, "give me a chance to explain."

Nothing she could say could take away the sick feeling in his stomach, in his soul. Ash had cheated on Susan. On top of being responsible for killing himself and his wife, Ash, who Coop had considered beyond reproach, had committed adultery. It was as if everything he knew about his brother was a lie.

"I met Ash in a bar."

"Ash didn't hang out in bars."

"And neither did I, but I had just put my father in a nursing home and I felt horrible, and I didn't feel like sitting home alone, so I stopped in for a drink. I just happened to sit beside him at the bar, and we were both drinking vodka tonics, and we got to talking. He said he was there because he and his wife were separating. He told me that they had been having fertility issues for years and after another failed IVF attempt, it was just too much."

Coop knew they had been trying to get pregnant for a while, but Ash never said anything about any negative effects on his marriage. If he and Susan had been separating, he would have said something to Coop. "I don't believe you."

"It's the truth."

"So why didn't he tell me?"

She shrugged. "I don't know. Maybe he was embarrassed? Maybe it was easier to talk to a stranger. All I know is that he had come from his lawyer's office, and they were going to sign papers the next morning. If you don't believe me, I'm sure his lawyer could confirm it. I'm sure with them gone he would waive privilege."

He would be sure to check that. "So you met in a bar…"

"We talked for a long time and had a few drinks too many, and we ended up back at my place. It was a mistake. We both knew it right afterward. He called me the next day to apologize and to tell me that what happened between us had knocked some sense into him. He and Susan had talked and were going to try to work things out. He begged me not to say anything to her, and of course I wouldn't. He was a great guy, and I was really happy for him. But a couple of weeks later I found out I was pregnant. I called him, and of course he was stunned and heartbroken. He wanted a child so badly, but to be in the baby's life he would have to admit to Susan what he'd done, and that would ruin his marriage."

"He would never do that. He would never refuse to take responsibility for his own child."

"He wanted to, but how would he explain the missing money? He said that Susan handled all of their finances. Things were already really tight. The fertility treatments were draining them financially."

If things were that bad, why hadn't he asked Coop for help? Coop *owed* him. He could have been the one to pay the support. Ash had made a mistake, and he should have owned up to it.

"It was a really terrible time for me to be having a baby. I was barely scraping by as it was, and I would have had to put the baby in day care while I worked seventy hours a week. I started to think about adoption, and when I found out I was having twins, I knew I couldn't keep them. I couldn't give them the sort of life they deserved. But I knew who could. I figured if the twins couldn't be with their mother, they could at least be with their dad."

"So why did Ash have to adopt his own kids?"

"He came up with the adoption idea so Susan wouldn't know about the affair. He was so afraid of losing her."

"And you just went along with this. You just gave up your babies to save a virtual stranger's marriage."

"I didn't have a choice. It was an impossible situation. Without his help, I couldn't keep them, and he couldn't give me any financial help without ruining his marriage. Giving them up was the hardest thing I ever had to do, but I did it because it was best for them."

"You must have been pretty happy when you heard about the crash, knowing you would get the chance to be with them again."

Tears welled in her eyes. "That's a terrible thing to say. And it's not true. If I didn't think they would have a good life with Ash and Susan, I never would have suggested the adoption. I would have given them to some other family who was desperate for children."

"You know what I find ironic? All this time I knew something wasn't right. I chocked it up to you having trust issues, when all along you were the one lying, the one who couldn't be trusted."

"I know it was wrong to lie to you, but I didn't have a choice. I didn't expect to fall in love with you. It's not something I planned, and I fought it. You know I did."

"Or that's what you wanted me to believe."

"It's the truth."

"What difference does it make now? It's over. I won't ever be able to trust you again."

She lowered her eyes, wringing her hands in her lap. "I know. And I'm sorry."

"And to think I was willing to marry you without a prenup. That's the last time I question my lawyer's advice." And he didn't doubt for a second that her insistence in signing one was all a part of her scheme. And what if he had married her? What if they'd had a child? The thought made his stomach ache.

"You didn't deserve this," she said. "And I know you won't believe this, but I do love you."

"You're right. I don't believe you."

She rose to her feet, her face pale, looking like she might either be sick or lose consciousness. "I'll go pack."

He laughed. "You don't seriously think I'm going to let you off that easy, let you leave your daughters?"

She blinked, confusion in her eyes. "But...I thought..."

"I may think that you're a miserable human being, but they need you. Do you really think I would rip them away from the only mother they have? But don't think for a second that you are anything but an employee."

"You want me to stay? *Here?*"

"Obviously you're moving back into your bedroom. And I'm going to treat you like the servant that you are. And you're going to take a substantial pay cut."

"You don't think it will be awkward, me staying here?"

"Oh, I'm counting on it. It's going to be that nightmare scenario you mentioned when you were telling me all the supposed reasons why you didn't want to get involved. You are going to live here, day in, day out, watching me get on with my life. Watching me exercise that revolving bedroom door."

"And if I say no? If I quit?"

"You never see the twins again. And you have to live with knowing you abandoned them twice."

She swallowed, tears welling in her eyes again, but he couldn't feel sorry for her. He flat out refused. She'd made him suffer, and now he was going to return the favor.

"Well then," she said, squaring her shoulders, trying to be strong. "I guess I have no choice but to stay."

Chapter 15

Coop had given it considerable thought and had come to the conclusion that he was an idiot.

He sat in his office, staring out the window at nothing, without the motivation to do anything but feel sorry for himself. The past two weeks had been the longest and most miserable of his life. If he thought making Sierra suffer would bring him some sort of satisfaction, he'd been dead wrong. He just wanted her to feel as miserable and betrayed and as *hurt* as he was. But knowing that she was unhappy and hurting was only making him feel worse.

He couldn't concentrate, couldn't sleep. When he was out with friends he wanted to be home, but when he was home he felt as restless as a caged animal. He didn't want to upend the twins' lives, but living in the same house with Sierra, seeing day to day how guilty and unhappy she felt, was killing him.

The worst part was that this was just as much his fault as hers. Probably more.

Deep down he had known there was something wrong, that something was just slightly…off. And instead of bothering to try to identify its real source, he'd passed it off as her shortcoming and left it at that, thinking that as soon as she accepted how wonderful he was she would be the perfect companion. When, in reality, he was the one with the bigger problem. He had lousy vision. He saw only what he wanted to see. He had pursued her with a single-minded determination that was almost manic. She'd resisted, and he'd ignored her. She pushed back, he insisted. He hadn't *let* her tell him no.

Looking back, he couldn't help but wonder what the hell he'd been thinking. Moving her into his bedroom after two weeks and planning a wedding six weeks after that. If she'd been pregnant he maybe could have understood the urgency. And speaking of that, the stretch marks should have tipped him off that there might be something she wasn't telling him. He had just assumed that she had been a little overweight at some point and they were the result. It wasn't the sort of thing a man could ask a woman. Not without getting slugged. Or so he wanted to believe. He never really asked her about her past. The truth was, he didn't want to know. It had been easier just to pretend that she was perfect, that her life didn't really begin until she met him.

What a selfish, arrogant jerk he'd been.

Though it had taken a little time to realize it, it wasn't even Sierra who was making him so angry. How could Ash, who had drilled into Coop the virtues of being a responsible adult and a good man, be so careless and self-centered? He should have supported Sierra, his marriage be damned. He should have owned up to the responsibility, so she could keep the babies, so they could be with their mother, where they belonged. Instead he had ripped them from her arms and taken them for himself. Coop didn't think he would ever understand it or ever be able to forgive him for what he'd done.

Yes, Sierra had lied to him but only because she thought she was doing what was best for her children. They were her number-one priority, as they should be. She was a good mother. She'd made more sacrifices for those girls than most women would ever consider. And he intended to make sure they knew it.

Ironically, now that he knew who Sierra was, warts and all, he loved her more than he had two weeks ago when he had her built up in his mind as the perfect mate. But after the way he'd treated her, why would she ever want him back? He told her that he loved her, that he wanted to spend the rest of his life with her, and at the first sign of trouble, he'd bailed on her. How could she love someone who had failed her so completely? And how could she ever trust that he wouldn't do it again?

He had really hoped by now that she would have come crawling to him on her knees begging for forgiveness, in which case he wouldn't have to admit what an utter jerk he'd been. Clearly that wasn't going to happen. He needed her a whole lot more than she needed him. Or maybe she just believed it was hopeless and didn't want to risk being rejected again.

He heard the doorbell ring and knew that it was Vlad, Niko and a few other guys from the team. Coop had met with Norris, who after some balking had agreed to their original terms. The deal was in place, and in just a few weeks Coop would officially be the new owner, so the guys wanted to celebrate. This deal had been all he could think about for months, yet now that he'd gotten what he wanted, he couldn't work up the will to be excited about it. It was as if losing Sierra had sucked the life right out of him.

Lita poked her head in his office. "Your guests is here, sir."

"Serve them drinks and I'll be right there."

She nodded and backed out.

He had no choice but to go out there and pretend as if everything was fine. But it wasn't, and wouldn't be, until Sierra was his again. And she would be. He would get her back. He just didn't have a clue how to go about it.

Sierra ignored the doorbell and read the girls their bedtime story. She had overheard Coop telling Lita—who seemed hopelessly confused by Sierra's abrupt switch from lady of the house to employee—that he was having a few guys from the team over. Was this him finally getting on with his life? Because she had been waiting, and other than a night out with friends in which he came home alone at an unimpressive nine-thirty and a couple of business meetings, he'd spent most of the past two weeks holed up in his office.

When it came to dishing out revenge, he wasn't very good at it.

That didn't mean she wasn't miserable and unhappy, and she missed him so much every cell in her body ached with it. Yet she couldn't deny the feeling that some enormous, cloying weight had been lifted from her, and for the first time in months she could actually breathe again. She realized now that if she had married Coop with that secret between them, she never would have been able to relax. She would have forever felt as though she didn't deserve him because everything that he knew about her was essentially a lie.

Unfortunately, the one thing that could have saved their relationship, *the truth,* had been the thing that killed it. Just like her pregnancy, it had been a lose-lose situation from the start, and she had been a fool for letting herself believe that it would work. For thinking that he wouldn't eventually learn the truth. And that it would end in anything but total disaster.

If he could ever find a way to forgive her, she would never lie to him again. But it seemed unlikely that would ever happen. He hated her, and that really sucked, but at least he knew the truth.

From the other room she heard men's voices. No doubt they would go up on the roof, drink and talk about what a waste of time she had been and the compromising position he had managed to trap her into.

Because she was in no mood for a confrontation with Coop's pals, she read the twins a second then a third book, realizing halfway through that they were out cold. She laid them in bed, grabbed their empty bottles and walked to the kitchen. Lita had already left for the night, and the dishwasher was running, so she dropped the bottles in the sink and washed them by hand.

She was setting them on a towel to dry when she heard the sound of footsteps behind her, but the cloying scent of aftershave tipped her off to the source. She turned to find Niko standing behind her.

"I need beer," he said, setting an empty beer bottle on the counter.

Was he just stating fact, or was he expecting her to wait on him? She was the nanny, not Coop's hostess. His friends could serve themselves, which Niko did.

"Coop tell us it's over," he said, walking past her to the fridge and pulling out a beer. Normally she didn't feel threatened by the younger Russian, but there was something in the way he looked at her tonight. His eyes roamed over her in a way that made her feel dirty.

"That's right," she said.

He stepped closer. "I like sister, maybe I like you, too."

Oh, yuck. "I'm not interested."

She turned to the sink and felt a very large palm settle on her butt. Repulsion roiled her stomach. And she couldn't help wondering if Coop had put him up to this, if that was part of her humiliation. But before she could turn and slap his hand away, it was gone. She spun around to see Coop pulling the Russian away from her, then he drew his arm back and punched him square in the jaw. Actually *punched* him.

Niko's head snapped back and he lost his balance, landing on his ass on the ceramic tile floor.

If he put Niko up to it, then why punch him?

Niko muttered something in Russian that Sierra was guessing was a curse and rubbed his jaw. He looked more annoyed than angry.

"What the hell is wrong with you?" Coop said.

"You say you and her is finished. So I think, why not?"

Coop glared at the Russian, then looked over at Sierra and said, "Are you okay?"

"Fine." Just mildly disgusted.

Coop turned back to Niko, jaw tight, and said, "I'm only going to say this once, so listen clearly and spread the word. The only man who's going to be touching this woman's ass is *me*."

Niko shrugged and pulled himself to his feet. "Okay, fine, jeez. I look but I don't touch."

"No, you don't get to look, either. Or *think* about looking."

Sierra planted her hands on her hips. "Excuse me, but do I have any say in this, since it is *my* ass we're talking about."

He pointed to Niko. "You, back to the terrace." He turned to Sierra. "You, bedroom, *now*."

What did he think, he could just order her around? And if he couldn't, why, as he stomped down the hall to his bedroom, was she following him? Maybe because the fact that he would punch someone to defend her honor was just a tiny bit flattering. But what she didn't appreciate was the part about him basically owning her. He'd lost that right when he dumped her.

He opened the bedroom door and gestured her inside, and she dumbly complied, but she wasn't a total pushover.

"Look. I don't know who you think you—"

That was as far as she got before Coop spun her around, slanted his mouth over hers and kissed away whatever she'd been about to say. His arms went around her, pulling her hard against him, and instead of fighting it and asking what the heck he thought he was doing, it felt so amazingly wonderful, and she had missed him *so* much, she couldn't help but kiss him back.

So much for not being a pushover.

He kicked the door closed.

"I have been such a jerk," he said. "A miserable excuse for a man. I am so sorry."

She tucked her face against his chest, breathed in deep the scent of him, knowing that she was home. Any reservations that she had been feeling before their fight were gone. "I deserved it."

"No you didn't. And when I saw him touch you…" He squeezed her so hard it was difficult to breathe. "Tell me you didn't like it."

"God, no! It was revolting."

"I don't want another man to ever touch you again. Only me, for the rest of our lives."

She cupped his face in her hands. "You're the only man I want, Coop. The only man I'll ever want. And I am so sorry for what I did. It was killing me having to lie to you. I should have told you the truth from the beginning."

"Sierra, it's okay."

"It's not. I should have come to your door, told you I was the twins' mother and asked you if I could be a part of their lives."

"You never would have made it to my door. The doorman would have to let you up, and he wouldn't have done that without permission from me, and I wouldn't have let you near the twins."

"So you're saying it was okay to lie to you?"

"Maybe not okay, but necessary. If I were in your position, and I thought the twins were in danger, I would have done anything to keep them safe. And what my brother did to you…" He shook his head, as if it was almost too painful to say. "It was so wrong, Sierra. He never should have taken the twins from you. He should have owned up to his responsibility."

"But his marriage—"

"To hell with his marriage. He made a mistake and he should have been man enough to admit it. I love my brother, and I appreciate all the sacrifices he made for me, but I just can't excuse the things he did. I'll never believe it was okay. And I will always take care of you and the twins, the way that he should have."

Her heart sank. She didn't want him to see her as some debt he had to repay. That just wasn't good enough for her anymore. "Because you feel guilty," she said.

He cradled her face in his hands. "No, because I *love* you. I asked you to marry me, and you put your faith in me and the first time things got a little hard I bailed. But it isn't going to happen again. I'm dedicated to making this work. I don't have a choice. I need you too much, love you too much to let you go."

"I love you, too," she said.

"And just so you know, I'm calling my lawyer first thing tomorrow and telling him to tear up the prenup."

Not this again. "But, Coop—"

"I don't need it. And I'm going to tell him to get the ball rolling on having your rights as the twins' mother fully restored."

She sucked in a soft breath. The most she had hoped for was to someday be their adoptive mother. She never thought that she would ever be recognized as their biological mother. "Are you sure, Coop?"

He touched her cheek. "They're your daughters.

Of course I'm sure. Then after we're married, I'll adopt them. They'll belong to both of us."

It sounded almost too good to be true, and this time she wasn't going to take a second of it for granted. "I'm going to be the perfect wife," she told him. "I'll figure out how to cook a decent meal and learn to clean if that's what it takes."

He shook his head. "Nope."

She blinked. "What do you mean?"

"I don't want the perfect wife."

"You don't?"

He grinned down at her, with that sweet, crooked smile—the one she would get to look at for the rest of her life—and said, "I only want you."

* * * * *

We hope you enjoyed reading
BILLIONAIRE'S JET SET BABIES
by *USA TODAY* bestselling author
CATHERINE MANN
and
THE NANNY BOMBSHELL
by *USA TODAY* bestselling author
MICHELLE CELMER.

If you liked these stories, which are a part of the
Billionaires & Babies Collection, then you will love
Harlequin Desire.

You want to leave behind the everyday!
Harlequin Desire stories feature sexy, romantic
heroes who have it all: wealth, status, incredible good
looks…everything but the right woman. Add some
secrets, maybe a scandal, and start turning pages!

HARLEQUIN®
Desire

Powerful heroes…scandalous secrets…burning desires.

Look for six *new* romances every month.

Available wherever books and ebooks are sold.

SPECIAL EXCERPT FROM

HARLEQUIN®

Desire

Read on for a sneak preview
of USA TODAY *bestselling author*
Janice Maynard's
STRANDED WITH THE RANCHER,
the debut novel in
TEXAS CATTLEMAN'S CLUB:
AFTER THE STORM.
Trapped in a storm cellar after the worst tornado to hit
Royal, Texas, in decades, two longtime enemies need
each other to survive…

Beth stood and went to the ladder, peering up at their prison door. "I don't hear anything at all," she said. "What if we have to spend the night here? I don't want to sleep on the concrete floor. And I'm hungry, dammit."

Drew heard the moment she cracked. Jumping to his feet, he took her in his arms and shushed her. He let her cry it out, surmising that the tears were healthy. This afternoon had been scary as hell, and to make things worse, they had no clue if help was on the way and no means of communication.

Beth felt good in his arms. Though he usually had the urge to argue with her, this was better. Her hair was silky, the natural curls alive and bouncing with vitality. Though he had felt the pull of sexual attraction between them before, he had never acted on it. Now, trapped in the dark with nothing to do, he wondered what would happen if he kissed her.

Wondering led to fantasizing, which led to action.

HDEXP0914

Tangling his fingers in the hair at her nape, he tugged back her head and looked at her, wishing he could see her expression. "Better now?" The crying was over except for the occasional hitching breath.

"Yes." He felt her nod.

"I want to kiss you, Beth. But you can say no."

She lifted her shoulders and let them fall. "You saved my life. I suppose a kiss is in order."

He frowned. "We saved *each other's* lives," he said firmly. "I'm not interested in kisses as legal tender."

"Oh, just do it," she said, the words sharp instead of romantic. "We've both thought about this over the last two years. Don't deny it."

He brushed the pad of his thumb over her lower lip. "I wasn't planning to."

When their lips touched, something spectacular happened. Time stood still. Not as it had in the frantic fury of the storm, but with a hushed anticipation.

Don't miss the first installment of the

**TEXAS CATTLEMAN'S CLUB:
AFTER THE STORM** *miniseries,*

STRANDED WITH THE RANCHER

by USA TODAY *bestselling author*

Janice Maynard.

*Available October 2014 wherever Harlequin® Desire
books and ebooks are sold.*

HARLEQUIN®

Desire

POWERFUL HEROES... SCANDALOUS SECRETS... BURNING DESIRES!

THE CHILD THEY DIDN'T EXPECT

by *USA TODAY* bestselling author
Yvonne Lindsay

Available October 2014

Surprise—it's a baby!

After their steamy vacation fling, Alison Carter knows
Ronin Marshall is a skilled lover and a billionaire businessman.
But a *father*...who hires her New Zealand baby-planning service?
This divorcée has already been deceived once;
Ronin's now the last man she wants to see.

But he must have Ali. Only she can rescue Ronin from the upheaval
of caring for his orphaned nephew...and give Ronin more of what
he shared with her during the best night of his life. But something is
holding her back. And Ronin will stop at nothing to find out what
secrets she's keeping!

This exciting new story is part of the Harlequin® Desire's
popular *Billionaires & Babies* collection featuring
powerful men...wrapped around their babies' little fingers!

Available wherever books and ebooks are sold.

Talk to us online!
www.Facebook.com/HarlequinBooks
www.Pinterest.com/HarlequinBooks
www.Twitter.com/HarlequinBooks

— www.Harlequin.com —

HARLEQUIN®

Desire

POWERFUL HEROES... SCANDALOUS SECRETS... BURNING DESIRES!

TEMPTED BY A COWBOY
by **Sarah M. Anderson**

Available October 2014

**The 2nd novel of the *Beaumont Heirs* featuring
one Colorado family with limitless scandal!**

*How can she resist the cowboy's smile when it
promises so much pleasure?*

Phillip Beaumont likes his drinks strong and his women easy.
So why is he flirting with his new horse trainer, Jo Spears,
who challenges him at every turn? Phillip wants nothing but
the chase...until the look in Jo's haunted green eyes makes him
yearn for more....

Sure, Jo's boss is as jaded and stubborn as Sun, the
multimillion-dollar stallion she was hired to train. But it isn't
long before she starts spending days *and* nights with the sexy
cowboy. Maybe Sun isn't the only male on the Beaumont
ranch worth saving!

Be sure to read the 1st novel of the *Beaumont Heirs*
by Sarah M. Anderson
NOT THE BOSS'S BABY

Available wherever books and ebooks are sold.

HD73346

HARLEQUIN®

Desire

POWERFUL HEROES... SCANDALOUS SECRETS... BURNING DESIRES!

Come explore the *Secrets of Eden*—where keeping the past buried isn't so easy when love is on the line!

HER SECRET HUSBAND
by Andrea Laurence

Available October 2014

Love, honor—and vow to keep the marriage a secret!

Years ago, Heath Langston eloped with Julianne Eden.
Their parents wouldn't have approved. So when the marriage
remained unconsummated, they went their separate ways without
telling anyone what they'd done.

Now family turmoil forces Heath and Julianne back into the same
town—into the same house. Heath has had enough of living a lie.
It's time for Julianne to give him the divorce she's avoided for so long—or
fulfill the promise in her smoldering glances and finally become his wife
in more than name only.

Other scandalous titles from Andrea Laurence's
Secrets of Eden:

UNDENIABLE DEMANDS
A BEAUTY UNCOVERED
HEIR TO SCANDAL

Available wherever books and ebooks are sold.

HD73345